DANCE OF THE JAKARANDA

PETER KIMANI

This is a work of fiction. All names, characters, places, and incidents are the product of the author's imagination or are used fictitiously. Any resemblance to real events or persons, living or dead, is entirely coincidental.

©2017 Peter Kimani
ISBN: 978-1-61775-496-8
Library of Congress Control Number: 2016935080

Front cover painting: William H. Johnson, *Jitterbugs* II, 1941, Smithsonian American Art Museum

Akashic Books
Brooklyn, New York
Twitter: @AkashicBooks
Facebook: AkashicBooks
E-mail: info@akashicbooks.com
Website: www.akashicbooks.com

Yusuf Wachira

Peter Kimani is a leading African writer of his generation. Born in 1971 in Kenya, he started his career as a journalist and has published several works of fiction and poetry. He was one of only three international poets commissioned by National Public Radio to compose and present a poem to mark Barack Obama's inauguration in January 2009. Kimani earned his doctorate in creative writing and literature from the University of Houston's Creative Writing Program in 2014, and is a faculty member at Aga Khan University's Graduate School of Media and Communications in Nairobi. *Dance of the Jakaranda* is his third novel.

Peter Kimani is a leading African writer of his generation. Born in 1971 in Kenya, he started his career as a journalist and has published several works of fiction and poetry. He was one of only three international poets commissioned by National Public Radio to compose and present a poem to mark Barack Obama's inauguration in January 2009. Kimani earned his doctorate in creative writing and literature from the University of Houston's Creative Writing Program in 2014, and is a faculty member at Aga Khan University's Graduate School of Media and Communications in Nairobi. *Dance of the Jakaranda* is his third novel.

In memory of my mothers, Esther Wangari Kimani and Rebecca Njeri Ng'ang'a,

and

for Lisa, Samora, and Tumaini, who continue their lineage

PROLOGUE

In that year, the glowworms in the marshes were replaced by lightbulbs, villagers were roused out of their
hamlets by a massive rumbling that many mistook for
seismic shifts of the earth. These were not uncommon
occurrences—locals experienced earthquakes across the
Rift Valley so often they even had an explanation for it.
They said it was God taking a walk in His universe. They
believed this without needing to see it, but on that day
the villagers saw the source of the noise as well. It was a
monstrous, snakelike creature whose black head, erect like
a cobra's, pulled rusty brown boxes and slithered down
the savanna, coughing spasmodically as it emitted blue-
black smoke. The villagers clasped their hands and wailed:
Yu kiini! Come and see the strips of iron that those strange
men planted seasons earlier—which, left undisturbed, had
grown into a monster gliding through the land.

The gigantic snake was a train and the year was 1901,
an age when white men were still discovering the world
for their kings and queens in faraway lands. So when
the railway superintendent, or simply Master as he was
known to many, peered out the window of his first-class
cabin that misty morning, his mind did not register the
dazzled villagers who dropped their hoes and took off, or
led their herds away from the grazing fields in sheer terror
of the strange creature cutting through their land. Neither
did Master share in the *tamasha* booming from across the

coaches where British, Indian, and African workers—all in their respective compartments—were celebrating the train's maiden voyage. Instead, Master was absorbed by the landscape that looked remarkably different from how he remembered it from his previous trip.

The mass of water appeared to have grown from a pond into a large lake. Maybe his eyes were playing tricks on him; or maybe after crawling through that very same land on either donkey or zebra, his lofty perch on the train now afforded him a very different view. To the left, a spring spewed hot water, the vapor casting clouds of woolly nothingness above it. *One of these should be named for Sally*, Master thought—the idea eliciting a mélange of soreness and softness that always came with the memories of his English wife, now estranged for four years. She was the reason he was looking forward to returning to England. A ship was waiting at the port of Mombasa, some five hundred miles away, where the rail construction had begun. The railroad tracks ended at the head of what he had named Port Victoria, memorializing the lake there with the same name, in honor of the Queen of England. So the rail that started by the shores of the Indian Ocean now cut through the hinterland to the shores of Lake Victoria. This was the mission that had brought him to the British East Africa Protectorate, and it had now been accomplished. He had been *discharged with full honor*, the cable from London said, echoing the military jargon that had regulated his life for twenty-three years. The cable also said a letter with full details of his release had been dispatched on SS *Britannia*, the vessel that would then deliver him home to England. Master suppressed a smile at the thought, and further subverted the thought by pretending to scratch his pate, whose receding hairline merged with his forehead to form what looked like a small crater.

"Happy are the pure at heart," Reverend Richard Turnbull, sitting beside Master, said over the rattling sounds of the train: *Kukuru-kakara, kukuru-kakara.* They held different sections of the shiny pole that served as passenger support, as though they were experienced pole dancers, though their bums never touched.

Master nodded and smiled ruefully but said nothing, retreating to the cemetery of his mind where memories unfurled. He wanted to absorb as much as he could from the land, a sudden burst of emotion clogging his throat. It was hard to imagine the space they were gliding through with such swiftness had been a blistering crawl that had taken them four years to complete. Four years in the wilderness. What had partly kept him going was the anticipation of the triumphant maiden ride. That moment had finally arrived, but Master felt somewhat deflated, the memories of his difficult past keeping him from fully enjoying the celebrations.

As if reading his mind, Reverend Turnbull bellowed, "Rejoice!" as the train approached a new township, which, like many other settlements they had encountered, seemed to have sprouted up out of the steps of the train station. On either side of the compartment, Indian and African workers, traveling in second and third class, made music from anything they could lay their hands on, rattling bottles with spoons, clapping, ululating. The walls that separated the different races were still up, just as they had been through the years of construction. The different racial groups, Master had written in one of his dispatches to London, remained separate like the rail tracks. Yet the rail was the product of their collective efforts—of black and brown and white hands.

The African and Indian workers on the train danced jubilantly and Reverend Turnbull joined them, nodding his head and waving excitedly. But Master remained unmoved through the razzmatazz. Still unable to savor the moment, he was still distracted, lost in his thoughts. He found it strange that he was starting to miss the land before even leaving it. He had anticipated this moment for four years, but now that it had come, the longing that he'd harbored fizzled into knots of anxiety—not just about the future and Sally's place in his scheme of things, but also about the present that would soon become the past.

Trying to rid himself of his anxiety, Master glanced outside. "That's where we left that Indian bastard," he said to Reverend Turnbull, his forefinger arching into a crooked arrow that pointed to a spot where rows of mud-and-wattle rondavels stood. The walls were plastered with white clay and the shingles on the roofs were aligned neatly, like rows of corn.

"The runaway father?"

"Yes, the f—the bastard," Master replied, checking himself just in time before cursing in front of a man of God.

"We have all come short of the glory of God," Reverend Turnbull said quietly, glancing outside, the rondavels almost out of sight. "I'm glad I took the baby into my care."

"Was our suspicion borne out?"

"What suspicion?"

"That it was his child?"

Reverend Turnbull shook his head quietly.

Master turned to face him. "What does that mean?"

"No."

"What do you mean?"

"Nothing."

"Why?"

"That's a secret only known to the child's mother."

Master opened his mouth, then sighed and shrugged. "Was the child Indian or Caucasian?"

"What's the difference?"

"Hair? Nose? I thought it was pretty obvious . . ."

"Nothing in life is that obvious."

"So, are you confirming the child was Indian or Caucasian?"

"What does it matter?"

"It does."

"Why?"

Master opened his mouth, flashed a wan smile. "Because . . ."

"What's done is done," Reverend Turnbull said. "I'm now the girl's father. I will raise her as my own."

Master opened his mouth again but kept quiet. He had burdened the man of God with enough secrets.

Both men returned to gazing out the window. Their arms were tangled around the shiny pole and their faces nearly touched as they craned their necks to peek outside—their bums still as far from each other as possible—stretched out at awkward angles so that they resembled ducks. The lake was almost out of view, only a sliver of light visible where it stood, and the clouds above the hot water spring appeared to have shifted.

"Reverend," Master said, facing him, "I know your Bible says heaven is somewhere else, but I think it must be close by."

Reverend Turnbull smiled, loosened his collar, and responded, "I'm afraid so."

"Why are you afraid?"

"Because God shouldn't live so close to heathens."

HOUSE OF MUSIC

1

God's *Country* was how Reverend Turnbull described the land in 1893 when he wrote his first pastoral letter to the mother church in England. He wrote about the marvels that he had witnessed during his travels—from the gentleness of the sands on the pristine coastal beaches, to the stunning lakes that seemingly appeared out of nowhere in the middle of forests, to the dramatic plunge of what European geographers had named the Rift Valley.

Although the natives do not know God, the perfection of their land raises serious doubts as to how this could have been created by heathen deities, Reverend Turnbull confided in his letters. What he failed to elaborate on was whether or not it was his mere presence that elevated the heathen land to God's dominion—but then again, it was pointless to state the obvious. In that age, God and the white man were one and the same; in fact, even the locals had an expression for it: *Muthungu na Ngai no undu umwe.*

When Reverend Turnbull started preaching in Nakuru, he liked to refer to his mission as God-ordained, for he was not destined to be there in the first place. He used the locals' idiom of the train as a snake to recall the story of Jonah, God's servant who had defied His call only to be swallowed by a whale and spat out in the city of Nineveh, where he was meant to be in the first place to spread the word of God. Reverend Turnbull told his congregations that Nakuru was his Nineveh, where he had emerged from the belly of the iron snake.

The Nineveh narrative was a white lie. Reverend Turnbull simply appropriated a line that Master had used to describe the dramatic events that followed upon reaching Mombasa to commence his return trip to England. The letter of Master's discharge from the colonial service was there all right, but it contained an unexpected gift. He had lobbied heavily for a knighthood for his service to the empire, and the letter from London indicated his bosses had acquiesced to his request and had granted him a title. But when the letter elaborated upon the details of his title, he realized his was a different kind altogether: it was a title deed to a parcel of land of his choice, anywhere in the colony. The only condition was that the portion of land had to lie between two natural boundaries for easy demarcation.

Master instantly recognized this as a bureaucratic slip that would be corrected in due time. But since he was already attached to the land, he saw it as his chance to kill two birds with one stone; he would accept the land, but this would not stop him from pushing for knighthood. He remembered the breathtaking hot water spring and the lake in the Rift Valley, and he decided that would be the land he would claim. Reverend Turnbull offered to accompany him on the trip back to the valley.

"This is your road to Damascus," Reverend Turnbull intoned, to which Master replied, "Feels more like that Nineveh fellow, reverend."

"Jonah?"

"Yes, Jonah must be his name. Here I am in the belly of what locals call the snake, destined for England, but fate conspires to return me to the African wilds."

Reverend Turnbull smiled and touched his collar, and said, "I hear you," which was his way of saying he had deferred participating in the conversation because he was distracted by a pressing thought. He was thinking *Nineveh* sounded both profound and spiritual. He committed it to memory for future use.

"You can build Sally a house," Reverend Turnbull said to Master when they arrived in Nakuru. "A castle between the spring and the lake."

Master thought that would be blasphemous but he did not voice his concern—building a house between two marvels of nature was like challenging God's creation.

It was the talk about the Indian who got away, the one who Master was reticent about, the one whose child Reverend Turnbull was raising, that helped clarify things.

"God says we should love our enemies, and He has brought you close to the Indian to test your faith," Reverend Turnbull said, adding immediately: "Build Sally a monument to love like that beautiful building in India . . ."

"The Taj Mahal," Master said triumphantly, as though the sheer intensity of feeling would somehow will such a majestic building into existence.

"And those Indian workers must know how to build such monuments."

"Technically, they are still under my command," Master reminded.

"Then command them to action!"

The legend about the house that Master built is that the construction went on for so long that babies born during that time were toddlers when the work was completed. Others said construction went on around the clock, with shimmering lightbulbs suspended off the trees to illuminate the workers' paths at night. Yet other villagers claimed they slept one night and woke up the following morning to find the towering structure sneering down upon them.

But the reason Master became a legend in his own life-time was because of what happened with the house. Soon after its completion, the windows of the Monument to Love were shuttered so that no light streamed in as Master mourned and villagers whispered of the loss of his mysterious love, who had dropped him like a piece of hot *ugali*. Some villagers disputed this, saying it was impossible for one to hide that long, burrowed like a *huko*—a rodent—and devised ways to test if anybody was home. A typical test entailed picking wild eggs from the lake that gave the township its name, letting them cook in the hot water spring, and then hurling them at the wooden shutters. Cooked eggs, the villagers said, bounced off better than raw ones, their intention being not to defile the building but to rouse the aggrieved Master—*ngombo ya wendo*, or the love slave, as they nicknamed him—from his slumber. Nobody appeared, so they concluded that Master was no more.

Then one day, as a gentle sun rose in the east, the shutters were flung aside, the windows slid open, and throaty shouts were heard to mark the reopening. Master had overcome his grief, but only after issuing a decree of a most intriguing nature: he posted notices around the property warning that females caught trespassing on the land would be shot on sight. He and women were done, *kabisa*. But since very few locals could read at all, and those who did were protective of the white man, it was hard to tell which aspects of Master's life and the house that he built were fact and which were fiction.

What happened for a fact is that Master turned his castle into a farmhouse and brought in dairy animals. He patrolled the large expanse on horseback watching his animals graze. This was a downgrade, as Master had spent years watching over humans at work and, like Jesus, rode a mule. The mule was preceded by a zebra, whose mouth was muzzled to ensure it did not bite Master. The dairy animals, beautiful in their brown, white, and black skins, grazed with white pelicans perched on their backs who watched as they mowed grass. Imagine an uninterrupted stillness of bovine bliss, the low hum of munching animals enhanced by whistling thorns in the distance. The stillness is broken by the muffled sound of a cow scratching where a tick has attached itself, but even that seems to be part of the natural ambiance. A pelican in soundless flight from the muscle twitch of its host, before relanding, the soft drops of dung at calculated intervals opening a floodgate of urine.

An electric fence surrounded the farm, dividing the animal kingdom. Wild animals that often streamed to the nearby watering hole would be jolted to their senses whenever they touched the fence, and most learned to keep their distance. By dusk, if the dairy animals had not been milked, their udders would swell and the drip-drop of milk from their teats would grow into a steady trickle, soaking the black-cotton soil to evoke notions of that ancient land where milk and honey flowed.

The wild animals watched the milky spectacle but none dared to touch the fluid, even when it formed a rivulet and coursed beyond the fence. They had the sense to stick to the pond water that they knew. A deer would mount another after quenching its thirst, which appeared to trigger other thirsts, while the hyena, convinced that Master's arm would fall from its rapid swings, stalked him on the other side of the fence, giggling at the prospect of a meal that never materialized. The giraffes would trot through the brown savanna, and the zebras, with their black-white zigzags, brayed for Master's attention, yearning to cross the line and leave the wilderness for his domestic dominion.

But that was before a plague wiped out the entire dairy herd yet afflicted none of the wild animals; they appeared to thrive through that period of strife.

The farmhouse was turned into a private club where white men in wide-brimmed black hats and knee-high boots sat in high-backed seats and waited, with guns at the ready, for wildlife streaming to the watering hole. They seemed to begrudge the wild animals for the plague that scuttled the Pipe Dream, as Master had called his grandiose plan to lay pipes across the country and supply milk in place of water. There would be plenty of milk for all to drink, Master had declared; even natives would have enough to drink and wash their dark skin if they so desired—it might just whiten them.

After the plague, men and, increasingly, women arrived to the shooting range and placed bets. With the carousing that went with the shooting, seldom were hands steady enough to make a proper shot, especially if it might interrupt the mating animals. As if on cue, the humans would try similar antics, reaffirming that years under the sun had not wiped out their primal instincts. The shooting range gained a whole new meaning.

Master's real name was Ian Edward McDonald, but there was nothing real about his identity. He could as well have been Wasike or Wanyande or Wainaina, as he fluently spoke the local languages. But since he privately enjoyed the sobriquet *Master*, he neither protested nor affirmed its usage. And there was nothing unusual about his name, for even the colony that he had come to serve for God and country had no solid name. It was called the British East

Africa Protectorate before it was christened the Kenia colony. In June of 1963—six decades after the construction of the Monument to Love—the country would gain yet another name: Kenya. And the house that McDonald built out of love would be conferred with yet a new name—the Jakaranda Hotel—immortalizing the jacaranda trees he had planted for his love, Sally. By then the trees had long wilted, just as his mysterious love had long dried up, but the passage of time had only served to renew the memory and enhance the mystique of Master's Monument to Love.

And while Master's house accumulated many stories over the years after its construction, it wasn't actually the first building in the area. Babu Rajan Salim, the Indian briefly famous for fathering the child that Reverend Turnbull raised, was the first settler to arrive by the lake, although his modest rondavel was not as prominent a landmark. Not being visible is not the same as not being there, he often reminded his Indian workmates who said McDonald had built his edifice to spite them. Africans arrived later and built their huts on the other side of the lake to complete the triumvirate of hostilities that had originated on the seashores of Mombasa, hundreds of miles away, when the construction of the rail had begun. And as Reverend Turnbull liked to remind any who would listen, the sins of the fathers would be visited upon their sons a thousand times. Local elders, too, had their own proverb. They said, *Majuto ni mjukuu*, which meant children would pay for the sins of their forebearers.

And so it came to pass that a sixty-year grievance between two old men—one brown, Babu; and one white, Master—fell onto Babu Rajan Salim's grandson Rajan. And in keeping with the tradition of the monument, it all started as a quest for love.

2

On that balmy night in 1963, Babu's grandson Rajan was at the Jakaranda Hotel, where he often could be found, waiting to take the stage with his band. While he was making his way toward the bathroom, the lights went out. The outage elicited a mixture of exasperated shouts, yells, and groans from bar patrons who instantly recognized the range of possibilities that the cover of darkness provided: scoundrels would flee without settling their bills, lovers would snuggle closer, and villagers would get a chance to hurl rotten eggs at the *wazungu*.

The latter arsenal wasn't as crude as it sounds; it was actually a downgrade from the stones that the revelers initially took to the establishment, because for decades racial segregation had been enforced at the Jakaranda Hotel, with a notice at its entrance proclaiming: *Africans and Dogs Are Not Allowed*. Actually, some Africans were allowed: the cleaners and gardeners and cooks and guards and those who ensured the *wazungu* patrons were comfortable. But dogs were strictly prohibited, for reasons few could remember, and which many found confounding given the centrality of dogs in *wazungu*'s lives. They were always talking or cuddling or walking with one. In another part of the colony, one *mzungu* had gunned down an African for stoning his dog when it attacked him.

So in June of that year, 1963, with the onset of independence, when word went out that all races were welcome in the previously whites-only Jakaranda Hotel, most Africans suspected dogs would be allowed in as well, and so carried stones as a precautionary measure.

When they did not find any dogs at the hotel, the revelers exchanged stones for eggs, because given their restive past with the *wazungu*, they thought it foolish to meet them empty-handed, especially when unhatched flamingo eggs ringed the lake that gave the township its name. The use of eggs, the locals further conceded, would confirm to the whites that they bore no hard feelings. So, an outing for drinks nearly always concluded with quite a few rotten eggs cracking on white faces.

Rajan stopped abruptly, torn between proceeding to the bathroom and groping his way to the safety of backstage. A moment or two passed before some illumination glowed in the distance. A candle beckoned in the walkway, stretching a tongue that licked the walls at every swoosh of the wind. Rajan made a fresh attempt for the washroom, making short, hesitant strides because he still couldn't see properly and the pressure on his bladder had slowed his walk. He had only shuffled a few steps when he felt, rather than saw, someone approach. He judged her to be a woman—her silhouette was framed by the faint candlelight, with tongs of hair looping a halo over her head. As she neared, he picked up her sweet, spicy scent; it descended on him like the sweep of an ocean wave.

Rajan turned to the right to dodge her but her hip was there already; when he turned to the left, the other hip was there too, curved like a strung bow. Without uttering a word, the stranger planted one of the softest kisses he had ever received and then drifted into the darkness. Rajan stood, momentarily transfixed, the tap-tap of the stranger's heels reverberating like bathwater trapped in the ear.

There was a clicking sound above him before a burst of light flooded the hallway, synchronized with appreciative shouts from the revelers assembled at the Jakaranda.

Rajan licked his lips—there was the gentlest hint of lavender. He found her scent fascinating. Some of the African girls he had kissed dabbed their mouths with Bint el Sudan balm, whose sharp, sweet taste turned their lips into sets of ripe guavas. But those were the chosen few, the urbanites who had outgrown their rural roots to acquire city tastes. Most village girls smeared their faces and lips with the milking jelly, because until very recently, man and beast had lived in the same quarters, virtually sharing food and drink.

The Indian girls were not any better, though their use of Vaseline on their lips was a bit ahead of the times. Rajan had not kissed a white girl, so had no idea how they tasted, though it wasn't for lack of trying. He simply had not come into kissing distance of any white girl, since everything in his life had been organized according to his color. He was a brown man in a black world which had been placed under white rule all his life. But now that *uhuru* was in the offing and barriers that had divided the races for generations were beginning to crumble, maybe this was his chance. People were testing the limits, exploring new horizons.

The lavender lips were outside his experience. The idea that he *could have* kissed a white woman in the dark brought Rajan to a screeching halt, and his bladder released a drop or two in his pants. He momentarily feared he had dripped something else, and he unsuccessfully tried to steer his thoughts in a different direction.

Rajan couldn't quite remember if the stranger's lips touched his lower or upper lip, or even whether he had opened his mouth properly to receive the kiss. Yet the taste in his mouth seemed everlasting. The burning sensation in his bladder subsided, and was replaced with a tingling of excitement. Although Rajan was only a few paces from the washroom, and could detect the acrid smell of the toilets in the air, he decided to scour the hotel and look for the kissing stranger.

Outside on the hotel grounds, Rajan slowed down when he reached an intersection. Wooden planks with sharpened edges formed a compass pointing to the different directions of the establishment. Black marks now blotted out the scrawl that had earlier announced, *Whites Only.* Rajan licked his lips again. The mysterious taste was still on his tongue, seemingly stronger than the last time he had checked.

He took the path that led to the clubhouse, or the farmhouse, as it was still known to McDonald and a generation of men who now spoke in croaky drawls from years of dust clogging their throats. Those men, skin birdlike with age, still came to the club and trembled as they pointed to where the farm once existed, unable to mouth the name because of the emotion it evoked. They remembered the peaceful days when their hands were steady enough to balance minuscule measuring cups to get the right dosage of medicine for a sneezing cow at night. Now such doses were being administered to humans.

Rajan cautiously stepped into the clubhouse and glanced over at a group of men sitting at the counter. Those men, once white, now looked pink, like pigs. They sat solidly in their seats, their thick necks holding heads that were once proud and erect, but were now drooping, defeated, hairy hands clasping tall glasses with frosted rims. There wasn't a single woman in sight and the four men seemed downcast. The only things that appeared alive were the three rhino and two buffalo heads hoisted above the main bar counter; glassy eyes stared vacantly, as though frightened by the bleakness of their future.

Rajan hurried out and took the path leading to the annex, which through colonial times had been reserved for Indians—yet even then, only a few token Indians were allowed in. The annex was almost empty now but for three men and two women. One of the women sat on the lap of a heavyset man, nibbling at the edges of his earlobe poking from under his turban. Rajan looked intently at the canoodling woman and instantly concluded she wasn't capable of kissing with the tenderness he had experienced in the dark. The other woman was drinking from a green bottle, lips crimson red. She turned when she noticed Rajan, pushing aside a strand of hair that had strayed to her eye with an air of sophistication.

"Beautiful *bhai*, you vant to breast-feed?" she giggled, touching her generous, heaving bosom with her two hands. "The milk is burning me up."

If the woman had the capacity to turn fermented barley and hops into fresh milk, and was still able to accurately note Rajan's good looks, then she must have been more sober than Rajan assumed. He had a handsome face with penetrating eyes framed by dark lashes, which further amplified an aquiline nose that seemed perfectly chiseled.

Rajan fled and took the path to the watering hole. This was simply a tarpaulin stretched across a frame of wrought iron that formed an outdoor sitting space. It was pretty new, created to accommodate Africans when the nation's political developments pointed to the inevitability of *uhuru*. Since Africans would ultimately be invited to the main table, the hotel management had decided it would be useful to allow them a forum where they could acquire some table manners.

But there was scant evidence that the management's ideals had borne fruit. The white plastic tables sagged under a forest of green and brown beer bottles—proof that Africans had yet to refine their manners and order one drink at a time. Although only a few token Africans were initially allowed on the premises, and most were generally wealthy enough to afford some trappings of comfort, they still found the display of plentiful alcohol irresistible.

When the Jakaranda opened its doors to Africans in June of 1963, some folks simply arrived barefoot or on bicycle and said they had come to see the property. Some saw with their teeth, unable to hide their surprise at catching glimpses of whites and Indians at such close quarters. Since most had no money to spend, they converged around a black-and-white TV set that had been installed in one corner and spent the evening watching the news. Undoubtedly nature, as well as man, produced interesting news on a regular basis. The Longonot crater was reported to have erupted the previous night, spewing molten lava that left a serpentine trail in its wake. But what most African revelers enjoyed hearing was the booming voice of their new leader, whose mystique had been considerable even before he took office. He was simply Big Man and all his lieutenants needed to do to get things done was invoke his name, or insinuate they were following his command. In such instances, they said they were "acting on orders from above." So Big Man, who presumably lived above, inspired awe and dread.

The watering hole, so named due to its proximity to the wild animals' drinking point, became a favorite spot for tourists, as well as locals across the racial divide. But since all the races had never before interacted socially, their initial meeting resembled nervous animals coming in contact for the first time; if animals started by nosing their opponents' horns, humans began by sizing each other up from a distance, commenting on news events, then finally warming up and sitting at the same table to share a drink.

Rajan scanned the female faces and settled on several sets of lips turned in his direction. They were mostly Indian and African lips, thickened with layers of Bint el Sudan and Vaseline. There were no white women present. Rajan's hopes were waning. He licked his lips again, shaking his head to fend off the gnawing thought: why would a single touch from a woman cast such a strong spell on him? The mysterious taste seemed to be dissipating now, which only heightened his despair.

He stepped out and walked aimlessly, before taking the path leading to the butchery, hoping the kissing stranger had somehow ended up there. The butchery was the spot where his grandfather Babu sat during his maiden trip to the establishment, a visit that was made after weeks of coaxing. Babu had simply said, without any elaboration, that it didn't feel right for him to venture into the Jakaranda for ancient historical reasons. When Rajan persisted in his demands for an explanation, Babu said: "A foolish child suckles the breast of its dead mother because he can't differentiate between sleep and death."

Rajan often wondered if the ancient history Babu had in mind related to McDonald, the elderly owner of the ranch that became the Jakaranda, and who still lived in a house on the sprawling property. McDonald occasionally dropped by to watch Rajan and his band rehearse. On such occasions, the old man would stand, nodding his head to the beat, before retreating as silently as he had arrived, the shuffle of his feet interspersed with the gentle knock of his walking stick. Rajan noticed McDonald had started paying more attention to him since learning Babu was his grand-father. "Greet the old cow for me," McDonald would say to Rajan as he trod away.

Rajan never conveyed the message because Babu grew tense every time he mentioned McDonald or the Jakaranda, though he still managed to convince his grand-father to shake off that ancient history and show up there to watch him perform.

The butchery was located in a building that had once served as the servants' quarters of McDonald's house. One wall had been removed to provide a view of the animal carcasses that hung upside down. This area offered a pan-oramic vista of the plains as well. The electric fence still stood between the establishment and the wilds. The an-imals still came to the watering hole but the mating had died down. Tourists' cameras had replaced guns on the shooting range. Most people suspected the animals found the flashing cameras intrusive, or perhaps the animals could tell camera flashes did not threaten their survival like the booming guns, and so did not feel the pressure to procreate. But few thought the animals could have been corrupted by the humans, whom they had watched doing their thing for many years. The animals had acquired the human habit of experiencing thrill only when under im-mense pressure.

Rajan considered the contrasting appearances of the cooking meat, the raw meat, and the animals roaming the wilds. One was at liberty to choose the animal he wanted killed for dinner. The majority of the meat was from goats, sheep—lamb and mutton—chicken, and turkey, all having replaced the dairy cows. The meat was grilled, broiled, fried, roasted, or made by the *tumbukiza* method, which in-volved throwing the meat, vegetables, and spices into one

big soup pot to cook together. A charcoal brazier, the size
of a man, sat outside the butchery—its wobbly, spindly legs
holding amazing amounts of meat, the multiple apertures
breathing laboriously, as if bogged down by the demand of
giving fresh life to coal from dead acacia stems and shrubs
and fossilized bones. Eventually, after spasms of seething,
sighing, and hard breathing, the brazier would spark gently to life, turning the layers of black coal to dawn brown,
before glowing evening red. The brazier was the glue that
held white, pink, black, and brown hands together, pointing at the pieces of meat they claimed as their own.

It was a site of unbridled desire as men and women
salivated over the cooking meat, while others watched
the animals and developed their own appetites. All were
there to eat their fill, and the task of feeding them fell on
Gathenji the butcher, with his reassuring leitmotif, "*Ngoja
kidogo!*" which meant one needed resolute patience when
dealing with him, for his "wait a minute" often lasted a
few hours, usually because Gathenji sold meat faster than
he could roast it, and some hungry patrons were more than
willing to induce his cooperation with a little extra money.

Rajan surveyed the butchery, reminded once again of
his grandfather. When Babu had visited for the first time,
he observed even with the promise of independence that
men were still hunters and gatherers; women waited at the
table to be fed. True to Babu's word, there was not one
woman at the butchery.

Babu and Gathenji had instantly hit it off. It was one
of those quiet nights when the month was in a bad corner,
which meant somewhere around the third week, when people had exhausted their midmonth advances and the next
paycheck felt years away. Babu, slouched and supporting
his frame on a walking stick, had barely settled in his seat

when Gathenji marched over to the table and bowed in unctuous deference. "This is the man himself!" the butcher had saluted Babu, placing a wooden tray bearing a piece of meat on the table. "This is *kionjo*, just a small bite to silence the pangs of hunger," he said generously, slicing the tangled meat open, the juicy parts yielding drops of oil as he proceeded to cut it into tiny pieces. "You know, we have heard so much about you, *mzee* . . ."

"I hope you have heard the right things," Babu had replied, glowing as he turned to his grandson Rajan. "He keeps asking me to tell him stories from the past. But I don't know how he retells them."

"He does it very well," Gathenji assured, then went on: "You know, now that we are about to celebrate our independence, you stand tall as one of our fathers of the nation."

"Not so loud," Babu cautioned. "Some don't think of fatherhood as a shared responsibility."

"Never mind, you are our father. Tell me, where did you learn all those languages? Swahili, Kikuyu, Dholuo, Kalenjin?" Gathenji pressed.

"Well, it was all in a day's work," Babu allowed. "I worked with men from different communities, so I learned their languages."

"And you know the most difficult part of it, my good *mzee*?" Gathenji said. "You built the rail with those hands of yours . . . the rail that now links the land of Waswahili to that of Wajaluo, Wakikuyu to Wakalenjin."

"It was all in a day's job."

Gathenji waved him down. "Hold it right there, *ngoja kidogo*." He had noticed Babu was not eating and still had his false teeth in. Gathenji dashed to the butchery and returned shortly with a mug of *muteta* soup and a glass of water into which Babu dropped his dentures, sipping the soup as he did so. They managed this exchange without a word.

"I hear this very house has an interesting tale to tell," Gathenji said conspiratorially.

"Careful," Babu smiled, flashing his bare gums, "walls have ears."

"I agree," Gathenji said. "Let's not gossip about the stream while sitting on its rocks."

"Words of wisdom."

Gathenji was summoned back to the butchery by a customer. Babu took another sip of the soup and sighed. It was spicy, just as he liked it. He took a bite of *mutura* and chewed nervously, wondering if the meat was halal. Although he wasn't very religious, he liked to eat right. The *mutura* was delicious, if a little oversalted.

Soon, Rajan took to the stage, calling the audience's attention to the special guest in the house. Babu waved his walking stick from his seat as the revelers ululated.

Bringing his thoughts back to the present and to the mysterious kissing stranger, Rajan paused by the brazier and warmed his hands absentmindedly. With the return of the lights, the brazier had lost some of its brilliance, but the intensity of the heat had not diminished. The meat was spread on a mesh above the hot coal. A rising blue flame was snuffed by a trickle of blood. A blob of fat followed the route the blood had taken but got caught between two glowing coals. After some moments, the white blob congealed into a black knot, its fatty juice trickling down with a sparkle. The flesh sizzled, its red-pink color turning golden brown. There was a popping sound as a kidney puffed and burst, spewing a splash of fat that ignited a fresh flame that sprinted across the brazier, like a shooting star on a dark night, before it went down in a flicker.

Rajan felt a light wind sweep through. He lifted his eyes and peered at the animals by the watering hole. They, too, had lifted their ears, listening for threats to their lives. The carcasses of the animals that had been killed for the day's meat nudged back to life, doing their upside-down dance at the butchery, attracting a fresh lease of interest from revelers. The sizzling of the meat and the heaving of the coals melded into the din of the night: the popping of a frosty, turbaned bottle losing its top, the clink of toasting glasses, the loosening of belts, the murmur of drunken men and women seducing one another.

Music came to the fore as someone bellowed: "Next onstage, the Indian Raj, the undisputed king of *mugithi* . . . Next onstage . . ."

Although Rajan was scarcely aware of this, he had gone almost full circle. He had combed the entire establishment in his search of the kissing stranger, to no avail. He had almost reached the washrooms again. The sound of the riff and the cheer from the crowd nearly brought him to his knees. There was something utterly overpowering about the music and the energized audience's response. Somebody called out his name, and the riff sounded once more as the drums throbbed and the guitar wailed.

He was suddenly aware of the pressure on his bladder, which felt like the prick of a thousand needles, drilling a mild, burning sensation. There was even something pleasant about the pain. He shuffled to the urinal and listened to the rhythmic drone as the jet of urine drummed the white bowl, a haze of steam rising lazily in the air.

He felt happy and light as he sprinted backstage without washing his hands, feeling safe in the dim light, now insulated further by the taste of the stranger's kiss.

He walked up to the microphone onstage and adjusted it to his height. He was small-bodied, like a stunted teen, with a clutch of jet-black hair held at the back by a red, gold, and green hairband. When fans saw him for the first time, they often remarked that fame does not match its owner, for his frame came up short of his towering reputation.

The instruments were building in tempo. Rajan trembled with delight and nodded appreciatively to the instrumentalists, tapping his right foot, responding to a rhythm that appeared to bubble deep inside him.

In his formative years as a singer, Rajan would shake with fright before the curtains opened, unsure how the audience might respond. Sometimes, lines that he had rehearsed for weeks would evaporate at the sight of hundreds of eyes. Now he was a lot more composed, but the dread before performing a show never really left him. It helped when he was under the influence of something. *Steam* is what they called preconcert intoxication; he'd had a few beers to "unlock" his mind.

Rajan let the instruments play on—the squeak from the keyboard, the wail of the guitar, and the throb of the drums building into a frenzy. He yanked the microphone from its stand and walked to the edge of the platform as dozens of hands rushed to touch him. He crooned in a low, mournful voice:

Barua nakutumia
Nikufunze ya dunia
Usije ukaangamia
Ewe wangu—eeeeeeeeeee!

He shut his eyes and let the music smother his face,

now contorted into a mask of pain and pleasure. The air was tense as revelers fell silent. All the sounds from the orchestra were suffused in his small frame, his voice releasing the energy in dribs and drabs. The fans were hypnotized. When he sang the chorus again, the audience joined in, turning the song into a call-and-response, uniting those seated in different sections that once separated the races, building gently before cascading into the main riff.

Rajan fished a pretty girl from the mass of hands that waved excitedly at him. He always picked the most striking girls for this dance, which was a precursor to the gentler dance that followed backstage. The girl wore high heels and ascended the creaky stairs as though she were stepping on eggs. Her skirt was too tight to allow a full stride, which elicited more ululation from the audience. Rajan's heart somersaulted at the flash of her exposed leg. He stretched his arm and held her dainty hand and pulled her onstage.

The music transitioned smoothly to a faster beat. Rajan turned his back on the pretty girl. She obviously knew the drill; she hoisted her hands on his shoulders. Other fans jumped onstage and lifted their hands onto those ahead of them, and soon the dancing troop had formed a convoy. This was *mugithi*, the train dance, bringing onstage the stories that Rajan's grandfather Babu had narrated about his life building the railway.

That night, even as he danced *mugithi* and led the brigade of old and young alike trooping through the Jakaranda's uneven and crammed dance floor to imitate the movement of the train, hands on shoulders and thick waists, feet falling with the perfect synchronicity of a centipede tread, his eyes were downcast, looking for the high heels that could only belong to the kissing stranger.

He had kissed many women. Since rising to prominence in Nakuru—the measure of his celebrity being his regular features in the *Nakuru Times*—female attention had never been in short supply. In fact, so many were on offer that he and Era, his childhood friend and bandmate, had developed codes to distinguish the women: *News in Brief* was the tag attached to the skimpily dressed; *Long-Term Investment* was reserved for the big-bodied; *Coming Soon* referred to the striking young girls about to blossom into womanhood; *Takeout* meant petite girls who could simply be packed away like a bag of chips.

Many other women, in shapes and sizes that defied codification, would steal backstage and commend Rajan for his singing. He would politely acknowledge their compliments, even when he was inclined to tear away and hide—from the drunks shouting because they were hard of hearing, from older women clinging to vestiges of youth. Or pretty girls with stinking mouths. In the spirit of *uhuru*, such yardsticks were waived and those wishing to test the limits of their newfound freedom were encouraged to proceed backstage.

It was hardly a backstage, just a tiny enclave where the musical equipment was loaded after every performance, sharing a wall with the butchery. Humans would pile on top of the stacked equipment and try to make a different kind of music, the neon lights flickering outside, the clouds of smoke from the butchery providing enhanced stage effects.

A week before the kissing stranger arrived on the scene, a horsehaired woman had wandered backstage and brayed her affection for Rajan. She tripped over the equipment, while still clinging to her glass of beer. Sprawled on the ground, Rajan had motioned for her to join him, but she was too drunk to lift a leg. Rajan walked over and touched her hair. Her horsehair wig fell off to reveal silly cornrows. He offered a hand and her plastic nails fell off. The false eyelashes dropped off when she cocked her head to look squarely at him. The woman removed her dentures and threw them into her beer glass. When she unhooked her bra, its stiff cups collapsed to reveal shriveled breasts. Rajan had fled and sought Era's intervention. Era took one look at the woman and said: "Ugly cows belong in the butchery!" And with that, the woman, animal naked, was rolled over to the butchery where Gathenji received her with philosophical gratitude: *Ciakorire Wacu mugunda*. That might sound like an attempt to redistribute resources, but in those days, the young men called it growing up. They sat and laughed and toasted their green-turbaned bottles the following day, then drank and laughed some more as they narrated the events of the night. They played music and more besotted fans crawled backstage for a repeat performance.

It was remarkable how few words were exchanged backstage, which some band members also called *kichinjio* or the slaughterhouse. Perhaps Era and his band saw no need for further communication; like animals, they used spoor to pick their prey. But not everyone was willing to play the game. Only weeks earlier, a girl called Angie had flatly declined to cooperate with Rajan, even though she went backstage and undressed. "What do I mean to you?" she had demanded in a calm voice.

Rajan had propped himself on his right elbow and looked intently at the girl. Even in the faint light, he could tell she was strikingly beautiful. Her naked breasts, like filled jugs, stood erect, the wide hips seemingly out of sync with her slight frame. Her calm and beautiful presence appeared misplaced amid the riotous din from the butchery, the chorus of drunks ordering fresh rounds, the whimper of music equipment under the weight of two adults.

Rajan had kept quiet.

"Soooo, did you hear my question?" Angie had repeated without any hint of annoyance. Rajan could feel his indignation rising, like heartburn after a good meal. What did the girl expect him to say? And why did she impose her expectation that she should mean anything to him?

Angie had gotten dressed and stood to leave. "If you want to see me, I will be at Moonshine tomorrow at four p.m.," she announced. "They serve nicely brewed tea." Moonshine was another previously whites-only establishment, and young African women were quickly catching up with white culture, like having four o'clock tea. If this was the new African woman, Rajan shuddered, he and his ilk were in trouble. The era of free things was about to end.

Rajan had grudgingly honored the appointment the following day but arrived half an hour late.

"There is no hurry in Africa!" Angie said cheerfully. "You must know you are worth waiting for." She was sitting by the pool, next to a whitewashed wall. An inverted image of Angie was submerged in the water, an image that threw Rajan's mind to his grandfather Babu's story of his treacherous journey by boat from India to Mombasa many years before.

Rajan had approached the girl. She looked remarkably different from his night visions. He remembered her spiky hair falling all over her face. Now it was pushed back and pinned, accentuating her forehead that shone against the sun. The high cheekbones were still sharp, perhaps sharper than an artist's chisel, and her calm face, almost childlike, contradicted the mature, worldly mask Rajan had seen at night.

Accustomed to the dark and the comfort afforded by multicolored lights, Rajan had blinked like an animal out of his lair. He realized for the first time how rare it was for him to face the daylight. He typically slept through the day and sang at night. He found the sun blinding. He did not know what to say, for he never had to say anything to women. They all arrived at his feet seduced by his music, and hurled their bodies at him without a word. The best effort he ever made was to stretch out a hand and pick his chosen few from the sea of besotted fans. His microphone was the magic wand that drew them to him; without it, he was powerless.

Angie held his hand and squeezed it, her eyes dark with power and mystery. He cringed and thought of the image in the pool, envisioning their gazes mirrored in the water. He felt like he was drowning in the pool of her eyes and his hand went limp in hers. Unable to keep his grip, he lowered his gaze and pulled his hand away, then excused himself to go to the bathroom, although he felt no urgency at all. He used the back door and made his exit. He had not uttered a single word.

Quite often, Rajan woke up in beds where he could hardly recall how he'd gotten there in the first place, but where he did not need to utter a single word to get things going. Quite a few times, it was with a hint of regret, dodging kisses from stale mouths or breaking free before his captors could grant his leave, extricating himself from a mess he did not wish to get tangled in. In such circumstances, older women were usually the culprit. He dreaded their insistence on small talk that could only end in hurt—he was there to have a good time, not chat about life. Worse still, some sought his thoughts on their immediate future under a black ruler. But the one thing that he enjoyed was bedding different generations of women and assessing their values and attitudes toward life and love. He had discovered that all women, whether young or old, sought an affirmation of love—or at least some declaration that they meant something to him. The truth was, they did not, and he suspected that they knew as much, yet couldn't quite leave him alone.

Then the kissing stranger arrived and disrupted everything. Just like that. For the lavender-flavored kiss on that balmy June night in 1963 breathed into Rajan a restlessness that infected his mind, and later his heart.

There were the awkward moments when he'd stop in his tracks, convinced a girl he passed on the street was the kissing stranger, only for her physique to transform into an image different from the one in his mind. At other times, he would walk into the washrooms at the Jakaranda to retrace her steps; he made so many trips there that his band members started speculating that he was suffering from a serious case of diarrhea.

In moments of despair, he stood on street corners scanning the women passing by before marshaling up the courage to confront one with a ready line, only to falter upon closer scrutiny. He thought the kissing stranger had dimpled cheeks, with a gentle smile playing on her full lips as she seductively swished away. But in other visions she would appear chubby and unsmiling. Occasionally, he found he had assigned her features from different women from his past until he got all mixed up. Then he would remember he'd never actually seen her face because it had been so dark.

One morning, Rajan went from door to door inquiring about young women who wore high heels. He pretended he was a fashion photographer looking for models to parody the flamingo dance, which was all the rage at the time. But no one ever remembered seeing anyone in high heels, the question only serving to remind many that they did not wear any shoes at all. The irrationality of his inquiry was amplified by a middle-aged woman who remarked: "Could anyone go tilling the land or carrying a load of firewood on her head in the kind of shoes you are describing?" The woman clasped her cracked hands to display her dismay and squeaked, "Yu kiini!"

He did not gain access to any white homes because no one answered the doorbell and he was afraid of venturing in unannounced, since most homes had signs warning of *mbwa kali*, or ferocious dogs. The search bearing no fruit, Rajan broached the idea of placing an advertisement in the Lonely Hearts column of the *Nakuru Times*. But who was he looking for? Was she tall or short, slight or heavy? How many Nakuru women would fit that bill? Was she white, black, or brown? He froze at that question. Who among the three groups could have kissed with such sophistication? Probably a white girl, but then Africans, Indians, and Arabs were racing to make up for lost time, and could probably give whites a run for their money after only a couple of months of freedom.

Had he known the ethnicity of the kissing stranger, would that have narrowed his search and yielded better results? He reckoned that would actually be problematic, for how could he describe the subject of his admiration without arousing his prejudices about her imagined history? After all, humans do not wear identities on their faces. Where would he place her in a land where dozens of communities existed? And how could he describe *himself* anyway? *A Kenyan of Indian ancestry seeks a lean, pretty woman who can wear high heels in the dark . . . ?*

And would it be accurate to describe himself as Indian when his only encounter with the subcontinent was through the stories he had heard from his grandparents? He realized to his horror the perils of history and the presumptions that come with symbols. A turban may be the mark of a Sikh, but the Akorino of Molo and Elburgon wore them too. In that place, anybody could be anything. And when things appeared set and certain, nature erupted to remind him of the temporal nature of man. A dormant volcano leaped to color the land ashen gray. A landslide tossed a mass of red earth to bury houses in the bowels of the earth, erasing the markers that people had used to define their existence.

Eventually exhausted by his fruitless search, Rajan returned to his routine at the Jakaranda of drinking and eating and performing.

The Jakaranda wasn't just home to Rajan's personal melodrama; the atmosphere of the hotel was also spiced up by the butcher Gathenji's own spectacle—his tools of trade a sharp cleaver, acerbic wit, and swift feet, which were unfailingly thrust in ill-fitting flip-flops, the big toes nosing the ground for any trouble. Picture the man in what was once a white dust coat faded brown with oil and dirt, a fleshy face grinning at an impatient customer, one hand caressing the carcass, the other gently tearing the strips of flesh as though it hurt the animal to cut it up.

"*Choma, chemsha, au tumbukiza?*" Gathenji would ask, pausing to look at the customer. "My friend," he would continue, "let me tell you, *undo kwo undo*. If you want this for a roast then you need a little fat. Just a little fat to help it sizzle," he would explain, the knife slicing through a hump the color of bad milk. He would meticulously gather the meat and the chops of hump and drop them on the scale with the violence of Moses crashing the clay tablets on Mount Sinai. The scale would perform a jerky dance before the meter rested on the exact weight requested. Gathenji would tap the metal lid to ensure the weights were right, then flash a toothy grin at the waiting customer. "*Sawa sawa?*" he would ask, piercing a metal rod through the pieces of meat, rolling them into a parcel before throwing it over his shoulder so that the bundle landed on the kitchen table with a soft thud. "*Hiyo ni choma!*" he would then shout, indicating that the meat was for roasting.

"How do you manage such accuracy?" a puzzled customer would pose, while handing Gathenji the money.

"My friend, let me tell you. *Undo kwo undo.* One by one. I'm the meat master," Gathenji would reply with a hint of pride as he retrieved the change—the hundred-shilling notes in the right breast pocket, fifties in the left, the *mashilingi* in the left side of his trousers, the twenties in the right. All other big notes were stashed deep inside Gathenji's layers of clothes, in a pocket sewn in his coat that he called *kabangue*, which meant he would rather die than part with its contents.

As the meat roasted, Gathenji would march around to different customers, complete with his chef's hat, like an admiral inspecting a guard of honor, and gently place a chopping board bearing sizzling meat on the table to placate some enraged customer who had been waiting for hours.

"This is *kionjo.* Just to whet the appetite as the meat cooks," he would say. Hungry patrons would grab the pieces faster than they were cut, and praise the butcher for a great job. And wait.

But when the meat they'd ordered was done, bewildered revelers would form a line at the butchery demanding their pound of flesh, for Gathenji seldom sold them the requested weights. Since the area was generally poorly lit, and drunks often dimmed their eyes as alcohol took effect, none of them ever noticed the thin, colorless string attached to the scales. No one ever wondered why Gathenji always wore flip-flops, which allowed easy pull of the string using his toes. Those who had been shortchanged threatened not just to go after Gathenji's *kabangue* but his throat as well. More often than not, the disputes tended to boil over and spill onto the music stage, ending in a fragile truce that would hold until Gathenji delivered the entrails, the only conciliatory dish available, but itself a subject of constant conflict.

"This offal is not equivalent to the meat you stole from us," someone charged one evening.

"Who said I stole meat from anyone?" Gathenji demanded, meat cleaver in hand, the naked lightbulb dancing above his head. There was a tense silence. Someone coughed nervously. Gathenji relaxed and dropped the cleaver and walked clumsily toward the complaining party, his large belly protruding, the flaps of his dust coat swishing like a duck's tail.

"One of these days, we are going to roast that belly of yours," someone declared, eliciting laughter.

"It would roast well in its own fat," another remarked.

"My friend, let me tell you. *Undo kwo undo*. The Bible says one eats where one works. I eat from the sweat of my brow. We have a saying that when someone is full, he should cover his stomach. But if there is a hungry man, that I shall feed."

"So what happened to our meat?" the voice that had accused Gathenji of theft insisted.

"My friend, let me tell you. *Undo kwo undo*," Gathenji

returned confidently. "Did you not hear of the fool who quarreled with the fire for consuming his meat? Or do you think fire eats vines and *mikengeria*?"

"*Wee*, barman, give Gathenji a Tusker," someone shouted. "Give him a drink. He has spoken like ten elders!"

And so, this type of dispute over meat and offal would be resolved with glasses of beer followed by: "Waiter, give us another round. And don't let Gathenji thirst. Hey, Gathenji, give us another kilo and a half. And don't let too much heat eat away the juicy parts. Give it some bones too!"

From his counter, Gathenji would shout: "Hey! Let the Indian Raj play us some music to seal the deal!" Era and Rajan and the rest of the band would have no choice but to oblige.

Such distractions kept Rajan's mind off the kissing stranger, and his angst subsided; he quietly wondered if it was the revelers' ability to endure that allowed them to bear his musical privations. But he still felt, without being able to explain it, that the kissing stranger knew him. That's why she had kissed him in that dark corridor. And even after he'd given up searching, he could not forget her.

Then one day she returned. Just like that. Rajan was onstage at the Jakaranda, stretching out a hand to fish a pretty girl from the audience, when he detected the unmistakable sweet, spicy perfume. Like a bee drawn to a flowering plant, he leaped offstage and strode over to the table where he believed the scent was wafting from. He found himself standing within a foot of a stunning young woman. Even in the waning light, she was quite a presence. She sat ramrod straight, with long, lush black hair that reached her waist. When she rose to greet Rajan, he saw how her tiny waist supported massive hips, or as

Gathenji the butcher liked to say, she carried her hips and her neighbors'. And when she moved, no matter how gently, her erect breasts shook lightly; her skin appeared to change from brown to white and back, as the oscillating lights did their dance around her.

3

In 1902, shortly after Master's Monument to Love had been built, Sally did make a trip to Nakuru, and experienced firsthand how the town got its name. As she hoisted a leg up to board the carriage which had been sent to fetch her, a cheeky whirlwind, *ngoma cia aka*—or the female demons, as locals called it—picked up pace and swished her skirt this way and that, before knocking her hat off. When Sally bent to pick up the hat, the wind blew her long, flared skirt up and over her head, exposing her hindquarters that resembled a Maasai goat's—if you ignored the cream drawers that resembled her light skin.

The African servants who had been sent to fetch her had the good sense to flee for dear life, fearing they might somehow be implicated in the ignominy. While they may not have conspired with nature to embarrass the English woman, seeing her nakedness carried with it a tinge of violation. After all, *muthungu* and God were one and the same. That's the story locals liked sharing while devouring mounds of food, although the connection between the whirlwind and Sally's naked truth and her rejection of Master, as most still called McDonald, was never quite stated outright.

But in a land where myth and history often intersected, what happened to the woman of England is uncertain. What's more certain is that McDonald vowed he would never speak to another woman after Sally rejected him— for the second time.

* * *

The first time Sally left McDonald was preceded by a confrontation in South Africa, his last station before his British East Africa Protectorate posting. It was early morning. He had returned home unannounced to retrieve a diary he had forgotten. He had left Sally in bed, perhaps staring into space, picking her nose, or doing those things that most housewives did before they could summon up their energies to rise and face another day.

For Sally, there was nothing to face, save for the sun that she shielded herself from by wearing a sombrero as she cut flowers from her lawns maintained by a full-time gardener, hands gloved against the prick of rosebush thorns. One could tell the progress of Sally's day from the trail of cups. The cup beside the bed was for the early-morning tea, taken in her nightdress, feet thrust in frog-shaped warmers, while leafing through a magazine bearing big images of thoroughbred dogs. The cup by the window was for the ten o'clock tea, consumed behind dark glasses or drawn curtains while admiring Table Mountain. The cup at the dining table was for the prelunch drink, consumed with a slice of lightly buttered whole wheat bread. The jar of butter was a locus of vicious warfare between Sally and McDonald: he liked the butter surface smooth and gentle; she liked to use the blunt edge of the knife, leaving ugly marks. To McDonald, this reflected the tangled mess of Sally's life that he was fated to deal with. Smoothing out the butter became one of the many chores in his daily routine.

The cup by the balcony was for four o'clock tea, taken with biscuits or fruit. This trail of teacups wouldn't be collected by their servant until Sally went out for her evening walk because she did not like her solitude to be interrupted. Solitude was the reason she gave for postponing motherhood.

"I can't handle children," she said earnestly. "Running noses and wet bums I can, but not the cries from toothless gums."

McDonald had long taken note of the trail of cups but voiced no concern. Like the wise soldier he considered himself to be, he had learned to pick his battles wisely. So on that fateful morning, afraid to disturb Sally's peace, he sneaked quietly into the house to collect his diary. He was tiptoeing out when he heard a moan from the bedroom. He paused and cocked his head. He heard another moan. It sounded like pleasure, and he doubted that Sally could have derived that from the big-eared thoroughbreds in her magazines. He made his way to the bedroom door, silently opened it, and entered. Sally's face was not burrowed in some magazine as he suspected; actually, he couldn't even see her face—the view was blocked by the back of a head he found eerily familiar.

He could see that it was a man's neck, sinewy from his present labors and engaged enough in his task at hand not to sense McDonald's presence. McDonald realized it was his black gardener; he had seen the man strike a similar pose as he worked—fondling soil to pick out a weed or pruning the bushes. Now he devoted similar attention to this chore, and for a while, neither the man nor Sally noticed McDonald. When Sally finally did, and screamed, the black man thought she was screaming because of something he had done, so he continued on. It was only when McDonald dropped his diary, his trembling hands unable to hold anything, that the man realized the intrusion. Where does a man hit another to inflict the most pain, without injuring one's ego that the invader's very presence under his roof seeks to quash? McDonald appeared hypnotized by the puzzle, much the same way vermin are dazzled by the sudden burst of light when emerging from a crack in the furniture. McDonald's soldierly instinct was to cut off the offending organ, but he had no idea what he'd do with it. A soldier had to envision a whole operation before setting forth. Should he throw it to the dogs? Keep it as a memento? He didn't even have a weapon in hand. Perhaps he could use his teeth, but that would intimate a certain rage. He wasn't a savage. Yet.

He obviously did not approve of the man's presence in his bed, but his training taught him to keep emotions out of his work. That's why guns had been invented—to create distance between assailants and their victims. He tried to catch a leg, but the man was as slippery as a fish. He noted how feminine the man's shin felt, bereft of hair or scars. McDonald was determined to leave a lasting mark.

He dashed out of the bedroom to retrieve a weapon from his bag in the sitting room, but quickly remembered it was in his rickshaw waiting outside. He was losing crucial time, so he sprinted back to the bedroom, only to find that the man had disappeared out the window. Sally had gathered herself and was sitting on the edge of the bed, downcast.

For several long moments, he glared at her, trembling with anger as well as the fear of what he was contemplating. He slapped Sally once, and being a soldierly slap, it left a buzzing sound in her ear.

When he was confounded, as he was then, words utterly failed him. And when he finally spoke, it was neither a personal rebuke nor a remonstration. "Even if you have to do these things, don't you want to be respectful of the law?" McDonald glared, before walking away. It was a useful reminder that under the apartheid laws in South Africa, miscegenation was outlawed, so Indians, blacks, whites, and coloreds were prohibited from mating outside their own races. While the statement conveyed McDonald's allegiance to the law, it was also his way of saying: *You can do what you want to do, but surely not with blacks.*

The incident was not discussed any further; they were giving each other what Nakuru folks liked to call "nil by mouth." Neither uttered a word to the other, McDonald humiliated into silence because there was no way he could broach the topic without raising doubts about his abilities as a man. After all, his wife had not been caught stealing food or clothing; she had steered her servant, her black servant, away from the flower beds to her own bed, to perform a role that McDonald had either failed to do or had not performed to her satisfaction. Sally, on her part, remained silent because she had lost hearing in one ear and was too upset to talk anyway.

So McDonald had seen his posting in the new colony of British East Africa as an escape from personal turmoil and humiliation. Perhaps he and Sally would even have another shot at their troubled marriage.

I shall be the lieutenant of the entire province, he had written to her. *With a dozen servants at my disposal so even when I cough, one is likely to check if I had called for him . . .*

Sally's response had been terse: *Even if you were the governor, I'm not going anywhere with you, now or in the future.*

Sally, whose rich background and royal roots had been a permanent source of ridicule from McDonald's peers, said she would remain in England for the rest of her life. He then prevailed upon her not to file for divorce—to give them a bit of time to review things.

McDonald then resolved to do what he knew best: work hard and earn a decoration for his service to Great Britain. Sally would be proud of him, he mused to himself, perhaps she'd even harken his word. If he was knighted, he would be a man of title, just like her father. That's what motivated him to go to East Africa—to head the project that even his bosses in London admitted was a little insane. Its London architects called it the *Lunatic Express*, wondering where the rail would start and where it would end, for nothing of value was to be found in the African wilds. But it had to be done, and McDonald had fully committed himself to the idea that the construction of a railroad across the African hinterland was his route to self-affirmation and validation. But soon after he arrived in the marshes that grew into Nakuru town, few locals believed he was anything but completely nuts.

Ian Edward McDonald's Years of Solitude—as his four-year seclusion came to be known in Nakuru lore—far surpassed the few hours that Reverend Turnbull was reportedly in the belly of the iron beast, and, if one were to allow his mythical parallel, the three days Jonah spent in the belly of the whale. And even the forty days and nights that Jesus spent in the wilderness. But where myth and history often intersect, and the past often collides with the present, it is imperative to clarify the circumstances surrounding McDonald's house and Sally, the woman for whom it was built. For one cannot talk about the Indian singer Rajan, the love slave, without talking about the original *ngombo ya wendo*, since the two narratives both start and end at the place: the house that McDonald built—set between a hot spring and a cool lake—which ultimately became a site of unseemly arguments and simmering loves. To absorb the full story, one must turn back the hands of time and think about the dry savanna where only stunted acacia stands, their spiky hands thrown up in surrender against the harsh sun. That was McDonald's inheritance of loss, the bitter-sweet consolation for the coveted peerage from the Queen of England that had fallen through the bureaucratic cracks between London and its colonial outpost of Mombasa.

So, as was typical of McDonald, he ignored any signs to the contrary and continued dreaming that another future was possible for him and Sally. He saw the virgin territory and trembled with lust. He would conquer nature and assert his control, make something out of it for himself and, in the process, leave his mark on the world. He had been to different territories in the colony where locals had adopted names of missionaries who had ventured there, and remembering them, he felt a clog in his throat, for long after those men of God were gone, memories of their life would linger. There was Kabarnet, named for Reverend Barnett who had pitched a tent in Nandiland. Or one could point at Kirigiti in Kikuyuland, where the Brits' love for cricket had earned them immortality in the name of the place.

Above all else, McDonald wanted to please Sally, estranged from him since the incident in South Africa, and for the entire duration of the railway construction. He would prove he had been worthy of her love.

So, soon after his discharge was confirmed, and London reaffirmed that the coveted title for his service to the empire had been erroneously replaced with a deed to a piece of earth he neither desired nor needed, McDonald wrote to Sally. His first letter went unanswered. And the second, and the third, and the fourth. She answered his seventh letter, clarifying that she had been prompted to respond not by his persistence, which she remarked was a sign of foolishness—a wise man has many ways of sending a message, she said—but because the last letter had arrived on her birthday. Any meanness of spirit wasn't permissible on her special day.

Sally said she would think about the visit, which to him meant his request had been considered favorably. He knew Sally was not the thinking type; she acted on impulse, so any claim that she was thinking things through was, in fact, an affirmation that she had already made her decision. Her final letter with confirmation of dates and itinerary arrived six months later. She would be visiting in another six months. She then added:

> I'm curious to how you use your fork and knife these days. I recall you had trouble drawing butter from the jar and putting it on the side plate. You liked buttering your bread direct from the jar, which ticked me off without fail. I suspect you must be eating butter directly from the jar since, in your military wisdom, bread and butter eventually meet in the stomach.

Sally wanted to find out if he had gone native, McDonald thought happily; he would prove to her he had only grown more sophisticated. He would demonstrate to her that he was as good as any Englishman; in fact, he was as good as her father, whose country home in Derbyshire he replicated in the design of the Nakuru house. He worked his men like donkeys, most of them artisans he had diverted from the team detailed to maintain the new railway, and so worked at no cost to him. None of them knew their old boss had been retired.

The concrete blocks were sourced from other faraway colonies like the Congo and Nyasaland and hauled uphill by African handymen. The blocks were used as cornerstones that were a slightly different shade from the rest of the wall, and were placed at calculated intervals to evoke the pattern of a staircase. Once again, McDonald maintained the division of labor he applied on the railway construction. African laborers teamed up with an Indian artisan. A white architect named Johnson—whom the African workers called Ma-Johnny—provided general oversight.

Workers sang songs to urge others; they cracked jokes to deflect attention from their backbreaking toil. "Hey, man, a bird is going to perch on your head thinking it's a tree!" one worker would tease another who was considered lazy.

"Maybe he will help build its nest," another would join in.

During the rail construction, McDonald had discouraged joking among the workers because he believed those busy using their tongues were misdirecting their energies. But he had become more tolerant during the construction of the house—not that the workers necessarily knew this. To be on the safe side, the workers continued to fall silent at his approach.

When workers fell short of their projected goals, McDonald organized overnight shifts. That's when the glowworms in the marshes were replaced by lightbulbs and locals who had never experienced electricity were drawn to the lights, just like the moths that buzzed around the bulbs, singeing their wings and doing their death dance before paving the way for more suicidal insects. The locals stood and marveled: *Muthungu ni hatari*, they said, admiring the discoveries the white man had brought to their village. In that spirit, few spoke about the builders who had been killed or maimed in their labors, or devoured by wild animals at night while working. And those who did speak of these casualties concluded with philosophical zest: an abattoir is never without blood.

The house was completed in ten months, sixty days ahead of the projected deadline. McDonald devoted the last months to supervising the gardens as well as the jacaranda trees that he ordered planted along the road that led from the train station to his house so that Sally would be garlanded by purple blooms when she set foot upon the land in 1902. The idea of the blooms came straight from the Bible, or McDonald's vague recollections from Reverend Turnbull's sermons about Jesus's dramatic entry into Jerusalem garlanded by palm fronds from enthused followers.

He thought the jacaranda reflected Sally's beauty, and the trees were in full bloom when a horde of servants in a horse-drawn chariot was dispatched to fetch Sally from the Nakuru train station, only a few miles away. Some of the trees had shed their leaves, turning the black earth into a purple carpet. McDonald stayed home to receive guests who had been invited for the banquet. A band had been invited all the way from Nairobi to perform, as was the chef and the kitchen staff. It was the same chef who had cooked for the first colonial governor in 1901, and would be detailed to cook for the Queen of England when she visited the colony years later. The freshest English pastries had been delivered on the weekly flight that brought in the mail from Nairobi. The smells wafting, the piped music floating on the air, combined with the modulated laughter from guests who had already arrived, provided a sense of joy for those assembled.

At the dining hall, a matron hired from Nairobi had drawn up a list to ensure the right sort of people sat together. Engineers from the railway department, for instance, would sit with hoteliers and civil servants and businesspeople. The idea was to mix all manner of professions to spice up conversations and put different perspectives to debate.

The lilting music from the cellos and wind instruments was exactly right for the light refreshments being passed around. Reverend Turnbull was seated between an anthropologist named Jessie Purdey on field research from the University of London and a retired district commissioner named Henry James. On the other side of the table was a youngish woman with a sunburned face and freckled nose. Her name was Rosemary Turner and she giggled when Reverend Turnbull introduced himself.

"How can a reverend have such a cocky name?" she drawled. She proceeded to spend the rest of the evening stepping on his shoes and pinching his thigh.

What followed remains a topic of heated debate to this day, without a discernible conclusion or concurrence. With the passage of time, previous rumors would acquire more sinister pegs so that Sally, the *malkia*, became a legend in her own right. But as local people like to say, where there is smoke, there is fire, and the smoke and smog that clouded Sally's visit had one consistent thread: she made a brief appearance at the party incognito before exiting fast.

There were claims that she sneaked into the party disguised as a beggar to test McDonald's kindness, and was promptly chased away by the guards. Yet others claimed that when she arrived on the coast, she had visited a medicine man who gave her special herbs and charms that allowed her to transform herself into a cat, to spy on McDonald's house and his friends before making her quiet exit, never to be seen again. Another rumor that became firmly entrenched in the Nakuru lore was that Sally arrived without any disguise, took one look at the edifice built in her honor, sneered that it resembled a chicken coop, and spat on the ground to show her disgust before walking away, with McDonald in tow, pleading with her to return to him.

So, to lay the debate to rest, here's the true version of the events of that day: Sally arrived on the train from Mombasa as scheduled and saw the African servants waiting to receive her. They were holding a placard carrying her name. On it was McDonald's looped scrawling, identifiable from a mile away. Sally waved at the servants, who scrambled for her luggage and packed it in the carriage. As she hoisted a leg up to board the carriage, that aforementioned cheeky whirlwind did its thing and she was left with her skirt briefly covering her face, mildly embarrassed but otherwise in good cheer, even after the servants abandoned their mission. The horse trotted back home without the distinguished guest but bearing her luggage.

McDonald panicked when he saw the horse return with the two suitcases but without the servants or Sally. He responded with mathematical precision: adding all the facts together, he concluded that the servants and Sally were together, as memories of that morning in South Africa flooded back to him. He paused to think further; there were four servants involved. Even with Sally's preponderance for bedding her servants, she certainly couldn't manage all of them at once. There was a wave of relief as he realized it was implausible that they were *all* together. Yet, the horse's presence with Sally's luggage showed she had met his servants. So where were they?

As guests continued to stream in and greet old friends, McDonald quickly organized a search party that tracked down all the servants within the hour. Recalling the abduction of some British engineers four years earlier, McDonald was fearful this could develop into another crisis, so he had ordered the servants to be restrained from escaping, using any means necessary—a coded message for what military men called "appropriate force." From the servants' cuts, bruises, and bleeding noses, it was evident that those unleashed on them had applied McDonald's instructions to the letter. Some inebriated guests joined in the flogging as the four men were delivered to McDonald's house, arms tied behind their backs and roped together so that if one fell, the others followed suit.

It was during this commotion that Sally stole into the compound, having spent the hour picking flowers while following the horse's trail. She was actually tickled by the whole episode and thought no further about what may have prompted the servants' flight. She instantly recognized the man who had been holding her placard. He had a wound under his left eye, and he looked pleadingly at her when she arrived. Sally thought of her naked truth, as she called her windy exposure. It was nature's way of reminding her of her vulnerability, much the same way a hurricane sweeps onto the shores to return all the waste the humans have deposited in the sea for ages. Or a shoe that filters to the surface long after its owner is drowned. Sally thought she was being reminded of her own ordinariness, her near-nakedness reminding her of a birth into this new world, bearing nothing but her skin.

Sally did not speak a word nor venture beyond the porch; she simply turned around and went back the way she had come, a shudder in her chest, a quiver on the lip, as memories of her college days flooded in. She had enrolled at the University of London to study history and, out of curiosity, took a minor in African history. A huge chunk of the study was dedicated to the transatlantic slave trade. Sally had nightmares reading about the inhumane treatment the slaves were subjected to on those trips. But what broke her heart was encountering her great-grandfather in the list of merchants who transported African slaves through Bristol to the new lands. How could a man related to her have been party to such injustice?

Sally staged a solo protest against slavery by making amends to the next black man she encountered—a bearded student she had seen in the library a few times. He was from Ghana, shy, somewhat awkward. She invited him for a drink, gave her room number, and fled before he found his voice. He arrived as agreed and knocked timidly. Before the man could say *Asantehene*, Sally smothered him with kisses and undressed him, and it could have been misconstrued as rape had the young man not relaxed and grinned.

Sally's one-woman protest did not end there; her tryst with the South African gardener was prompted by the same instinct: an unspoken guilt over past mistreatment of blacks through slavery and her patriarch's complicity in it. After reading Joseph Conrad's *Heart of Darkness* days after its publication in 1899, her estrangement from white privilege was complete. How she rationalized that it was right or moral to enjoy the trappings of comfort acquired through slave labor—the backbone of her family wealth— nobody knows. It may well have been what prompts a soldier to lay down his life for country, even when the cause that takes him to the front line is fraudulent; or for those inclined toward the divine scriptures, it is the same principle that leads a righteous man to lay down his life for sinners. Sally's salacious behavior made her neither profligate nor righteous—her actions may have been an affront to the laws of the land but one could hardly consider them divine. Yet, it was difficult to divorce the simple privilege that her past afforded her, which freed her from the rigors of earning a living to fornicate at will. That fact of her life had been secured decades earlier, so her communion with black males, whether students in London or gardeners in

South Africa, could only be seen as returning a favor of sorts—thanking the black forebears who had made possible her comfortable future.

So when Sally caught a glimpse of McDonald's brutalized servants, it brought back that resentment. She walked away in silence.

She may not have spoken a word, but many words were spoken about her, especially after the assembled guests were told by a deflated and defeated McDonald that the guest of honor was unlikely to grace the celebrations due to some unexpected developments. He had been unable to extract any information from the servants, beyond the wind mishap and their flight from the station. But guests who had had a little too much to drink shouted that McDonald was lying because some had reported sighting a mysterious guest arrive and depart almost immediately. And since no one in the colony had met her previously, they all remarked on her skin, which was whiter than anyone they'd seen, her springy and dignified gait, as well as her manner of clothing, which was heavier than the Nakuru weather required.

It was Sally's letter from England a month later that finally broke McDonald's heart, resulting in a depression during which he locked himself up and mourned his loss. By then, McDonald had confirmed that Sally had arrived on the coast as scheduled and departed soon after, but he had no way of verifying whether or not she had visited his house:

I am distraught to write this letter, the last to you from me. Your cruelty toward me and fellow men, which I have borne and witnessed over the years, is the ground on which I'm filing for divorce. Yours is the Heart of Darkness.
Sally

Had locals been privy to this missive, they would have concluded that Sally was a witch, able to cast a spell and unleash a spirit. For the house that McDonald built soon turned into a veritable heart of darkness, with the windows shuttered for years and signs warning women to keep off the premises posted all over the property. Only male servants were allowed in the compound. They, too, were ordered to wear black uniforms because their master was mourning, although he did not specify his loss. Some overzealous workers chose to wear sackcloth as a mark of their loyalty, and those who learned about the secret code on the posters also abstained from touching their wives in solidarity with their master.

And when the doors and the windows to the house were finally opened, the villagers were surprised to see cows rearing their big heads in the doorway. That's when the edifice was converted into a farmhouse that later gave way to the segregated social establishment, which further gave way to the multicultural outfit named the Jakaranda, the letter *k* for Kenya replacing the *c* in the jacaranda that McDonald said sounded "colonial."

Now, on the cusp of the new republic and a new dawn for its multicolored citizens, the Jakaranda was about to acquire a new identity, yet again.

4

istory has strange ways of announcing itself to the present, whether conceived in comforting darkness or blinding light. It can manifest with the gentleness of a bean cracking out of its pod, making music in its fall. Even when such seed falls into fertile soil, it still wriggles from the tug of the earth, stretching a green hand for uplift. The seed of wonderment that germinated from the flicker of a kiss in that darkened night had, in a few months, grown by leaps and bounds. And so it came to pass that the ancient history that Babu had dodged for two generations suddenly arrived at his doorstep, unfurling with the slow, deliberate motions of a burning rope, embers crawling from knot to knot. What was perplexing was the precision of the revelations: like the biblical plague that reached every household that did not bear a lintel, the dregs from Babu's past rose to the fore, sliding beneath his locked door to sweep him off his feet.

But that's rushing the story, burying the inimitable drama that unfurled the night Mariam made her grand return to the Jakaranda and reordered the lives of those who she touched—not just with her already famously flavored tongue, but with words rolled off the selfsame organ. So let's hold it right there and absorb the moment when, lured by the smell of sweet, spicy perfume, Rajan descended the dais and stretched a hand, like a leaf dying for light after months in darkness. He stretched a hand toward the woman he suspected was the kissing stranger, and on whom he seemed utterly dependent for survival.

The young lass sat unmoved. She obviously did not understand the dance etiquette at the Jakaranda, and Rajan's slight frame silhouetted against the dancing lights struck a statuesque pose, hair pulled into a ponytail, his lower lip trembling with both anticipation and trepidation, a hand stretched out to receive the reluctant girl. All this was witnessed by the hundreds of pairs of eyes that seemed hypnotized by the act. A hesitant beat broke the enveloping silence as Rajan knelt at Mariam's feet, words instantly forming on his lips:

> *Malaika, nakupenda malaika*
> *nami nifanyeje*
> *kijana mwenzio . . .*

The crowd roared appreciatively as the band started to play the slow love song they all knew by heart. Mariam flashed a coy smile and rose to her feet. The instantaneous clamor was enough to lift the roof off the Jakaranda, so that even Mariam could no longer resist the serenade. She made a few strides toward Rajan, who led the way toward the stage, doing a little dance because he could hardly contain his elation.

When she hesitated at the staircase leading to the dance floor, Rajan swept her off her feet, rocking her in his arms. She proved heavier than he had anticipated and Rajan staggered, nearly missing a step before regaining his balance. She swooned with pleasure, or perhaps fright, as he took the stairs before depositing her onstage. She steadied herself, her wide, circular silver earrings shining against the oscillating lights. Her mass of thick hair reached her waist.

She smiled broadly, revealing twin dimples, straightening a crease on her long skirt as she did so.

If this was the kissing stranger he had encountered in the dark, Rajan thought, she certainly wasn't afraid of the spotlight.

The love song faded and was replaced by a *mugithi* tune, bringing onto the stage the stories that Rajan had been told by his grandfather Babu about his experiences building the railway. The dance imitated the movement of the train and Rajan guided Mariam to join the trail of revelers doing their rounds through the dance floor, their feet spread wide apart to imitate the railway, every lap around the premises marking a completed journey.

The next tune was called the dance of the *marebe*. It involved thunderous drumming followed by the wail of the guitar and the blow of the sax. It was called the dance of the *marebe* because it told the true story of the Indian trader who encountered a lion in the Tsavo forest as he led his mule to the camp. The mule carried on its back pails of paraffin and when the lion struck, Babu had narrated to Rajan, its claws got stuck in the ropes holding the pails. The mule attempted to flee but was paralyzed by fear and the additional load on its back. The lion could not extricate himself from the hessian ropes. The pails of paraffin clanged together as the mule hee-hawed, trying to shake the beast burdening his back.

The song climaxed with even heavier drumming that represented the clanging pails, an act Chege the drummer delivered with great drama. He would glide from one drum to another, teasing revelers that the skin drums were not taut enough and needed heating. He would make as though to head toward the butchery, but fans would wave him away, hurling coins onto the drum that Chege accepted with comic deference. It someone offered a note, especially if the giver was a woman, he would direct them to deposit it into the waistband of his pants, his bare chest glistening with sweat.

Rajan was tongue-tied when he was finally alone with Mariam backstage at the end of the concert.

"Sorry for the late introduction," Mariam said, finally introducing herself properly. When Rajan stated his name, she smiled sweetly. "Who doesn't know you . . . ?" she breezed.

Rajan simply stared back, dazzled by the beauty that seemed to radiate out of her every pore. Her face glowed at her every turn, and her circular, silvery earrings danced, oscillating in the darkened space. She was in high heels, and Rajan realized to his horror that she was taller than he. She was so beautiful, he couldn't imagine her doing any of the ordinary things ordinary folks did, like having a bowel movement. He couldn't imagine such ugliness from her gorgeous form.

"You are suddenly very quiet," Mariam whispered.

He wanted to shut his eyes and be serenaded by her cooing voice. His mind was racing through the past few months, when the mere thought of Mariam diminished his hunger pangs and set off such an acute desperation that he feared he was losing his mind. He remembered the many sleepless nights he had agonized about her, and now here she was, in a poorly lit space close to their original point of collision, looking even more lovely than he remembered her. The memory of the kiss resurged with such power that Rajan staggered toward Mariam and pulled her toward him.

"Hey, hey, *pole pole*," she protested. "Don't jump on me as though I'm a stolen bicycle."

Rajan laughed. "You just can't imagine how long I have waited for this moment . . ."

"I thought we barely met an hour ago," Mariam replied.

Rajan stopped himself before blurting about their first kiss in the dark and how it had affected him. He needed to kiss the girl again to confirm she was the one.

"I want to go home," Mariam said.

"You want me to take you home?"

"That'd be nice," she smiled.

"Where do you live?"

"Where do *you* live?"

"You mean my home?"

"Where else do you call home?"

"I am home right now!"

"Stop pulling my leg."

"I wish I could pull your leg!" Rajan smiled even as a knot of panic congealed in his stomach. Home meant the house of his grandparents, Babu and Fatima. This girl wasn't possibly thinking he'd take her there on their first night out.

Rajan was suddenly awash with shame. At twenty-one, he still had not moved out, and possibly wouldn't ever leave home because he was a Punjabi boy. He was bound to live with his grandparents his entire life. He envied his band-mates who all had their private spaces outside the family homes. Era had his small dwelling that was detached from his mother's house. It wasn't much, just a tin shack—ten by ten feet, meat paper on the walls, a single bed, and an earthen floor. But Era derived great prestige when he told the other band members: "I have to rush home, I got a bird in the cage . . ."

Rajan could never dream of saying such a thing. The backstage operations at the Jakaranda served to minimize such complications.

He had never taken any girl home to his grandparents, but then again, none had ever expressed such a desire. They seemed content to consummate their lusts backstage. But this was no ordinary girl; he had searched for her for nine months and she wanted to be handled *pole pole*. She was not a stolen bicycle.

That night, Rajan and Mariam ended up at Era's tin shack on the fringes of Lake Nakuru near the *kei* apple trees and fence that separated Indian from African quarters. The white quarters towered above, close to where McDonald had built his house, the layout of the township forming an unstable triangle, each race on a far end of the lake.

It was at that hedge separating the Indian and African quarters that Era had first encountered Rajan fifteen years earlier. Era was nine; Rajan was six—his small head appearing one day just above the hedge that stood between his family's house and Era's.

Era's principle memory of that first encounter was how Rajan resembled the portrait of Jesus that adorned their living room—only the crown of thorns was not standing on Rajan's head, it hung around his neck where the hedge reached.

"*Maze, umeona mpira?*" Rajan's had asked during that first encounter, his tender voice trilling like a flute.

"Eeeeehhh?" Era shouted.

"Our cricket ball."

"Where is it?"

"It just rolled under the fence," the boy with the thorny garland said. "Have you seen it?"

Era pretended to be looking, although the tiny hard ball was under his heel. "*Sioni!*" he said in a voice that declared the search over.

"*Sawa!*" the other boy replied with resignation, and walked away.

Era had hoarded eighteen balls by the time his mother discovered them: tennis balls, cricket balls, and footballs. "I'm not rearing a thief in this house!" she said as she administered a beating over the transgression. "Return them where you got them or else . . ."

Era's mother left her unspecified threat hanging, but he had a pretty good idea of what would follow. He was the oldest and the only male of her four children, and his mother was determined to make him a good example to his younger siblings. Their father was in a colonial detention, where thousands were being held.

"We may be poor, but we are not thieves," Era's mother reminded him. He walked heavily to the fence and hurled the balls over, tears rolling down his face.

The noise of the returning balls drew Rajan back to the fence. He got a glimpse of Era as he disappeared into their mud house and noticed that the older boy had no shoes.

Rajan went back inside and picked out a pair of shoes that he had outgrown and returned to the fence. "*Maze! Maze! Maaaaaaaaaaaazeeeeeeeeeee!*" His voice floated in the air.

Era stayed away. Rajan returned to the fence several times that day. He wanted to reciprocate the return of the balls that he and his cousins had been searching for for months, so he decided to dispatch his gift that evening.

The shoes landed on the tin roof where Era's household was waiting to cook a meal on the open fire. Even from a child's hurl, the shoes arrived with reasonable force, sending coils of soot tumbling off the roof into the cooking pot.

Initially, Era's mother did not know what to make of the whole episode. She armed herself with a hefty piece of wood and stepped outside, looking for the offending party.

The government had announced a state of emergency and had placed the entire colony under virtual curfew. Communities' social interactions had been reduced to a whimper and cultural life was disrupted as no one was allowed out before sunup or after darkness. The animals in the wilds were freer. One could not move from one part of the country to another without clearance from the local headman, who derived his authority from the white district officer. And every local had to bear the *kipande* on his neck like a dog, announcing his name and address. The parallels did not end there; as a dog's collar attests him to be disease-free through a raft of vaccinations, a *kipande* around a man's neck was his proof that he had been cleared by the colonial powers and did not pose a threat to his fellow man.

So everybody kept to themselves unless it was absolutely necessary to travel, making the crashing sound on the roof that much more perplexing. Era's mother stepped out and was confronted by the sight of two tiny black boots, their surfaces scratched to reveal a brown core.

"*Maze! Maze! Chukua viatu mimi nampa yeye!*" Rajan sang from the fence.

Era's mother sighed, dropped the piece of wood, and returned inside. "These Indians are full of *madharau*. If they want to give something, why not do it like a good neighbor? It's a child who is delivering them . . ."

Era was beside himself with excitement. He had never worn shoes, and the sight of the black boots was overwhelming. But from the look on his mother's face, he knew he had to employ caution.

"Go!" she urged Era in a savage whisper. "Go pick what has been thrown at you as one hurls stale *ugali* at a dog. If I see you in those shoes . . ." Once again, she left the threat hanging.

He waited until his mother went to work the following day before trying on the shoes. He dashed outside and got the washbasin—the heavy metal tub feeling light as he carried it, imbued as he was by the joy singing in his heart. He knelt at the water tank and opened the tap, the gentle trickle drumming a soft drone as it filled the basin.

"Don't dare drain the tank!" Ceeri, Era's younger sister, shouted.

He turned off the tap and sat on the grass patched unevenly on the red earth and washed his feet, then dried them quickly with a cloth. He was breathless with excitement as he tried on the shoes.

He attempted to squeeze in one foot but it was too wide for the shoe. He hopped into the kitchen and got a spoon, but even that proved futile in forcing the foot in. He used milking jelly to line the back of the shoe and thrust one foot in, then used the same trick on the other foot. But the shoes were so tight he could hardly stand, and he felt like a baby taking its first steps.

Era grudgingly removed the shoes and hid them, hoping to pass them on to a younger sibling when his mother softened. Months later, he couldn't remember where he'd hidden them, turning Rajan's generous gift into a terrible waste.

With Mariam's return to the Jakaranda, Rajan could have finally and proudly proclaimed: *I got a bird in the cage* . . . even if the cage was borrowed. But Rajan was still unable to believe his good fortune. He remained hypnotized by her beauty, which shone through the dim light coming from the kerosene tin lamp in Era's shack—the languid flame throwing shadows from one wall to another. Her eyes had a hint of blue, and they sparkled delightfully when she looked at him.

Upon arrival, Mariam had dumped her two bags on the floor and slumped onto the bed as though she had lived there all her life. Era returned with fresh linen for the bed before excusing himself to join Chege the drummer for the night. The band members were at liberty to arrive at another's house without warning or explanation. Such was the brotherhood in the band; each understood that these adjustments had to be made to free up room for overnight guests. As the young men liked to say, they were fine even if they slept packed like sardines because sleep resides in the eyes.

Rajan motioned to Mariam to help him make the bed. She held one edge of the sheet and remarked: "I thought I was a guest but I can see I'm the housemaid already!"

Rajan laughed and said nothing.

As Mariam lifted her end of the sheet up, the slight breeze from this movement blew out the lamp's flame, sending the room into darkness. There was a momentary silence, before they both collapsed onto the bed in a fit of giggles. It was in this state that Rajan received a kiss from Mariam. It bore the unmistakable lavender flavor.

This was followed by the rustle of clothes as Mariam undressed, before snuggling close to kiss Rajan's neck and face. He undressed reluctantly, waiting for her to prompt him to shake off this or that garment. She was all over him, her warm, wet tongue coursing along his body with the swiftness of a serpent. Rajan remained completely still, paralyzed with fear.

He was trying to reconcile the different visions of Mariam that he had experienced. There was the Mariam lodged in his mind from that first kiss in the dark and the events that followed through the search. Then there was the returned Mariam, easygoing and seemingly at home wherever he took her. And now there was the Mariam in the darkened room, animal naked, her warm breath scorching his skin. When Mariam's searching tongue reached his navel and coursed farther down, he went limp.

"What's going on?" she asked calmly.

He said nothing.

"What's going on, my friend?" she cooed again.

"I don't know," Rajan said earnestly.

"Relax, baby . . ." she soothed. "Relaaaax."

And relax Rajan did—over the next few days, their naked bodies marked the passage of time. Clandestine meals were sneaked in to the two lovebirds at appropriate intervals from different kitchens. Arrowroots and sweet potatoes from Era's mother's kitchen, buttered naan bread and samosas pilfered from Rajan's grandmother Fatima's kitchen. Sweetened tea with milk came from both homes. Social mores decreed it was taboo for girls to spend the night at boyfriends' houses, so it was sacrilegious to spend several nights together.

When Mariam was unable to find the keys to her suitcases, Rajan sneaked home yet again and returned with some of his own jeans and T-shirts. They were a perfect fit.

"Looks like you've been keeping my clothes," Mariam remarked joyfully, slumping back into bed and snuggling closer. It seemed they could live this way for the rest of their lives.

A day is a long time for anyone whose singular preoccupation is to eat, drink, and sleep. Actually, one should say day and night, for if one spends the day eating and drinking, then he or she is unlikely to be sleeping. Establishments were starting to sprout up in Nakuru, declaring themselves to be day- and nightclubs. One presumed the daytime pa-trons would be different from the night owls, though that was not necessarily the case—Rajan and Mariam were par-tying day and night, albeit in the solitude of Era's house.

By their third straight day together, Rajan trusted Mariam completely. He told her things he had never shared with anyone, not even Era.

There is something curious about humans' desire to unburden themselves to complete strangers. Perhaps it's because strangers, like a stream, flow on with their jour-neys by daybreak, minimizing any prospect for what has been shared being used against them. Or it could be that strangers make no judgment at all. Mariam had proven to be nonjudgmental on that first night when Rajan, over-come with fear, had failed to rise to the occasion. She had simply urged him to relax, and chuckled that she didn't know anybody who had died from lack of sex, much the same way she had rebuffed Rajan the next morning when he complained she was taking too much sugar in her tea.

"Ever heard of a bee being hospitalized for having too much honey?" she responded.

It was her easygoing nature that encouraged Rajan to share his secrets, despite the fact that she said little about herself and her mysterious locked suitcases. But Rajan felt no qualms about sharing his story. He briefly told her about his search for her, avoiding the embarrassing parts.

"You are a cow, all right," she swooned. "What you need is a fine milking of the foolishness in you."

Rajan laughed along with her, and then continued telling her about his life, too fearful that asking ques-tions about hers would drive her away. So he told her about his grandfather Babu and grandmother Fatima, his father Rashid, who had gone to study in England and stayed, his mother Amina eventually joining him.

"He left at the height of the emergency, when I was about ten," Rajan said of his father. "Now I'm twice as old."

"Do you miss him?"

Rajan paused and looked at Mariam. "You are the first person to ask me that," he sighed. "It's been ten years of solitude. And all Grandpa says when I inquire about my father is: *We came in dhows to build the rail, and left in planes.*"

"Do you miss him?" Mariam pursued after a brief silence.

"I don't know." He shrugged a naked shoulder. "There are times," he went on after a moment, "that I wonder how my life would have turned out if he had been around."

Mariam wrapped her arms around him. "You shall be fine," she assured in a tone that suggested she was speaking to a child. "*We shall be fine . . .*"

It was on their fourth day together that Rajan took her back to the Jakaranda and composed a song for her. Just like that, or as locals would say, *Hau hau*. Later that night, as he sought to refine the lines, infusing words from local languages, Mariam asked where he'd learned Kikuyu, which was spoken widely across Nakuru but seldom used by Indians. So Rajan told her about the journey that he had taken three years earlier, when he'd turned eighteen.

"I thought it was a joke," Rajan confessed. "My grandfather was making his usual rail jokes, only this time he said he and I would be taking a road trip the following morning. *We came in dhows to lay the rail, so let's hit the road*, he told all of us."

Babu had surveyed the table where the two dozen friends and family members had assembled to celebrate

Rajan's milestone and said: "This country has been generous to us. It's a decent thing to return the favor." He then
paused and looked in Rajan's direction. "I'm passing the
baton on to this young man. Now that he's come of age, it's
his turn to go see the world . . ."

That's where Babu left it and Rajan thought no further
about the issue. But the following morning, he was informed that Babu was waiting, ready to embark on a journey to serve his country. Initially, Rajan thought Babu was
bluffing—until he got to the driveway where Murage, the
family "boy," as Fatima liked to call him, was revving the
engine.

"What's going on?" Rajan asked. "Where are we going?"

"No need to argue, young man," Babu replied calmly.
"We'll talk on our way to Ndundori. You are going to become a fine teacher."

"Where, when, why?" Rajan was frantic as Murage
pushed him into the car.

Once inside the vehicle, Babu said calmly: "If American
children can travel halfway across the world to serve as
volunteers, what's the excuse for an Indian boy wasting
his youth in funny occupations like producing sounds im-
itating the train?"

"I felt like I was being banished from the land," Rajan told Mariam that day. "I was angry at my grandfather.
Angry that I had to leave all my friends without a proper
farewell. Angry that I was being forced into serving my
country as a teacher in some far-off location."

With the emergency laws still in place, the land was
desolate and they encountered very few people along the
way, most of them security agents—middle-aged men in
khaki shorts, their long, ashy legs resembling marabou

storks, their homemade guns lethal beaks.

When they reached Ndundori, Babu directed Murage toward a dirt road that led to a modest one-story wooden house ringed by eucalyptus trees. It was eerily silent and Rajan asked, with panic in his voice, if this was the school he'd be teaching at.

Babu smiled and explained, "This is the home of the Karims. They have a small business here. When Indians crave homemade roti or samosa or biryani, this is where they come. So you will be lucky to eat home-cooked meals every day."

Rajan said nothing, so Babu went on: "I want you to know my friend and his family. You know the story of our dhow being shipwrecked on our way here to build the railroad. Karim was on that dhow. These are good people. We were like family when we were young . . . Yes, I was once young," Babu chuckled. "And Karim has a granddaughter just about your age. Actually, you two knew each other when you were smaller."

Rajan shrugged and said nothing. This was too much information. In any case, why should he care about an Indian family in the middle of nowhere? All he needed was to return home and carry on with his life.

No sooner had the engine turned off than a little balding man emerged, with a big smile that Rajan found irritating.

"Karim, my good man," Babu greeted. They embraced, then paused to examine each other.

"You don't look a day older than the last time I saw you," Karim said. "The gods have been kind to you."

"We are not complaining," Babu replied. "You are looking hale." He glanced across the compound; it hadn't changed much over the past few decades.

"And this must be Mr. Rajan," Karim enthused. "You know, I first saw you when you were like this." He bridged his open palms as if rocking a baby in his arms. "Now you are taller than me," he added, standing beside Rajan to compare heights.

Rajan said nothing.

Two tiny windows creaked open simultaneously, as Karim's chubby-faced wife Abdia appeared. Upstairs, Leila, their granddaughter, peeked through the lace curtains to spy on the goings-on below. Instantly, Rajan took a dislike to them. He vowed to himself to keep away from these nosy women.

Babu waved at the woman in the *duka*.

"Abdia, come greet our guests," Karim called out to his wife. "You too, Leila," he waved to his granddaughter, whose silhouette was visible through the curtains.

As the two women made their way toward the men, Rajan shuffled uncomfortably. Karim and Babu spoke in Punjabi, which Rajan barely understood. Abdia joined in the conversation. Murage made for the woods to pass water, leaving Rajan and Leila standing awkwardly, eyeing each other suspiciously.

"Get to know each other," Abdia pressed. "Leila, ask him where he goes to school."

Leila did as told, but Rajan answered gruffly, "I don't!"

"You don't go to school?"

"No!"

Rajan walked a little farther away from their grandparents. Leila got the message and followed him.

"How come?"

"How come *what*?"

"You don't go to school?"

"Well . . . I do."

"Really?"

"I'm joining a new school."

"Really? You must be excited!"

Rajan sized her up. She was an excitable little girl, he thought. Not more than fifteen years old. "I'm not a student anymore," he said with a hint of arrogance. "I'm going to be a teacher."

Leila was wide-eyed. "You mean you're the guy my grandfather talked about?"

Rajan was about to respond when Babu called them back. "I don't have the whole day, but you two will have plenty of time to get to know each other."

Abdia winked at her husband, who cleared his throat and smiled.

"All right, all right. Mr. Rajan, now that you have another home away from home, I'm sure Leila would be happy to show you around . . ."

There wasn't much to see in the sparsely furnished rooms that Leila rushed through before escorting him to one with a foldable safari bed tucked in a corner.

"This is your room," Leila said. "Remind me to get you some sheets."

They heard Babu calling again and Rajan rushed out.

"You need to get your luggage out of the car, young man. What shall I tell your granny when I return?"

Rajan shrugged and said nothing.

"The schoolmaster expects you tomorrow. Get some rest, do some reading, get ready."

Rajan nodded.

He neither rested nor prepared for school. He just sat, dumbfounded by the turn of events. Had anyone told him he would have encountered half of what he had in the preceding twelve hours, he would have thought it a cruel joke.

He cast a look around the room. The Karim household was noisy. Abdia spoke like a sewing machine, Karim smiled day and night. Leila sat cross-legged and giggled at Indian songs blasting from her transistor radio. When Karim and Abdia weren't looking, Leila rolled her eyes at Rajan.

Dinner was served in this chaos, and it wasn't long before Rajan excused himself. Leila offered to get his bedsheets, and as he made his way to his room, tired to the bone, she tried to trip him. He pretended not to notice, so when she delivered the sheets, she rolled her eyes and stuck out her tongue. Rajan laughed quietly and bid her goodnight.

The school comprised a block of mud-and-wattle rondavels with grass-thatched roofs. A small party was hosted in Rajan's honor by a dozen other teachers. The schoolmaster was short and mustachioed, with his hair parted in the middle in a style called a "lorry" because the gulf was wide enough for a truck to drive through.

"We are honored and privileged to have you here," the schoolmaster said in a quivering voice because he had never been so close to an Indian.

The children stared openly at Rajan. "*Haiya, muthungu! Muthungu!*" those streaming into classes after break time screamed, alerting their friends to come and see a white man. It appeared that a few hours on the road had turned his brown skin white.

Rajan volunteered to teach history, but the diminutive schoolmaster had other ideas. "Why don't you teach English? The children think you are a white man!"

There were about twenty kids in the class, three or four sharing a desk so that each had to give way for the other to write or else they'd elbow each other.

"Good morning, class," Rajan smiled on that first day.

"Good morning, madam!" the class returned.

Rajan took no offense, correctly guessing that the previous teacher had been a woman. "Boys are males, girls are females," he started, pointing randomly to different pupils. "Tell us, are you a male or a female?"

Several boys said they were females while a number of girls said they were males, eliciting lots of laughter from their classmates.

In the second week of Rajan's posting, Leila arrived at the school one afternoon. "My mother said an Indian boy must miss samosa and masala tea, so she made some especially for you," she gushed.

Rajan nodded his appreciation, silently wondering if the treat couldn't have been served at home. He invited Leila into the humble staff room and poured the steaming tea into the only cup available. All the other teachers were in class.

"*Karibu*," he invited her to partake of the tea.

"You go first," Leila returned.

"No, you first."

"I asked first."

"I am your host."

"I made the tea!"

"I thought you said your mother did."

"She and I did."

"So who did what?"

"She made it. I listened to her. She said a cup of tea is like love: it is sweeter when shared."

Rajan blushed. What did this child know about love?

"Do you agree with that?"

"What?"

"The idea of love as a cup of tea," Leila said with a grin.

"I thought your mother was talking about you, not me."

"But now here we are. With a cup of tea to share."

"Why?" Rajan responded cautiously.

"Because you have only one cup . . ."

They ended up taking sips from the cup while quietly giggling. Despite his initial misgivings, Rajan realized he enjoyed Leila's company immensely, and he continued to in the weeks that followed. What Rajan liked the most were their evening walks. Sometimes they played games along the way that occasionally ended up in Rajan's room. Once, as they wrestled on his bed, Rajan came to the sudden realization that Leila's childlike frame was developing into womanhood. She had sizable breasts that she hid under large sweaters. She became aware of his discovery when Rajan loosened his grip and gently stroked her face. Just as they were about to kiss, Abdia's voice filtered into the room: "Leeeeiiiiilllaaaa!"

Leila rushed out of the room without a word, and what followed was a crackle of violent Punjabi inflexions finished off with the whack of a slap.

That night, Rajan remained holed up in his room and skipped dinner, awash with the shame of being caught fooling around with Leila. He also started taking long walks through the village after school just to avoid being confronted by Abdia. At school, he drifted from hour to hour, day to day, still without any clarity as to what could have prompted his grandfather to consign him to the wilderness. The other teachers were all older than he was, and at first, a few invited him to their homes, but Rajan declined all the offers. It was in this period that he started reading the books that Babu had given him: Mahatma Gandhi's *The Story of My Experiments with Truth*, Booker T. Washington's *My Larger Education*, Jomo Kenyatta's *Facing Mount Kenya*, and Kwame Nkrumah's *I Speak of Freedom*.

During one of his solitary walks, he met a young boy around five or six years old. The boy spoke nonstop in Kikuyu, while holding a bowl of porridge that he sipped between bouts of mucousy sniffles. The kid's khaki uniform implied he went to the school Rajan taught at, but Rajan could not tell him apart from the other three hundred pupils. As the boy continued with his Kikuyu monologue, Rajan just nodded and smiled and kept walking along.

One day, the boy followed Rajan to Karim and Abdia's home, bearing a gift of chapati rolled in a paper torn from his math book. On another day, he brought a liter of milk in a soda bottle; another, an egg cracked open in a minor accident along the way. After a few weeks, Rajan realized he could not only understand the boy perfectly, but could even engage in short conversations. Leila sulked at Rajan's new subject of affection. Abdia and Karim totally ignored the boy. By the end of the term, Rajan was fluent in Kikuyu.

"My grandfather wanted me to give something back to society. Instead, I gained something. A language that made me a proper Kenyan," Rajan told Mariam that night. "He was smiling from ear to ear when he came to fetch me at the end of the term. He did not say what he was happy about, but he seemed proud that I had survived, and as a bonus had acquired a new language. So the trip to Ndundori was a preparation of sorts for what lay ahead . . ."

"How do you mean?"

"If I didn't speak any local language, I feel like my art wouldn't be as authentic. I would just be another *muhindi*."

"Why do you say that?"

"I am Indian, am I not?"

"What does that mean?"

"I don't know," he shrugged. "My skin color has . . ."

He paused. "At least in the past it had political implications. Whites at the top, Indians after them, then Arabs, and finally Africans. That's political privilege."

"What's changed now?"

"We are waiting to see, but with independence, Africans will be at the top."

"And . . . ?"

"I don't know. Indians in the middle? Whites at the bottom?"

"What do your friends say?"

"Which friends?"

"Your bandmates."

"Era, of course, has been my friend since I was five or six years old. We don't have political conversations. He's simply my friend."

"Does he feel the same way?"

"How do you mean?"

"Does he consider you his friend without condition?"

"Absolutely."

"Then what's this pressure about speaking local languages?"

"You got me wrong, it's not about my friends; it's about myself. I want to be more than just an Indian. I want to be a Kenyan immersed in other cultures."

"I can't believe this," Mariam said softly, shaking her head.

"Why? I'm telling you the truth."

"I'm not questioning the facts of your story. I just can't believe you went to my village. I grew up right next to that school!" she exclaimed. "As a matter of fact, my foster family started the school."

"Really!? Then you must meet my grandfather, he surely knows your family."

"I said foster family."

"What's the difference, it's still your family!"

"Not quite. That's why the word *foster* comes first."

"Which means?"

"They are a family of sorts."

"*A family of sorts*. My goodness, where did you learn to speak like that! Seriously, though, who is your *real* family?"

"I wish I knew!"

"You can't be serious."

"Yes, I am. I don't know and I don't care. Well, I do care, but I don't know."

"Which makes you . . . ?"

"*Mkosa kabila*."

"Be serious."

"I am. I have no tribe." After a moment, Mariam added, "I have no family."

Rajan peered intently at her. She looked like a cross between an Arab and Indian, or Caucasian and African. Or a mix of all four. "Come to think of it, what's your race?"

"What does it matter?"

"It doesn't really . . ."

"Exactly. It shouldn't bother you. But I'm bothered about this Leila girl. What happened to her?"

"When? Before or after?"

"You mean you *did* it!?"

"I meant before my trip or after my trip."

"Stop being clever. Did you do it or not?"

"What do you think?"

"You tell me!"

"Why should that—to use your own word—bother you?"

"It doesn't, I'm just—just curious."

"Okay, let me tell you what I found most curious. Leila's mother gave my grandfather the impression that Leila and I were tight. Yet while I was there she did everything she could to keep us apart."

"That is weird," Mariam conceded. "Still, it doesn't answer my question!"

"I have no question to answer," Rajan declared.

Babu had noticed the erratic hours that Rajan was keeping, barely sitting for more than a few moments at a time, and had remarked to his wife Fatima, "I think he has woman problems. He is behaving as though he has ants in his bum."

Fatima cleared her throat. "I have also noticed his restlessness."

"Rajan has been spending a lot of time over there," Babu went on, looking out the window toward Era's family home. "See? Those are his footprints. I think they even made a hole in the fence." He gestured toward the hedge where Era had first met Rajan, which was now a towering mass of foliage that completely blocked the view of the other side. On the lower part of the fence was the hole that Rajan used to sneak through.

"Young people have to go through these stages, don't they?" Fatima said calmly.

"I'm not saying they shouldn't," Babu replied defensively. "Everybody has to learn these life matters his own way." He paused for a moment but Fatima said nothing. "I should have told him," Babu said finally, then sighed as though the admission lifted a weight off his chest. "I should have told him."

"I told you, but what does the proverb say? *A woman's prophecy is always taken lightly until it comes to pass.*"

"There is nothing to prophesize about. Nothing has happened."

"You don't know that for sure," Fatima countered.

"I know."

"You just said you think he has woman problems," she reminded Babu.

"I said I *suspect* he does. But that's not the end of the world."

"It could end many things . . ."

"We still have time to tell him, don't we?"

"You have to tell him soon. He needs to know before it's too late."

"It's never too late."

"That's what you've been saying all these years," Fatima said, a hint of irritation creeping in. "Do you know the kind of reputation we would have if he broke off the engagement?"

"Just let the young man be," Babu said, leaning back in his seat.

"If you don't tell him, I will!" Fatima threatened.

"I meant to tell him three years ago when he came of age. But things have been difficult with the emergency."

Fatima walked to the window where Babu had stood moments earlier. "Things will be even more difficult if he doesn't know. He needs to know so that his heart may be at peace."

"Who says his heart is not at peace?"

"Why does everything have to be so difficult?"

"Didn't I just say I will tell him? I mean, I introduced him to the family, he met the girl, and they seemed to like each other. What can one do other than wait?"

"Were it not for this music thing, which again you approved against my will, he wouldn't be running around with all these girls."

"He is not running around with any girls."

"Didn't you just say you suspect that he is? Or do you want to deny your own words before they dry on your lips?"

"Don't put words in my mouth."

"Tell me, which respectable Indian boy plays music in this town? Eeeh? Tell me!"

"I see you have *maneno*. First it was about the news of the betrothal, then the running around with girls, now it's the music . . ."

"I tell you, you are spoiling that boy, but will you listen? I wish his father were here."

"Go on, go on! I can see what this is about. Now it's about me spoiling the boy because his father isn't here."

"But it's true, isn't it?"

"You never cease to amaze me," Babu said, shaking his head. "I'm the one who alerted you to this thing, so together we can monitor the young man, and now you—you—you just amaze me . . ."

Theirs was a most interesting union. "Wife," Babu had said to Fatima upon her arrival in Nakuru, after being apart from each other for several years while Babu was working on the railroad, "we are in an arranged marriage, so we might as well make an arrangement that will work."

Fatima had merely sighed.

"First off," Babu started, "I swear I will never ask about that child of yours if you promise never to raise a word about the babies that you've heard attributed to me. Secondly, we shall have no obligation to touch one other, unless it is to apply medication or exchange greetings at family gatherings. And neither of us should be worried where one is going for some touch-touch."

"Really?" Fatima asked.

"Yes, really," Babu said briskly. "To ensure this rule is enforced to the letter, let's bring that child of yours to lie between us, in that space called no-man's-land, to make sure we don't touch accidentally while we sleep. Finally, let's agree that this child of yours shall become *our* child and he need not know about his story, provided he leaves my house at the age of eighteen. What say you?"

Fatima was silent for a while before she responded hesitantly. "You—you appear to have given this a bit of thought, so perhaps I should think it through first as well."

"No need to think, wife, there is nothing to think about. All I need is a yes or no."

"You may believe that," Fatima quipped, "but it's not that easy."

"This is pretty easy, *mboga kabisa*, as the Waswahili like to say. Easy like munching a handful of vegetables. The only thing that might require a bit of thinking is where one shall go for touch-touch moments since that shall not be provided at home. But from the look of things, you shouldn't have any trouble finding that."

Fatima was silent.

"Is that a yes or no?"

Fatima said nothing.

"I shall take that for a female no, which could mean yes."

"Babu Rajan Salim, are you out of your mind?"

"I thought you knew that already," Babu responded as he rose to go.

So it was Mariam's revelation about the Ndundori school that prompted Rajan to introduce her to Babu so early in their relationship. Rajan was elated that the first girl he would be taking home shared something with his grandfather.

Rocking in his swivel chair, cigar in hand, reading glasses on his forehead—held up by strands of hair that appeared bristly in the morning, curly in the afternoon, and soft in the evening—Babu spent most of his day on the veranda, which is where Rajan and Mariam found him.

Babu was now eighty-three years old, and the singular event that gave meaning to his life was rising early to prepare for what he called the "morning roll call." Showered and smartly dressed in fresh khaki pants and shirt, Babu routinely rushed to the gate overlooking the main road to wait for the whistle from the ice-cream man hurtling down the road, pushing a cart of goodies.

Babu would salute him, *"Afande!"* raise his right hand, and return to the house smiling because, he said, he had been acknowledged as present in the workers' register for the day. As little children, Rajan and his cousins Asha and Saida had participated in this morning ritual, competing to deliver Babu's cane, reading glasses, and dentures as he basked in the sun. The patriarch's playacting excited his brood, though when Rajan grew older he feared his grandfather was mildly unhinged. But as an adult, he fully understood this was Babu's way of getting a little exercise while maintaining something to look forward to every morning. He was occasionally forgetful, which meant he would retell stories, but in general he was sound of mind.

Babu flashed a smile when he saw the two approach, but remained in his chair, the dimple under his chin showing. When Mariam extended a hand in greeting, he commented casually, "I see you have brought me a beautiful girl." He did not release her hand immediately, so Mariam remained slouched at an awkward angle, their faces only inches apart. "What's your name?" he asked tenderly.

"Mariam."

"And the other one?"

"Mureni."

"What's your father's name?"

"Baba! Can't my guest be allowed to have a seat before being interrogated?" Rajan protested, playfully pulling Mariam away.

Babu did not relinquish his hold of her, and she pretended to cringe from the tussle.

"Mu-re-ni . . ." Babu said thoughtfully. "That's a name from Maasailand, right?"

Mariam nodded.

"In that case, you should greet me properly," Babu said, finally letting go of her hand.

Mariam dutifully bowed her head and Babu placed his open palm on it, as demanded by Maasai tradition, in which the youth defer to elders and receive blessings in return. Babu completed the ritual by lifting his shirt and issuing a sprinkling of spittle.

"Baba, Mariam is from Ndundori," Rajan revealed with pride.

"Is that so?"

"Yes," Rajan said before Mariam could answer. "She even knows the people who founded that school where I taught."

"Really?" Babu enthused.

"Yes," Rajan replied. "But that's a story for another day."

"Welcome home, *mrembo*," Babu said as Mariam and Rajan made their way inside the house.

Rajan excitedly showed Mariam around, whispering as they went along so they wouldn't disturb his grandmother who was napping. He took Mariam to his room and joked that it would be their wing of the house, where they would live as man and wife once they got married—to which Mariam giggled so loudly he feared she would wake Fatima. And Fatima did wake up, possibly because she had heard the giggles, or perhaps because her maternal instinct told there was another female in her territory.

"*Rajaa! Rajaa! Mama akuita!*" It was Kioko, the servant, announcing Fatima's summon.

Rajan smiled at Mariam. She straightened her T-shirt, which was actually Rajan's, and brushed her hair out of her face, asking him: "How am I?"

"Beautiful," he assured.

Fatima was standing on the landing of the staircase waiting for the young couple. She was a short woman, the tangle of sari leaving a large space that exposed her uneven ribs. Her skin was slightly wrinkled and her hair had thinned in the middle so that the tufts that fell down her back were lopsided. It looked like the mane of a lion, and she could be as fierce as one. But when she smiled, twin dimples poked her cheeks, revealing a beautiful woman.

As Fatima turned to face Rajan and Mariam, however, her smile failed to light up her eyes. "What kind of host are you? You bring in a guest and go into hiding," Fatima reprimanded as she adjusted her sari, her voice still heavy with sleep. "Did Kioko give your guest something to eat?"

"Yes, Mama," Rajan confirmed cheerfully. "The guest is well fed."

"Have you spoken with Baba?" Fatima pursued.

Rajan was familiar with the tenor of her voice. It was a cue that trouble was afoot. "I think so . . ." he said uncertainly. "We said hello when we arrived." Babu was still basking outside, the silhouette of his lying form visible through the glass panel of the door.

"One doesn't say just hello when he brings a guest home, you sit and talk," Fatima said.

Rajan now understood that she was checking to see if Babu approved of his guest, because obviously she did not.

"Go on! Go on and talk to him!" Fatima said.

Rajan grudgingly returned to the veranda. Mariam remained standing in front of Fatima.

"Oh, please take a seat, my dear. Would you like something to drink?"

"No thanks," she returned. "I have eaten my fill. Actually, what I need is a little sunshine. I have been indoors all—" Mariam checked herself just in time, before revealing what was classified information, as far as Rajan was concerned. It was true they hadn't enjoyed much sunshine all week—because they had been hibernating in Era's shack.

"Suit yourself," Fatima said generously. "Go join the men if that's what you like. I thought we would have a woman-to-woman chat . . ."

"Another time, certainly. I only crave a little heat from the sun." And with that, Mariam turned away from Fatima and joined Babu and Rajan outside.

"So," Babu said, sitting up and placing his feet on a low stool. "You told me you are from . . . Ndundori?"

"Yes, Ndundori and Laikipia," Mariam replied.

"So you have two homes . . . ?"

"Baba, why are you giving my friend a hard time? Let her relax."

"She is my friend now, and I'm at liberty to ask her anything," Babu responded. "Isn't that right, *mrembo*?"

She nodded, smiling.

"Go tell your mama to make us some tea," Babu said to Rajan.

"We had tea already."

"She didn't make it; somebody else did it."

"What does it matter?" Rajan challenged.

"On the first day you bring such a beautiful girl home, it is only right that your bibi makes you the tea."

"Is that so?"

"That's the way it should be," Babu said.

The confluence of events that had placed Babu and Mariam together, an elderly Muslim man and a young woman—born sixty years apart—transcended any explanation other than fate intended to bring them together. But even with its cynicism, fate undercuts its own import by presenting a deceptive calm about very extraordinary events. In those fleeting moments, even as Rajan requested a fresh pot of tea and Mariam said her mother was Rehema Salim, whose mother was Seneiya, daughter of Chief Lonana—uttering what had remained unspoken for sixty years—the birds went on with their singing. One hummingbird even hurled its chalky dropping onto the veranda; military planes cut through the sky practicing for the independence celebrations that were only months away; a dry twig broke off a nearby *muiri* tree; a duck in the compound mounted a female, hissing upon climax to reveal its springy organ. Downstairs, Fatima pounded ginger with a wooden pestle; Kioko used to a piece of cardboard to fan the coal brazier, having lit it to prepare for the evening meal.

Although none of them were aware, the moment had come and gone, and the house of Babu Rajan Salim would never be the same again, pulled asunder by the mysterious young woman whose tongue cast spells on other humans. It was a power that Mariam was unaware of, and when she uttered those words, though innocent and well-intentioned, they felt to Babu like body blows. He cocked his head from his reclining seat, unsuccessfully tried to sit up straighter, then shot to his feet before remembering that he did not have his cane. He buckled upon his second attempt to flee from the scene. His glasses flew off his face and the dentures fell out of his mouth, while his shock of neat white hair stood up on his head as spiky as a porcupine's. A loud bang was heard as his chair tipped over, Babu following suit. He crawled on all fours, making a guttural cry.

"The horn, the horn," Babu wept. "Somebody blow the horn, the horn . . ."

Fatima moved unsteadily toward Rajan, trembling with fury, her double chin twitching like a hen about to lay an egg. "See what you have done, you foolish child?" she said in a savage whisper. "Brought a curse upon your own family. Now the spirit of the sea is upon us. Didn't you know you were betrothed at birth?"

HOUSE OF SILENCE

5

Babu was barely a man when he set sail from India for Mombasa—a lanky teen, reed thin, and one of the forty adults and six children on the boat. They were aboard the MV *Salama*, destined for the British East Africa Protectorate. Eight of the men were the dhow's crew led by Nahodha, the captain who had a pronounced limp in his right leg and spent most days sitting in solemn dignity, peering into the distance through his binoculars. The sight of his skullcap and the black protuberance of the binocular lens gave him the surreal look of a pouting rhino.

Of the nine men going to take up work in the protectorate, five were accompanied by their wives, including Babu. The rest were older women joining their husbands in the colony where they had been working as technicians and craftsmen for a year. At nineteen, Babu was the youngest among the craftsmen. With his spiky hair and high forehead, one could not look at him without smiling. During his childhood in Punjab, his peers had directed their attention to another part of his anatomy that they—that is, the little boys—found comical as they ran around naked. Girls wore tiny wraps but boys were allowed to roam around in the nude. It was good for their manhood, the mothers giggled. Set them free and let them grow to their full potential.

But by the age of four, Babu started wearing a longish shirt that served as shorts as well—his distended navel had become a plaything for other children. A boy had squeezed it during a fight, issuing a high-pitched squeak. Since then, the navel had become the subject of constant humiliation. Overnight, he became the boy with the whistling navel. Even tots without teeth knew about Babu, the singing-navel boy. So his mother provided him with the long shirt, but that cover-up attracted even more ridicule: *We know what you are hiding,* children sang. *You got a gourd for a navel!*

Worried that the navel business would turn into a permanent distraction, his parents enrolled him in a madrassa. There, they reasoned, every child wore a kanzu and Babu's navel would be quickly forgotten.

At the new school, Babu kept to himself. His teacher was a disappointment; each morning he would assign which *ayah* and *surah* they were expected to memorize. He would then bury his face in the Koran while the boys studied. No one was allowed to even use the bathroom until they had memorized the assigned segments of the Koran. Babu resented this and gradually developed a dislike for authority in all its manifestations, particularly when affiliated with religion.

Babu never really got over his self-consciousness about his navel. So even as he and Karim sunbathed like giant lizards on the dhow's deck, his belly was not exposed. Karim was twenty when the two met on the voyage to Mombasa. While Babu and Karim relaxed in the sunshine, they drifted off to the soothing voices of the women below. The older women spent their time chatting incessantly as they coaxed the kerosene stoves to boil water for rice or rolled out dough to make chapati or roti. Food was carefully rationed, as was drinking water. The trip was projected to last about three weeks, but, as most sailors liked to add,

Inshallah, meaning they were submitting their journey to the will of God.

There was a feeling of camaraderie about the dhow. Women had broken into song when they set sail, as children played *bano* in the small spaces not occupied by the adults or the cargo; some of the men played cards while others read. Babu found himself at peace on the ship, and he would drift off to sleep counting stars while wondering what the future held for him, excited to be starting a new life in a new land, with a new wife in tow.

Nature provided a response on their sixth day at sea. It started as just another ordinary day. The sun rose shimmering in the east; when the glints touched the ocean, they bounced off it, producing a golden hue. Babu inhaled deeply and brought his two hands to rest on his chest. *"Alhamdulillah! Alhamdulillah!"* he sang in appreciation of the beauty that abounded. Soon, everybody was up and about. A muscled crewman squatted to fetch liters of seawater for bathing. The women served tea and chapati for breakfast. Children ate the few remaining dates and hurled seeds at each other. The lateen mast was hoisted, flapping excitedly. They were on the move again, with Nahodha peering into the distance through his binoculars.

Babu and Karim were back up on the deck. Over the past few days, Babu had learned that he functioned best by going against the tide—sleeping when everybody else was awake, and staying up at night as everyone else slept. The main reason was that he couldn't stand the blinding daytime light, and found the dark of the night comforting.

So, as had become his routine, Babu was drifting off to sleep underneath the warmth of the morning sun, listening to the women singing, the shouts from playing children, and the grunts from men playing cards nearby. But just as he'd fallen asleep, he woke with a start, covered in a thin sheen of sweat. He opened his eyes and blinked against the bright sun, catching sight of Nahodha as he skipped past the women and children with a look of panic on his face. The vessel had come to a halt. The mast was up but limp. Nahodha rushed over to the mast clutching something in his hands. They were dry leaves, which he crushed in his palms and hurled into the air. It was a common trick used to detect the direction of the wind. Even hunters on land used it. The dry leaves fell straight down on top of Nahodha's head. Babu flashed his big grin and elbowed Karim, who laughed out loud. Nahodha's head resembled a bird's nest.

"What's so funny?" Nahodha glared.

Karim sobered up, but Babu kept grinning.

On that day, the crew changed the masts from big to small, then back again, six times. The dhow traveled only a few hundred yards, the most remarkable movement being the sudden jerk when the vessel lurched forward and then halted with the violence of a drunk man skidding on mud. The women's singing died down, their prattle as they cooked disappeared. Even the garrulous men who shared stories as they played cards now just groaned or sighed. Only the children played, but they resented the adult attention as nobody did anything but stare at them, and they happened to be in the way of everybody no matter which direction they ventured.

All the adults wore long faces. Even Babu's grin had shrunk, although it wasn't gone completely. He elbowed Karim again when he caught sight of Nahodha, who was bent over in prayer, kneading knots of *misbaha* in his shaky hands.

"The captain has surrendered his vessel to the will of God," Babu said.

Karim grunted, suppressing laughter.

"There is nozing like being young," one of the men playing cards said in a tone that was neither castigating nor complimenting. "Just shoving teet all te time!"

Babu smiled on.

"We reckon there isn't much else to do but surrender to the will of God!" Babu shouted. Although the workmen were mostly Indian, they spoke different languages and dialects, so English was their common denominator.

Nahodha interrupted his prayers and stepped forward to face Babu. He had removed his skullcap to reveal a receding hairline. He looked like a lion without a mane, yet still bore a fierce demeanor that temporarily scared Babu. Nahodha did not have his shoes on, and his right leg appeared even shorter than Babu remembered it. His *churidar* pajamas conveyed a certain vulnerability, like a little boy stepping out of bed. He addressed Babu in Gurmukhi, a language that the younger man understood perfectly.

"Why do you mock God when I'm making an earnest prayer for help?"

Babu did not respond.

"Why do you mock my prayer?"

"Why do you think your prayer is so important? Everyone on this dhow is praying," Babu responded defiantly.

"Why do you mock my *dua*?" Nahodha repeated as if he had not heard the response.

Babu's patience snapped, his simmering resentment of authority finding an outlet. "If your commune with God is as important as you imply, then I expect farmers to plant when you pass water," he said, then added with as much spite as he could marshal: "And that this vessel will move if you break wind."

Nahodha's next statement was a war cry, delivered in a

fearsome trembling timbre. Even those who did not know the language understood his gesture of ripping hair from his depleted pate. He was issuing a curse against Babu. "I think you have water instead of brain in that head. May Allah, the Almighty God, whose faithful servant you have scorned, curse you and your bloodline!" he wailed. "May blood flow to your doorstep, may your women be barren, may your seeds dry up! May enemies triumph over you! May *laana* from Allah descend upon your family!"

Babu froze, turning his gaze away from Fatima, as the memory of their wedding night, only days earlier, flooded in. The wedding had been hurriedly organized by his parents and he had only met his bride hours before the ceremony. He had known about his betrothal for years, but had never met his future bride. He had hardly thought of his future wedding at all—his energies consumed by his curiosity about the world. Visions of Africa, the impenetrable, dark forests, the rivers that flowed endlessly, apparently without a source, captured his imagination. So he jumped at the opportunity when he read notices announcing jobs working for the British colonial government in Africa.

With his impending trip, it was decided between his family and Fatima's that the time was nigh for them to marry. He had gone through the ritual with bored indifference, and showed little enthusiasm when he was finally presented with his bride, a little girl whose dainty hand dripped with flowered henna patterns. She looked down when he peered into her eyes, and Babu felt a slight tremor shoot through him when he held her hand—just about the only visible part of her body.

Babu became more interested and curious as he undressed her that night, peeling off her sari and calico clothing as though unwrapping a package of food, until she finally lay naked before him. He hadn't seen a naked woman before, but he found Fatima too bony for his liking: her ribs showed through her skin; there were hollows around her pelvis. Still, it was thrilling for him to see a naked woman. He touched her glowing skin, stroking her carefully and smoothly. By the time he reached the middle of her legs, he had worked himself into a froth of excitement. He jumped on her with urgency, just as the tension that had been building up in him, like a rising tide, finally gave way to a whitish fluid that coursed over Fatima's belly.

Babu lay on his side, sighing with relief, which soon turned to desperation, as the fluid that he had emitted dissolved into the white sheet that had been spread beneath Fatima to test her virginity. Babu dreaded the sight of the clean sheet. He was now limp, and try as he might, he was unable to rise to the occasion. The absence of blood on the white sheet would arouse the suspicion that he had been fooled into marrying a woman who was not a virgin; conversely, it could also mean that he had been unable to consummate his marriage. Either way, he was going to end up with egg on his face.

Babu stroked his bride anew, touching different parts of her body but eliciting little reaction; his anger welled up inside of him as he considered a course of action that could salvage his pride and reputation. Throughout his boyhood, he was known as the striking cobra, a notoriety fanned by fights with boys who teased him over his distended navel, his weapon of choice being his pronounced forehead.

Babu lightly kissed Fatima's breasts, then her neck and face. He glanced into her eyes briefly before striking the bridge of her nose with his forehead. There was a flash of panic and anger in her eyes, but Fatima sobbed silently, as though she was bracing for a worse attack. Babu quickly grabbed the white sheet spread beneath and wiped the drops of blood that issued from Fatima's nostrils. His idea of her virginity test, it appeared, was directed at the wrong hole.

The passengers were marooned at sea for six days and six nights. Fatima lay in a corner weeping, her hunched shoulders supporting her tiny head, her hair covering her face, tears gluing the strands together like corn silk. Babu and Karim had retreated to a corner of the dhow. Both noticed the massive wave approaching, but made no sense of it until was too late. After six days and nights of zero movement, something was stirring in the sea.

The building wave was swirling and twirling as it drew near, before landing on the side of the dhow. The vessel reeled from impact, tossing sideways as women and children shouted for help. When stronger and swifter waves descended, the dhow went into a spin as men, women, and children did what their forebears had done for generations: they banged on whatever they could lay their hands on to calm the sea spirits; Nahodha blew the horn and knelt to pray, his voice trembling but still impassioned. The sky had turned from blue to gray; it was difficult to tell if the distant ocean was lifting up to the heavens, or if the heavens had melted into the sea. A gray nothingness held the ocean and the sky. All Babu and Karim felt from the edge of the dhow was the sludge of salty water on their feet, before it jumped up to slap their faces. The storm doused all the cries from the women and the children below. Nahodha's praying was the last voice to be heard on the ship, its tenor panicky and pained.

Against all odds, all the adult passengers aboard MV

Salama from India made it to the shores of Mombasa on the night of August 1, 1897. Three children had drowned during the voyage. The Mombasa fishermen administered first aid to the surviving children and adults. Most had distended bellies, which they pressed to expel water. One child had shrunk to the size of a shoe. It was hard to differentiate between men and women because the women had lost their round forms and breasts. Many were too weak to walk and got on all fours when they touched the land, like giant crabs scurrying across the earth for a hole to hibernate in. Some seamen stole suspicious glances at them, unsure if the creatures they had rescued were humans or jinn as some of them feared. Three more children remained unconscious; two of them never recovered. After crouching in a waterlogged corner of the dhow for so long, Fatima had lost the use of her legs and had to be dragged away, leaving a trail behind her, like that of a slug. She instantly believed Nahodha's curse had taken effect, but it was Babu's encounter with McDonald days later that fortified this notion.

That night, as the shipwrecked passengers were taken in safely to shore, a full moon hovered above, its silvery glow setting the ocean alight. Mombasa's single street was bustling with life. Flickering candles beckoned in food stalls where tin kettles sat on glowing coals to make chai. In other stalls, women who resembled bats, because only their eyes were visible beneath their black robes, prepared food to sell. One dropped dough in a large pan to make *mahamri*, the sizzle of oil dancing. Another vendor fanned her *jiko* to roast *mshikaki*. The food market was teeming with activity as vendors called out to passersby to try their delicacies. But all those sounds were muted in the ears of the new arrivals. Only Nahodha would have understood Swahili, but he had passed out by this point.

Babu would remember their arrival into Mombasa as the walk of the dead, for he could not tell whether or not he was still alive, or if the child in his hands was alive or dead. He could not even tell whether he was still at sea or on dry land. The roar of the sea was close by, as were the voices speaking all around him that he could not understand. All he heard inside his head was an incessant buzzing sound, like a radio searching for a transmission frequency.

They were taken to an inn and those who were conscious were given hot soup. Two traditional medicine men were summoned to the inn by the fishermen. They prescribed herbs to revive those who were still unconscious. They also lit incense to ward off evil spirits that may have been stalking the survivors.

Early the following morning, the inn's window opened to a panoramic view of Mombasa, then a mishmash of rondavels of coral and lime plaster, their *makuti* thatch and rusty metal roofs fanning out like a colorful oil painting.

The market was an open space ringed by palms. Although it was still early in the day, the market was almost completely full. Every sound competed for attention. A fetid wind lifted from the sea. A mongrel squeaked from the kick of a brown boot. A monger swished the tail of a tilapia, hailing its freshness. Another vendor sliced soundlessly through a ripe mango. A woman displaying hand-printed garments chuckled, revealing a fake gold tooth. A merchant clanged a knife on ivory. A rooster crowed. A donkey pulling a cart brayed, spilling drops of *mnazi*. A trader swore at a haggling customer. A mother admonished a child strapped to her back. A worker quarreled with his tools. The sea roared to assert its authority. The muezzin called the faithful to morning prayers. Mombasa turned into a Tower of Babel as Swahili, Arabic, Punjabi, Gujarati, Hindi, Marathi, and English tongues sought coherence.

Babu peered through the window and a wave of anticipation swept through him. He wanted to touch the soil, hurl a pebble into the sea and wait for its response. He was still weak, but his spirit wanted to fill his lungs with fresh air as he stepped outside. It was only when he saw two women helping another woman that he remembered he had not seen his new wife since their arrival. He had been at sea longer than he had been married, so his temperament remained that of a carefree boy, with the world at his feet. Feeling somewhat ashamed that he'd not thought of Fatima until then, he dashed back inside to check on her, but his mission was cut short by a man in a white uniform and a wide-brimmed hat. He was carrying a baton that he waved in the air while exclaiming: "This way, coolie! All workers are meeting now!"

Babu pointed to the women: "I need to see my wife."

"Coolie, you have not been here for a minute and you are missing your wife already?"

"My wife is unwell," Babu said firmly.

"What language do these people understand?" McDonald asked in clear exasperation, turning to his assistant, Superintendent Patterson. "Can you call these coolies to order? We need a head count." McDonald clutched Babu's wrist in a playful way, but the grip was tight enough that Babu could not extricate himself.

Patterson made his way to the spot where the newly arrived Indian men were playing a game of *bao*, tiny cups of *kahawa thungu* at their feet. Patterson called to the local drummer, Nyundo, and gestured to him to sound the drums. Soon, music filled the air as the instrument throbbed. Like crickets peeking out of their holes, men emerged from the houses and spilled into the dusty street.

"I have made a citizen's arrest!" McDonald said to Babu with a smile.

Babu smiled back but didn't speak. It was the first time he'd ever been this close to a white man, his white fingers encircling Babu's brown wrist.

"Where are you from?" McDonald asked.

"Punjab," Babu replied swiftly.

"How long have you been here?"

"Just arrived today . . . yesterday? I have lost sense of time."

McDonald relaxed his grip on Babu. "Are you the guys who were shipwrecked?"

Babu shrugged. "I guess so."

"Goodness me! And you are on your feet? You must get some rest."

Babu shrugged again. "I-I'm fine."

"You don't have to come now," McDonald told him. "You can come tomorrow, or whenever you are ready. We do a head count every other day."

Babu instantly took a liking to McDonald. He decided to stay on and watch the proceedings from afar. Once the beach was clear, he would touch the water of the ocean, toss a pebble in.

McDonald bore a handlebar mustache that served like the whiskers of a cat. He ran a forefinger over his mustache when nervous, curled its edges when amused, and the mustache twitched when he was irritated. McDonald had ordered his men to round up all Indian workers and direct them to Fort Jesus, the phallic building in the center of the town whose decaying stones had turned brown like the crust of bread, with green moss sprouting in its crevices. It had no windows, the only visible opening being the mouth of the cannon that faced the sea. It had been built by the Portuguese four centuries earlier when they occupied the coast. It took nearly two hours before all workers were assembled in front of the building.

McDonald stood before the gathering, his black boots shining so brightly one could see his reflection in them. His white pants were so well pressed they could have stood up on their own. His white skin, now full of pink blotches from the sun, made him look like a fish out of water. But the rays of the sun and their reflection on his white clothes made it difficult for one to look directly at him without lifting a hand to deflect the light. McDonald grabbed a whistle from Patterson and blew, puffing in and out. His voice grew shrill as he tried to compete with the roar of the ocean, which sounded louder now that all the workers were silent.

There were 249 workers in all; they had arrived on different days over the past week. From their long exposure to the sun and salty waters, their pale skin had faded to the deep brown of grasshoppers in the savanna. Babu quietly joined the meeting, buoyed by his burning desire to throw a pebble into the ocean. He stood at the edge of the gathering, impatiently listening to McDonald.

"On behalf of the government of Her Majesty the Queen of England, I would like to welcome you all to the British East Africa Protectorate. Thank you for enlisting your support in the service of Her Majesty. Now, I will make this short because I know you have all had long trips. Some of you have endured great hazards to get here. I appreciate your commitment to the service of Her Majesty. I want to start with a word of caution: in this service, there are rules of engagement. I am a soldier—well, I was one in my past life—but since soldiers never retire nor die, I can say I'm still one, which is to say I take rules rather seriously. Those who run afoul of the law shall be guests of the state in this building . . ."

McDonald pointed at the decaying phallic building. This strategy was straight out of the missionaries' manual: the fear of the Lord is the beginning of all wisdom. Getting potential offenders to fear their future dungeons should certainly serve as deterrence. There was an instant stampede as men on the brink of collapse from exhaustion and dehydration streamed into the rustic building. They had misunderstood "guests of the state" to mean that this would be their new guesthouse. The workmen grumbled in Urdu, Punjabi, and Gujarati, but their disapproval was unanimous: *Why does this inn look so unkempt?*

McDonald decided to let them wander. There were three levels to the building. The top floor was well lit and ventilated and had a beautiful view of the endless sea. In his notes, McDonald had labeled the top floor *White*. The lower floors were labeled *Others*. Even his jail was designed according to racial hierarchy. Whites took the best available space; other races would take what was left. The middle floor was poorly lit although some light from the *White* area filtered through, and one could see the outline of the sea where crevices had not been filled in with weeds. The bottom level was cloaked in virtual darkness—echoes reverberated when the workmen spoke as bats flitted around soundlessly. When one got accustomed to the dark, one noticed the stone walls were perspiring from the intense heat and poor air circulation.

McDonald blew his whistle, a sharp screeching sound

that the workmen understood was a signal for them to stream out of the building. They obliged and converged where they had first stood, but most left their luggage in the best-lit corners of the building. When the men learned that the dark building was the jail awaiting offenders, six of them took off instantly, three of them rushing to the vessel that had brought them from India and begging the merchants to return them home.

But the dhow merchants swiftly hauled two of them on their shoulders and dropped them at McDonald's feet like sacks of potatoes. The third man, who was the heaviest, was dragged off and similarly dumped with the others. McDonald smiled for the first time, revealing a cleft under his chin. He didn't really open his mouth when he smiled, his cheeks just puffed out a bit and his lips twitched. He handcuffed the three men to each other.

"These three have made history as the first inmates in the British East Africa Protectorate," McDonald announced, before starting to drag the man in the middle, pulling the other two along, the network of arms crisscrossing like tangled ropes. The three captives spoke Gujarati, Urdu, and Punjabi, crying out in frustration at their inability to understand each other.

McDonald had neared the mouth of the dungeon when one of the captives let out a raw cry: "Woooooooiiiiiiiiiiiiiiiiiiii iiiiiiii." It wasn't just a cry from the fatigue of the journey, or from the hunger that showed in their eyes—it was the recognition of their base humiliation. They had survived horrendous calamities at sea, only to land in this hellhole. It was hard to discern who among the three had cried out first, but it echoed against the walls, building in tempo and resonance so that the three men's voices came together as one. The response from the other workers was instant.

They, too, cried out: "Woooooooooooooiiiiiiiiiiiiiiiiiii." The blustering gale appeared to carry the cry and cast it to the sea, resurging moments later with more intensity. The water lapping on the shores seemed to sweep the cry and multiply it a thousand times. The crashing waves appeared to roar in anger bearing the cry, as did the smallest and weakest of waves that diminished as they approached the shores, crashing into frothy foam on the white sand.

Babu started walking toward McDonald. He wanted to help translate what the three captives were saying, but a group of technicians followed in his step. They were waiting for someone to step forward and fire the first shot before they could join in. Their walk found traction with the workers' cries, each step synchronized with the sound.

"Woooooo—iiiiiiiiiiiiii. Wooooooooo—iiiiiiiiiiiiii."

Babu was now very close to McDonald.

"Woooooooooo—iiiiiiiiiiiiii. Wooooooooo—iiiiiiiiiiiiii."

McDonald moved his lips but he did not speak. He could swear Babu's face looked very familiar, but he couldn't quite place him. Where had he seen that massive forehead? The men marched faster than his mind could spring a response. McDonald blew the whistle again but he appeared to be out of breath and only a whimper was heard. His lips trembled. By now, most of the marching workers held crude weapons in their hands, retrieved from the assortment of tools in their possession. They were armed with crowbars and saws and mallets and pliers and pincers and machetes and hammers. Local men who had been hired as porters joined in the march. Even the palm trees that had stood silent on the shores for hundreds of years appeared to open their mouths for the first time, the rustling of their leaves adding a lively soprano to the song. The traders and their customers and the mongrels in fright seemed to join in the wail, gaining such momentum that even the vessel standing at sea appeared to jerk, as though in the grip of an epileptic fit.

"*Wooooooooooooooo—iiiiiiiiiiiiiiiiiiiiiiiiiiiiiiiii.*"

McDonald released the captives from his grasp and retrieved his pistol. He shot once in the air. The sound was so muted, it was like cracking firewood on a bent knee. McDonald fired all the rounds until his gun was empty. The shooting only managed to scare sparrows out of their nests to join in the song.

"*Wooooooooooo—iiiiiiiiiiiiiiiiiiiiiii. Wooooooooooooooo—iiiiiiiii iiiiiiiiiiiiiiiiiiiiiiiiiiii.*"

The sparrows somersaulted and performed all manner of aerial displays. McDonald ran in panic into the dungeon. He scaled the steps to the watchtower with the stealth of a spider. He reached the armory and headed straight to the cannon whose mouth jutted out toward the sea. He fired the cannon once.

Yet again, a new legend had been invented, and for days and weeks and months to come, young men sat under the *mnazi* and listened to Nyundo tell and retell the story of the day the cannon was fired. There is nothing the Swahili enjoyed more than a well-told story.

"*Wacha kiswahili!*" one would shout lightheartedly at Nyundo when they suspected he was conflating the order of events, which most loved doing.

"*Wallahi!* I'm telling you, I saw it with these two eyes," Nyundo would counter, waving a hand to ward off a fly hovering over his cup of black tea, before taking a swig and belching with satisfaction. "I swear, *haki ya mama*. I'm telling you nothing but the truth," Nyundo would insist, then invoke the serious consequences that could befall him if he lied—including bedding his own mother.

Very few Africans had witnessed the firing of the cannon. When the melee started, most of the porters had retreated, for they had a saying about keeping a safe distance in the face of a disaster, lest blood be spilled on them.

"*Sikiza*," Nyundo narrated, "I never knew I would live to see such a day. You know, these white people made us retreat with tails between our legs, after displaying their small pieces of metal emitting smoke. We treated them like little gods. Now I know they're nothing! Their medicine is *muhindi*. The Indian, I tell you, is bad news. Just leave him alone! He's the cure for the white man's oppression. I saw an Indian give a white man a taste of that medicine, with these very eyes . . .

"*Aisee!* Chai! Chai *hala hala!*" Nyundo shouted, ordering a fresh cup of tea. "I want these people to understand the story, and my voice is getting croaky with fatigue. Chai *hala hala!*"

A fresh cup delivered, Nyundo sipped, then went on. "*Ushaona bwana?*" he asked to call his audience to attention. Although Nyundo did not know Babu by name, he accurately described his pronounced forehead. "*Sokwe mtu*," he said, then reenacted how the Indian had marched toward the *mzungu* holding a gun and demanded the immediate release of the three wailing Indian workers.

"And Bwana Mkubwa, the one whose clothes competed with the sun for brightness, trembled like a leaf as this Indian man walked toward him. Not a very tall man, but intimidating enough. I think he had planned to use the forehead to smash the white man. But the *mzungu* was wetting his pants with fear."

Nyundo sipped his tea again. "I was just seated there with my drum as this Indian jinni marched on. Bwana

Mkubwa, his mustache doing its dance because he was terrified out of his wits, got his small *chuma* and fired at the approaching Indian. *Phaw! Phaw! Phaw!* One, two, three—"

"Pumping bullets like that?" somebody in the audience interjected. "*Weee*, Nyundo, stop your *kiswahili.*"

"*Sikiza bwana*," Nyundo pleaded. "I'm telling you, *haki ya mama*. In the name of my mother. *Risasi, phaw, phaw, phaw!* But this Indian jinni was not feeling anything. It's as though the bullets couldn't penetrate his skin. They just zoomed past and fell into the ocean or melted in the air."

"Not a single bullet hit him?" another voice asked.

"Not a single one of them. That's why Bwana Mkubwa took off and disappeared into the building."

"Did he go there to hide?"

"No, just wait and listen. I'm the one telling the story. Listen. Listen, my friend. If anybody ever told you there is a louder blast than a cannon's, they are telling a lie," Nyundo continued. "Mark my word: a cannon blast has no equivalent; it is the mother of all blasts." Nyundo claimed that sparrows suspended their fluttering to listen to the blast, for they had never heard such a sound. The roaring sea waves, he said, flattened out to duck the cannon fire so that the sea lay flat like a mirror reflecting the sun above.

"I think the sea must have acquired a similar plane when that famous prophet that Cow Man preacher was talking about walked on water. The palm trees dropped all their fruit—mature, immature, raw, and ripe." Nyundo dropped his voice and said sotto voce, "Like a woman losing a pregnancy." Then, resuming his narration in a well-modulated tone: "The swinging branches were suspended in midair, the leaves arched awkwardly like a dreadlocked head . . . *Maajabu!*

"If you see *muhindi*, hats off to him, man. The Indian is

the medicine for the white man. Since I witnessed that, I have stopped fearing the white man," Nyundo concluded, ordering another cup of chai. "Good tea brings the brain to a boil."

6

McDonald recorded the events of that day, August 2, 1897, as the first organized labor protest in the British East Africa Protectorate. A career soldier, McDonald was experienced in information management. Had he called it a mutiny or even a siege, he knew his bosses in London would have been hysterical, perhaps even recalling the colonial governor, Charles Erickson, who was en route from the colonial capital of Nairobi, some five hundred miles away, to commission the railway construction in Mombasa. So McDonald only volunteered information that would be beneficial to his interests, and his key interest was to have the rail construction commence.

McDonald still trembled when he remembered the moment Babu marched toward him. He knew he had seen that forehead elsewhere. He thought maybe he was a porter sent to deliver an urgent message to him, but he wasn't carrying anything. When McDonald saw the other Indian workers join in the march, he realized he'd been wrong.

There was something terrifying about the forehead. It took one's attention off the eyes, so one lost focus and couldn't quite tell where the forehead appeared to be headed. That initial misinterpretation of Babu's intent would sow seeds of discord and blossom into a grudge that would last a lifetime.

The scare also prompted McDonald to do what soldiers call "going back to the drawing board." To grasp what he was up against, he needed to understand the local scene. He knew he would find ample information from the notes left by his predecessor, Captain John Adams, whose file he had put off reading.

From: Captain John Adams, Outgoing Commissioner of the British East Africa Protectorate
To: Ian Edward McDonald, Commissioner of the British East Africa Protectorate
Date: December 12, 1896

Receive my greetings, many as the sands in the ocean, or the leaves in a bush! That's my way of saying I have lived here long enough to acquire local sensibilities, like their exaggerated manner of speech. Welcome to Mombasa!

I must state from the onset that this place has lived up to its reputation as a destination that's easy to travel to, but hard to depart from. I fully concur with those sentiments. So, don't say you were not warned about the allure of the place . . .

Things did not seem that way when I arrived that distant evening two years ago in the company of two mules and two men. You shall inherit the two mules, but you cannot inherit the men—one Wanyika man, although I hear they consider that name derogatory and insist you call them the Giriama, and one Kikuyu tribesman. You cannot inherit the men because they have since deserted. The only reason I'm sharing this information is to ensure you don't hire them back, or even hire their kinsmen to run your domestic affairs. They are bad people.

The Kikuyu tribesman that I hired as a cook, apart from being lazy like all the natives, had this dreamy look that I found scary. I later came to learn that any Kikuyu, while serving you, is always scheming as to how he will steal from you so that one day he can sit at the table and be served by others. The Wanyika or Giriama tribesman that I hired as a gardener was so lazy he cut down my trees so that he didn't have to sweep the compound every morning!

But I am digressing. See, like I said at the start of this letter, it's been such a long two years I have acquired the natives' roundabout ways of speaking! What I mean to say is that you should arrive here in good cheer because you shall find many cheerful and cheering things. First off, Mombasa is a complicated place. It's an old port town that goes back several centuries, but it seems to be stuck there—frozen in time is a good way to think of it. The Portuguese, or Wareno, as natives call them, arrived in the fifteenth century. The Arabs came hot on their heels. The Portuguese brought corn to Mombasa. The Arabs shipped away all the grains. When the grains were in short supply, they started abducting natives for sale. The Indians and the Chinese have been here all along, doing their business in their usual shady way, which means you can't quite understand what they do, yet they are forever lurking.

I think you are now starting to get the picture that I'm trying to paint. You can think of Mombasa as a petri dish of cultures, and the end result has been many uncultured people put together because they seem to pick the worst from everyone. You might ask why I find that troubling, yet it is our work to civilize them. As long as we have uncivilized natives somewhere in the world, an Englishman's work is guaranteed. But the degree of their uncouth behavior can be startling, even overwhelming at times.

I don't know if I mentioned the port of Mombasa has a quaint feel, reminiscent of Britain's port towns, like Brighton or Southampton. I should add that the local social scene is remarkably close to that of ancient Athens, where locals spent their days arguing about nothing. There are similar groupings in Mombasa, particularly among Afro-Arabs, or Swahili as they are known here. It's a group that has emerged from the intercourse between Arabs and Africans, and they seem to be copulating all the time because they have spawned a whole new nation, complete with its own language. A sprinkling of Indians will be found in such idle gatherings, but the real loudmouths are the Afro-Arabs. They will sit and talk about anything under the sun. It could be a silly argument about which fruit is ripe enough to eat. But rather than settle such a mundane issue by climbing up the tree, they shall wait for the fruit to fall. That means they might spend several days arguing about a specific fruit, while waiting for nature's intervention!

You may be tempted to ask why I'm telling you all this. It's because the malingering crowds have serious implications on local labor supply. These meetings—or vikao, as the Afro-Arabs call them—have negatively impacted our local labor supply. Finding laborers for paid work is extremely frustrating, and remember we are talking of horrible, lazy, thieving natives, not quality workers. They cannot be forced to work, even on the pain of death. Their attitude toward work is amazingly unhealthy. This is partly because farm work is considered a woman's task. Real men go to the forest to hunt. It's only women who bend their backs and battle with the soil. A contingent of local porters were so ridiculed for carrying loads on their heads—other men said they resembled women returning from the stream to fetch water—that the entire expedition disappeared into the bush with our merchandise still on their heads. Of course, the thieves in their midst were looking for any excuse to flee.

The other factors for poor labor supply are grave. Since the abolition of slavery in Great Britain, Arabs and their local henchmen, mainly the Wakamba and Wanyika or Giriama, as they prefer to be called, have discovered new destinations for their human cargo. The sultan of Zanzibar, Seyyid Said, has established clove plantations in his country to recoup the income lost from the slave trade.

The clove plant, I should say, is a spice in the garlic family. It is a labor-intensive crop since harvesting is done year-round and each clove cluster has to be harvested by hand without damaging the branch. This is followed by days of drying before selling. The plant behaves like a chameleon, changing colors—from purple when still in the bud, to green when cut, and brown when dried. Let me tell you why you need to know all this, or even why we should care if it takes slaves on Arab plantations a year to harvest a handful of cloves.

The sultan of Zanzibar owns the coastline, so it is in our best interests not to antagonize him unnecessarily. When our men in London insisted we should not tolerate slavery of any nature, I was encouraged to offer modest recompense to Arab slave masters for every slave released. That's something you may have to continue. Secondly, Afro-Arabs have a measure of experience in administration—albeit gained by riding roughshod over others—and we need them to establish our administration in the hinterland.

Which leads me to my first proposition: given the complex histories around the coast, we have to find ways of accessing the hinterland population, which by far exceeds the transient and economically superior groups of Indians and Afro-Arabs. I shall address this question more substantively in a short while. But first, allow me to elaborate on the social scene.

As if we didn't have enough problems on our hands, nature unleashed her wrath upon the land. We experienced a crushing famine for the two years that I have been here. I suspect the superstitious natives must already have concluded that the disappearance of the rain has something to do with our presence in their midst. Which is not a particularly bad

*thing for them to believe! If they think we have the capacity
to meddle with the rhythms of nature, they might be more re-
ceptive to our instructions. I did not have a lot of success with
that.*

*We brought in a psychoanalyst from London with the
hope that we could understand the degree of superstition
among the locals. He had a clever sampling methodology that
required respondents to narrate the kind of dreams they had
been having since the arrival of the white man. Since dreams
often draw from the subconscious, we had hoped to find out
if their dreams would reveal their attitude toward us. But all
the natives said they had stopped dreaming since we set foot
here! So that's the sort of cunning you shall be dealing with!
It's inborn for a majority of the natives.*

*But the worst was yet to come. When we saw things go
from bad to worse due to the famine, we decided to do something. We went to the hinterland and conducted a malnutrition survey. We mapped some 50 families accounting for about
2,000 children and adults. Out of these, about 30 percent did
not have enough to eat, meaning they had an occasional meal
every few days, while 10 percent suffered acute malnutrition,
most of them children. We instituted measures to mitigate the
situation by shipping in corn from India, which had probably originated in this place. The monsoon winds couldn't have
been better. But our intervention was a bag of mixed fortunes.*

*Natives flatly declined to receive the grains, fearing it was
an inducement to lure them into captivity and slavery. This,
it has come to our attention, is an offshoot of the unorthodox
methods used by Arabs over the past years. The waterfront of
Watamu, I am told, derives its name from the sweet dates that
the merchants dangled before capturing natives for shipment
abroad. So they feared our gift of grains and no one would
touch the corn.*

Now, if you thought that was surprising, listen to this: the Wanyika natives, who have been hardest hit by famine, and who wouldn't touch a grain offered by a white hand, have been pawning their wives and daughters to Arab merchants in exchange for grains. The deal is that once their fortunes improve, they shall pay off their debts and their women will be returned to them. I cannot grasp, for the life of me, the logic behind such actions. But apparently, it is a time-tested tradition and families that fall on hard times have no hesitation pawning wives or daughters.

Yet other natives have migrated to farmlands near the Sabaki River and have succeeded to such a degree that they are able to supply their tribesmen in other parts of the hinterland. This is demonstrable evidence that natives, if subjected to stringent conditions, can start to use their heads to survive. I have always had this lingering question, wondering if the natives would have fared differently if they had freezing temps throughout the year instead of the blistering heat. I mean, they certainly wouldn't be walking about naked, or waiting for fruit to fall from the trees. They would have found ways to dress warmly and perhaps store food for a snowy day.

I think I'm giving these natives more credit than they actually deserve for just being able to put food on the table. After all, even birds, which have no hands and only very tiny heads, possess adequate imagination to marshal such feats. Anyway, I'm digressing yet again. I guess all I'm trying to say is that I have had such low expectations of the locals that whatever modest thing they achieve does not escape my notice. So that rare demonstration of initiative by natives on the banks of the Sabaki stands out for this reason.

It might surprise you, therefore, if I tell you even this cultivation on the banks of the Sabaki has put us on a collision course with the locals. Yes, we have a problem when natives *sit and talk, and we have a problem when they rise and work!*

Here's why: The Wanyika's, or the Giriama's, homes are organized in enclosures. Several of these form a village, under which a council of elders arbitrates over community disputes from a kaya. You must be aware now about the superstition associated with primitive cultures. Even if you have encountered that elsewhere, the mother of them all is to be found here. The kaya, the Wanyika believe, is the hallowed seat of their god, and they feed the trees with meat and honey. I suspect it is this healthy nourishment that led the figs in those kayas to grow to such gigantic scales that several men cannot hold the girth of one such tree. The people have mortal fear of those elders, while the fear of someone bewitching another is so commonplace that you will find children wearing protective amulets from birth to keep them out of harm's way.

This offers a chance for us to tap into this illogic psychology and make inroads in turning natives' minds in another direction. Reverend Turnbull is doing a good job of it, and he's a man I propose you should meet and get to know. He is with the Church Mission Society and has a native lad he uses for translation. Not particularly good, but something is better than nothing.

I seem to have lost my train of thought again about native superstition. Oh yes, now I remember . . . The migration to the Sabaki settlement by the Giriama has eroded the influence of the elders over the youth because they have left the kaya in their old village. Without the kaya and its associated mystic power, fathers have no say over their sons' affairs. In turn, the elders' influence over the community's spiritual and political welfare is waning. This means that if we are to make demands on the community as a whole—for instance, taxation—there is no central authority to impose sanctions. So if the young men choose to talk and wait for fruit to fall on their heads, the par-

ents cannot compel them to do anything. Further, if the loose coalition of elders was the ineffectual pillar of administration, things will only get harder because they have dispersed to the four directions of the wind.

The most immediate battle, which you will have no choice but to wage, is over the Sabaki settlement. I am certain you are familiar with the Imperial British East Africa (IBEA). You must have encountered them in your previous work in India. I think they traded there as British India Steam Navigation Company Limited. Now, these gentlemen and their affiliates have an eye on the Sabaki. They think they can invest in rice cultivation. Now, that is what we call hitting two birds with one stone. On the one hand, you would have something to ship off, and make use of the rail once it is laid, and then there is the European capital injection, which should attract even more investors from England and the larger Europe. Even Americans won't hesitate to invest once IBEA comes in. But what stands in the way is how to get natives out of their new settlements and get them to engage in wage labor. That's the only way to get the railway laid. I think you should use this line as your mantra to all the natives: Get off the land, get on rail!

Finally, here are some suggestions on how to proceed. These are random thoughts just bubbling off the top of my head, and may appear incoherent or utterly useless. Feel free to discard what you can't use. But they are worth thinking through. For starters, you can impose a tax. Make every household pay, and demand that those who default will be taken off to work on the rail for free. No one can claim this to be slavery, or a replacement of slavery, because they have the option of working for a wage.

The other way is to appoint headmen and use them to collect the tax—hoping they won't steal all of it—so that public resentment, if any, will be directed at them, not you. The other *suggestion is banning the killing of the wildlife. The Wanyika hunt elephants for their tusks to sell to Arabs, or to buy trophies from other tribes for sale on the coast. Reducing their ways of earning a living is the safest guarantee that they will be available for wage labor. If all these mechanisms fail to get the Wanyika to work for you, you can undermine their capacity to produce food. Although this is not said too loudly, there are ways in which we can decimate their domestic animals. Rinderpest is one. Fleas can also immobilize the natives en masse because they do not wear shoes. And when all else fails, violence is still a viable option. There is no better medicine to native obstinacy than a good beating.*

As I said, these ideas are random and might not hold up to scrutiny. But they are worth sharing.

All the best, my dear friend. Best wishes in your new job. Don't hesitate to ask should you need any further information. The only caveat is that you should be prepared to get tons of rambling before you can get anything of value from this compatriot who seems to have been on the verge of going native, in a manner of speaking. To use a common local expression, I hope you and I will meet in this life, in London or some other station elsewhere in the Empire, for we are people, not mountains. Mountains do not meet because they can't move.

Yours Sincerely,
John Adams

McDonald had picked up many useful lessons from the day of the riot, the most crucial being that brute force was the only language that the locals and the newly arrived Indians understood. And to ensure that locals and Indians did not join hands, McDonald formulated what he called a divide-and-rule policy. A new compartment was created in the dungeons. Now there were three dungeons, with *White* at the top, *Brown* in the middle, and *Black* at the bottom. He decided to wait and gauge the Arabs' attitudes. If they were hostile to the British presence, he would lump them together with Africans in the *Black* section. But if they behaved properly, they would be categorized as *Brown* and grouped with the Indians.

McDonald then turned his attention to Babu. His training at Sandhurst told him the man was up to no good. So he applied the principle that he learned long ago at military school in England: dig up as much information on your opponent as possible, and you have halved the problem. McDonald considered his options: Deporting Babu to Punjab was one of them, but the monsoon would not be blowing westerly for another four months. And that would mean a free ride when Babu hadn't earned it. Such rascals should be made to walk back home. But if he waited for the monsoon to reverse its direction, the conspiracy to abort the railway construction that he suspected was being hatched would mature, if not immediately nipped in the bud. McDonald considered detaining Babu at the fort. Finding an appropriate charge should present no problem whatsoever. The description of the colonial government as "the long arm of the law" was not invented for nothing. If he wanted Babu really quickly, he could pick him for something minor like urinating in the open. This misdemeanor attracted a raft of charges under English law, from indecent exposure to threatening a breach of public peace.

But McDonald knew he could extract his pound of flesh if he caught Babu defecating. In addition to all the charges one incurred from the misdemeanor of urinating in public, defecating in public carried the additional charge of jeopardizing public health through poor hygiene and unsafe waste disposal. And Babu could be kept in prison as a quarantine measure. *Hey, coolie, finish off and let's go!* McDonald relished the thought of Babu caught with pants down, dragged away on tiptoe by a policeman whose grip at the back of his pants ensured the suspect's manhood would be on the brink of strangulation. Defecation was a charge no magistrate could dispute, and Indians appeared to enjoy the breeze in their most natural form.

Detention without trial was another option still open to him. The English common law permitted that. All he needed was to prove the suspect was a threat to British national interests, and the railway construction fell within that realm. The wealth of the British East Africa Protectorate could not be accessed without the rail, and the British government expected a return on its investment. But that strategy was fraught with risks: Babu could be turned into a martyr and symbol for future protests. That could be problematic if Babu's band of supporters—and McDonald had no way of assessing how many there were—rallied to his cause. The locals appeared to communicate with the Indians in ways he could not decipher, and he didn't wish to be caught flat-footed again. That was a scary experience! He didn't want to have to fire the cannon again. That was meant for external aggressors like the Portuguese or the Germans, who threatened the colony from the nearby Msumbiji and Tanganyika, not defecating coolies and their local collaborators.

Blacks and browns joining hands could be dangerous. He had seen it happen in South Africa, and he didn't wish to have that replicated in East Africa. McDonald decided to place Babu under surveillance. It was then that he remembered where he had bumped into Babu previously—he'd been on the shipwrecked vessel. McDonald knew where to find Nahodha, the ship's captain.

* * *

Fatima remained bedridden, barely seeing Babu for more than a few minutes each day. She had no idea what was keeping him away, although she suspected he felt complicit in the calamity that had befallen her. She blamed him squarely for the loss of the use of her legs. She had heard the ship's captain with her own two ears: Nahodha, a pious man of Allah, had cursed Babu and his family. Days later, she lost use of her legs. She would never walk again, and her new husband, the proper target of the curse, could barely stand still. Her initial anger was replaced by bitterness. She regretted having left home to join a man she now considered completely mad. She replayed such thoughts over and over, but always returned to the beginning—she had married a crazy man, and would have to bear the consequences. Her father had appeared hesitant about her accompanying her husband to the new land. It was her mother who'd been pushy, telling her to think of the Indian Ocean not as a barrier but a link to the new land and to new opportunities. She had encouraged her to travel. When they were ready, they would return, especially if they found prosperity while in Africa. A woman could belong anywhere, her mother had said. She could put down roots wherever the soil was fertile. Fatima had simply nodded and said nothing. Even at the tender age of sixteen, she knew, as her people said, acceding to something was not a burden, nor did it mean being bound to that decision.

The morning after surviving the shipwreck, Fatima had been in a state—her eyes shut but ears wide open—when she heard voices and instantly recognized that of Nahodha next door. His voice was weak, but it was unmistakably him recalling their trouble at sea. Fatima instantly knew Nahodha was talking about Babu.

"Yes, I recall the man. His head is full of water, that's why his forehead is so pronounced," Nahodha said.

Fatima heard another man laugh. "The people here call such a man *kichwa maji*. I don't know a lot of Swahili, but I do know *kichwa maji*. It means a head full of water. There are plenty of those around here."

"But he is trouble, I tell you," Nahodha went on. "I believe our shipwreck stemmed from his misconduct. How does one mock a man in prayer unless one is the agent of *ibilisi*, the devil himself?"

Fatima heard the other man laugh again, but this time the laughter did not last. "If he is looking for trouble, he has come to the right place," he said. "The locals here have an expression: *If you want to catch a man, you place a tail in his path. Once he steps on it, the cat will show him what she does best . . .*"

Fatima was very attentive now. None of those recuperating knew she was related to Babu, for he had spent his time on the deck throughout their sail. Nor did anyone know that she had recognized Babu to be the subject of discussion by Nahodha and the visitor. She had to warn Babu about the conspiracy against him. She would deal with him on her own terms—no one but she would seek revenge against Babu. Nahodha had cursed Babu, but Fatima was suffering the consequences. The stranger with his cat tricks would not get the better of her.

The sentry detailed to monitor Babu reported to McDonald that he had noticed almost no movement, accurately recording the few instances Babu stepped out for air or walked to the hedge to pass water. Twice, the sentry said, he noticed Babu emptying a tin gallon before returning inside the camp. "He appeared engrossed in thought the entire time," the sentry said. "It's as though something is troubling him."

McDonald shuddered. That probably meant Babu was planning some revolt against him. But he thought the man's lack of movement was strange. He had expected Babu would be all over the place, building new alliances. One does not make trouble in the solitude of one's own mind. "Do you think he suspects he is being watched?" McDonald asked.

The sentry, keen to have the assignment called off, lied, "Maybe," although he knew Babu hadn't really displayed any such anxieties—he didn't look over his shoulder or appear self-conscious. As a matter of fact, Babu appeared to be mumbling to himself. But the sentry wanted his isolation to end so that he could return to his regular spot under the *mnazi*, where Nyundo told his tall tales. Spending his days in treetops watching other people go about their business would soon become public knowledge, and the sentry would be ridiculed by those who knew him. They would say strange things were happening since *wazungu* had arrived—they had turned some in their midst into birds, perching on treetops eating figs all day.

McDonald was puzzled. If Babu had discovered his surveillance, then they must be dealing with a more complex adversary than he had originally assumed. That could only mean one thing: that Babu probably had military training, as the instinct to cover one's tracks does not come naturally, especially if the garrulous temperament that Nahodha had described, and what he had personally witnessed at the fort, were accurate. Stalling, so he had more time to figure out his next move, McDonald told the sentry without conviction: "Let's watch him for one more day."

On the third day, the man espied Babu escorting Fatima to the fence to relieve herself. Initially, her feet swept the ground before Babu lifted her comfortably and deposited her near the hedge. She waited for a few moments as Babu retreated to a respectable distance. She crouched in a kneeling position and swiftly lifted her sari to reveal a smooth brown bum. She glanced at what she had deposited, then scooped earth in her palms and buried her waste, just like a cat. Babu walked aimlessly while keeping an eye in the general direction of the hedge. The spy watched Fatima lift a hand to wave at Babu, who returned and helped her back to the camp.

McDonald was unable to disguise his joy at this new discovery. If Babu had a crippled wife who kept him busy day and night, that was good fortune. Even his trainers at Sandhurst had a term for it: soft target. It meant his initial plan to administer a quick, sharp attack against his adversary would now be changed to a long-range, long-term strategy of annihilation. His visions of Babu taking care of his sick wife invoked the sour memories of Sally and his mind flashed back to that morning in South Africa when he had found her in bed with his black gardener. He would teach Babu a lesson. He suspected the hospital would be Babu's next port of call and planned accordingly.

Fatima went to see Dr. Casebook over the next few weeks. Dr. Casebook dutifully administered bad medicine as McDonald had instructed. The intention was not to maim Fatima, only to slow down her recovery. As long as she was unwell, McDonald had decided, Babu would be fully absorbed in caring for her. Dr. Casebook told Fatima she would have to learn to live with her condition as the nerves in her legs had been dead for the week they were shipwrecked and could not be revived.

Babu's daily exchanges with Fatima were confined to her health status. How was she feeling, had she remembered to take the medication, did she feel like a massage? To these questions, Fatima responded with a simple yes or no, and theirs became a house of silence.

This was part of Fatima's strategy to keep Babu out of harm's way. As long as he was with her, Nahodha and the mysterious man plotting against him would have little prospect of succeeding. She had told Babu she had nightmares day and night and begged him not to leave her alone. He spent the day attending to her, cooking for her, coaxing her to eat, shifting her from one corner to another, gingerly lifting her like delicate cargo. Once she was done eating, he applied herbs that had been offered by the two Swahili medicine men. One of the healers said it was pretty common for people to suffer cramps after crouching for long periods. They provided some herbal ointments that they believed would ease the cramps.

Every few hours, Babu applied the ointment, his gentle rub getting more aggressive until she sighed. "Does it hurt?" he would ask, more a statement than a question, but she would only venture that she was fine, and he would continue rubbing the herbs onto her legs. He knew where her purple veins converged, and where the skin receded like a dimple, where the ankle creaked when turned.

Babu watched Fatima sleeping calmly, her deformed, spindly legs lying uselessly, as if their owner had run off and forgotten them. A pang of guilt overcame him. He needed to take her to see the doctor but he had practically no money left. If she did not improve over the next two weeks, he would have to look for money for her treatment. He was getting sick with worry, and though he couldn't verbalize his fears, he still suspected her ailment had something to do with Nahodha's curse. He wondered what Fatima felt about him. She had barely spoken since they'd arrived.

"Do you feel like eating pilau? The vendor close to the mosque sells really good pilau. It's made in coconut sauce," Babu had ventured earlier that day.

Fatima only shook her head.

"How about some chai? Strong chai with cinnamon and cloves? They're nice, warming spices."

"No."

Presently, Fatima turned and mumbled in her sleep, but she did not open her eyes. There was a wheeze in her chest. Babu listened keenly, as his mind raced to another place and time, when he was younger and had first encountered another crippled, bedridden girl who had a whimper in the chest. He was in Punjab, and he had gone to visit his mother's sister, Dharma Aunty, on his way home from school. She was back from work when he arrived, and Babu was drawn to a low, mournful sound coming from the squat house. It was a low wail, the sort of lament dogs sing when afraid of their own shadows under a full moon.

Dharma Aunty arrived within no time and once they were inside the house, muted light filtered in through a tiny window, its feeble illumination revealing a bed in a corner. Lying there was Dharma Aunty's youngest child, Reena. The light weakly illuminated her yellow face, fingers curled into her drooling mouth, her deformed legs lying lifelessly on the bed.

Dharma Aunty cracked firewood on her knee, her shin shining above her looped skirt, and blew into the cold hearth. A cascade of butterflies fluttered in the room, some ash settling on her scarfed head. A shower of kerosene doused from the tin lamp was followed by a strike of the match. Once the match was hurled into the pile, tongues of fire leaped like serpents from a hatched egg. A sooty pot was placed near the fire to warm, as Dharma Aunty scooped food—a mishmash of potatoes, vegetables, and meat—into it. She sat astride a low stool, her skirt folded inward, dishing food with meticulous calculation as the ladle tapped the pot rhythmically. Babu tasted the food; it was too hot. Dharma Aunty was known to enjoy heavy spices a little too much. Babu's mother said Dharma Aunty made her food spicy to ensure children did not touch it. Babu coughed and asked for some water.

The shaft of light from the tiny window had shifted to the legs of the bed, silhouetting Reena's sleeping form. The bed's broken black rubber hung loose like entrails from a beast, Reena's tender rump forming a slight bump beneath the bed. Her flat chest rose and fell, the hum of her sad song buzzing in Babu's ears.

A glassy tear now blurred his vision momentarily as he realized Fatima was awake and watching him intently.

He is a coconut, Fatima thought, as she watched Babu; hard on the outside but soft inside. An idea came to her suddenly and she smiled brightly at the simplicity of it.

She continued to make incessant requests for food and medicine, ensuring that Babu returned to her every night after work. As rail construction advanced toward the hinterland and Babu's trips back to see Fatima became few and far between, she decided to pursue her idea. She could tell Babu had already survived her worst fears. He had not been harmed by the men who were plotting against him. What she needed now was to save herself. She sought a good traditional doctor. If her problem stemmed from a curse, then she was wasting her time and money seeing the white doctor. She meant to see a fortune-teller, but the local woman took her to a Swahili herbalist who also did palm readings. The man, face dripping with ocher and draped in animal skin, took her foot and twisted it this way and that.

"Ouch!" Fatima cried.

"Ooh, if you can feel pain, then leg is not dead," the man said. "You shall walk again," he assured her, speaking through a translator. "But all that depends on a few things."

Fatima sat with rapt attention. "What things?"

"How would you describe your relations with the other people in Mombasa?"

Fatima shrugged; she only knew her husband.

"Have you or any member of your family been at loggerheads with others?" the medicine man pursued.

Fatima shrugged again.

"Any arguments of late with men of authority?"

"What authority?"

"A government man or a man of God."

"I'm not following."

"The medicine used against you is quite strong. It could only come from a man in authority."

"My husband quarreled with Nahodha," Fatima confessed.

"Did he issue a curse against you or your family?"

Fatima's voice dropped to a whisper: "Yes."

"Were you present or did you learn about this from others?"

"I was present."

"What did the man do after issuing the curse?"

"He blew a horn."

"What color was it, can you remember?"

"Black, it was black in color."

"Did you cry?"

"Yes."

"Why did you cry?"

"Because I was afraid."

"Fear not!" the man pronounced. "Evil triumphs when we are afraid. I will give you a horn, black like Nahodha's. *Dawa ya moto ni moto*. You shall blow to ward off the evil spirits he cast on you. And you shall keep the horn in a place of pride in your house. Blow it only when you detect evil spirits. They mainly come in the form of women."

Fatima paused. "I am a woman. Am I an evil spirit?"

"The man whose spell you want to break will consider you an evil spirit. But that will not make you one."

On that very day Fatima received the horn. She smoked the herbs given by the traditional healer from the horn, while boiling the rest of the herbs in water that she then used as an ointment. Within a few weeks, Fatima had regained complete use of her legs. She waited to surprise Babu, but he repeatedly postponed his next trip back to Mombasa; instead, he kept dispatching money for her treatment, unaware that she did not need it anymore.

Fatima used the money to start her own business, growing her *duka* step by step.

7

When the railway enterprise began in earnest, Mc-Donald was troubled by the increasing attacks on his caravans by local youth—two engineers had even been reported missing after they chased some attackers. Sections of track that had been laid were stripped off, the iron used by local tinsmiths to forge hoes and machetes. Communication cables were also cut to make decorative ornaments. He decided he needed to demonstrate the enormous power of the colonial administration, so McDonald visited a Giriama village accompanied by twenty-five policemen.

Villagers said the elders were at the *kaya*, but warned against venturing there without an invitation. Not one to heed heathen customs, McDonald decided to visit the *kaya* regardless. While his presence and that of his team was considered sacrilegious, the *kaya* being the hallowed abode of the coastal community of the Mijikenda, he was welcomed with a gourd of *mnazi*. The *kaya* elder poured some of the *mnazi* into a horn, and then he poured some of the libation on the ground, took a sip, and spat on his own chest.

"That's for the spirits of those who have gone before us," he explained to no one in particular, then handed the horn to McDonald.

"I thank you very much for the offer, but I cannot afford a drink before work. It is supposed to be after work," he said through an interpreter.

The elder retracted his outstretched hand uncertainly. "I hope you are not saying that making *mnazi* is not work." The *kaya* elder chuckled, making light of the rebuff.

"Not from some of the stories I have heard," McDonald said easily, remembering the notes he had read from his predecessor about locals' laziness. "I hear some of you wait for fruit to fall from trees."

"That's certainly true of people my age. I doubt if you can climb the *mnazi* tree yourself," the *kaya* elder challenged, sipping his drink as he did so.

"I doubt it," McDonald said, tilting the brim of his hat and running a forefinger across his mustache. It was doing its dance to show his growing irritation. "Thankfully, I'm not here to climb trees, or to have a drink. As a matter of fact, that drink is one of the things my government will consider banning."

The *kaya* elder fell silent. McDonald realized his mistake and kept quiet as well. He had said too much.

"This drink is our way of life. We found it here because our forefathers had it," the elder finally said in a shaky voice. He was not afraid, only angry. "Is this why you have brought these men with you, to arrest an old man for having a drink?"

"No, I'm not here about the drink. That time will come. I'm here because young men from this village have been attacking my men doing work on the railway and stealing supplies they are assigned to carry."

The elder's face darkened. "That's a grave charge," he said.

"I am demanding compensation from your people," McDonald went on.

"That's a difficult task you demand of me. How can the aggrieved become the aggressor? Your people have trespassed upon our land. And you have come to the *kaya*, the abode of our gods, uninvited. *You* must pay a fine in goats to cleanse this abomination."

"That's why I have come to you," McDonald responded slyly. From his reading, he had discovered the *kaya* elder was the highest-ranked man in the community's political and religious system.

"Why?" the elder posed.

"Your people need to know things have changed. You are going to be my chief."

"Chief?"

"Yes. Chief. I am appointing you as of today."

The elder hesitated. "What chief?"

"The paramount chief," McDonald said swiftly. "You shall be in service to the Queen of England."

The elder smiled broadly. "I shall marry the Queen of England?"

"Who said that? The Queen is the leader of my country."

"Men in your country are ruled by a woman?"

"Yes," McDonald conceded grimly.

"I hear some tribes in *bara* are ruled by women," the elder said. "I hear in one tribe, the woman leader sits on a man's back instead of a seat."

"Yes, women rule in the hinterland, I hear as well."

"What's this world coming to?" the elder said thoughtfully.

"That's why I feel you will make a good chief . . ." McDonald persisted.

"Every village here has an elder," the man said, his brow creasing in thought. "I am only one of nine elders in our community."

"I shall make those elders chiefs as well, but they shall

all report to you. You shall be the chief of chiefs."

"I'm not following you."

"I shall work with you. You shall be in service to the Queen of England. And you shall get paid for it."

The elder paused. The question of money was interesting, but he did not understand this chief business properly. He was silent for a while before speaking again.

"You told me a moment ago that you were here because of the *mnazi*. Then you said that time will come. You then told me, and I heard with these ears, that you were here to extract a fine because our men have been stealing from your caravans. Now you say you have offered to pay me to work for you. Those are many things to ask of a man all at once!" he laughed.

McDonald struggled to keep his composure. "Let me state my case," he started, looking at the young translator. "It is true caravans on the railway works have been targeted and their wares stolen. It is also true two of my men are in your people's custody. I am demanding my men's release immediately. Some natives working as porters have also taken off to hide in their villages, bringing their supplies with them. I am seeking compensation for that. And I shall accept payment in kind only, by having young men come and work for me. Is that clear?"

"It is not clear," the *kaya* elder replied. "It is dark, like the night."

"What's not clear?" McDonald asked, slightly uncomfortable because he did not know where this exchange was going.

"Everything!"

"What?"

"Our people say one does not hurl words like a club. You have hurled so many words, some of which are hurtful. And you have stated your case and passed a judgment without hearing the other parties. That does not sound just. We have another saying: *Justice bends a strung bow.* But I don't think your bow can be bent by anything."

"I wish I understood all your nice proverbs," McDonald said impatiently through the interpreter. "But I think you get the message. I need five hundred men this time next week to work on the rail. That's the punishment I have decreed for their attacks on my caravans and abduction of my men. I will be back."

8

Drumbeats sounded that night, hesitant and mournful, across the nine villages. It was the code used to summon the community to a meeting in the *kaya* the following day. It had been four seasons since the last such drumbeats were heard, when the community met to sacrifice and commune with the ancestors after the rains failed, triggering the famine that had devastated huge swaths of the population. Although the rainy season had not yet started this year, those on the banks of the Sabaki River grew enough crops to feed those who had remained in the villages.

People wondered what the new threat was to the community's survival that merited a summon to all to come to the *kaya*. So they streamed in the next morning—tots strapped to their mothers' backs, slouched elders supporting themselves with walking sticks, youths playing games along the way while waiting for others to catch up with them.

The *kaya* elder, Wanje, who represented the Giriama village, had been joined by eight other elders representing the villages of Chonyi, Duruma, Kauma, Digo, Bajuni, Kambe, Rabai, and Jibana. Together, they had offered their sacrifice to the gods at sunrise, and now awaited the community to settle so they could address the gathering. Drumbeats filled the air with greater intensity, conveying the urgency of the meeting.

By noon, several thousand were assembled. Wanje, resplendent in his bark dress and colobus monkey hat, addressed them.

"*Habari zenu!*" he shouted his greetings, then added wryly: "We always say we are well, even when we are not. We always say we are well because it is in our tradition to smile at adversity . . ."

A bubble of agreement vibrated through the crowd.

"We have gathered here because we know there is strength in unity, and two heads are better than one. A hundred heads are better than ten. We are here because our collective future is under threat. I alone was presented with a challenge, and I said I would share it with my people, and share it with our ancestors who went before us. We stand in this space where we draw inspiration and guidance from our forefathers, and so that they may bear witness to what we do, for they are the bridge between our past and our future.

"That future appears to be threatened. The events I shall narrate happened last evening. I am not talking about the day before yesterday or even days past—but yesterday, so my mind is very clear. I received a visitor. He is from Uingereza, which is ruled by a woman, I think the Queen is what they call her. The visitor first arrived here without an invitation. I ordered him to return here with animals to sacrifice and cleanse the abomination he and his ilk may have left upon our land.

"When he visited yesterday, he refused to sit down, or even take the drink that I offered him. In our culture, we know who doesn't accept food or drink from others!"

"*Mchawi! Mchawi!*" shouted the crowd, meaning *witch*.

"We are not afraid of white medicine!" Wanje went on, seeming energized. "We know who has the more potent medicine . . ."

"Toboa!" roared the crowd. Imploring, *Tell us!*

"I will not tell you," teased Wanje. "But when you see Bwana Mkubwa, let him know his medicine is cooking! One more boil and it shall be ready for serving . . ."

The whistles and shouts from men and ululations from women were deafening.

"But that's not why we called you here. Bwana Mkubwa has committed a heinous crime against our people . . . He has laid a serious charge against our people. He has called us thieves."

Murmurs of disapproval rose and fell sharply.

"Yes, he said it and I heard it with these very ears. He says we are stealing from his caravans, and that the few youths who have taken work with him are also in the habit of stealing. And that we are holding his two men illegally."

People shook their heads in disapproval.

"That's not all. He has imposed a fine on our community. He wants to be paid—not in terms of money, not in terms of grains, not in terms of animals, but in terms of humans. He has asked for five hundred strong young men to work for him. This thing that the white man is building on our land is the snake that Me Katilili warned about. And for an appetizer, he is asking for five hundred men to push into the belly of the beast . . ."

The speech elicited more violent eruptions. Women issued a curse against the white man, done by displaying their genitals, and tore off their loincloths, dancing around naked. Young men retrieved their swords from their sheaths and demonstrated how they would demolish the white man. Elderly men wept openly at what they saw as an unjust intrusion into their way of life.

Eventually, Wanje told everyone to quiet down. "We are not here to lament. We did not come to our fathers to express our helplessness. We are here to draw strength from them. To seek inspiration from them so that we may overcome. Just like our ancestors overcame the Wareno, just as they overcame the Waarabu. We shall overcome the Waingereza. And so, on these hallowed grounds, we shall take the oath to defend our land to the last man, to the last woman, to the last child, to our last breath."

McDonald received reports of the ceremony in the *kaya*, but he did not know what to do. First, he deployed forty policemen to swoop into three villages and arrest all the men. The policemen went through the first village, but the search only yielded women and children. All the elders and young men had left, and the women did not volunteer any information. Most did not understand English, and the policemen's gestures to illustrate they were looking for men, not women, ended up as a lewd display and groping of women's breasts.

The police went to the second village; the result was the same: all the men had left. In the third village, a young policeman tugged at the breast of a young woman he found baking *mandazi* by the roadside. The woman squeaked her protest and shook off his hand. In the brief tussle, the pan tossed oil on the open fire and a fresh inferno leaped into the air and burned down the nearby huts. The fire spread quite quickly and an entire village was razed. Since there were no men around to defend the village, the policemen went on with their mission and trekked to the next village.

McDonald was alarmed by the reports from the policemen, and it didn't help matters when he confirmed that the two missing engineers had not been abducted at all. They had eloped with local girls, which would strain his relations with the villagers even more. He realized what he needed to do to stop the building rebellion from developing into full-blown warfare: he had to swiftly pacify the community. It was a military tactic that found traction with the local expression, *Kuuma na kupuliza*. Blowing hot and cold. The community's spiritual warfare needed a spiritual response. He sought out the English preacher from the Church Mission Society.

McDonald had no trouble locating Reverend Turnbull in Mombasa. With his baggy corduroy trousers squeezed into ill-fitting socks, a thick collar on his neck, a wide-brimmed hat over the flowing gown, and an umbrella tucked under his armpit, Reverend Turnbull looked like a scarecrow. He was in a field with his servant, Tsuma, a scrawny, light-skinned lad who carried the reverend's tent and its accessories.

In their early days, when the reverend did not speak Swahili or any other local language, Tsuma had acted as his interpreter and had translated Richard Turnbull's name as "the lizard that turns into a bull." The name stuck, and only changed to Cow Man when Reverend Turnbull started artificially inseminating the local zebu cows to produce better milk-producing breeds.

This cross between agricultural extension officer and veterinary services was a way he used to interact with the locals, introducing them to Christianity in the process. One of the local debates was whether the reverend's pants had been chewed on by a cow to acquire their crumpled feel, or were made from the innards of a ruminant, since his life appeared to revolve around livestock.

McDonald did not divulge everything to Reverend Turnbull. He lied and said that he wanted to enlist his support in negotiating freedom for the missing British engineers. The reverend agreed to accompany him to the *kaya;* he had no problem helping his compatriots.

But Reverend Turnbull soon realized he did not fully understand their mission when they encountered Nyundo dragging along two rams, one black and one white, near the edge of the forest. That encounter was something Nyundo later shared with his many followers under the *mnazi* with remarkable accuracy, yet few believed him. They accused him of spicing up his narratives—*kuongeza chumvi*, as they called it—doubting that what he was narrating could have actually transpired.

Nyundo said that McDonald—Bwana Mkubwa, as he called him—had asked him to meet him on the fringes of the *kaya*. Nyundo honored the appointment and dutifully appeared dragging two rams as McDonald had instructed him. Sipping his favorite cup of chai, chanting his leitmotif, *Ushaona bwana*, Nyundo explained that Reverend Turnbull had appeared perturbed at the sight of the rams.

"*Ushaona bwana?*" Nyundo recounted. "There I am with my two rams, the black ram on my right, the white one on the left. I am dragging them with ropes of reasonable length, and I'm happy to see Bwana Mkubwa and I shout my greetings excitedly. Then Cow Man starts pointing at the rams, as one would point accusingly at a thief." Nyundo sipped his cup and said, winking as he did so, "I was a bit worried because I couldn't quite follow what Cow Man was saying about the rams. I hoped he wasn't asking to be given one. I certainly couldn't have trusted leaving Cow Man alone with a ram in a secluded part of the forest"—this last comment referring to the reverend's methods of inseminating the local cows by thrusting his polyethylene-covered arm inside them.

Nyundo roared with laughter and called for more chai

from the roadside vendor. "And although I couldn't understand most of their words, I could see Bwana Mkubwa and the Cow Man were having a serious argument about the rams."

Nyundo's observations were, in fact, accurate. Reverend Turnbull was furious with McDonald for taking animals for what he considered a heathen ritual to appease pagan gods. "The supreme sacrifice was laid by Jesus on the Cross for all our sins," he had protested. What followed was a detail that Nyundo told with relish, soothed by his fresh cup of chai.

Finding Reverend Turnbull's temper rising and threatening to boil over, McDonald had modified the story and offered that the rams were actually the ransom demanded by the *kaya* elders.

Nyundo took a swig of his chai, belched, then flashed a smile. "*Ushaona bwana?* I don't understand their language, but I can tell the Cow Man is unhappy with the presence of the rams, me, or both. He seems to be particularly unhappy with the colors of the rams, or something close to that. By this time, I have slackened my pace considerably. I am looking for an escape route, just in case I have to make a hasty retreat. You know, I don't want blood of the feuding whites to spill on me when they fight. But before I can say *kahawa thungu*, I hear: *thwaaaaack!*"

"*Kofi?*" asked a young man seated at Nyundo's knee.

"Yes, *kofi*. A proper slap on the face."

"Who is slapping whom?"

"*Sikiza, sikiza.* Listen. I'm the one telling the story. It is the Cow Man slapping Bwana Mkubwa."

"Really?" said another listener. "I thought Bwana Mkubwa carries a gun, and the preacher only carries a Bible . . ."

"Yes, tell us. Which is mightier between the two, the Bible or the gun?"

"Listen, listen, my fellow people," Nyundo pleaded. "I'm telling you what I saw with these two eyes of mine . . ." Another cup of chai was delivered. Nyundo sipped. It was too hot and scorched his lip. He swore and everybody laughed. He licked his lip then shouted at the vendor, "Those plans of yours to cut off my tongue won't succeed!" He blew into his cup and sipped carefully, broke into a grin, and went on: "*Ushaona bwana? Wazungu* are very interesting people. These white people come all the way from their land, cross the ocean when they are good friends and everything. But the moment they land here, they fight it out like dogs! *Wenyewe kwa wenyewe.* One against another. Can you imagine that? *Wenyewe kwa wenyewe.*"

"Did you just watch and do nothing?" an older listener asked.

"*Weeee,* have you not heard the proverb: *When two brothers fight, take a* jembe *and go till the land?*" Nyundo replied. "I was about to flee for my safety when I heard Bwana Mkubwa calling out for help."

"Had he been overpowered by the preacher?" asked the older man.

"Listen, listen, my good man. The preacher, who had started the fight, was fleeing from the scene of the crime. Bwana Mkubwa clung to his coattails. But Cow Man just shook off the coat and Bwana Mkubwa was left holding it. He grabbed Cow Man by the scruff of the neck, but the shirt came off too. He ran after him and held his pants. But Cow Man was willing to let go of those as well and run the way he was born. That's when Bwana Mkubwa called me to help restrain him."

"Did you?"

"Listen, my good man. You are asking too many questions. Now listen: when Bwana Mkubwa gives a command, you are most likely to obey. So I did. I dropped the ropes holding the rams and rushed to secure the Cow Man. I feared losing the rams, but they did not flee. They had stopped bleating to stare at the man who was behaving like one of them. We dressed Cow Man and dragged him along until his clothes threatened to tear. That's when Cow Man decided to behave himself . . ."

Many of Nyundo's fans only half-believed the story, but it was all, in fact, true. Initially, Reverend Turnbull had decided the best way to salvage his reputation was to disassociate himself from McDonald and attempted to flee from the scene. There was no way a minister of the gospel would be part of a heathen ritual, no matter the cause. But as McDonald and his servant Nyundo dragged him along, Reverend Turnbull suddenly realized this was a God-sent opportunity to defend his Christian faith. He would preach to those heathens and challenge their ungodly ways. And so he decided to play along and carry on with McDonald's suspect mission.

"I'm a disciple of Jesus Christ and I'm here to bear testimony that he is Lord and Savior," Reverend Turnbull announced to the *kaya* elders, through a translator, when they arrived.

"Then you are in the right place, preacher. You are in the abode of our gods, the truly living gods," one elder returned.

"Those are idols you are talking about. There is no other god than Him," Reverend Turnbull snapped.

The *kaya* elder gave a laugh that sounded like cracking wood, sharp and dry, then turned to face Reverend Turnbull for the first time. "Do not be like the fool who quarreled with the river about the direction of its flow, and jumped in to disprove the obvious, and drowned."

Reverend Turnbull kept quiet. McDonald shuffled and cleared his throat.

"Do you want to say something, my friend?" the *kaya* elder asked McDonald.

"Not at all," McDonald said uneasily.

"All right then. What can I do for you?"

"We are here to atone for our sins and seek forgiveness from you," McDonald explained in a clear voice. "We have brought you some goats."

"It is good you have come," the elder said quietly. "There is a small problem, though: you have trespassed our holy ground. No foreigner is allowed into the *kaya*. You have done it twice."

"I perfectly understand," McDonald said. Reverend Turnbull shot him a quizzical look. McDonald couldn't tell if the preacher was troubled by the insinuation that he had accepted that the forest was a holy place.

"Very well. Very well," said the elder quietly. "I shall receive your sacrifice. And since our people say we should never talk to a hungry man, we shall offer you something to eat."

Two elders received the rams and led them away. The white ram was slaughtered and its blood was collected in a calabash. Some entrails were cleaned and beads of droppings were added into the mix. This was stirred into a fine paste. One *kaya* elder took a fly whisk and dipped it in the calabash and splashed its contents around the clear enclosure, chanting a song that was later picked by other elderly men who emerged from different corners of the sacred grove. They were nine in all, each representing a village, and had been freshly enthroned to join the *kaya* eldership. They wore bark clothes and hats made from colobus monkey skin. Their feet jangled when they walked to the beat of the soft drumming above their chants.

The carcass of the ram was unfurled, now spread-eagled with its skin pinned to the ground using wooden pegs. Small intestines were disentangled from the maze of spongy offal and stretched out. The tubular skin was knotted around the fig tree, serving as a protective charm against adversity. A fire was lit at the foot of the fig tree and meat placed for a slow roast. Ceremonial herbs and shrubs were thrown in and the smoke was dispersed using the fly whisk, sending it toward the top of the fig tree. The nine elders guided the youths, all of them animal naked, in swearing to protect their land and invoking their forebears to destroy them should they falter in their commitment.

McDonald sat stonily and stared ahead. Reverend Turnbull, overcome by this open idol worship, moved a few steps away and sunk to his knees. Initially, those assembled thought he was coughing from smoke inhalation. But he was actually praying and speaking in tongues.

That was the day Nyundo, who had been hired for the afternoon to beat his drum and lead the goats to the *kaya*, switched sides and declared he would work for the *kaya* elders and the community. He would use his drum to mobilize the community. The motivation for his actions, true to his character, remained debatable, although some whispered he had been emboldened by the Indian workers' act of defiance against McDonald at Fort Jesus, and now the *kaya* showdown in which the elders had carried the day.

McDonald agonized over what to do next. He had attempted unsuccessfully to recruit local elders to serve as his chiefs. The same elders had humiliated him into dragging rams into the *kaya*, yet remained adamant that local youths would not work on the railway even if they were paid. This was because the elders saw the construction of the railway as a continuation of the slave trade. Not only was the railway cutting through the tracks used by slave traders, its shape also imitated a snake, just as local seer Me Katilili had predicted. Me Katilili was a direct descendant from the lineage of the great seer, Kajuma wa Kajuma, who long foretold the onset of men with soft hair and long faces who would scour the land with men yoked like cattle, a prophecy that many saw fulfilled with the arrival of Arab slave traders. Me Katilili had warned about a long silvery snake that would slither across the land, swallowing crops, man, and beasts to fill its large belly.

The *kaya* had become the centerpiece of the local resistance. And now, that very *kaya* which McDonald had initially thought he'd be able to count on, with the help of the elders, to mobilize the community for his own gain, was being used as a force against him and British interests.

McDonald shuddered at the thought of what he knew he had to do. He had done it in India, but there was no telling how things would turn out in East Africa. If his plans backfired, he would possibly be on the next ship back to England. What the natives needed is what his trainers at Sandhurst called short, sharp shock.

McDonald returned to the kaya under the cover of darkness, accompanied by fifteen policemen. The mangrove and the palm trees appeared conjoined, while thorns, thistles, and dry leaves covered the ground. To add to the eerie feeling about the forest was the sound of crickets and birds that fluttered around the massive trees.

It became so dark inside the forest, the policemen

started grumbling and threatening to turn back. But most froze at the thought because they couldn't even remember how they got there. The farther they walked, the louder the troop's grumblings grew, but they continued on, feet blistered and hands lacerated by the thorns they had to clear to make their way. Only McDonald carried a gun, the rest had batons, coils of wire, and heavy equipment.

Eventually, the British troops came to a wide opening in the forest. There were several hundred young men, animal naked, bodies smeared with clay. They had clods of clay on their heads as well, which they later peeled off and threw into the bonfire. Smack in the middle were a dozen elderly men, hunched over a boiling pot.

The policemen secured the perimeter of the *kaya* quite quickly and ringed it with dynamite. Then they retreated to a safe distance and waited for McDonald to act. When he did, a flash of lightning lit the dark forest, followed by a clap of thunder. Those who survived would tell their children and their children's children that they had never heard a louder blast. Others said they had never imagined that humans could possess such power as to cause lightning and thunder and literally uproot trees and hurl them into the air. Nyundo, who witnessed it from a corner in the *kaya*, was so traumatized by the destruction that he lost his voice, so there was no one to marvel about the enormous power of *mzungu*, or even debate whether it was the cannon or the dynamite that caused the greater damage or made the louder blast. What was most evident was the deafening silence from the community, its fighting spirit momentarily crushed.

9

There was a big bang on the day Babu set foot in Nakuru in 1900. A cloak of darkness spread across the blue skies just as the morning sun was peeking through the clouds, just as the wild dogs were lifting their legs to urinate and shake off the heat of the night, just as the *wazee* in the villages were spreading their ox hides to bask in the sun, or smearing on shea butter to smooth out their wrinkles. Babu noticed the sudden change in the sky. He thought it was a rain cloud that would soon pass, but the oppressive heat did not offer any signs of rain. So many strange things had happened of late that his past knowledge appeared to bear little use to his current circumstances. He had walked from the desert where the sun penetrated from the head to the soles of the feet, to rain forests where torches were needed to illuminate the way—all in a matter of days. He and other railway workers had been on the road—if one might call the trek through the bush, valleys, rivers, and mountains that—for nearly three years. He did not keep a calendar, only slips of payroll that came every month. He had thirty-four slips the size of a palm, whose scribbling needed a palm reader to decipher. He could hardly tell where the sun rose or set. Even when he bowed in prayer, he relied on his faith that he was facing the right direction.

They were organized into gangs of two dozen men comprising African and Indian artisans, technicians, engineers, menial laborers, and carriers under the supervision of a British officer. The division of labor was strictly racial: the menial laborers and carriers were African; Indians did the technical work, the British supervised them all. Babu's supervisor was Superintendent Patterson, a man with halting speech and rickety legs. But it was McDonald who handled workers' wages. Every evening, Patterson, with his uneven gait, would confirm the yards covered by every worker and McDonald would enter the details in his small black book. He would calculate the yards not covered from those assigned, and work out the rupees that would be docked off a worker's pay slip. The figure would then be multiplied by three so that the surcharge would be way above the corresponding wage for the day. Initially, workmen grumbled that this was plain theft, which was true in the case of Babu. McDonald secretly chopped a percentage of Babu's wages in ways he could not detect. This was his retaliation for the trouble Babu had given him, and also his way of ensuring Babu kept out of mischief. A hungry man, McDonald reasoned, would be too absorbed by matters of survival to think of organizing others and foment labor unrest.

Since the workers were paid by the yard, they toiled hard to cover the assigned distance, sparing little time to catch their breath or break wind. Babu knew every little detail of the track like the back of his hairy hand. He knew the spot where a dry branch broke off a *mukinduri* tree and workmen fell over each other in flight, and he laughed at their folly. He could point to the spot where a man stood on a rock in the Athi River and collapsed as his legs disappeared in a river of blood, his anguished cry only coming in bubbles as the crocodile's nostrils flared for breath. Babu knew the sudden dip where Abdullah the donkey rider broke his leg.

He could point to the site where his assistant, Ahmad, found a dry log riven with ants, which came to life when he hauled the python on his back. It missed Ahmad's head by inches, but when Ahmad flung it off, it crashed into the tripod that had been set up as Patterson opened fire—four bullets that all missed the target but grazed the tripod—leaving scratches that Ahmad felt every day as he set up his equipment, reminding him of his great escape, but also of the danger that lurked. Babu could point to the tree that Muchoki the workman had climbed to escape a buffalo after he had come upon it with his scythe; Babu had watched the animal wet its tail and swish it this way and that to spray urine on Muchoki, hoping the irritation would make him fall off the low branch.

Still, that did not stop the men from earning an honest day's wage. There were yards to be covered, and there was Patterson with his crooked gait verifying the distances crossed. Not even the strike of a hammer on a thumb would deter a worker from pounding again. And when an ankle gave way from a fall down an escarpment, its owner kept walking, perhaps a little less springy, maybe a lot more cautious, but determined still.

Their jungle-green tents had grown threadbare; what once provided a cool shade was now like a shredded palm leaf, offering more relief from the rustle of the wind than shielding against the sun. The workmen's black boots were worn out, and most walked barefoot, the cracks in their heels deep enough to hide a rupee coin. But the rhythms of men crushing stone went on uninterrupted, as did the swish of the scythe nipping vegetation with every swing. Within no time, one hundred feet would open where thorns and thistles had existed since God had created the world, and other men would follow closely with *makarai* full of crushed stone, which was spread out over the space where the rail would lie.

Carpenters followed with their saws and wood, pencils slotted behind their ears. They would mark where to cut, and the saw would hum its ceaseless song, the pitch different for every man. A saw in the hands of an impatient man squeaked and wailed. More often than not, the saw would break, and a replacement would be delivered, almost always accompanied by a slap from Patterson—because words didn't come as fast—plus a surcharge on the carpenter's account. Patient and skillful artisans, however, had very different outcomes. They would commune with the timber, starting with smelling to assess its maturity, then knocking the piece along the grains to check for defects. Then they would wet their forefingers and point where the pencil had drawn so that the shavings would not screech with dryness but soak in the moisture. The pitch of the saw would remain even until the cutting was midway, when the tool would acquire a deeper tone—the sound muted by the long distance covered, and the remaining distance still to be completed. The homestretch brought yet another tone that carried the relief of separation of the waste from the useful timber, and the carpenter's celebration of the successful completion of the task.

There were distinctive sounds that came at certain hours of the day: the muted wails of knives or machetes on file; the clang of pots that announced it was lunchtime, when black, white, and brown workers would cross the train tracks to their respective kitchens. Just like the rails that remained separate—in spite of their common interests—the workers of different colors kept to different kitchens for lunch and dinner.

Once they had eaten their fill, some would lie on the

grass, tummies distended like spiders carrying eggs, and count the daystars. Some would follow a sparrow in flight, and marvel at its gymnastics before it was joined by more birds, each trying to outdo the others. A few would somersault, others would stay still, and the dozing worker would wonder if his eyes were playing tricks on him. He would wonder if the clouds had stopped running to watch the birds, or if the birds had stopped flying to watch the clouds, as they appeared to toss and turn before scuttling in different directions.

Some workers lay with their eyes shut, listening to dull pains in their limbs, the nudges of tightness in the small of their backs. They would try to determine the moment they may have injured themselves, but their minds yielded nothing concrete. A short, sharp bleep would interrupt their reveries as Patterson blew his whistle to indicate the end of lunch break. The men would resume their toils and the tools would converse again in their own language.

Babu listened to these sounds as he worked, the only noise from his tools being the clank of his tripod as he set the telescope, after which he stood to the side as Ahmad noted the measurements and set the surveying coordinates. The two would then place the beacons on the exact positions where the rail would be laid. They would further mark the span of the railway so that all encumbrances were cleared. A metal bar would be sunk and a mix of cement and sand would follow to solidify the base, cast around the bar smoothly and carefully. That, too, was called a beacon, and when Ahmad saw a woman who he liked, he would say to Babu: "*Yala*, my *bhai*. Me vant to place a beacon in there!" Ahmad said he wanted to leave a trail of women who could make a line from the coast to Lake Victoria—"with a big-eared kid at ewery station," he would add with a big smile.

It was his way of provoking a reaction from Babu, whose passive tendencies toward local women evoked both mystery and contempt from Ahmad. In one breath, he would sneer at "Imam Babu" because of his pious deportment, and in another, praise his silence as synonymous with still waters that run deep. Babu paid scant attention to Ahmad's monologues. He blazed the trail, walking ahead of those who cleared the way when the grass was still silvery with dew, when the mounds of dung from wild animals were still warm and vapory.

The only women the workers encountered were those who brought firewood to sell to Patterson for cooking needs, or to run the steam engine. When Patterson was not at the station, Indian workers teased the local girls a lot, and some would steal into the bushes with them. Many moons later, some girl would return with a child strapped on her back.

"Have you seen him?" the girl, practically a child, would ask the first Indian she met.

"Seen who?"

"The father of my child," the girl-child would answer. "I know he works here."

"Is that so? What's his name?"

"Patel," she would say, eyes brimming with hope.

"There are two hundred men here called Patel. Don't tell me you . . ."

"I'm not a bad woman." The girl would start crying.

"You must have enjoyed, I tell you, two hundred Patels!"

Humiliated, the girl and her baby would head back the way they had come, the prospects of making Patel take responsibility fizzling before her eyes. If Patterson was at the station when such a girl arrived, he would gather all the workers and ask her to identify the man.

An interrogation between Patterson—through an interpreter—and those girls went along these lines:

"Was it an Indian or an African?"

"It was a white man."

"How white? You mean British or Indian?"

"Yes, that one."

"Which one between the two? British or Indian?"

"British Indian."

"You mean it was a joint effort? Both at the same time? A Briton and an Indian?"

"Britain, India, all same to me," the girl would maintain. "They all have long noses and big ears."

Patterson's stutter, as well as the unwieldy nature of the conversation, would compel him to organize an identification parade featuring Indians only. He did not bother with Africans, for they were hardly ever implicated by the girls. Neither were the British men. He said the British men were not capable of deflowering dirty local girls—"It's against the B-Bri-tish way of li-ife."

But Indians looked the same to those girls. They couldn't even distinguish between white and brown. "They all have long noses and big ears," was all they would say.

Ahmad was never picked, although he swore to Babu to have deflowered some of the girls who returned with children in tow. But again, he would add, he could be mistaken, as all Africans looked the same to him.

"A thief has forty days," Babu reminded him. "At least I'm proud to display my paper trail," he would say, and flash a wand of pay slips that said he was a British subject from the colony of Punjab hired as a surveyor for twenty-four rupees a month for three years. Half his earnings went to Fatima who was still in Mombasa, five hundred miles away. A quarter of the pay went to his parents in Punjab. He lived on the other quarter.

It was impossible to predict what lay ahead of the workers as they slowly progressed forward, but Babu's puzzle that day in 1900 came from above and not from the ground in front of him. He knew breaking from his work would make him lose momentum and run the risk of losing a few rupees in Patterson's rickety march. But curiosity got the better of him. He had always been a curious lad, and his deep gray eyes were still filled with wonder. At the age of twenty-two, Babu may have rightfully invoked the words of that wise man from across the seas: *Like all great travelers, I have seen more than I remember, and I remember more than I have seen.*

He fished a black polythene bag from the cart drawn by a donkey tethered nearby and shook off the peppery sands that had accumulated from the years of trekking. He looked through the opaque paper but saw nothing, not even the faintest hint of the sun's presence in the sky.

"*Bhai*, this is darkness at noon," he mumbled to no one in particular.

Ahmad, who was setting surveying equipment nearby, asked without looking: "Boss, vot are you saying?"

Babu strode to where Ahmad was squatting and tilted the telescope from its clamp on the tripod, directed it toward the sky, and peered up.

By this time, Ahmad was following his gaze, and Babu could hear his muffled exclamations as he tried to make sense of the spectacle unfolding in the skies. There was pitch darkness. The sun had given way to darkness without resistance; no struggle at all to shine for a few more minutes, no softening of the light to signal it was cooling off. Just a sudden gush and *poof*, the light went off. That was the mystery that drew Babu to the shores of East Africa. He had read in school of the European explorers who spent decades on expeditions cruising down massive rivers without sources, or mountains that spewed lava, hot as *jehannum*'s fire, yet were capped with snow, and forests where the sun never penetrated. He was enthralled by the prospects of venturing there, and Africa did not disappoint. Here he was, in a marshland with only a bunch of trees, but the sun had been snatched away by darkness at noon.

After a while, Babu noticed some movements. The skies cleared somewhat but the sun was still invisible. He saw the silhouetted forms that appeared like flying ducks, though their necks were elongated like a snake's. But the forms in the sky also had long, spindly legs. Did these flying snakes have legs? He wondered if these were overgrown chickens, oversized hawks, or what.

"*Achi bhai*," he mumbled. "*Bhai*, can you see this?" He turned to Ahmad.

But Ahmad was already in full flight, as were the other workers who had noticed the specter in the sky, all of whom were shouting with the full volume of their lungs: "*Alhamdulillah! Siku ya kiama imefika! Alhamdulillah! Alhamdulillah! Siku ya kiama!*"

The flying forms were leaving a hole in the dark sky that permitted a shaft of light to pour through, blinding those who looked up. The combined wing flapping and the hissing from the flying creatures grew to a roar as they descended and the full sun returned, bright and blinding, and the workers did not know whether to shut their eyes from the sun or struggle to watch the clearing canopy. The flying forms crashed into a nearby water mass, their splash producing one of the loudest bangs ever heard in that part of the world. By now, every worker had abandoned what he was doing and taken off, not quite certain where he was going, or even what he was running from. Mules kicked their tethers to freedom. A traction engine derailed. Patterson fired in the air in panic. The only people who were left behind were the three men whose legs had been crushed by heavy steel dropped by their fleeing colleagues, but even they managed to crawl the one mile to the assembly point, watching a spectacle totally out of this world.

The strange creatures, with wings flapped open for balance, fluttered soundlessly in the breeze, amazingly effortlessly, without crashing into others. They glided on the lake's surface, their webbed feet slicing the thinnest film of water whose iridescence flashed like the flip of mirror toward sun. They dived in, coiling their necks at awkward angles to scoop algae, before repeating their aerial displays and feeding afresh. Those that had eaten to their fill flew to the head of the spring pouring into the lake. Once the spring water hit the foot of the rock beneath, it yielded a steady flow of steam that cast the entire area in a misty wrap. All this while the cooing and squeaking and the hissing from the pink-colored flamingos rose and fell with the harmony of a philharmonic orchestra.

For decades to come, Babu would narrate this story to explain his decision to settle in Nakuru. He simply followed the instincts of the alien birds, he would tell friends and family, and repeated it so many times that when Rajan was young and begged for a story, he would provide the caveat: "But not the flamingo story, Baba . . ."

The other version of the events of that day of darkness that Babu told with equal regularity was that he pricked his right foot during the pandemonium as workers fled to safety and limped off without stopping, for he too feared the end of the world was nigh. When the commotion died down, Babu removed his right shoe and examined his foot.

There were four drops of blood on his sock. Ahmad grabbed Babu's foot and squeezed it. Four more drops oozed out and lingered on the surface of the black land momentarily, before merging into a fudge of nothingness.

A bit of thorn was still lodged in the sole of the boot, which Ahmad expertly wedged out using another thorn.

"*Bhai*, you should become a cobbler."

"Boss, your wish be my command. If cobbler you vant me, cobbler I be!"

Ahmad was a small man, only twenty-five, with thinning hair already. He was also from Punjab although he insisted on speaking in English. He had traveled to Bombay earlier on assignment, which is where he was recruited to work on the *Lunatic Express*—to join men of lucid mind and free will who had given up their lives and submitted to wanderlust, and discovered rather late in the day that they had gone too far to turn back, in part because they had no way of retracing their steps.

Babu sat on the freshly cut tree trunk and considered the sock soaked in blood. His body had yielded eight drops of blood. His people said bad blood did not survive the day; it had to be spilled. Ahmad appeared to read his mind when he walked over and said: "I'm not super . . . superstition, boss . . ."

"You mean *superstitious*?"

"Yes, tat one! Tat super ting! You know, *bhai*, you lucky, bossman, you go to school. You go to school to learn to speak like vite man. Te ting is, someone be trying to derail you from tis journey. Someone or someting be telling you: *Alight from tis* Lunatic Express."

"*Bhai*," Babu said, lowering his voice, "are you telling your boss to abscond?"

"Tat be te last ting on my small mind, bossman."

Ahmad walked as Babu limped the one mile back to their camp. In the melee, their donkey had gone missing but the telescope was still hoisted where Ahmad had set the tripod.

"Let's go," Babu said when they heard Patterson's whistle commanding his gang back to base. He saw Ahmad was stifling laughter. "What's the matter?" he asked with mild annoyance.

Ahmad pointed at Babu's backside. The fresh sap from the stump had left a round outline on his threadbare pants. "Someone or someting make mark of Nakuru on bossman. Someone be telling you someting . . ."

"Take that off." Babu pointed at the telescope while trying to wipe the sap from his pants.

Ahmad peered through the telescope. "Vot is tis, boss?"

"What is what?" Babu said, growing more irritated.

"Come see for youself, boss."

Babu's version of what followed was that using the telescope, he panned through the plains and caught a group of white men in sombreros, flitting around like butterflies against the brown background of the savanna. They were demarcating land, he could tell, because they were placing planks to note the boundaries.

That was all true. The segment that he edited out in future narratives of the events of that day of darkness was that he also saw, in the frame of his telescope, six young women. They were coming in his direction to sell firewood, he could tell from the loads on their backs, as others had done at every other station along the way. The local women walked naked save for a tiny cloth that covered the area between their loins. Men wore a piece of cloth knotted on the shoulder that served as shirt and pants. He zoomed in on one woman with a pretty face and watched her generous behind swirl gently, like a record playing on a gramophone.

"*Yala*, my bossman, I'm going to plant a beacon today!" Ahmad shouted. "Today is today, he who say tomorrow is a liar!"

Babu did not respond, but as usual that didn't dampen Ahmad's enthusiasm. Ahmad went to meet the young women who were actually girls, with legs thin like stilts, just sturdy enough to carry their own weight, not to mention the loads of firewood.

Babu could tell the girls were enjoying Ahmad's banter, but they tensed when he said something and pointed in his direction. All the girls cast their eyes down. Ahmad lifted the chin of the most striking girl Babu had noticed through the telescope. The girl walked hesitantly toward him, dragging her feet like an animal being led to the slaughterhouse.

The sun was setting in the west, and its rays had softened. The light hit the girl smack in the face. She raised her hand to shield her eyes. Babu stepped sideways and blocked the sun with his head. The girl looked up. She was shorter than he, and her eyes had such a piercing intensity he almost had to protect himself from her gaze. He did not know what Ahmad had told the girl, and since she was within his grasp, he figured he was supposed to do something.

He stroked her brow and she averted her gaze. He touched her breasts, first the left one, then the right. She sighed and shut her eyes. She walked on, as if to lead him, and he followed meekly. She threw down the load of firewood and sat next to it. They were in a marshland and cooing flamingos could be heard in the distance. He wanted to ask if she'd heard about the arrival of the birds, but decided against it. The linguistic barriers were just too immense. It was best to undertake what could be communicated by touch. He spoke to her in a mix of Punjabi and English and broken Swahili. The girl spoke the local language, Maa, which Babu did not understand. She shut her eyes and made no effort to resist his touch, which kept probing and probing.

They finally lay side by side. The girl said something and started sobbing. She looked at him, her eyes pleading as she moaned: "*Mubea, mubea.*" She turned and lay prostrate. "*Mubea, mubea.*"

Babu had dropped his pants to his ankles, and he went on with his probe, looking for the dark tunnel that he hoped would lead to some light. He swelled with excitement at the sight of her nakedness, as a vibration surged through him and built to a momentum he could hardly contain. He felt relief at the release of the tension that had been welling in him, while a knot of anger and frustration began coiling in his belly. But then he went limp, as his mind flashed back to the sea. He heard Nahodha hurling his curses in a furious torrent: *May your women be barren, may your seeds dry up! May enemies triumph over you!* He wondered if Nahodha's curse had something to do with his failure to rise to the occasion, but he recalled he had failed similarly on his first night with Fatima, after their hurried wedding before they set sail for East Africa.

Afterward, when Ahmad sought to know how he had fared with the local girl, Babu deflected the question and responded that undressing a Maasai girl was like skinning a goat. "Everything is all sewn up."

Ahmad laughed heartily and said: "*Bhai*, hope you found the right place!" Then he sobered: "Did she say *mubea?*"

"Yes, she did," Babu responded, puzzled.

Ahmad's guffaw resurged, now with a new intensity.

Babu stood intrigued by Ahmad's line of inquiry. He opened his mouth to speak but decided against it. Six months later, he wished he had.

10

It seemed inordinate that the infraction would bear such grave consequences. But those were different times, when honor came before all else. On that memorable day of Mariam's visit, as Babu lay on the floor whimpering like an old dog, he remembered his awkward copulation with that girl delivered by Ahmad.

Babu was back in the swamp and the sun was on the girl's forehead. He lay on top of her, shifting his weight around until his head finally shielded her from the direct sun. A bunch of droplets converged around the girl's nose and he wiped them away with one stroke of his tongue. He kissed her lips lightly, but his tongue felt dry and the girl seemed indifferent to his probing.

Mubea, mubea! he remembered the girl whimpering, again averting her gaze as she sobbed.

"Must have felt something like being born again," Ahmad had said when Babu rejoined him. "After all those years of celibacy."

Babu had assented with as much enthusiasm as he could muster: "Something close to that . . ."

Ahmad's conclusion about Babu's sexual encounter as some sort of rebirth would prove prophetic in a startling manner. Months later, when news spread that the girl was heavy with child, it spawned a scandal that nearly derailed the rail and yet again resurrected McDonald's grudge against Babu.

The girl's name was Seneiya; she was the daughter of a traditional Maasai chief, Lonana. She was royalty among the locals, for a traditional chieftain was an inherited title handed down from father to son. To complicate matters further, Seneiya was not only betrothed to marry Lempaa, son of another powerful traditional chief in the neighboring village, she was also the favorite daughter of Chief Lonana.

Again, that might not mean much, except for the fact that Chief Lonana had made it into the history books, although most of his exploits were grossly misrepresented.

This is how Captain John Adams wrote about his expedition across Maasailand and his first encounter with Chief Lonana:

Situational Report: The Maasai Land Agreement of 1896
Commissioner of British East Africa Protectorate

When the history of the Lunatic Express is finally written, a reasonable chunk should be devoted to the initial assessment of the Laikipia Escarpment. Our experience there should also inspire policy change to embrace divide-and-rule and other forms of unconventional warfare, which have paid great dividends in Maasai land.

The Maasai are a fierce, warlike tribe who thrive on milk and blood from their long-horned zebu animals. For initiation, young men known as morans kill lions with their bare hands and are reputed for their womanizing. All one needs is to plant a spear outside a hut and the man who lives there will quickly understand his wife is busy with someone else and move on, perhaps to plant his spear at another man's hut.

Since the sociocultural setting of the Maasai seems ripe for deeper intellectual inquiry, I will confine my observations to the preliminary surveying of the railway line, which I con-

ducted between June 1, 1895 and December 2, 1895. Our aerial reconnaissance using flying boats operating from Lake Kavirondo had confirmed to us that the shortest route from the coast of Mombasa across the Nyika plateau was through the Rift Valley. What we did not know was that the fierce Maasai tribe occupies the whole region. We were also unaware of their strong aversion to foreigners. The terrain around the escarpment works to the locals' advantage. The railway workers would be spotted from afar and taken down with well-aimed poisonous arrows, well-slung stones, or were speared in an ambush. After losing four men in such attacks, and worried that the railway assessment would not be completed as scheduled, I devised other tricks to access the Laikipia Escarpment.

I played the divide-and-rule card on two blood brothers after spies confirmed Chief Lonana was feuding with his brother Sadaka.

Our spies reported the nomadic community to be thriving through livestock production, shifting to new pastures according to the rhythms of nature.

We were thinking hard how to exploit the rift between the two brothers. But God works in miraculous ways. As we were cracking our heads on the matter, I learned that our School of Tropical Medicine was about to open a field station in the colony.

The recent discovery of foot-and-mouth disease in Europe couldn't have come at a better time! Our spies were given pellets containing the virus that they dropped in select paddocks. Before long, the Maasai herds started dropping like flies from the virus, or nagana, as the Maasai called the disease. Unable to move in search of pasture and with gums too diseased to chew any food, herds starved by the thousands.

With livelihoods destroyed, the community started blaming Chief Lonana for not advising their medicinemen to

concoct something to counter the white man's medicine. We
used that window of opportunity to prop up Sadaka against
his brother by sending in agricultural extension officers who
sprayed Sadaka's paddocks with a foot-and-mouth antidote.
A resurgent Sadaka staged a palace coup, so to speak, and de-
throned his brother as the chief. I elevated him further to make
him the Paramount Chief of the Maasai.

The Maasai Land Agreement of 1896 is the enduring trib-
ute to that shrewd diplomacy that led to several million acres
of rich, arable land being signed over for British occupation
and exploitation. The lease agreement is for 100 years—far
longer than I suspect the rail will live.

What Captain John Adams omitted in his report was
the fact that Chief Lonana's band of warriors, spurred on
by the strong medicine of Kioni—the seer who had warned
about invading white butterflies long before the onset of
the British—halted the railway reconnaissance for one
whole year as they defended their land.

But that was well before McDonald arrived on the
scene and steered the rail construction from the coast to
the hinterland. They were about sixty miles from the Nakuru station, and on the homestretch to the lakeside town
of Kavirondo, where the train was to end its run, when the
news of Chief Lonana's daughter erupted, and McDonald
picked up the intelligence that trouble was afoot.

Locals had been grumbling that the foreigners were out
to erode their morals, just as some seers had prophesied,
and various colonial chiefs had submitted dozens of cases
to McDonald's office complaining about the womanizing
conducted by the railway construction staff, a vice that appeared to enjoy subtle official backing. The evidence that
the foreigners were complicit in promoting immorality

was that *mubea*—a preacher, a man of God—was adopting children born out of such relations between local girls and foreign men. That was why Seneiya had been sobbing. She didn't want to surrender her baby to *mubea*, as other girls had reportedly done in other villages.

The man known as *mubea* was, of course, Reverend Turnbull, and his adoption campaign, which in later years morphed into a large humanitarian organization dedicated to orphaned children, was promoted by McDonald for two reasons: It was a conduit for the disbursement of huge sums of money that McDonald gave the reverend as an expression of gratitude for his willingness to step in when needed to negotiate with the local communities. The other reason was that while he was not interested in preserving local customs, McDonald feared mixed-race children would encourage integration when he was busy keeping racial segregation policies in place. Treating multiracial children as an isolated special group was his way of enhancing the stigma, thereby nullifying the prospects of widespread miscegenation.

But what elevated Seneiya's pregnancy from a case of personal choice to communal humiliation was the renewed interest in the seer's warning that the white butterflies would scorch every plant dry and push entire villages to the throes of starvation, a vision that was interpreted in spiritual terms. The community elders concluded that the foreigners traversing their land would lead to the community's moral decadence and its ultimate decay. They had heard that the invading men had left a trail of yellow children in the villages that they had coursed through, after planting the mysterious iron snake in the earth.

Without the cultural practices observed by the community since the beginning of time, Kioni had prophesied, the community would be decimated within the blink of an eye. And while social mores looked down strongly on those who conceived before marriage, those who bore children with foreigners acquired a special blemish—no man was willing to take them, even as a second or third wife. So news of Seneiya's pregnancy was seen as a serious assault against the community. The Maasai youth organized quickly to fight back, razing one camp and uprooting all rails leading from Nakuru to the Laikipia Escarpment.

11

McDonald sat under the eaves of his camp house burrowed in thought. He was out of his depth, unable to figure out how to surmount the new challenge facing his railway enterprise. He recalled his tribulations at the coast, when he'd had to use every trick in the book to coax the locals to work. He shook his head in disbelief at the memory of that day when he had appeased the locals by offering rams for sacrifice in a heathen ritual. That was before his patience snapped and he exploded in violence, ordering the use of dynamite to destroy the *kaya*. It was an episode recorded in local lore as the day the figs walked and birds froze in midair. Alternatively, it was remembered by some as the day of the earthquake, for the powerful blast upturned trees, casting light upon the dark enclave that had preserved the power and the mystery of ancient gods for generations.

From his soldierly experience, McDonald knew the destruction of a place of worship was considered an act of terror—which was prohibited in conventional warfare—but nothing about the locals was conventional. The destruction, however, did end up leading to a predictable outcome associated with conventional wars: the locals submitted. And his railway work had progressed, slowly but surely. All that was now in serious jeopardy because, yet again, his vision of the future of the colony was in conflict with the locals' past, which defined their present. If the railway construction was derailed by the Maasai resistance, then all he had strived to achieve over the past few years would end in ignominy. He would be remembered as the captain who ran the train into the wilderness.

McDonald rose and kicked a table in fury, spilling the cinnamon tea that he had been served, the china crashing to the floor. The noise drew a male servant outside who silently picked up the broken china and retreated back to the kitchen. He did not inquire if there had been an accident, or if McDonald needed a fresh cup. He was used to his boss's tantrums.

McDonald waited until the servant was out of sight before removing a shoe to inspect his foot. His kick had left red splotches on his toes. Now his foot resembled his face. McDonald examined his foot further, noting the rough edges of his toes that had been smoothed out by his shoe. He winced in pain as he sat back and propped up the hurt foot on a stool, cursing under his breath. He was still cursing when Reverend Turnbull arrived. Both men paid each other visits without advance warning, but on this occasion McDonald had sent for Reverend Turnbull because he wanted a sympathetic ear to help him think through the task ahead.

"We have only sixty miles to go, then this." McDonald gesticulated toward the open expanse, looking to the west where the sun was setting. A solitary cactus was silhouetted, its trunk thrusting a three-finger salute.

"As locals say," Reverend Turnbull responded quietly, similarly looking toward the setting sun, "it's like eating the whole cow but failing to finish off the tail."

"My friend," McDonald said, mildly irritated, "since you understand these people so well, why don't you ask them to lay off the rail?"

Reverend Turnbull smiled. "And they will ask you to lay off their land . . ."

"I can see whose side you're on!" McDonald charged, rising, one foot still in a boot, the other bare, causing him to limp slightly.

"I'm glad you do!" Reverend Turnbull countered enthusiastically, which McDonald mistook for sarcasm. "And I suppose," Turnbull continued in the same tenor, "since you think this is a spiritual warfare, it must be met with the full force of our spiritual arsenal!"

"There is no need to be sarcastic." McDonald recalled, once again, the incident on the coast, when he'd dragged Reverend Turnbull to the sacred *kaya* grove where he offered the rams. "This time, I'm done with appeasement. I plan to crush these savages into smithereens."

"And how do you intend to go about that, my good friend?"

"That's why I called you, isn't it?"

"You are the soldier. I am a preacher. I can only offer prayers . . ."

At that point, the servant reentered with fresh cups of tea: cinnamon for McDonald and *tangawizi* for Reverend Turnbull. He had served Reverend Turnbull enough times to remember his preference. The servant smiled gently. "*Hujambo*, reverend? *Karibu* chai."

Turnbull returned the greeting and inquired about the servant's family, addressing the man by his name. Hemedi said he was fine, but he remained rooted, his left shoulder stooped awkwardly in the reverend's direction.

McDonald was about to dismiss the servant when he addressed Turnbull directly. "The cow—the cow has calved," Hemedi said.

"That's wonderful news," Turnbull replied enthusiastically. "Is she producing enough milk?"

"Not much. Just enough for our baby and the calf."

"Don't tell me you had double blessings: a baby and a calf!"

"Yes, reverend, we have been blessed twice."

"Are you suggesting that cows here deliver babies instead of calves?" McDonald sneered.

Hemedi started to explain that his wife had delivered in the same week the calf was born, but Reverend Turnbull cut in. "Don't mind him," he said, waving toward McDonald.

"Can we wean the calf yet?" Hemedi asked.

"No, not yet," the reverend responded. "But you can save a lot of milk by milking the cow instead of letting the calf suckle. Mix the milk with warm water."

"Thank you for the tip. And thanks for the good seed," Hemedi went on. "The calf is very strong."

"It's my pleasure, Hemedi. Do you have a name for the calf?"

At this point, McDonald sprang to his feet, wincing in pain before limping off to the edge of the courtyard. He looked over at the Laikipia Escarpment that separated the railhead from its final destination. On the horizon, rain clouds were gathering. He intently watched the skies, taking in the clouds of different hues. The skies resembled islands in the ocean, bearing a permanence that he knew would not survive the wind of night.

"I see you are admiring God's canvas," Reverend Turnbull said, startling McDonald out of his reverie.

"It's wonderful, isn't it?"

"God's wonder to perform."

McDonald limped back to his seat. "Have you finished dispensing milking tips?" he grumbled. "Or is it donating sperm? Why don't you teach these folks to milk the elephant and the rhino? There are plenty of those here."

Reverend Turnbull sat next to him but remained quiet. After a moment, he said: "This is my flock. I am their shepherd."

"Now," McDonald replied impatiently, "I have more urgent matters than discussing your flock and shepherding ways. I want to blast these savages into oblivion." McDonald pointed toward the escarpment.

"You need prayers to do that?"

"More than that. I need to infiltrate the land. Assess their manpower, distance, topography, things like that."

"I told you, I am not a military man. Why don't you try appeasement? It worked at the coast, even though you put my Christian faith on the line."

"That's what you preach about Jesus. He laid his life for others."

"You need prayers, seriously."

The two men fell silent, each absorbed by his own thoughts. Then Reverend Turnbull rose. "I think I have an idea. It's a wild idea, but it's something you can work with."

McDonald said nothing but fixed a skeptical eye on the reverend. When Turnbull finished outlining his suggestion, McDonald leaped to his feet, a big grin on his face, and rushed toward Reverend Turnbull, momentarily forgetting about his hurt foot. Although McDonald's intention was to give him a hug, Reverend Turnbull lost his balance and they toppled over. They were both in stitches when they rose, dusting off their clothes as they did so.

"Not so fast," Reverend Turnbull cautioned. "It's only a suggestion."

"My friend, that's the stuff of genius," McDonald returned. "Pure military genius. Did you read all that in the Good Book?"

"All that I am and will be is because of the grace of God. His word keepeth me—"

"I guess all soldiers should read the Good Book."

Reverend Turnbull smiled. "You may say so. And if you haven't considered it, you can start by drafting that Indian fellow who has given you so much trouble over the years. That's a good place for him to be."

McDonald spent the next day drawing up a list of technicians he would enlist in his mission, per Reverend Turnbull's advice. It comprised all those who had entered his bad books over the past three years, with Babu topping the list.

Others included a man named Kiran, who led what became the *karai* movement—a group of workers who protested the small food rations by rioting every Monday, tossing their tin plates in the air, ostensibly to donate the tin to make large cooking pots that could produce enough food to satisfy them. Then there was Rasool, who led a band of technicians to protest working past official hours without compensation. After working the required hours, he would lead a peaceful sit-in during which workers folded their arms and legs and said they were withholding their labor.

And of course there was Wazir, who helped release some locals who'd been arrested for vandalizing telegraph wires. His motive was not fully established, even though he was busted weeks later with the sister of one of the suspects. So McDonald knew he had to handle the matter carefully, because he was dealing with very dangerous men.

He summoned these workers and addressed them collectively. He had considered dealing with each of them in-dividually but realized that would cost him more time than he had. He needed to dispense with the matter at once.

"I want to state up front how pleased I am to announce that you have all been recommended for promotion by your supervisors," McDonald started. The declaration elicited a wave of chuckles from the assembled workers. There was a quiver in McDonald's voice when he spoke next as his mustache did its dangerous dance. "Listen, lis-ten, gen-gentlemen . . . I said that's what your supervisors think. I have been asked to consider that position and I have imposed one condition before I can proceed with my consideration of your promotion."

The workers stood with rapt attention. Earning a little more money, after all, never hurt anyone.

"I hold the view that workers should demonstrate competence in all spheres of life, from sportsmanship to spirituality. Being a good technician is not enough, one has to excel in other things." He now had the workers' full at-tention. Even his dancing mustache stabilized somewhat. "My assignment for you is very simple: I want you to par-ticipate in a cultural parade. The specific emphasis is on traditional worship in your communities."

This was met with a chorus of disapproval from the technicians, but McDonald continued, undeterred. "Trust me, it's not that complicated." This was the make-or-break moment, McDonald told himself, and being a seasoned soldier, he knew how to camouflage the most important aspect and pass it off as the least of his concerns. "Listen, my good men, listen carefully. My assignment for you is very simple. But allow me to first explain my motivations. As some you might be aware, there has been quite a bit of misunderstanding between us and the locals." He nearly

clipped his tongue when he uttered *us* to imply the workers were a single collective, while in actual fact, he was ac-
tively balkanizing them along racial lines. "We want them
to know we are not all work and play. As a matter of fact,
the locals think we are all play, judging from the accounts
of those messing with their girls. We also pray where we
come from. And we have culture."

"I'm lost," Babu spoke up. "What exactly do you want
from us?"

"I'm equally lost," Rasool chimed in.

"And so am I," said another technician.

"I want you to organize a pilgrimage to the Laikipia
Escarpment," McDonald revealed, as though he was in a
hurry to get the words off his chest.

There was a momentary silence before the men spoke,
all at the same time.

"Listen, my good men," McDonald pleaded. "Listen . . ."
When the protestations died down, he explained further:
"Don't get me wrong. This is not missionary work. It is
a cultural parade. To raise awareness about your cultural
and religious heritages. None of you require spiritual or
artistic acumen to do that. You only need to dress the part
and go to the Laikipia Escarpment."

"Who would you take us for? Fools?" Babu posed, before he continued in an even voice: "We all know that the
construction of the railway has been suspended due to hostilities from the Maasai. What's all this nonsense about?"

McDonald smiled painfully, one red blotch on his face
appearing to enlarge. He shifted uncomfortably from the
pain in his foot and faced Babu. "I like you for—for . . ." he
searched for the word, "for thinking ahead. You are right
to ask why we are doing this. The first thing, as I said, is
to foster better understanding with the community. They

will look at us differently. By demonstrating our own faith, they will know we respect their faith and way of life . . ."

"But do you, or is this just for show?"

"Then vot?" a technician named Imran persisted.

"I am not a magician!" McDonald shot back. "So this *then what* business has to stop. I have no way of predicting what will happen to each of you. What's important is achieving our goal, which is to penetrate the Maasailand as pilgrims."

"Are we supposed to get new converts?" a technician named Assad asked. He was a short, bearded man with a turban.

"No need for converts." McDonald managed a short laugh. "What we need is information."

"Information?" the technicians chorused.

"Yes, we need information. I forgot to tell you that you are to observe as much as you can. Count the number of people you encounter, the distances covered from village to village, that sort of thing . . . You shall use special surveying equipment disguised as items of worship."

This revelation elicited another round of protests. A technician named Warah said that sounded like intelligence gathering, which was not part of their work. Babu argued that although the dozen technicians were all Indian, they had different faiths, and such schemes of deception could be construed as idolatry. Rasool demanded insurance—payable to their families in the event of death—before proceeding. Another technician named Kamani wondered why Reverend Turnbull, who was more experienced in missionary work, was not part of the expedition.

McDonald was starting to panic once more. He breathed hard and fought to stay calm. He drew in a deep breath and explained that the information gathered was only to help in future expeditions. "Watch for anything else that strikes you as odd," he said. "Like groups of people huddled together and doing nothing."

The workers continued to voice concerns about coming into harm's way during the expedition. A number of caravans had recently been attacked while coursing through the escarpment.

To McDonald's surprise, it was Babu who now came to his rescue, appealing to his fellow technicians to take up the challenge without further delay. "We have faced wild animals of all kinds for the last several years. Why should we be so scared of our fellow men?"

His argument was met with silence. None of the technicians wanted to be thought of as cowardly. And when Rasool argued that the problem was not their perceived cowardice but the workers' exploitation by the employer, McDonald stepped in and assured them that they would be well compensated when they returned.

"Vat vill happen to tose dat don return?" Rasool pursued.

This produced more grumbling, reminding McDonald about the mutiny at Fort Jesus, years earlier. A sudden chill ran down his spine. He needed to act fast and nip this in the bud. He cleared his throat and conceded that he had considered providing some form of insurance, but was waiting to secure a budgetary allocation from London.

Rasool said that the technicians would have to wait until the funds were availed for their insurance.

"I'm pleading for your understanding," McDonald replied in clear exasperation.

"And how come you only picked Indians for this mission?" a technician named Raheem asked.

Once again, McDonald calmly explained that the locals were already familiar with Reverend Turnbull. What they needed to know more about were the Indians.

"No money, no vork," Rasool insisted.

McDonald promised to draw up contracts providing twenty rupees—the equivalent to nearly one month's wages—to each technician's next of kin.

"Make it two hundred!" Rasool shouted. "No money, no vork."

McDonald waved everyone down. "Not so loud. I will make it fifty, but only if you deliver helpful feedback." Imbued by the positive spirit that Babu had demonstrated, McDonald nominated him to head the mission. "One last thing," he called out. "Treat this with the utmost confidentiality."

On the night before their mission, Babu dreamed he had turned into a guinea fowl. His skin was covered with thick black feathers, but his neck was bare because Maasai warriors had used it as a whetstone. His head had been replaced by a crown. Babu the guinea fowl was foraging when a sudden thought hit him: was he male or female? He peered between his legs but couldn't see any genitals. He elongated his neck to look from the rear but still couldn't see anything.

He crowed in horror, fearing his fowl genitals had been mutilated by the Maasai warriors. His anguished cry mobilized other guinea fowls in the forest. They arrived by the dozen, but Babu found their cries guttural and different from his. It soon dawned on him that guinea fowls from different parts of the forest spoke in different tongues. He could see the other fowls squeaking excitedly, as though there was something weird about him. They were whispering in each other's ears, then elongating their necks to point toward him. Babu the guinea fowl decided to gesture his own query to the others. He pointed with his beak toward his tail, then lay in the sand and lifted his rear and swished it.

The act elicited a trill of squeaks from other fowls. Some spat in obvious disgust. Babu realized they must have thought that he wanted to relieve himself, so he assured them in the fowl language he had acquired—*Ti kumea ngumiaga, ni itina ngumemagia!*—that he wasn't shitting, only flexing his rear muscle.

The explanation appeared to excite even more fury from the other fowls. Some danced around him as others clawed at those who stood in the way. He did not understand what the fuss was about until an elderly fowl walked over to him and whispered in a language close to the one he had acquired: "They are upset because of your indecent exposure. Some want to snatch your head for your golden crown. Better flee and save your life."

Babu thought to declare his innocence and explain it was all a misunderstanding. He simply wanted to know if he was male or female, and his crows were not intended to offend. But instead, he turned to the elderly fowl and thanked him. He sprinted and dived in the air, then came crashing down. A few feathers were broken. He tried again but stalled. One aggressive fowl caught up with him and snatched more feathers from around his neck.

Pain shot through his frame and the sight of fowl blood horrified him. It was like human blood and its smell attracted even more fowls to his spoor. He sprinted for dear life as a new idea surged. He clawed the earth and hurled as much soil as he could behind him. He heard shrieks from the fowls whose eyes had been soiled. He repeated this stunt after every sprint and the number of fowls that chased after him dwindled.

He knew it was only a matter of time before he collapsed from exhaustion, so he decided to climb up and hide in a nearby *muiri* tree whose thick foliage would conceal him adequately. He clenched a branch with his beak and used his short legs to hoist himself up. Midway, he took a break to catch his breath and look for some water to drink. He found some gathered on a large leaf where several earthworms and flies had been trapped. How could he drain the water but get rid of the contaminants? He was about to tilt the leaf and drink at an angle when he saw his own reflection. He was a guinea fowl now and the worms and flies would make for a very good fowl meal!

The flies were easy to suffocate. He pecked one at a time and held his breath for a moment or two before they went limp and he was able to swallow them. The worms were a little problematic. They did their dance and tangled themselves up, so that he couldn't tell their heads from their tails. He found the answer in holding them down and pulling out each worm individually, then placing it under his claws. Away from the cool habitat, the worms withered fast and he swallowed leisurely. He washed down his meal with the cool water. "Not too bad for a maiden fowl meal!" he mused aloud. "I can live with this!"

It was on that happy note that Babu the guinea fowl fell into a deep sleep. He couldn't tell how long he had been out when he slipped and started his descent to the earth. He was shouting at full volume before realizing his cries would only attract the same fowls that had expelled him from their midst for indecent exposure. He remembered in the nick of time to spread his wings to prevent his fall to the earth. Magically, the wings halted his descent and reversed his movement. He was now suspended in the air, flying higher and higher.

Before long, he was heading over Fort Jesus. It was nearly unrecognizable from above. The only thing he could make out was the unmistakable red and blue of the Union Jack. There was a large assembly of men. Several shot at him, but he managed to fly higher. African porters threw stones excitedly at him. Some shot arrows at him shouting, *Kanga wewe! Ndege mweupe tutakukaanga!* meaning they would make a good stew out of the white bird.

White technicians also hurled their arsenal at him with equal intensity. "Black bird of omen!" they chanted. Some rounds were fired and Babu the guinea fowl reeled from the impact. African porters started laughing; they did not think *kanga* was worthy of this volley of gunfire.

The exchange allowed Babu the guinea fowl enough time to fly away, as the line of argument among the workers changed suddenly: Was the *kanga* a black or white bird? Who had the right to kill and eat it anyway?

Babu jerked from his nightmare with a start. He was sweaty and thirsty. His thoughts instantly went to his skin. He examined his arms carefully, searching for the wings he had worn in his dream. He touched his mouth, looking for his beak. He touched his genitals. Everything was in place; he had not evolved into some hermaphrodite. He was awash with relief. He was about to relapse back to sleep when he remembered their pilgrimage was slotted for the following day. He was perturbed by the dream, whose vividness surprised even him. He hardly remembered any recent dream that had come with such clarity.

Soon his thoughts turned to his wife Fatima, long forgotten in Mombasa. Babu reprimanded himself for abandoning her for so long. What would happen in the event of his sudden death in the mission to the escarpment? Although it was dubbed a pilgrimage, Babu knew it was a spying mission. And the reason McDonald had assembled the men he picked—all well-known troublemakers—was because it would be good riddance if they perished. Would McDonald keep his word and deliver Fatima the modest insurance money? Would a fellow worker deliver his bloodied clothes as evidence of his demise? He had known families that had suffered this kind of fate. Such was the case with Manchura, a draftsman who was devoured by a lion. His fellow workers collected the fragments of his *kitenge* shirt which they dispatched to Manchura's family through another colleague visiting India—two years after the man's death.

Babu shuddered at the thought of his remains—or whatever would signify his life—being delivered to Fatima to convey his departure from the world. He would prefer a more personalized approach. After all, death and grieving were very private affairs even when one suffered a public death, serving a suspect assignment from his employer. An Indian, in service to the empire, in the heart of Africa.

Babu knew he needed to do something, but what exactly he did not know. He wanted to convey his uncertainties without appearing cowardly. Moreover, there was the question of keeping their spying mission confidential. Perhaps he would confide in a friend and make his final wish. He flipped through the names of fellow workers he considered his friends. Very few, he realized with horror, passed muster. Most were colleagues, not friends—there were quite a few friendships that did not survive the railway construction, sometimes strained by a transfer to a new station, or a misunderstanding attributable to cultural differences. For although the different races ate and slept separately, workers mingled socially during weekends. Some organized games drawing teams from different races, one of the most popular being cricket. Other workers tried more dangerous sports, the most legendary of them being Abu Nuwasi. A short man of slight build and a shoe-shaped nose, Abu Nuwasi single-handedly caught a buffalo and tethered her to his camp. How he managed to subdue the animal, nobody knew, but the animal appeared to regain her strength when Abu Nuwasi returned with a bucket and milking oil. He was convinced that the animal belonged to the cow family and could be coaxed to produce some milk.

No sooner had Abu Nuwasi touched the buffalo's udder than the animal launched a massive kick with her hindquarters, sending the man—together with his empty bucket—flying through the air. The animal broke free and returned to the wilds while Abu Nuwasi lived with the ignominy of the foolish man who tried to milk a buffalo. Some claimed his nose had been disfigured further while others alleged his modest height had lost a few inches after his bones compacted from the heavy fall.

Babu thought the best man to confide in was Karim, but Karim had been posted to another station. His next best option was his assistant, Ahmad. Babu's primary concern was that Ahmad tended to be a loudmouth and considered everything to be a joke. Babu's other concern was that Ahmad was not very discreet. In their weekend washing rituals in the stream, Ahmad had no qualms about stripping naked and cleaning all his garments, then basking in the sun while waiting for his clothes to dry. If anyone commented about his manhood, Ahmad remarked cheerfully: "Vot you see is vot you get, maybe much more . . ."

Regardless, Babu reasoned, it was better to leave his last wish with a loudmouth than to take it to the grave.

"I had a very disturbing dream," Babu said lightly to

Ahmad when they met for breakfast. "I dreamed I had turned into a guinea fowl and was flying over Fort Jesus."

Ahmad burst out laughing. "*Yala*, my bossman! Don't make me laugh. You have become that super-ting?"

"Superstitious?"

"Yes, tat super-ting!"

"Not quite," Babu said seriously. "I'm curious what it could have meant."

"My bossman, not so serious. It's just a dream. Dream, dream, dream . . ."

"Yes, it was just a dream, but don't dreams tell us something about our lives?"

"Vat do you tink your dream tell you about you?"

"I don't know. I wish I knew." After a moment, Babu continued: "It feels as though I was being made to decide where I belong; whether I am black or white. I am neither . . . Then there was the question of gender. I am a man, but that wasn't clear in the dream."

"Relax, bossman, relax, it was only a dream! But tell me: you have a doubt if you are a man, no?"

"Listen. I want to ask a favor. Should anything happen to me on this mission to the escarpment, I want you to travel to Mombasa and relay things as calmly as possible to my wife Fatima—"

"Vait, vait, my bossman *bhai*," Ahmad interjected. "Are you making some dead vish or vat?"

"Just stating my wish—"

"Your vish be my command, my bossman, but you don't expect to drop dead . . ."

"The Maasai warriors could decide to shoot us on sight."

"Why shoot you?"

"Never mind," he brushed off the question, realizing

he had already given too many details about his impending trip to the escarpment. "I hear you, my friend, but I don't understand what I was doing at Fort Jesus in the dream. Fatima lives very close by, and I haven't seen her for ages. And . . ." Babu hesitated, "and you know the situation with her legs. She can't walk."

"Okay, my bossman *bhai*. Your vish be my command. Should you be struck by lightning or shot wit a poison arrow, I vill make the trip to Mombasa, see your Fatima, and tell her of your dead vish . . ."

"It's not my death wish; just a wish."

"No worries, my bossman, your vish, dead or alive, be my command!"

Gutire utathekagwo. Even the gravest of matters can provoke mirth. And such was the case on that morning when the dozen workers assembled for their risky mission—for what some feared would be their last journey alive—and found themselves to be a rather comical, motley group. First, the sartorial. At McDonald's insistence, the workers were instructed to wear clothing associated with their community's religions. Since none of them were particularly religious, their request for sacred regalia was largely treated with suspicion. Understandably, the religious leaders who were asked to lend their garments were circumspect about giving their official wear to men who seldom patronized their temples; instead, most of them opted to donate clothes they had outgrown, or those that were so torn they no longer hid their nakedness. It did not help matters that none of the workers wore the same size as their benefactors—some squeezed tightly into the garments while others wore clothing that floated on them, so that they looked like puppets.

To complete this picture of absurdity, and again on Mc-

Donald's instruction, they all carried musical instruments that few could play.

"You have to play something for the locals, that's the only thing they understand," McDonald had insisted. When the workers protested that few of them had any musical talent, McDonald swiftly responded: "You are playing for the natives, for heaven's sake, not the Queen of England. They have no idea what to expect whatsoever."

So play they did, or they attempted to, which instantly drew other workers. Picture a dozen men in ill-fitting clothes, their faces ashen from the fear and uncertainty of venturing to a place some suspected they would never return from, their hands clumsily clasping musical instruments most had never seen or held in their lives, their eyes lit up in surprise at the philharmonic orchestra they had managed to concoct. Upon sighting the pilgrims, other workers laughed long and hard, before joining the ensemble, ignoring the ones who tried to wave them away. It took McDonald's intervention to get the other men back to work and let the parade commence, which only aroused even more curiosity. Some workers thought this was a new type of punishment that McDonald was administering, and silently wondered why he had not considered it earlier.

Babu led the pack. He was dressed like a sadhu bearing a special rosary with one hundred beads. He was immersed in his counting; every tenth bead was larger and represented a thousand paces, which meant his fingers walked in tandem with the swift movements of his sandaled feet, his long, loose-fitting clothing dancing in the wind. Babu's task was to ensure he recorded the precise distance covered. Gadgets for recording altitude were disguised as watches and carried by other technicians.

Babu stared stonily ahead, wrestling with the idea

that had been fomenting in his mind since McDonald announced that he would head the spying mission. He ignored the complaints from other workers lamenting that their clothes were hampering their movement and urged them to keep going as this was the only way they stood a chance of making it across the escarpment and back before nightfall. Moments after their camp was out of view and the Laikipia Escarpment was within sight, Babu abruptly ordered his troop to stop. He slumped to the ground and lay spread-eagled, trying to catch his breath. Some of the workers crouched, while others lay down to stretch their limbs.

After several minutes, Babu rose and surveyed the group. "Comrades, we have come to the end of the road . . ."

A cornucopia of queries swept through, many of the workers unsure what he meant, but obviously relieved that they were not marching on to the escarpment.

"We all know we have been conned," Babu announced, which elicited instant nods and affirmative grunts. "Our madman, McDonald, wants us dead. He has chosen all the troublemakers and pushed them into this pit, where we risk instant death . . ." There were more enthused responses. "You all heard him—our madman, that is. He enticed us with a promotion. When we were hooked, he spoke about a pilgrimage to demonstrate our faith. Now the song has changed to spying. He thinks we're children, and cannot see through his lies . . ." The workers were unanimous in their agreement.

"Can you imagine?" Rasool exclaimed.

"But we shall not give him the pleasure of succeeding," Babu went on, to which jubilant workers responded with more shouts. Babu raised his hands to shush them. "Let's keep quiet . . . lest we warn our enemy what we think of him. Here's the plan: We are not going beyond this point. We are going to lie low and map out our return. Our madman thinks he is a military genius, but he is mistaken. We shall teach him a lesson from a book he never read in school."

"Comrade power!" Rasool shouted. "Let's make the bugger wet his pants!"

"Teach him a lesson he will not soon forget," said Wazir.

A cloud of dust. A shaft of light. A thump on the ground. Shuffle of feet on dust. The waning light brightening. Then . . . white apparitions. McDonald lifted his binoculars and wiped his eyes, unable to comprehend what he was seeing. He had spent the entire day peering through the binoculars in the direction of the escarpment and had not witnessed anything untoward. Now, the light from the setting sun and the dust had given way to apparitions, and he could not discern whether it was man or beast.

As the forlorn figures drew nearer, he realized the white apparitions were fragments of clothing, though he still couldn't tell if the forms in the distance had animal hooves or human feet. With every step made by the beasts or men, he gained more visual clarity. They were men all right, but why were they so gigantic? As they came closer, he noticed they were huddled in three groups, each carrying a load of something.

By the time the workers arrived at the camp, it was dark; McDonald left his binoculars and raced to meet them, unable to contain his curiosity. The workers delivered their delicate cargo and some started wailing hysterically as others tore their loose garments and raced around in circles like mad dogs. It took awhile for McDonald to calm everyone down so they could tell their story—all

starting to speak at once, as the three men who had suffered injuries sighed in pain. Rasool, who claimed to have
broken a leg, wailed uncontrollably when anyone touched
him. Assad had a sling on his right leg, and Wazir said he
had been shot in the back.

None of them offered any details of their mishap, beyond saying it was an ambush. Babu explained that they
had barely managed to escape with their lives from the
"forest of people" where everyone was "armed to the
teeth." But what scared McDonald the most was the weap-
onry the workers had witnessed. It sounded as though the
Maasai community had mobilized and armed thousands of
youth to defend their land.

"What sort of weapons?" McDonald pursued.

"Poisoned arrows and bows and clubs," Assad said.
"Like the one that was used to shoot Wazir in the back."

From where he lay, Wazir groaned in mock pain, clutching his back. *He's a great actor*, Babu thought silently, while
McDonald directed the injured to proceed to the clinic for
treatment, a deep crease spreading across his face.

As the wounded were led away, McDonald noticed
none of the workers had lost their musical instruments.
"What the hell is going on?" He shrugged. "This place is
full of strange things . . ." It slowly dawned on him that
it'd be futile to fight this battle. While Chief Lonana had
been vanquished by his brother Sadaka, the outrage at the
railway workers' exploitation of local girls had obviously
found traction with the people across Maasailand. And if
the community was mobilizing to wage war against his
caravans or even attack his camp, he stood virtually no
chance, since, based on Babu's intelligence, they were seriously outnumbered.

* * *

Some ancient sage counseled about the wisdom in trusting the tale, not the teller, but the invitation here is to neither trust the tale nor the teller. That's a difficult proposition, especially when the Nyundos of this world are not there to counterbalance what's witnessed and recorded as the history of mankind. And since the English bear the special gift of transforming even the most humiliating spectacle into a historical epoch, it is a safe bet that the truth resides somewhere else other than where it is presumed to be.

The writing on the wall of the British Museum, dripping with bronze arrogance in that hallowed space where the supreme truth is supposed to reside, proclaims: IT IS NOT UNCOMMON FOR A COUNTRY TO CREATE A RAILWAY, BUT THIS LINE ACTUALLY CREATED A COUNTRY.

This was probably true; what the statement concealed, however, were the obstacles that nearly derailed the rail, and the men who nearly brought the construction to a halt. Those are the stories that never made it into any museums, like the story of Nyundo, who initially harkened the call of the British, but changed sides after the destruction of the *kaya*.

Then there is Babu, a man who remained in McDonald's crosshairs. Babu had taken a liking to McDonald when they first met, but that's as far as it went. Their lives remained separate like the rail tracks, one's suspicions about the other fortified over years of silence, one scheming to bring the other down even when there was nothing to gain.

Before the mission to the escarpment, McDonald had shifted his attention away from Babu, convinced that caring for a crippled wife would distract him. But Babu continued to bring trouble for him; what was remarkable was that Babu was hardly aware of this.

One evening, for instance, when the workers, returning

to their camp, found that a lion had stolen into the sick bay and carried off a man who was recuperating, Babu did not hesitate to address the issue. He immediately headed over to Patterson's cabin.

"We did not leave our country to provide meals for the wild animals," he calmly stated. "We came here to work. You are our employer. You owe us duty of care. What are you doing to guarantee our safety?"

When Babu turned around, he found that a dozen workers had joined him. "Yes, tell us!" they choroused. "What are you doing about it!"

Trembling, Patterson radioed McDonald and said he needed urgent assistance. When McDonald arrived, Babu repeated his question. "It's good you have come, we want this addressed at the highest office possible."

"Who has control over the lions?"

"You do, absolutely," Babu said in his gentle tone. "That's why you don't live under a tarpaulin tent like the rest of us. Or out in the open like the African workers. By choosing the most secure accommodation for white workers, you consciously shield them against such attacks while the rest of us are left to the elements. So you have control over who the lions can reach."

By now, several dozen workers had congregated, and they cheered Babu on. "Yes, tell them! Tell them, our man! No safety, no work . . ."

"You have heard for yourself," Babu said to McDonald. "The workers demand reassurance about their safety, or else they shall withhold their labor."

To keep the meeting from turning into a full-blown protest, McDonald conceded that his team would provide security to all workers, which he did by deploying armed soldiers to keep the wild animals at bay. Babu was carried shoulder high by the jubilant workers.

But things came to a head over Babu's mission to the escarpment, when McDonald's gesture of entrusting him to lead the expedition was repaid with nothing but schemes of deception. Babu had connived with the rest of his team to hoodwink McDonald into believing that the locals were planning a major retaliation to derail the railway enterprise.

So, it was in this frame of mind that an anxious McDonald had resolved to appease the locals and avoid fighting altogether by organizing a lineup in which Chief Lonana's pregnant daughter would pick out the man responsible.

This "sex parade," as many amused workers called it, availed yet another opportunity for McDonald to get even with Babu. He was initially conflicted about including Babu in the lineup. The man did not fit the billing at all, being married and hardly ever involved in any of the sexual escapades that had been reported to McDonald's office. And all the spies who he had instructed to monitor Babu said he was a model worker. He rarely socialized, and he devoted all his energies to his work. McDonald had not disclosed to Superintendent Patterson his motivations for undercutting Babu financially, and Patterson had expected Babu to confront him over his pay, but Babu never did. He appeared willing to endure it all.

Patterson found this discomfiting. He knew in his heart he was stealing from an honest man. Unknown to McDonald, when he went away on trips, Patterson gave Babu fair payment or even topped it up by a few rupees to restore what had been stolen from him; but Patterson always relapsed to McDonald's old rates when the man returned.

Babu simply did not notice these pay fluctuations. He was totally absorbed in his work. Sometimes those de-

tailed to spy on him reported seeing him stop by a molehill
and pick up a mound of its refined soil, letting it fall slowly
through his fingers. At other times, he would be mesmer-
ized by multicolored pebbles that he examined against the
rays of the sun, like a goldsmith confirming the carats in a
piece of gold. He pocketed the most striking pebbles and
had them delivered to Fatima, who kept them in a glass jar
he had bought her from an Arab trader.

But all that changed with the mission to the escarpment. McDonald soon had a hunch that Babu wasn't telling
the whole truth. And as his military trainers had drilled
into them at Sandhurst, it was better to be safe than sorry.
Babu would have to be included in the lineup. McDonald
pored through workers' records to isolate those who were
at the Nakuru camp around the time the Maasai girl could
have conceived, although no one knew for sure the stage of
her pregnancy. To be on the safe side, he worked within a
three-month window, then checked through the names to
weed out men who had accompanying spouses. Bachelors
were most likely to be the ones chasing after local women.
Then he dropped from the list a few elderly and pious men
and those whose public notoriety did not involve women.
In the end he had a list of fifty-two young men, all of whom
were notified they would be required at the lineup in the
late afternoon.

McDonald was particularly pleased he had included
Babu in the lineup for another reason: one enduring lesson
at Sandhurst was to push your enemies down, and keep
them down. Although McDonald felt a little contrite about
holding his grudge for so long—not to mention his role in
stunting Fatima's recovery with the fake treatment from
Dr. Casebook—Babu had not helped his case by acting so
suspiciously throughout the debacle at the escarpment.

* * *

The lineup was conducted in an open space. The fifty-two men, naked to their waists, stood in the sun, while a small group of elders sat under a large *muiri* tree. Among them was Reverend Turnbull, who was translating, and Chief Lonana, who sat in solemn silence in a pith helmet gifted to him by McDonald that morning. McDonald had told him he'd been appointed Paramount Chief, to which Chief Lonana had responded that though he did not know what that meant, he did not care for it. But he had taken the hat and tried it on, then left it on, as it shielded him from the sun. At that juncture, Chief Lonana informed McDonald that he had appointed a Maasai elder to act on his behalf in the dispute.

"I'm the complainant, so I cannot be expected to be impartial. My role here is simply to observe," he had said, before slumping into silence.

Everybody else at the gathering did nothing but observe Seneiya, a small bump discernible as she walked hesitantly before the line of bare-chested men. She had been instructed to stop at the feet of the man she recognized as the one responsible for her pregnancy. There were dramatic pauses whenever she lingered to peer at a face closely; the man under scrutiny virtually stopped breathing, then sighed with relief after she walked on.

When Seneiya first discovered she was pregnant, she had fled to her favorite aunt in the nearby village of Witeithie. She had hoped she could secure refuge there until she gave birth. But since she was her father's favorite daughter, her aunt knew it would only be a matter of time before she was summoned back home. In any case, since the fallout with his brother, Chief Lonana spent most of his days outside his hut brooding, rarely calling for meals from his wives, and rarely eating if the food was not delivered by Seneiya.

"You can't abandon your father in his hour of need," her aunt reprimanded. "I shall take you back home. We shall rear whatever it is that you bear."

Seneiya and her aunt returned under the cover of darkness, and for a while the awareness of her pregnancy was confined to only them. When the aunt divulged the news to Seneiya's mother, she was silent for a long while before she sighed: "This will kill him. He thinks he failed when his brother wrenched power from him. Now he will hang his head in shame for failing to protect his own daughter."

Inwardly, Seneiya was burning with shame. What she had considered a very private act was now playing out in the open. She had once attended the trial of another girl who had conceived before she was married. The girl and the young man responsible for the pregnancy had been summoned to appear before a group of elders and asked to recount what had happened, every tiny little detail, from how he had taken off her kilt to the method used to remove her *muthuru*.

Seneiya knew she wouldn't divulge certain information. It was enough humiliation for her to go through the lineup like a thief. Nobody had sought to know how she felt about the whole thing. If the intent was to smoke out the culprit who had stolen her innocence, they could have simply asked her for the name. But it was presumed she didn't know his name. She felt numb from the ordeal, momentarily wondering if she should pick a few different men from the lineup, which would mean she wasn't even sure who it was. This would cast her in very bad light, but she didn't care anymore. In any case, that would only further humiliate her parents. Then and there, Seneiya resolved she would do it her own way: she would pick the man who had the kindest face.

Seneiya walked toward where Babu was standing. She glanced at him and acted as though she was about to move on, but then did not. She could remember encountering him but couldn't remember where. In any case, all Indians looked the same—though this one had the kindest face.

Babu froze as their eyes met. The girl who he had first seen through a long lens, and later lay beneath him on that day darkness came at noon, when the moon and the sun became one, on that day flamingos arrived in Nakuru, was standing right in front of him.

She looked at him and bowed. An excited murmur went around the group, as two well-built men dashed toward Babu, each grabbing one of his arms and dragging him away.

12

The news of Babu's arrest for impregnating Seneiya came as a shock to many. Ahmad's joke about Babu being hit by lightning during the pilgrimage to the escarpment had turned stunningly prophetic at the sex parade. Who would have thought it possible? Many men giggled, glad to have escaped what some silently feared was about to befall them. Ahmad also escaped unscathed and his heart went out to Babu. He wondered if Babu had been nailed for that one instance he pimped a girl for him in the swamp on that day flamingos descended on the lake. He wanted to make amends, do something to make him feel better. He decided to keep his pact with Babu. *Should anything happen to me on this mission*, Babu had pleaded, *I want you to travel to Mombasa and relay things as calmly as possible to my wife Fatima . . .* And so on the third day after Babu's arrest, Ahmad took the goods train to Mombasa to look for Fatima.

Ahmad was in his khaki uniform; that was the only way he was going to get a lift from the train driver. He had lied to Patterson, telling him he had an urgent family message to telegram to India, and needed to go to the post office in Mombasa. He found, with relief and trepidation, that Babu's news preceded him there, if somewhat distorted, for every man who greeted him in Mombasa asked if it was true some coolie had been arrested for putting all the girls in one village in the family way.

Babu's arrest had been received with lighthearted

cheerfulness by men who had survived the lineup, some of whom confessed to having slept with a local girl or two, and who had feared being picked out. But as Ahmad neared the spot where somebody had said Fatima operated a *duka*, he got increasingly worried about how the conversation was likely to go. Relaying news about someone's death may be considered grave, but breaking news about an impending birth, presumably from a spouse's suspected infidelity, carried with it a hint of scandal. One might take it out on the messenger; alternately, the messenger could be made to mop up the mess if the spouse simply couldn't handle the news.

Through his inquiries to Karim, Ahmad had established that Fatima had been bedridden after losing use of her legs during their long sojourn from India. He had expected to find her resting at home, a little sulky, resentful even. Instead, he found a cheerful, beautiful woman on her feet, going about her business. She ran a small shop that opened into Mombasa's fish market, a semicircular outlay of dwellings that brought in men, women, and children to the *duka*. The space couldn't have been bigger than a cupboard, so how Fatima fit in there and was still able to take in sacks of cereals and cooking oil and sugar and salt and spices and cigarettes and kerchiefs and *simsim* and mango and coconut and guava and toothpaste and bread and *andazi* and *mahamri* and *kaimati* and what-have-you, seemed a great accomplishment. There was a small glass case on the counter that held the sweets and toffees and *tamu tamu*; the main face of the shop displayed a mesh on which the kerchiefs and rolls of tobacco were knotted. Sacks of cereals leaned on the outer structure, as though to secure it from being blown away. The only space inside or outside that wasn't laden with goods was the tiny aperture Fatima's pretty face filled to greet a customer or slide through a commodity that had been requested or receive rupees to pay for the goods. Fatima's own torso appeared to grow out of those wares, her pale yellow melding with the colors and textures of her products.

Ahmad watched customers come and go: a little boy came for a pinch of salt, which Fatima measured in a spoon and rolled in a piece of paper, admonishing the boy for holding it clumsily; a woman wrapped in *khanga* wanted a cake of soap, which Fatima sliced expertly with a thin string; yet another woman wanted flour because the *sima* cooking on the stove was soggy. She promised to bring money when the meal was done. Men, too, arrived at the shop. Some simply said they wanted *kawaida*, and Fatima dutifully rolled sticks of their favorite cigarettes. In other instances, when a little boy came for *kawaida*, she would roll a wand of toffee for him or give him a donut.

Watching all this, Ahmad was confounded. This woman was no cripple; she was part of a thriving community—actually, she was the centerpiece of that community. She was not the neglected cripple that he had imagined her to be. Ahmad cleared his throat and peered into the small aperture, wondering if he had been directed to the wrong shop.

"*Shikamoo ndugu, nikuuzie nini?*"

Ahmad perfectly understood the Swahili greeting, but he responded to her in Punjabi. "I am your visitor," he said hesitantly.

A flicker of doubt flashed through Fatima's face as she recognized his khaki railway uniform, before she replied cheerfully. "A visitor who arrives without knocking on the door?"

"Knock knock," Ahmad intoned, ramming his knuckles in the air.

Fatima grinned.

Ahmad relaxed. "I bring you news from afar."

"It better be good news, coming so early in the morning."

Ahmad was silent.

"Can I get you something to drink?"

"I'm not thirsty," Ahmad lied.

"A guest who arrives without thirst must find others with thirst for news, no?" Fatima smiled.

"You may say so."

"If it's about Babu it must be bad news," Fatima said in an even voice.

"Yes, it is."

"It is bad news?"

"No—not quite. I said yes to confirm it's about Babu. I wasn't sure I am in the right place."

"So you bring me good news?"

"Uuuhm, uuuhm . . ."

"What does that mean?"

"I'm not sure what to make of it."

"Why . . . ?"

"Sister Fatima, I need some baking powder," a new customer cut in.

Fatima's voice regained her cheerfulness as she made the transaction, then another customer arrived to place another order.

The third customer was a man who glanced at Ahmad's uniform and asked, "Is it true what we are hearing?"

"What have you heard?" Ahmad asked cautiously.

"About the coolie who has been stringing girls along, building a railway of women."

"I-I don't know what you are talking about," Ahmad stammered.

"You sure do!" challenged the man. "We hear the man

was even arrested and castrated. Would they have done that for nothing?"

"Rashidi," Fatima said, "my guest has had a long trip."

"Ooh, I'm sorry, Sister Fatima. I thought—"

"Never mind what you think, Rashidi. This is my cousin Abdul. He traveled overnight to see me."

"My apologies, Sister Fatima."

When Rashidi left, Fatima's face filled the tiny aperture again. "My cousin Abdul," she smiled, "better finish this family tale before the entire village descends on us. What was that about coolies and the village girls?"

Ahmad tensed. "There was only one."

"What one?"

"One coolie."

"And how many girls?"

"Just one girl."

"Who did what?"

Ahmad paused. "Pregnant. She got pregnant."

"With the coolie?"

"You may say so."

"Was Babu involved in any way?"

Silence, then: "Yes."

"Is Babu the coolie in question?"

Silence.

"Has he been arrested?"

Pause. "Yes."

"Is that why you are here?"

Another silence.

Fatima retreated inside the shop. Ahmad couldn't see her face, only coils of ground tobacco swishing against the wind as white kerchiefs flapped about.

A female customer arrived. "*Dada* Fatima?" she called out.

Fatima was momentarily silent as she gathered herself before answering. They exchanged greetings as Fatima peeked through the hole, glassy tears lingering in the corners of her eyes.

"Mama Suleiman, meet my cousin Abdul," she called out as a distraction.

But Mama Suleiman was perceptive enough to notice the sadness in her eyes. "I hope your cousin has not brought bad news from home," she said.

"No, he didn't," Fatima replied.

"Nobody has died . . . ?"

"Not at all!"

Mama Suleiman relaxed and effused, *"Watu wa Mombasa ni watu wa raha, hatutaki matata,"* meaning that Mombasa people wanted nothing but happiness, before she placed her order of *kawaida*, a dish of quail eggs, onion, and garlic. That was her regular breakfast. The result was there for all to see: a smooth face with round arms and an extended round bum. A small child could ride on it without falling.

It was only ten in the morning and the sun was still soft. Fatima had not spoken directly to Ahmad since he'd broken the news; the teary eyes were the only response he had seen thus far.

Fatima stepped outside; she was an imposing figure in her own right. She grabbed the sacks of cereals without much of an effort and cast them into the shop. From inside, she pulled in the metal bar that propped the window open. Like a folding umbrella, the outer merchandise collapsed to lie on the mesh. She bolted a latch and stepped outside again.

"Let's go," Fatima said to Ahmad, who walked uncertainly along. He did not know what to say, lest he aggravate what he had already revealed. Neither did he inquire where they were going. Instead, his mind swirled with a hundred thoughts, unable to reconcile the stunning woman walking beside him and the image of the invalid lodged in his mind. Along the way, they met some of Fatima's customers, who asked why she had closed the shop so early, and how soon she expected to be back. She said she was attending to her cousin Abdul before returning to the shop, *chap chap*.

After a ten-minute walk, Fatima led Ahmad to a cluster of huts plastered with white coral and entered her house. He instantly recognized the jar filled with colorful stones that he had witnessed Babu collecting during their first year of the rail construction. There was hardly anything else suggesting that this was Babu's house. All else belonged to Fatima: the multicolored *uteo* hanging on the wall, cowrie shells by the window, a ringed black horn suspended in a corner, a large mirror. Ahmad admired a pebble that had the feel of a ruby while Fatima walked quietly about the house, opening or shutting windows. Ahmad wasn't paying much attention to her as she did this, but when he turned around, he found Fatima standing behind him, animal naked, the rays of light streaming through the grass thatch on the roof landing on different parts of her body. Like a sun goddess, she was all lit up.

13

Yet again, Ahmad's words had turned prophetic: his vision of placing beacons in women who stretched from Mombasa to Nakuru had come poignantly true. But his copulation with Fatima was special. She was a virgin, which enhanced his thrill and wonderment. How could it be that Babu had a virgin wife and was now in trouble for consorting with a chief's daughter? How could it be that his wife had remained untouched all these years? Ahmad did not dare ask these questions, at least not yet. All Fatima said, between her gasps and moans, was that she needed him to fill her and make her whole, which Ahmad did with his regular leitmotif: *Your vish be my command.*

Fatima did not seek any further information about Babu; her only comment about his reported infidelity was a simple lament: "I spared myself for him all my life, and this is what I get in return?" She then chuckled and said in Punjabi: "I guess he was always drawn to the wild side of things; maybe I'm too domesticated for his liking."

That day and night, and over the next few days, Ahmad and Fatima remained in bed. She was hungry for experience, and Ahmad was patient and generous in his lovemaking. On the second day, he announced he was willing to elope with her and live happily ever after, to which Fatima reminded she had a shop to run and he had the rail to build. When their work was done, they would explore the future, she said after learning the punishment that Babu was likely to get for his transgression.

The goods train to Nakuru was to depart on the fifth day for overnight travel. When Ahmad made it to Nakuru, he found Babu's story had taken an interesting turn.

14

Rajan's absence from the Jakaranda was elevated to a mythical plane when news spread that a mysterious woman was behind his disappearance. And Gathenji the butcher was among the few people who could attest to having rubbed shoulders with the woman.

"Let me tell you, *undo kwo undo*, I have never seen such beauty, and I suspect neither have you," Gathenji told revelers who sat in rapt attention. He described her face as brighter than the flash of sun upon a mirror, her cheeks rounder and softer—even though he had not actually touched them—like a tomato growing in *iganjo*, while her bosom was so well endowed, it hurt to imagine what a man could do with such assets.

"What was her voice like?" some curious reveler inquired. Gathenji hesitated. "Ooh, she didn't talk to you?" the reveler persisted.

"Aaaah, what are you saying?" Gathenji returned. "Let me tell you, when she greeted me, my heart went *paragasha!*" He explained her voice was like the croon of the nightingale, the chatter of a weaver, and the coo of a dove all put together.

Most of the band members conceded that Gathenji had likely served Mariam at the Jakaranda, although some silently questioned the butcher's detailed descriptions of Mariam, given the fleeting nature of their interactions. But there was no doubt that Mariam was a striking woman.

Even those who had not seen her trusted the assessment.

Finding concurrence that the mysterious woman was a fine catch, focus shifted to why she had fled the scene and who between Rajan and her was leading the other on. "*Mubira niugarurukanagwo*," Gathenji said, meaning that even in a game of soccer, the underdogs occasionally win against great odds. Maybe it was the mysterious woman who had driven Rajan out of town. Most of the musicians nodded in agreement, silently acknowledging that since Rajan had chased after the same girl for nine months, it was likely she was returning the favor. The only problem with such analysis was that since the girl had returned to Rajan of her own volition, it made little sense for him to flee town.

Or maybe it did make sense to leave, some revelers argued, especially if Rajan had unmasked the mysterious woman and decided it was in their best interest to get out of town before everyone learned who she was. Some said she was probably McDonald's illegitimate daughter, who had to suddenly take off after realizing the Jakaranda's owner was a man she wasn't supposed to meet.

"You know how it is these days," one elderly reveler said. "The white man has brought many strange things to our homesteads. Daughters without fathers . . ."

Yet others claimed the strange girl had found she was somehow related to Rajan and had run away to avoid scandal. As to why Rajan found it fit to flee with her, no one had a satisfactory answer.

When those explorations hit a dead end, all the attention shifted to Era. He was the last person to see the couple, some of the members charged. "Are you telling us the whole truth?" they demanded.

Era explained, with as much sincerity as he could muster, that he had returned to an empty house the previous evening and had been as surprised as anyone else to find Rajan and his girl gone. None of them knew about Rajan and Mariam's visit to Babu and Fatima and none of them expected the lovebirds to call on their grandparents. It was the last thing any of them would have imagined.

So no one checked with Babu and Fatima to see if Rajan and his guest had ended up at their house. Unable to produce any solid explanation for the missing duo, revelers probed Gathenji further but he provided no additional insights.

When darkness fell, the mood at the Jakaranda changed. A sudden restlessness settled when the band started in on its repertoire, playing instrumental versions of some of their popular songs. Without Rajan's energized singing, the sounds rang hollow. Theirs was a ship drifting without a captain; the music floated aimlessly before fizzling out. The din from the crowd confirmed that very few, if any, were paying attention to the band. An occasional whistle or a shout for Raj cut through the noise, which sounded like the buzz of bees in a hive. But these were idle bees, and it took no time before they indulged their idleness. An empty beer bottle was hurled onstage, splintering softly. The act inspired copycats and several more bottles were thrown. One hit the main lightbulb and plunged the establishment into darkness. The last was an unopened beer bottle that produced a loud explosion upon hitting the floor.

HOUSE OF LIGHT

15

Allah is the Light of the heavens and the earth. The example of His light is like a niche within which is a lamp, the lamp is within glass, the glass as if it were a pearly star lit from a blessed olive tree, neither of the east nor of the west, whose oil would almost glow even if untouched by fire. Light upon light. Allah guides to His light whom He wills. And Allah presents examples for the people, and Allah is Knowing of all things.
— Koran 24:35

This inscription, encased in a gold frame, still stands on the mantelpiece in Babu's house in Nakuru, and the words sprung to his lips as he lay in bed that night of Mariam's visit, shutting his eyes against the harsh glare of the solitary lightbulb above his head, the act calling to mind the time he had shut his eyes—over sixty years earlier—against the scorching sun after his arrest over Seneiya's impregnation. As he tossed and turned in bed, calmed by the hooting of Fatima's horn, yet another piece of memory spooled lazily from the vault of his mind.

It was a bright day and he was back at his haunt at the chief's camp, a shirt wound around his waist, a scythe in his hand as he nipped grass with every stroke. It was the second day of his incarceration for the transgression against Chief Lonana's daughter. He had been ordered to remain in custody pending Seneiya's safe delivery of her child.

"The womb is the heart of darkness," Chief Lonana had said, speaking for the first time on the matter. "The day shall come when truth shall be revealed. We shall make no haste in passing a judgment until that truth is evident to all," therefore saving Babu from the instant justice that McDonald and others had proposed. "Truth bends a strung bow," Chief Lonana added, acknowledging the merit of verifying facts before unleashing punishment. The chief spent his day in his courtyard, still clad in the pith helmet, staring stonily ahead as he sipped a traditional brew.

Reverend Turnbull regularly appeared at the court, mumbling his newfound line: "What's done in the dark always comes to light."

"You are essentially a prisoner of war," McDonald had told Babu in one of their rare encounters in the courtyard. "I'm glad about not fixing you earlier as I had planned, coolie. Now you are going to roast here and become a burnt offering."

It was appropriate for McDonald to think of Babu as a prisoner of war. There were rumors of war in Europe and it wasn't clear how things would play out in the British colonies abroad. The Germans, or Wajerumani as they were known, had finished connecting the railway from the land they christened Salisbury all the way to Tanganyika. Their spies had strayed into the British East Africa Protectorate several times, as had the Portuguese, or the Wareno, from nearby Msumbiji. But what really concerned McDonald the most was Seneiya's much-anticipated delivery. It was as though the birth of the new colony depended upon the safe delivery of the baby.

Babu took everything in stride. He did not regret what he had done in the marshland that day the flamingos descended on Nakuru. He did not harbor, no matter how he tried, any ill feeling toward Seneiya, his inamorata whose future appeared inextricably linked to his. But what he did regret was the conversation he had with Ahmad.

The truth of the matter was that Seneiya could not have produced a child, any child, black, white, or brown, from him. Unless of course siring a child was the same as planting a crop of potato, when farmers rejoiced in finding *waru wa maitika*, the nominal harvest that sprouted from the accidental drop of seed during harvesting.

On that day at the chief's camp, while Babu clipped grass using a scythe, he smiled at the small group of women who had arrived to steal glances at the village bull, as he had been nicknamed, and watched them giggle and compare notes.

"He doesn't look that well hung," one young woman said.

"You've got no idea," another responded. "That man is hung like a donkey. That's why he has draped his shirt to disguise his true value."

Babu had not seen Seneiya since the lineup and he wondered where she was. He had considered the different sentences that awaited him. One possibility was that he would be asked to marry her. How would they communicate? The same way he had done in the marshland, using touch and gestures? And whom, between Seneiya and Fatima, would he settle for, if he had a choice? He had not chosen Fatima, he did not know her, yet they were expected to share their lives together, tolerate each other, love each other, and raise children together. Wasn't betrothal at birth a little ambitious in its expectations? How could strangers hit it off within days of marriage and live happily ever after? There was comfort in the knowledge that he had chosen Seneiya, if filtered through the long lens of his telescope before Ahmad delivered her to him.

Even after she had subjected him to public humiliation, he had no doubt in his heart that he could learn to love and care for her.

Regarding the child growing in her belly, the seed from another man, how would he deal with that? There was a sudden weight around his neck and he choked with hate. That was too much to ask of one individual.

He had reflected on Nahodha's curse on him and his lineage. Would the offspring in dispute be spared that wrath? Babu suddenly stopped cutting the grass and paused to ponder the facts: Since the disputed baby was not his bloodline, then it should be spared the wrath that would befall his own brood. He whipped the grass with new vigor.

There was the possibility that the baby had been fathered by another Indian, in which case his features and the baby's might be similar. But there was also the possibility that it had been fathered by a man from a different race. He considered, between strokes of the scythe, the different genetic possibilities and their likely outcomes. If Seneiya had lain with an African, the baby was likely to be black and hard to pass off as an Indian. But then, he had seen very dark individuals in Punjab and no one had ever questioned their roots. A child sired between a white and black could sometimes look yellow. Some Indians looked yellow as well. If an Arab was involved, the outcome would still come close to what a Punjabi and African could produce. Babu concluded that any child, as long as it drew features from the two parents, could easily pass for his. Perhaps some good could come out of the mess: no one would ever doubt his ability to sire.

But there was a bit of him that was still repulsed by the idea of accommodating a lie to fit his own lie. It was true no one would ever question his ability to transmit life to another, even though he doubted his own ability, and the whole development would be so public he was likely to secure more offers to make babies in the future. He shuddered at the prospect. Nothing good could come out of this charade, and the sooner he stopped it the better. Maybe he should have asked Chief Lonana to organize a physical examination to prove he could hardly sustain an erection. But who in their right mind would make such a proposition, let alone to another man? Babu had heard some Christian denominations conducted such tests to determine if men were fit to train as priests. This was to ensure they were not joining the church to escape societal judgment over personal dysfunction. The test entailed throwing a naked woman oozing sex into a room packed with men and monitoring their responses. Those who had no voice, as an arousal was called in religious jargon, would be rejected on that basis, even though their call of duty required they remain celibate all their lives. Babu did not know if that was true, but it didn't sound right to him. After all, why deny a man for not possessing something he would never need to use to serve his religious vow?

These were the thoughts floating around in Babu's head when Reverend Turnbull had arrived at his cell after his arrest. Babu did not trust Reverend Turnbull one bit. There was something about him that he couldn't quite place, but the man of God seemed somewhat uneasy at times—*shifty* is the word he would have applied if he were dealing with a worldly man.

"I'm curious about one thing, coolie . . . I-I mean, what's your name?" Reverend Turnbull started.

Babu told him his name, though Reverend Turnbull did not seem to hear it.

"Yes, uuh-uuum, coolie—I'm curious about one thing.
Did you do it or are you being framed? I mean, as a churchman, truth is essential. Did you, as they it put in law, have
carnal knowledge of the lass?"

"It wasn't that ugly."

"What wasn't ugly?"

"Don't put it in such ugly terms."

"What's ugly?"

"The term you used, *carnal knowledge*, is ugly."

"It certainly is, and it is even uglier coming from an
old cow like myself. Now, there are reasons for my inquiry,
and I should declare my interests here and now: I wear two
hats—a churchman and a man of letters. I don't know how
familiar you are with female circumcision, or what they
simply call *the cut*. Was this girl cut?"

"You should find that out," Babu responded. "You can
ask the father. I thought you two were friends."

"Such impertinence won't help you, coolie. The Bible
says pride comes before a fall . . . Look, if one puts a girl in
the family way in this part of the world, one is compelled
to marry her. I hear coolies leave a trail of children wherever they pass. But here, we are dealing with the chief's
daughter, so you can't marry her. That would be considered a mark of honor, but not after your disgraceful act—
do you understand that?"

"So, how do you intend to help me?"

"The Bible says only the truth shall set you free. Tell
me what you know, and I will determine how to share the
information that will serve you best. As it is, only God can
help you out. You will need enormous favors to extricate
yourself from the mess you are in. But you should count
yourself lucky because I am on your side. I want to help
you. As I was saying . . . where were we . . . ? The cut . . . let

me explain. The Church of England that I work for has asked me to compile data on the social impact of female circumcision. I am to assess whether it is an adequate deterrence against premarital sex, unwanted pregnancies, and so on. Let me put it this way: you know, I have a medical background, and my understanding is that the cut is such a traumatic procedure—a punishment inflicted on women—and so it should be stopped. It takes away the pleasures of procreation, and complicates deliveries. So, what do you know about it?"

"About what?"

"Was she cut?"

Babu kept quiet, heaved, then: "I don't know. I didn't look."

"It is not something for you to see; it is something for you to experience. Maybe I should explain. From what we know—that is, I and others involved in African anthropology—a cut is supposed to suppress sexual urges in girls and young women by removing some parts that trigger desire. So if it didn't quite succeed in this specific instance, then it offers a window for us to look again at the whole ritual. The impression that we get is that once cut, it suppresses sexual desire, and I don't think the organ can grow back. In any case, some preventive garb is also sewn around the area that would make . . . what's the word . . . *penetration* impossible. Was that the case?"

"You fucking bastard!" Babu thundered, and stalked off to the fields to cut grass.

Reverend Turnbull kept visiting the courtyard but it wasn't until the fourth week that he built up the courage to talk to Babu again.

"My dear coolie," he started, "I am making what we call a last-ditch effort to help you. Listen carefully to what

I have to say. You don't have to respond. As Jesus said to the stones in the wilderness, even if they didn't respond, at least they heard His message. This is what I have to say: Your case appears to be growing more difficult than anticipated. Opinion is divided over what should happen to you after the baby is born. On the one hand, there are those who feel that being a foreigner, you should be subjected to British law and not customary Maasai law.

"The idea of commuting your punishment until the baby is born is already testing the patience of the Maasai. That's never been done. Young men think Chief Lonana is getting senile and are conspiring to overturn his edict. They insist culprits must get instant punishment. But this stay of execution is creating tensions and there are those who want to bring this drama to a close. Young, randy men who impregnate girls among the Maasai are put in hives full of bees and hurled down a cliff. At times the hive is set on fire to allow it to burn brightly as it flies down. You will appreciate there is an escarpment nearby, so pushing you downhill should provide no challenge whatsoever. From my understanding, this could happen as soon as tomorrow. Don't say I didn't warn you."

Babu was petrified. He had been determined to wait to prove his innocence, or even sit through his sentence before ultimately walking to freedom. That was the best way to clear his name. But if they opted to get rid of him now to save face, he had an obligation to preserve his own life. He did not know why Reverend Turnbull had volunteered the information about what was afoot, nor did he seek to verify if it was true. But as he knew all too well, dead men tell no tales, and sometimes it's better to flee and live to fight another day.

Through the years of hardship on the railway, Babu

had never considered leaving his work. He had seen men drop off and wave away to start a new life, their only possessions being the clothes on their backs. Some became farmers who supplied vegetables from the strips of land they had cultivated while working on the rail. One zealous farmer had tried to domesticate a rhino for milk, and as locals put it, the rhino taught him a book that the man had not read in school. Then there were those who became timber and transport merchants, contracted whenever such supplies were needed. And of course there were the *dukawallahs* who supplied general merchandise.

Babu had envisioned a different future. He had wanted to build the rail to the end, to stand beside the last coach with a grin on his face, shoulder to shoulder with other technicians in solidarity and triumph. In particular, he had wanted to see the last station, which Colonial Governor Charles Erickson had decided ahead of time would be named Port Elizabeth for the princess of England. The construction would go on for another six months, just about the time remaining on Babu's contract. The completion of his contract would come with two paid tickets back to Punjab and, he kept hoping, the possibility of an extension of his contract as part of the railway maintenance staff. All that was now in jeopardy because of what he was plotting. He was going to run away, walk away with his life.

Babu considered his various escape options. He could try to bribe the sentry, yet he had no money on him, and there was no way of telling if the man would blow his cover and provoke McDonald to enhance his surveillance. Maybe what he needed was to befriend the sentry so that once he dropped his guard, Babu would make a dash for freedom. But that would take time, and if Turnbull was right, he had to run now.

His handcuffs had been removed for the night, and the sentry had already taken his position by the fireside, which he lit to keep wild animals at bay. Babu thought he saw him nod to the nudges of sleep, and grew worried for his safety. He moved toward the sentry so as to warn him about the fire, then quickly realized this was his chance. He should let the sleeping dog lie.

He walked stealthily toward the edge of the fence and stretched two strands of the barbed wire to create a gap in between. He crouched through the hole but one tong of the wire clung to his clothes. As he tried to extricate himself, the sentry appeared to wake up. Babu froze. The sentry glanced around before he fell right back to sleep. Babu gently unhitched himself from the wire and crouched a few meters away for several moments before fleeing into the darkness—and freedom.

He knew he had to keep off the railway or any other white settlements. They were scattered all over, and many of them bore names of English counties where their new owners were presumably from: Devon, Surrey, Brooke, Sheffield, Anglia, Redhill. All of them bore the word *Estate* to invoke their new owners' desire for perpetuity; estates were legal entities that were meant to outlive their owners. *What were these places named before the arrival of the whites*, Babu asked himself for the umpteenth time, *and how do locals feel about the new names?* Babu was constantly surprised that the hinterland was already heavily populated by whites. It was another country away from the railway line that changed terrain every few miles.

Here, there were paddocks of rolling hills where merino sheep bleated or locked horns, while the foolish ones trooped after their leaders, their white coats standing out against the endless stretches of green; there, coffee bushes in straight lines spread out at calculated intervals, the bushes trimmed into circular shapes that looked like bobs of neat hair. Walking farther down where the temperature was cooler, there were the tea estates, blocks of neat green ringed by patches of red earth where walkways demarcated one section from another.

Babu had a sudden revelation. He had seen similar enterprises in Punjab—what was pending here was the means to ship away what the land could produce. That's where he and the others came in—they were there to lay the rail to transport the crops to the coast.

This was the turning point in Babu's life, one that, unknown to him, established links with local seers like Me Katilili and Kioni, who foresaw the train as a beast whose belly would require communal feeding for an eternity, accurately presaging the years of colonialism that lay ahead. It was in that walk through the bush that Babu made a silent vow to do something. What, exactly, he didn't know. He just knew he had to do something about the white domination taking root before his very eyes.

In that moment he realized whites and blacks had not been subjected to the so-called sex parade. In McDonald's mind, crimes of different natures were consigned to different races. And only Asians were capable of crimes of passion, the sort that he had been plunged into. His thoughts turned to Reverend Turnbull and he wondered what was in it for him. Although the man had declared his interests in the matter as both scholarly and spiritual, Babu suspected this was a cover-up for a far more sinister intent. *Who knows, he could have been the one who fathered Seneiya's baby,* Babu laughed to himself.

Babu walked at a modest pace so as not to appear too anxious to depart from the land, or too rushed to get to his next destination. He did not even have a destination yet; he just needed to open up a reasonable distance between himself and the railway builders, particularly the white supervisors who were likely to betray him to McDonald. He was therefore walking in the opposite direction of the railhead.

Along the way, he picked enough wild fruit to eat and save for dinner, and slept close to a stream where he bathed and drank to his fill, before setting off at dawn to repeat the process. By the end of the third day, he encountered Mujibhai, an Indian farmer who had jumped off the moving train, as all deserters called their flight. Mujibhai wore a turban and had his mustache curled at the edges so that he looked like a catfish. He welcomed Babu heartily, but tensed when he heard his full story. He said he feared McDonald would boycott his crop if he knew he was hosting an outlaw.

"Obviously, tat be too big a market to lose for no good reason, no?" Mujibhai posed. "It's not tat am chasing away a good friend and eweryting. It just won't look good and eweryting. You know tis tings, my friend."

"Yes, I do," Babu said with a tinge of sarcasm, which Mujibhai did not seem to notice.

"You know, we Indians came here to look for money and eweryting," Mujibhai added. "And if I had found it on the Indian Ocean, I voulda made about-turn and head right back to India. So to come here and not make someting is a bit foolish . . ."

Babu sought refuge at the next farm. Chetan was another Indian farmer and he grew French beans. Babu volunteered his labor to earn his keep but said nothing about his work situation. Chetan said he was afraid what other Jains would say about him hosting a Muslim.

So Babu was elated when the next farmer turned out to be a Muslim, also from Punjab, and whose name was Nazir. He took Babu in. Babu marveled at nature's ways. The seeds from a rotten tomato that Nazir had squeezed onto fertile ground, and then had shielded using mulch from dried grass, had grown into a sizable crop.

Babu's hands and feet were soon blistered, although he made nothing from his labors other than a cup of sorghum porridge every morning and spinach and roti for lunch and dinner. On a good day, Nazir got ghee and lentils at the market where he sold his tomatoes. Babu would have waited for the tomatoes to mature but his stay was interrupted.

"My friend . . . you know, I didn't realize you are a Sunni Muslim, and not a Shia like me," Nazir said to him. "You know, we may be away from home and everything but our values have not changed. Sunnis and Shias are like water and oil: they don't mix . . ."

Yet again, Babu was beside himself. The Jains, the Patels, the Hindus, and the Muslims may have left India, but India had not left them. They had taken with them the caste systems and prejudices from their villages, so they may as well have never traveled.

It was in that moment of despair that Babu crossed paths with Karim, his old friend from the shipwrecked dhow they'd arrived on from India. Since the shipwreck, they had hardly seen each other, losing contact through the years of the railway construction since they had been deployed to different departments. While Babu had been sent ahead of the pack, surveying and mapping the possible train routes, Karim was among those deployed to maintain and repair trams that were used to test the rail once it was laid.

Karim had put on a little weight, and he appeared to be in good cheer. When Babu calmly explained his predicament, Karim laughed so long and loud that his eyes teared. When he calmed down, he said, even as a fresh bout of mirth bubbled, "My good friend, you are the master of shipwrecks. First you were stranded at sea. Now you are stranded on dry land."

"At least I can't drown on dry land." Babu chuckled at his own joke. "I just can't help myself. Forces of nature are totally beyond my control."

"You are absolutely correct," Karim teased. "It's hard to control a call of nature, especially the sort regulated by a zipper."

"I certainly do control my zip," Babu replied defensively.

"My good friend, tell that to the birds," Karim said with a smile. "But listen. You arrived in the nick of time. I'm about to jump ship, or is it the train, but I'm not sure where I'm going. All I know is that I have to get going. If you want to join me . . ."

Babu thanked him for the offer, but explained that he would have to lie low for a while, until the heat died down. But they promised to look for each other.

Babu decided to hibernate for a season, his next abode being a cave that locals called *ngurunga ya itugi*, because solid rocks stood erect like flagpoles at its mouth. He had left Punjab a young technician only four years earlier; now he was a caveman. *That's what the British do to you*, he thought bitterly.

For some reason, Babu was cheered to find that the spring emanating from the cave fed into other springs downhill that drained into the massive lake where the flamingos had made a home nine months earlier. He was even more elated to come across the tree stump where he had sat to remove the prick on his foot. What he found intriguing and pleasing at the same time was that the sharp-edged tuber that had pricked him to extract eight drops of blood had grown into a massive crop.

It was the first sisal crop in the colony; its seed had been dropped accidentally by settlers headed farther up in the Rift Valley where an entire crop had failed due to harsh climatic conditions. And the wild seed that had fallen off in the bush had found easy nurture and grown without any human intervention. The plant now stood a meter high, with broad, sword-shaped leaves that jutted in every direction. The plant looked like an upturned star and was ringed by tiny suckers that Babu knew from his recent vegetable and tomato cultivation were the seeds.

As Babu knelt to begin planting some of the seeds using the machete he had picked up at his last outpost, he thought about the range of tasks one could not complete satisfactorily without kneeling: a man earnest in prayer, a thief picking a lock, a man in copulation. In all those instances, there is some expectation of a reward, some yield from the toils. Through his labors, Babu lazily wondered about Ahmad and whether he had managed to inform Fatima what had befallen him. But his mind would immediately get absorbed in the work at hand. He did not care that this crop did not bear any visible fruit; he was only intrigued by its majesty and size.

He cleared a small patch and gingerly sliced off the sisal suckers and transferred them there. He planted the suckers at intervals, using his steps to measure because he had no other equipment. He returned to the mother plant days later and found new suckers sprouting. He cut these too and transferred them to a new patch he had cleared. Babu's instinct was that something of value could be harnessed out of that crop, but he did not know how or what.

He did this for the next month, rising every morning from the cave to attend to his mysterious plant, watering the seedlings in the morning before going to forage in the forest for something to eat. By the end of two months living by the lake—and the fourth month since he gone on the run—he had put an acre under sisal cultivation.

Chief Lonana's daughter Seneiya delivered at the end of the third month of Babu's disappearance. She gave birth to a baby girl with the bluest of eyes and broadest of grins, as if to mock the gloomy circumstances of her arrival. She was named Rehema Salim, her surname picked from Babu's name. Were it not that she was exiting the loins of a black mother, one would have thought she was a white child; it was as if the mother had served as mere vessel for her conception and delivery, much the same way train wagons would be used to ferry goods that they had played no role in creating.

Chief Lonana took one look at the child and declared they had the wrong man. It had been proven that the coolie was not the one who had broken the leg of his goat and they would have to start looking elsewhere.

When Ahmad heard about the blue-eyed baby, he realized it would be his opportunity to deliver some good news to Babu. But fate had a way of disrupting his plans. Although Ahmad had lied to Patterson when he'd said he had to go to Mombasa to dispatch a crucial telegram home, his words returned to haunt him when a telegram arrived from Mombasa on the train that very day. It was from Fatima, and the black blocks of ink read: *COUSIN ABDUL, WELCOME TO THE FAMILY. I'M WAITING EXPECTANTLY.*

HOUSE OF DARKNESS

16

Hadithi Hadithi! Paukwa? This is an invocation to confirm that the reader is still there, lest one is tired of being dragged through the crooked jogs of history, trying to untangle mysteries that never quite unfurl. There is the story of the horn that stands on the mantelpiece of Babu's house in Nakuru, the one that Babu remembers when he convulses about the past; tied to it is the curse of the sea. Then there's the story of the betrothal, the one that involved Rajan, although he wasn't privy to it; there is also the story of the virgin bride; and now, the mother of them all, the messenger sent to the convey news of a man's illegitimate child, but who only returned with news of his illicit affair that had produced a child.

So let's end this pregnant wait and reveal the succinct truth, some of which will elude Babu the rest of his life. Just as the task of the consummation of his marriage fell to Ahmad, not Babu, Ahmad would similarly be the first man to know how Fatima came into the possession of the horn that stills the sea spirits, and which was linked to the two questions about her virginity and the miraculous healing of her legs.

When Babu and Fatima were aboard the MV *Salama* on their maiden trip to the British East Africa Protectorate, and the vessel went into a spin on their seventh day at sea, flipping around until everyone collapsed in fits of dizziness, Fatima feared she would not survive the trip. In the heat of the moment, when the vessel dipped and drank water to its fill, chugging back and forth as though hiccuping from the effect, and Babu hurled insults at Nahodha—who then returned with a curse—not knowing his young wife was present and listening, Fatima, frightened, cold, and lonely, sobbed for the rest of the journey, her crammed legs numb from the salty warm waters of the Indian Ocean.

When Fatima learned that Babu had turned to a native girl for comfort while she waited for his return to surprise him with the good news about her ability to walk again, she was determined to repay him in kind, an eye for an eye, a man for a woman, a baby for a baby. The news that she was carrying Ahmad's baby took three months to reach Ahmad, by which time Babu's baby saga had taken a new twist. Babu had been exonerated, but he did not know about it. And Ahmad, the man who was about to relay the news to him, cut his trip short after discovering news about Fatima's own pregnancy. For how does a man look another in the eye and say: *My friend, when you sent me to see your wife, I gave it to her like nobody's business and now she is heavy with my child. Call it our child. But you are off the hook over the chief's daughter. It has come to light that you only did the deed but left no seed . . .*

So Ahmad waited a few more weeks before he mustered enough courage to face Babu. By that time, he was coveting something else in Babu's possession which would solidify his ties to the family for the long haul.

17

Rajan and Mariam's disappearance coincided with the onset of the season of anomie. Strange things were rumored to be happening in different corners of the land and one did not know what to believe and what to discount. Gathenji the butcher gained a new name—he became Gathenji Rumas because his greetings to customers started and ended with: "Have you heard the rumor . . . ?" There were rumors on just about everything. Some unspeakable things had reportedly happened to Indians of Ruiru, a township about three hours east of Nakuru. Then there was the rumor of the white man who painted himself black, a humiliation that was reportedly supervised by naked men dancing under a bright torch, faces dripping with ocher and chalk and holding roosters that crowed at every nudge.

The rooster was a symbol that made sense of everything: it was the symbol of the leading political party. But what spurred Gathenji and other Nakuru residents to indulge in the rumors more intently was the one circulating about Rajan and his disappearance from the Jakaranda.

Gathenji narrated the Ruiru incident as follows: The new leader, Big Man, had made an impromptu visit there, on what was called a "meet the people" tour. This meant stopping at trading centers where elderly women did dust-raising dances, digging in their heels in their syncopated steps and swinging their hips—whose outlines were enhanced by sisal kilts. In moments of inspiration, Big Man would leave his car and join in the jig, swinging his fly whisk or stroking his beard to show he appreciated their efforts. He would address the crowd for a few minutes, usually from the open roof of his limousine, urging the people to welcome and support *serikali ya Mwafrika*, the black man's government. He would then ride on to the next destination.

According to Gathenji's narrative, things had initially gone smoothly at several stops along the way for Big Man and his convoy. The security detail included soldiers, regular policemen in pith helmets, teargas, and other weapons such as truncheons—or *manogore*, as Gathenji called them because they had the power to relax tense muscles if applied properly—as well as heavy clubs that the locals called *mathiukure* because they were known for their ability to crack open human skulls with a single strike. The clubs also came in handy when bringing down locked doors.

Big Man's heavy security detail was understandable. Although Gathenji did not know it, there were many enemies of *serikali ya Mwafrika*. The new republics of Togo and Dahomey, or what's known today as Benin, had already tasted the bitter fruit of a coup and their French masters were back at the helm, saying they had realized their mistake in leaving the continent too early. There were rumors that something was cooking in Ghana as well, because the British were not too happy with what Kwame Nkrumah was doing—barking, they said, like a mad dog about African unity, after they had spent decades dividing the continent. But Gathenji's reasoning for Big Man's need for a large security detail was more simple: he had been hit with rotten eggs at a few public rallies, so he was not taking any chances.

The heavy security, Gathenji said he had heard, was also an affirmation of what many had suspected, and what Big Man had persistently denied: that he was the spiritual and political leader of the group known as *Kiama kia Rukungu*—Party of the Dust—which rampaged farms in the Rift Valley, harassing white farmers.

So, many Indian traders, ambivalent about the new black leader, decided there was no need to feign adulation toward a man they did not quite trust, and whose attitude toward foreigners was suspect. They opted to keep their shops open and wait for customers instead of attending his "meet the people" tour.

"You know how these Indian are," Gathenji said. "I heard a rumor that they keep their money under their mattresses, so they can't risk venturing out and leaving their treasures unattended."

But it wasn't just Indians who chose to ignore Big Man's tour. Although Gathenji did not know it, other locals in Ruiru skipped the fête as well, so that Big Man's entourage found only a hefty old man in tight khaki shorts and shirt selling bananas by the roadside, likewise using a whisk to ward off flies as goats nibbled at the peels that had been thrown at his feet. Big Man was instantly drawn to this man who seemed to be nearly the same age, but when the goats bleated and one of them issued a trail of droppings, Big Man thought the locals were staging a farce to mock him, especially when the goats began shitting. With the blink of an eye, the old man in khaki was lifted *juu juu* by Big Man's security detail, and when they put him down, the vendor seemed to have been punctured—his nose was runny, his eyes teary, even his ears perspired, and a small patch of his pants looked wet. He was saved by his goats when they started nibbling at the uniformed men.

Gathenji's rumor did not reveal the full story though; he quickly forgot about the old man and spoke about the horrific fate that befell the Indians of Ruiru after the soldiers went around to inquire why there were more goats than humans to meet Big Man. They were asked to find out what could have kept the traders from a national event in which the black man's government was being inaugurated and its leader was there to meet his people. Since Indian traders occupied all shops in the locality, they were the main casualties. Some sat sipping chai, balancing books, so that many of them were open-mouthed when the soldiers descended. One moment, a shopkeeper was preparing to greet an approaching customer, a smug smile ready to be dispensed; the next moment, the smile froze when the soldier announced his mission, his choice tool of communication being the drop of a truncheon to the shoulder. This type of blow was not strong enough to break the bone, but it left no doubt that some bones would be broken if cooperation was not fostered immediately.

One unspoken rule about warfare—some Indian traders instantly recognized this as warfare—is that neither the victim nor the villain is willing to tell what truly happened afterward; the motivation for the former being to minimize the degree of hurt and loss, which intensifies at every bout of recollection; the explanation for the latter being to disguise the full extent to which one's humanity is diminished by brutalizing others. So the trail of blood left on shop floors was wiped away silently by the women who had lain there spread-eagle—the stream of tears sufficient to wash the drops of blood away—while traders who had lost entire life savings kept under the mattress denied losing more than the day's collection. Either way, the books were balanced: in one strike, lifetime gains were wiped out, while the inflicted pain left scars that would last a lifetime.

The soldiers' strike on the traders did not last more than fifteen minutes, but then soldiers are trained to eat in less than one minute. Yet the power of their punch in Ruiru reverberated across the land, whispered from ear to ear until it reached Gathenji's butchery in Nakuru—some two hundred miles away—without losing any of its potency. What had been visited upon the Indians of Ruiru would serve as a strong warning to others that the incoming black man's government meant business and could only be ignored at one's peril.

Another story that Gathenji told repeatedly, and which many revelers dismissed as mere gossip, was the one of the white man who reportedly painted himself black to save his skin. The white man was said to have been surveying his farm on horseback when he encountered adherents of the dreaded underground sect *Kiama kia Rukungu*. Supposedly, that evening, as the sect members went around villages beating their drums, singing and dancing, the white pigment on their faces melted so they looked ashen. When they encountered the white man on horseback, they asked him to climb down.

"Come down, only birds should perch so high," the sect leader was reported to have told the white man.

But the old man was hard of hearing, and when a rooster was hurled in his face and then fell to the ground and began doing an odd sort of dance, he mistook that to mean that he would be in a lot of trouble if he did not cooperate and do as the rooster was doing. So he dismounted and did the rooster dance. The *Kiama kia Rukungu* believed he was attempting to turn himself into a black man, much the same way they had turned their black faces white using the pigment.

"Gathenji, tell us another one!" a skeptical customer prodded when the butcher finished his story.

"Let me tell you *undo kwo undo*," Gathenji insisted. "I'm telling you the truth of God . . ."

Gathenji's ramblings came to an abrupt halt one evening. Many had already arrived for their regular dose of beer and roasted meat, as well as for the camaraderie— shortening the night, as they called it. The communion with fellow men was useful, many whispered. But since the music had stopped, people's attention shifted from the raised stage to the corner where the black-and-white television stood in relative darkness, its flickering light picking the eyes and teeth of those assembled. "Sssshhhh . . ." somebody hissed when the image of Big Man filled the screen, his beard styled so that he looked like a billy goat, and sounding exactly like one when he spoke.

"*Wale wanaoleta nyoko nyoko walikuwa wapi ile miaka tuliyokaliwa mabegani na beberu? Kumanyoko!*" A translation was not availed on the TV set, though the crowd roared with laughter, possibly tickled by the rhyming words like *nyoko nyoko*, which meant trouble, or *beberu*, which meant billy goat, but in this usage was a derogatory term for *colonialist*. Or it could be the swear word that triggered the jovial reaction that threatened to lift the roof off the Jakaranda. Those assembled did not listen to the rest of the bulletin, even after many of the patrons ordered others to keep quiet. Big Man bleated for two full minutes before finishing off with his favorite swear word, *kumanyoko*. At the end of the broadcast, the Jakaranda erupted with chatter as everybody began speaking at once.

18

An elaborate account of the pronouncement by Big Man appeared in the following day's issue of the *Daily News*:

The father of the nation, better known as Big Man, has directed that all foreign nationals residing in Kenya, and who were over the age of eighteen by June 1, 1963, to regularize their status for continued stay. It is understood that the decision does not affect British nationals domiciled in the country, many of whom arrived as colonial administrators at the turn of the century.

An estimated 30,000 Indians arrived as indentured laborers during this period as well to build the 500-mile railway that started in the port city of Mombasa and terminated in Port Elizabeth, nestling the second-largest freshwater lake in the world, named for the Queen of England. Of the 30,000 Indians who arrived to work on the railway, an estimated 5,000 perished, devoured by the lions of Tsavo, or victims of tropical diseases like malaria and tsetse infections. Many of them lived to tell the story and some 6,000 workers stayed on after the project completion to build the new colony as administrators, clerks, and policemen. But a majority of them are in private business and the withdrawal of their private capital is expected to slow down the economy, if not derail it altogether.

This development is expected to pose a legal minefield on several counts. Many of the migrant workers were granted papers defining them as British subjects, not citizens, ostensibly

*because their country of origin was under Britain's domin-
ion until 1947, when India gained independence. Such families will have to decide whether to fortify their British ties
by choosing to migrate to Britain, return to India, or take up
Kenyan citizenship. The option of settling in Britain is a gray
area since British subjecthood may not necessarily mean au-
tomatic citizenship. Already, the campaign to ban Indians of
the British East Africa Protectorate from migrating to Britain
has gained traction with the Conservative Party, with one senior member of Parliament warning there would be "rivers of
blood" if thousands of Indians are allowed there.*

*Remaining in Kenya is equally problematic. India was a
British colony until 1947 and Indians were seen as part of the
colonizing agents by Kenyans. They also enjoyed significant
leverage during the seventy years of British rule in East Africa, hired as administrators, managers, and technicians. In
the social hierarchy that defined colonial rule, Indians ranked
second after the whites, with Arabs third and Africans at the
bottom. Now that order is about to be reorganized with the
onset of black majoritarian rule, with Africans at the top of
the social ladder, and it remains to be seen where Indians will
be consigned in the new world order. But the real complexity
lies with groups of families from countries that have since been
dissolved, like Punjab, once an autonomous region but now
amalgamated into the larger India and Pakistan. Punjabis
were encouraged to migrate to the British East Africa Protectorate, as Kenya was then called, to work on the railway as
technicians. This situation limits the options open to Punjabis,
because they simply have no country to return to. They can
either stay on in Kenya or migrate to Britain. Should Britain
shut their doors on them, the Punjabis will have to make do
with Kenya, where their future, for now, appears somewhat
difficult and uncertain.*

A recent episode of unprovoked violence targeting Indian traders in Ruiru township after they failed to close shops to cheer Big Man's entourage inspires little confidence that they are likely to enjoy the full protection of the law. This development comes hot on the heels of sporadic attacks on white farms across the country. The band, calling itself Kiama kia Rukungu, or Party of the Dust, is a pseudopolitical and religious group that has vowed to show "dust" to white settlers and overrun them to take their farms. The attacks have terrified many farmers who have since started relocating to southern African colonies like Rhodesia and South Africa.

Speaking in Swahili at a public rally in Elburgon, Big Man distanced himself from the Kiama kia Rukungu adherents and reaffirmed his commitment to protecting private property against what he called "enemies of development."

Predictably, not many people read the Daily News, so they had to make do with third-, fourth-, or fifthhand information, which meant no one could quite tell the vetting criteria, or even where the vetting was conducted. By the end of the week, a number of social halls had been opened for the exercise, as well the Kenya Farmers' Association field that ultimately became the Nakuru District Stadium.

Some interactions went better than others. One Indian man, a cobbler, arrived at a government office with his children and their children, along with all their mattresses and beddings. He wanted the authorities to see for themselves that he did not keep any money under the mattress as it was alleged of Asian businessmen. He told the screening officials he was too constrained feeding his family to spare anything for the mattress.

"I know some of our people like to keep one leg here

and another leg there, like the hyena. But I have not sent any child to Britain. We are all here, we don't have another country. We shall prosper or die in this very land," the man said, and his testament appeared to move the three immigration officers, for they all nodded their agreement and stamped all the papers for him and his family without even opening a page.

Some were not so lucky, like the senior government clerk who sent his African junior to queue for him because he had too much work to do in the office.

"My friend, we shall not accept such insults anymore. Why do you think your work is more important than ours?" a short official asked.

"And to make matters worse, you send one of our own like a little boy to queue for you. *Kwani*, you don't know things have changed?" another one, quite tall, pursued.

A third officer kept quiet, only stretching a hand to check the man's papers.

The Indian clerk produced a file, explaining, "This is a recommendation from my boss, Mr. Anderson. This one is from—"

"Do you think this is a job application?" the short official interrupted. "Who told you we need to see recommendations from white men? Don't you know an African who can also recommend you? Or do you think they don't know how to write in English? Oooh, you think that's beneath you, isn't that it? I can tell from the look on your face."

The clerk, now sweating profusely, loosened his tie and responded: "I think there is a misunderstanding . . ."

"There is no misunderstanding," the official exclaimed. "You just need to open your eyes and start seeing clearly. This is the new Kenya, my friend. We are the people in charge. So go get recommendations from black Kenyans.

And if you can't find one, come and ask me quietly. I might be in the mood to help."

The second officer was less generous; he told the Indian clerk, "Go bring your entire clan here, even the cat that meows and the cow that moos. Come to think of it, you people worship cows, don't you? In that case, don't bring us your god, just a little milk from your god cow. And since the milk must be boiled, don't forget to bring something to cool it with."

This roundabout way of communication left many Indians confused, and it would take them awhile to understand that the officials were soliciting bribes.

As days progressed, and word spread that one could secure the right papers without breaking a sweat—as long as the bribe was correct—many Indian businessmen stashed envelopes with wads of cash between their papers and presented them; these were swiftly stamped without verification.

But not everyone could offer a bribe, so the queues remained long and families grew more desperate as the deadline for registration drew closer. Some families opted to divide their children and send them to relatives in Britain or Canada or the United States. Many returned to India. It was better to be somewhere other than waiting to be wheeled out the door.

It was in this troubled season that Karim's family arrived at Babu's household one Saturday afternoon. Karim was accompanied by his wife Abdia and their daughter Leila, who appeared to have bloomed into womanhood overnight. Her slight frame had gained weight in all the right places, while her shoulder-length dark hair accentuated her pretty face.

Fatima received them cautiously. She was afraid that

the family had heard about Rajan's philandering in Nak-uru, and had come to call off Rajan's betrothal to Leila. Rajan and Leila never actually knew they were betrothed because Babu had hoped to have a proper ceremony, but this now seemed unlikely with both Rajan and the country spinning out of control. Fatima had never forgiven Babu for keeping this a secret from Rajan, and her anger was bubbling as she waited in the kitchen for the kettle to boil, adjusting her sari that kept unfurling from her strained, uneven breathing. And in that moment of anger, pacing around the kitchen, thinking of the humiliating conversation she was about to have, she contemplated hurling the steaming water at Babu's bare belly in his sanctuary up-stairs. He should be the one to do all the explaining, she thought bitterly, and she was so consumed by the thought that she didn't sense Abdia approaching.

"These are difficult times," Abdia said softly, noting the gloomy expression on Fatima's face.

Fatima nodded gravely.

"But it's not the end of the world," Abdia added.

Fatima sighed. "It's the end of a wonderful relation-ship."

"Wonderful people," Abdia said.

"So, you are not angry?" Fatima asked, puzzled.

"Angry with what? What will anger help?"

"You are right . . . You were always right about these things."

"As the holy book says, everything that has a beginning must have an end."

"But I never thought the end would come this soon."

"As Christians like to say, we must get ready, for no one knows either the day or the hour."

"Were you . . . ready?"

"I can't say I was ready. Nothing in life would prepare you for such a thing. I just wasn't surprised."

"Really?"

"Yes."

"Why?"

"Just like that."

"I don't understand."

"I mean, I didn't have any expectations at all," Abdia said.

"Excuse me?"

"I mean, I prepared for the worst and wished for the best."

"You mean it was *that* bad?"

"I mean, it's different for you guys . . ."

"How do you mean?"

"I mean, Babu is different."

"Babu is . . . is . . . he is no longer in charge!"

"Still, he is different. He's not like other *wahindi*."

"Excuse me?"

"He will be spared."

"Why? What are you talking about?"

"Actually, that's why my husband thought we should come see him. He might be able to help."

"Are you listening? Babu has lost it. He can't speak. This thing has crushed him."

"At this stage, we are desperate for anything. You mean he can't even recognize his old friend?"

"Abdia, you are as difficult as Hindi script. Why can't you understand such a simple explanation?"

"Because one can't just rise and walk away like that."

"I understand. And I'm sorry."

"How can you understand? You have nothing to worry about. At least you and Babu will survive it."

"What makes you think so?"

"I know so."

"Why?"

At this juncture, Karim's frame filled the kitchen door.

"Sorry, ladies. I couldn't find the old man on the porch. Is he napping somewhere else?"

"He has been—for two weeks now. Can't tell between night and day. I think it's what doctors call a vegetative state."

Karim was alarmed: "What are you talking about?"

Fatima tensed. How could she let them in on the family scandal? "It happened faster than any of us could comprehend," she sighed. "One moment, Babu was alive and well, the next he was fighting for his life."

"Was he alone?" Abdia asked.

"Yes—no—I mean, he was alone when he fell. But we were in the house."

"You should have alerted us. We should have come and said *pole*. Our hopes are dashed," Karim said, his voice breaking. "I never knew it would come to this. Babu was our last hope . . ."

"What's done is done," Fatima snapped. "And stop weeping in my kitchen. Don't you know it's a bad omen for grown men to weep?"

"How dare you say that. Don't you feel our pain?" Abdia said with clear indignation.

"Yes, yes, my dear," Fatima hissed. "But what can I do?"

"If you do anything," Karim said, sobering up, "please find somebody who can stop this. If not Babu, then who?"

"Stop what? There is nothing to stop!"

"I wish we came earlier," Karim said. "We know Babu would have come to our rescue."

"But how do you know?" Fatima asked, puzzled by his insistence that Babu could have somehow salvaged Rajan's betrothal to Leila. "That wayward boy—"

"Pardon me, *memsahib*, has Babu become a *boy* now that's he is unwell?" Karim posed.

Fatima reeled from the revelation. She now understood with great relief that the Karims were there to seek Babu's help in stopping their possible deportation, not to harangue them for failing to safeguard their daughter's betrothal to Rajan. Fatima moved calmly toward Karim. "You are right, you are right," she said, backtracking from her blunder. "Maybe Babu would have been able to help."

Later that night, long after the Karims had left, Fatima lay awake and wondered what had prompted them to think Babu could have stopped their deportation. *There are way too many things I don't understand about this man.* She shrugged and turned on her side to sleep, as Babu's breathing rose and fell in a seesaw rhythm. They had spent years of their married life in separate spaces on the bed, the dividing line being Fatima's child, before Babu ultimately moved to a different room. He had seldom returned home before midnight, and when he did, he tiptoed into his room without a word. *Where does he disappear to for such long periods?* Fatima had often wondered, and a savage thought would creep in. *The bugger*, she'd say to herself with a pang of envy, *is seeing another woman*. But she could not figure out how sleeping around extended political leverage that the Karims believed Babu enjoyed.

A gang of *Kiama kia Rukungu* adherents descended on the Jakaranda a day after Big Man's memorable appearance on television. They were about a hundred men, most of them young, some middle-aged. Feathers jutted out of their

258 ọ DANCE OF THE JAKARANDA

heads, faces dripped with white chalk, and all wore sisal kilts decorated with bright colors. Their leader carried a torch whose flame threw grotesque shadows on the assembly. Initially, the customers at the Jakaranda mistook them for the new resident band since Rajan's group had stopped playing. Momentarily, revelers joined in the jig that was punctuated by the rhythmic chime of *karing'a ring'a* and deep drumming. But everybody scrambled back to their seats when the man holding the torch announced they were there to see the owner of the Jakaranda. They wanted to personally deliver the message they had been giving to other white farmers in the land: *Mzungu aende ulaya, Mwafrika apate uhuru*. The white man must return to Europe for the black man to gain his freedom.

Many took it as a joke even as they pointed to the distant part of the farm where McDonald still lived, all alone—in yet another cycle of solitude—and returned to their drinks. "Better be warned, the old dog keeps a gun," someone said over the throbbing sounds of the drums. "If ever there was *mkoloni*, then that's him." The party drifted away, the chime of *karing'a ring'a* accompanying them.

McDonald, almost ninety-two, was still in perfect health, running most of his affairs with minimal assistance. His day servant had come and gone and he had been lounging on the upstairs balcony of his one-story wooden house smoking a pipe. He heard the dancers approach his farm and felt a mixture of curiosity and anger. He had heard stories about white farmers being humiliated by the gang at their own farms, so he was not surprised that he would be targeted. What surprised him was how calm he felt. But he was also angry that anyone dared trespass upon his land. To keep his anger at bay, he puffed on his pipe, standing in the shadow of the floodlight that illuminated the band of men beneath him. He noticed that in addition to the white chalk and spikes of feathers jutting out of the men's heads, some wore animal masks that reminded him of England during Halloween. One man wore a pig snout; another wore rhino horns. McDonald thought the movements of some of the dancers was eerily familiar—he could have sworn he had seen them perform in the past. Or it could be that some had been his workers.

The throb of the drums continued in earnest, with some of the dancers throwing lewd gestures in his direction, others indicating that he should descend from his balcony so they could stomp on him. McDonald did not mind the threats at all. He was relaxed enough to let his mind wander off to another time, another place.

The cacophonous drumming faded in McDonald's mind and gave way to the rhythmic rattling of that misty morning when the train made its maiden trip from Port Elizabeth to Mombasa, and the bewitching beauty of Nakuru that stunned and startled him, and compelled him to return when his coveted knighthood was substituted with a title deed to a piece of land.

As a soldier, McDonald had felt somewhat cheated that the land he claimed as his own had been won without the firing of a single shot. There could be no glory in that. What he found even more frustrating, however, was Sally's rejection of him and the land on which he built a house in her honor.

McDonald had watched townships grow out of the steps of train stations. All townships followed a similar trajectory: Indian traders would build temporary stores selling refreshments. This encouraged other traders to hawk their wares near those stores. Before long, a market had ringed the place. Indian traders ventured into African villages to bring back sacks of *sukuma wiki*, potatoes for *bhajia*, *dhania*, and *brinjals* that they sold mainly to white settlers. Soon, there were different market days in different townships, each specializing in distinct merchandise. Livestock was procured from Kajiado every Monday; tanned hides were bought to Athi River every Tuesday; grains could be found in Kiambu every Wednesday, bales of cotton were sold in Port Elizabeth every Friday.

The presence of traders from different parts of the colony led to the emergence of modest boarding facilities, and with these came other support services: transporters ferrying goods and people; petty traders selling yards of cloth and *mukima* toothbrushes; torches and sandals made from old tires. Different eateries emerged too, catering to the growing cadre of workers, all of whom remained organized along racial lines.

Leading this brigade were the white settlers who, clinging to vestiges of white privilege, transformed many farmhouses into golf clubs, whose membership they offered only to their own. So every town that evolved from the train stations boasted one such club where whites socialized and whispered their fears of what the future held for them. Soon, many established reciprocal agreements so that a member of one golf club could patronize facilities in other parts of the colony at no extra cost. And in this way, the dream of making Kenya a white man's country, even with a sea of resistance, would survive another day.

The one group that defied this racial stratification were the twilight girls, most of them African, who migrated from one township to another like birds, scavenging for rich pickings. They could smell from afar which crop was about to flower and descend on the farmers awash with cash and relieve them of their hard-earned money with the blink of an eye. Actually, some would later confess, these city girls could steal with their eyelashes—all they needed to do was look at you and your money was gone.

Occasionally, there was melodrama when men caught up with women who had stolen from them in other towns. An Indian transporter based in Port Elizabeth encountered a woman while she was entertaining another man in another town and claimed she had "eaten" his truck. The Indian did not want his money back, but he asked an unusual question of the man who was being entertained: he wanted to know if the man had heard an engine roaring when he was inside the woman.

The new man, naturally, wanted to protect his woman's honor and was about to swing into action, but stopped short, puzzled by this business of trucks roaring inside his woman. He thought the Indian meant breaking wind, but he couldn't have been that uncouth. So he waited for some explanation, which the man supplied without any prompting.

Before meeting the woman, the Indian said, he operated a profitable enterprise ferrying goods from point A to point B. After meeting the woman, she confused him with *mapenzi moto moto*. The man conceded he hardly enjoyed *mapenzi moto moto* at home, only his wife's constant nagging. So at the twilight woman's prompting, he had left home and settled at a local lodging with her. In the meantime, he left his assistant—or turn-boy, as he called him—to run the business. Because of the turn-boy's inexperience on the road, mainly due to poor driving skills, the truck kept breaking down. The Indian said he was a competent mechanic and had been servicing his own vehicle for years. But since he was too busy servicing the *memsahib* in bed, he told the turn-boy which part of the vehicle he thought needed fixing and gave him money for the parts. But the turn-boy did not buy quality parts, having seen this as a chance to keep a little money for himself. The truck soon began falling apart again and was in need of further fixing.

Before long, there was hardly any money available for proper servicing of the vehicle, the entire savings having been spent facilitating *mapenzi moto moto*, so the breakdowns persisted. The man said he only left the twilight woman's bed when he was told the truck had been grounded. Even then, the woman persuaded him that it was better to sell it rather than keep pouring good money into it, or incurring parking costs as he awaited its repair. So he left the bed to sell off the truck and returned quickly to enjoy the proceeds with the woman.

"Now, do you understand when I ask if you hear engine roars when you are inside her? This woman ate my truck!" the man exclaimed, and left before the new man could even respond.

After McDonald's efforts to tame the African wilds failed, and his pipe dream to produce enough milk for all to drink and even bathe in collapsed, he became the laughingstock of the white highlands. After the farmhouse had been turned into a whites-only private club, other settlers, between tots of brandies and slender glasses of wine, would mock McDonald's naïveté. How could a man leave his own land to tame another's? Did it not make more sense, and require much less energy, to simply conform and flow with nature? the white settlers asked themselves. While many admitted they had fled England to escape its horrible weather, they had no hang-ups about their motherland. They were happy to experiment with life and do what they wouldn't dare back in England. Like sleeping with another man's wife, or swapping wives with other men, or keeping a dozen servants. Yes, slavery had been abolished in Europe, but not in her dominions. And the master could fornicate with the servants and produce yellow babies without raising an eyebrow because the sun would tan them to acceptable social hues. As long as they bore white skin in the black land, the English would always have something to eat. And drink.

This was the lot that in later years came to be known as the Happy Valley Set. Their debauchery entered the annals of history because that's all they ever produced. Well, there were the bastards too, though they weren't very many, given the amount of copulation that the group managed in those heady days of the empire. McDonald was scandalized when he learned some of the sordid things that had been conducted on his premises—that the space could be debased so deeply by his compatriots shocked him into silence. But the salacious-minded Happy Valley Set did not just live their lives; they also poked noses in other people's business. Of McDonald's indifference to women, they whispered that it was not entirely innocent. The man had tried dairy farming not just for milk; he must have enjoyed touching cows' udders, they whispered. Bestiality, after all, was as old as mankind.

McDonald ignored the gossip and threw himself into farming. He would grow wheat and feed the nation; he would introduce the colony to a culture of baking cakes and bread and pastries. The crop did remarkably well until 1939, when the war in Europe frustrated his importation of pesticides that could have saved the harvest from virulent weevils. That was McDonald's turning point. He'd had enough with trying to domesticate the land and its people. He simply walked away, leaving farm equipment and the diseased crops still standing.

That's when McDonald turned his efforts to conserva-
tion. He would let the land be. He built a sanctuary away
from human habitation to observe the wild animals. He
learned their habits and noted their habitats. Soon, all important guests to the colony would look to him for guided
tours to experience nature at its best. The only thing Mc-
Donald had to keep away from wild animals was the local
poacher who sought them for food. As the chairman of the
all-white Farmers' Association, he had no trouble pushing
through legislation that banned poaching.

McDonald's farm, whose acreage was expanded during
the 1923 land adjudication to include the lake and the hot
water spring, was certified as his with a shiny red seal; the
embossed letters announced that Her Majesty had granted
him a hundred-year lease for the thousand-acre piece of
land. The revision of the land map meant that McDonald
now encroached on Babu's initial settlement by the lake.
The long-term lease meant his control of the land would
outlive him. Over the years, McDonald had agonized about
the land and what would become of it once he was gone.
He had neither an heir nor spouse to survive him—Sally's
exit from his life having sealed a certain void in his heart
that never needed filling. Where others felt a void that
needed constant replenishing, McDonald didn't—his loss
of love had firmly bolted the door to his heart. He would
be fine, he had vowed to himself, all by himself. A man
alone.

In rare moments of reflection, McDonald thought about
how many families had been displaced to accommodate
him. He used his leverage in 1923 to formulate a policy that
was given the lofty title of the Devonshire White Paper
that would prevent Indians from owning land in the colony,
under the pretext that African land ownership would be

given priority. In the meantime, white farmers occupied all arable lands, which they insisted they were holding in trust for the Africans. Once they were ready to receive the land, it would be granted unto them.

McDonald had heard his African servants talk of their anticipated lurch into adulthood when they would be bequeathed by their fathers a portion of the earth to build their own houses, after which they would marry. Yet, for all the land under his custody, McDonald would never take another wife. Failure to take a wife meant a man would die childless, a fate that his servants dreaded, because upon death, childless men would have ash smeared on their buttocks signifying they had produced nothing more than a mound of impotent soot.

For the most part, however, McDonald felt good about himself and his circumstances. He had left home at seventeen with nothing more than the clothes on his back and with little prospects in life. An apprenticeship as a locksmith, to inherit his father's business, was all that awaited him in England. But he had envisioned a different life for himself. He had chosen the army, and after twenty-three years of service to his country, he had started a new life in the colony as a pioneer farmer. And he had thrived, even in his solitude. Other lone men arrived on his doorstep and sought permission to camp on his farm. Trout fishing was possible in the lake, and steam-bathing in the hot water spring healed diseased or broken skin. This was the seed that grew into a thriving enterprise combining tourism and sports. Wealthier tourists arrived on hunting expeditions. They lived in tented camps where they could shoot kudu for dinner, trail impala for lunch, and fell rhinos for trophies to take home. It was the only resort of its kind in the entire colony, where man and wildlife lived in such close contact.

Had he returned to England, McDonald suspected, he would have ended up in drab council housing, spending unbearably cold days staring at a blank wall and feeling pity for himself—a grumpy old man haunted by his unfaithful wife. He may have been unable to control one scrawny woman, but in the colony he had thousands of men under his command. Here he was the master of his universe. It was, for all intents and purposes, a proper universe, with natural and manmade features: a cool lake and a hot spring, and animals and servants to lord over. His landholding qualified him as a baron in the colony. Only men of title controlled such lands in England, and most of it had been handed down through the generations. He had inherited nothing from his father other than his receding hairline and a short temper.

The high point of McDonald's life in the colony was when the colonial government notified him they had chosen his lodge to host an important couple from London. The year was 1952 and the colony was in the grip of an armed insurrection that was pushing for the expulsion of whites from the land, what historians agree was the precursor to *Kiama kia Rukungu*. McDonald, with his military background, had been instrumental in organizing a neighborhood watch, which buoyed his other credential as the chairman of the Farmers' Association. He had risen to meaningful societal recognition even without the knighthood that he so coveted. So it was a cruel twist of fate that the important couple destined for his lodge turned out to be a young royal by the name of Princess Elizabeth, only twenty-five at the time, and her young husband.

McDonald personally escorted the couple around, ducking into the woods when he sensed they were about to kiss, but intervening when they wandered too close to dangerous animals. McDonald navigated that space with ease, availing himself when needed, lurking in the shadows when he was in the way. He was proud to be of use to his country, even prouder that he had stayed on and harnessed the African wilds to accommodate his royal guests.

As the couple's visit neared the end—they were to leave in two nights—the princess invited McDonald to sit with them for dinner. "What can I do for you?" she asked gently. "You have been an exceptional host."

McDonald said he was glad to be of service, particularly to the royal family.

"Sleep on it," the princess prodded. "Think about it."

McDonald did not sleep that night. He was thinking how, nearly fifty years earlier, he had unsuccessfully lobbied for a title from the queen. And here was her daughter, sleeping under his roof, pestering him to state his wish. McDonald tossed and turned in bed that night, wondering whether to make the belated confession about how his quest for knighthood had kept him going. The lass would almost certainly let her family know there was an Englishman who deserved recognition for his contribution to the empire.

But the couple woke early the next morning to startling news from England. The girl's father had died in his sleep. The princess was now the queen! Once again, fate had conspired to deny McDonald his rightful inheritance. As a gracious host, he bowed to the new queen and inquired: "What can I do for you, Your Majesty?"

That's not to say McDonald was left empty-handed. The news that he had hosted the royal couple during that dramatic transition of authority would ensure a steady trickle of important guests arriving on his doorstep wanting to sleep where the young girl had gone to bed as a princess and woken up a queen. Through fees charged for accommodations and the concierge services provided for next to nothing by African laborers, McDonald made a comfortable living without seeming to do so. When in a good cheer, he'd donate to a local school or a church, even to charities formed by white conservationists. But he kept the bulk of his money for himself, unsure how he'd use it and what would happen to his vast land once he was gone, perhaps with a sprinkle of ashes on his buttocks.

McDonald's revelation came in 1953, the year after the new queen's visit, and like many aspects of his life—in which fate so often conspired to direct where he should go—it started as a call of duty. The colony was in a restive mood, so much of it placed under emergency laws. This meant all natives had to wear tags around their necks that announced their name and tribe, and special permits had to be secured for the Kikuyu, whom the colonial authorities had identified as supporting the insurgency. The emergency laws also meant the colonial police, comprising mainly Punjabi, Sikh, and British officers, had been ordered to shoot to kill any locals who stood in their way. Tens of thousands of locals were pushed out of their villages and placed in concentration camps for screening. Rajan's friend Era's father was one of them. A man torn from his family, subjected to hard labor for years, only because he had been suspected of aiding those fighting in the forest; the evidence of the man's alleged complicity stemmed merely from his name and a perceived communal allegiance.

Their animals were confiscated and villages razed. Overnight, villages that nestled the forests or rose gently over the rolling hills were crushed to smithereens by fighter jets that attested to the white man's might.

Nothing pained Reverend Turnbull more. God's country was gone. And the aspects of cultural life that he built his ministry around had been disrupted. Men had been separated from their wives. Mothers had been torn away from their children. McDonald and Reverend Turnbull had never felt further apart. McDonald provided strategic and military support to the colonial police; Reverend Turnbull went to console the new widows and orphaned children. He was among the few Englishmen who entered and left Kikuyuland during those years of strife without being threatened or harmed. He still stepped out in his scarecrow attire, complete with an umbrella, calling on the locals to repent for their sins and turn to the Lord.

Following the completion of the construction of the railway, Reverend Turnbull had dedicated his time to spreading the gospel, establishing missions in different townships over the next several decades. He considered himself the quintessential mustard seed that had found nurture in the most propitious of circumstances. He had set up churches all over the colony, literally following the railway line. He took particular pride in the fact that he had been there to watch the railway take shape, and in turn had helped shape the country. But he always went back to Nakuru, which he thought of as home and where he met regularly with his old friend McDonald—whom he considered family—to recall their shared past.

Although the mother church considered him to be in retirement, Turnbull insisted he would preach to his grave because his faith came before all else. At the advanced age of nearly ninety-two—locals said his face was now paper-white—he hardly traveled. And when he did, it was only short distances that ensured he'd be back to base by nightfall.

But this changed when *Kiama kia Rukungu* started its

campaign to oust white farmers from the Rift Valley. Turnbull felt he needed to participate in fostering peace among
the communities because he had been there since the for-
mation of the colony. He personally knew almost all the
parties involved in the political process, and he believed
God's voice should be allowed to prevail.

Even at his advanced age, Turnbull retained his usual
cheerfulness as he went about his business, ministering to
women and children in villages because all men had fled
to the forest to fight, or were detained at various camps
by the colonial authorities. Occasionally, he was invited to
the prison to administer final rites to the inmates about to
face the noose. Wherever he went, Turnbull reminded that
God existed for all human creeds, because there was only
one God. All were children of God. And all had come short
of His glory.

But what really prompted Turnbull to visit the villages
surrounding Nakuru was that he'd heard all the local preach-
ers had been intimidated into submission. Almost all of
them had received handwritten letters from the fighters in
the forest warning that they would be punished for treason
if they continued working for the white man. One preacher
received a letter warning him that he had been exposed as
a hyena pretending to lead his herd to the grazing fields,
while all he really wanted to do was feast on them.

One afternoon, while delivering a sermon mainly to
women and children in an open-air camp, Turnbull received a hand-delivered letter from little boys who said
they had found it by a tree near the church. It was written
in Kikuyu and signed, *The Leader of Kiama kia Rukungu*.

You came to our country and told us to close our eyes to pray.
When we opened our eyes, our land was gone. The Bible in

your hand had been replaced by a gun. Have pity on yourself
and depart from our midst, for killing a man your age is like
mocking God. Do not tempt us . . .

Turnbull continued, undeterred. He was inwardly
sympathetic to the African cause to liberate their country,
for he had relatives in Ireland who had spent their life-
times resisting the English rule and demanding their land
back.

Another warning was delivered a week later, this time
containing a more ominous warning: *We know what you are*
doing under the cover of darkness. We shall come for your head . . .
This second letter was unsigned, and Turnbull thought no
further about it. He simply crumpled the paper and hurled
it into the fire with philosophical contemplation: *Those in-*
tent on killing don't go around talking about it. They do it. If they want
me, they will find me.

That day, Turnbull gave a moving sermon before a
group of seven young women and two boys, elaborat-
ing on Jesus's travails in the wilderness, which lasted a
whole forty days and nights but presaged His redemption and everlasting life. To climax the sermon, Turnbull asked, as he always did, if there was anyone in the
congregation who wanted to commit their life to Jesus.
A young woman rose to her feet, followed by a second,
then a third . . . until all seven female congregants were on
their feet.

The reverend was beside himself with happiness.
He gave all of the women hearty hugs to receive them in
Christ's communion, he said, each hug lasting longer than
the previous one. The assembled women then broke into a
song that Turnbull joined with unalloyed joy:

Mwathani wakwa njakaniria tawa
Nyumitwo thutha ni nduma nene
Mbere ciiruru ihana mahiga
Kuria thu ciakwa injetereire . . .

Lord light my way
I'm pursued by impenetrable darkness
Ahead lie shadows darker than the rocks
Where my enemies lurk . . .

Turnbull wore a big grin as he continued to receive the new converts, even as his thoughts wandered to that maiden ride on the train and the lie about Nakuru as his Nineveh mission upon which he founded his church. He embraced the next convert absentmindedly, distracted by his memories. The two remained locked in an embrace as the singing continued a bit longer, before abruptly ending. Turnbull had slumped to the ground, with blood oozing from his chest. The faithful wailed in flight, as Turnbull's attacker, a man who had been disguised as a woman, brandished his weapon and chanted: "*Mzungu arudi kwao, Mwafrika apate uhuru.*"

Turnbull's wide-brimmed hat was still on his head, somewhat tilted as though to shield him from the sun, his trousers still squeezed in his socks. Even in that state, the reverend seemed full of life, his eyes staring intently at the blue sky. But for the single fly that buzzed around his open mouth, lured by the dried blood from his chest, one would have thought he was asleep.

When McDonald received the news, the twitch of his mustache—which like a dormant volcano had laid undisturbed for years—resurged with such violence he feared he would lose it. McDonald spent the whole day considering the best ways to avenge Reverend Turnbull's death. A note stashed in his pocket pointed an accusing finger at the *Kiama kia Rukungu:*

> *You came with the gun and the Bible, the note charged, now you reap what you sowed . . .*

Years earlier, McDonald had declined to join the war against the insurgents, partly because he was still traumatized by his experiences in Mombasa. In any case, he was officially retired; it was up to the colony to defend its citizens. Only now he had a personal stake in the matter. He had lost a good friend and he could not just sit there and grieve. He had laid the base for the new colony, each aspect of its life compartmentalized like the train coaches. Segregation was applied in deciding where one could live, as well as how much one could earn and for what kind of work. Some white farmers had started allowing black workers to stay on their farms in the hope that they could convince their black brothers to leave the places alone when they came calling. But the black workers were not allowed to keep animals on their masters' farms, lest they imported diseases into the white paradise.

McDonald's household had more stringent regulations. Nobody was allowed to stay overnight. All his domestic workers came and went. He felt more comfortable living with wild animals. The only staff that stayed on were those running the transport service that picked up guests from the train station, and the housekeeper who ensured clean linen was available and water ran in the taps. It was on that day that McDonald thought through the entire colonial enterprise and came to a sudden recognition that

the British Empire that he and other settlers had been assured would last a lifetime, the empire upon which the sun
would never set, was slowly plunging into darkness. The
colonial enterprise was not sustainable. The train brought
in soldiers and missionaries and took away bales of cotton
and bags of cereals. The soldiers and missionaries spent
their days persuading the locals to toil hard through the
threat of violence and the hope of redemption.

But these were hardly sensible choices for people who
had nothing to eat. The British had taken the people's land,
of which McDonald had kept a thousand acres. What had
been previously communal sources of fresh water and fish
was now in private hands, and trespassers were threatened
with persecution. On top of that, McDonald had fashioned
his own lodge as a private ranch for wild animals and hunting was prohibited. So communities that had for centuries
depended on the land to feed and clothe themselves could
neither own the land nor what it could produce, nor even
tread on its surface. Even locals' movement was confined
to where a passbook, the *kipande*, issued by other white
men, determined where one could venture and work. The
vast majority of the population had nothing to lose, other
than their chains.

"I see darkness everywhere," McDonald mumbled to
himself on that day of reflection. What had his life been
about? What had he achieved after ninety years on the
planet? And once again, Babu the Indian technician began
seeping in and out of his consciousness. McDonald remembered that it was Reverend Turnbull who took in the child
that the Indian had been suspected of siring sixty years
earlier. As McDonald went to the window and looked
out, what he saw in his mind was the misty morning he
first arrived in Nakuru and the conversation that he'd had

with Reverend Turnbull. Did it matter, the reverend had asked, the color or creed of the illegitimate child? He had declared, "I'm now the girl's father. I will raise her like my own." Turnbull had doted on the child as he watched her grow and blossom into girlhood. And McDonald had marveled at the girl's development as she matured into womanhood.

With the reverend's words ringing in his mind, Mc-Donald knew the only way to honor the memory of his departed friend would be through fostering better race relations and promoting tolerance. In this instance, he knew what would happen to the land bequeathed to him by the Queen of England in place of the knighthood that never was. He would build on it, using the money he'd accumulated over the years, a school named after his friend. The few conditions he would impose would include strict anonymity of the donor, as well as a fusion of the Christian principles that Reverend Turnbull had lived for with a slight emphasis on sportsmanship and physical fitness, the latter an offshoot of the military discipline that had shaped McDonald's life.

The school, named CMS Nakuru, for the religious order that had sponsored Reverend Turnbull's trip to East Africa, was completed mere months after the preacher's death and quickly established itself as a multiracial, non-religious institution. Before long it had satellite campuses across the colony, including in Ndundori. Its reputation caught Babu's attention and inspired his decision to send Rajan there to work as a volunteer. His other motivation was to ensure Rajan spent time with the Karims so he'd meet Leila, to whom he was betrothed.

19

The fall of the house that McDonald built was as spectacular as its rise; it did not go down without drama, or without spawning new legends to add to what had been in circulation for many decades. Many village folks who heard the news for the first time interrupted the speaker and instructed: "Can you repeat what you have just said?" And when the news was repeated, they interjected, "*Atia atia?* So, it's true . . ." A majority refused to believe the news and opted to walk to the Jakaranda to see the ruins for themselves or asked those traveling in that direction to detour there and confirm the story.

Travelers alighting from the train paused on the stairway, turning to their fellow passengers to ask: "Have we not arrived in Nakuru?" To which the reply would be that he, too, thought they had reached their destination, although the town looked remarkably different from the way he remembered it. Perhaps the township had moved a little farther? he might speculate. So the travelers stayed on the train, convinced they hadn't arrived, only to hail the train master to stop again when they started moving out of the station. It took them awhile to figure out why Nakuru looked so different; the edifice that had defined the township for generations had been erased from the face of the earth. And as Nakuru dwellers liked to add, just like that. Dissolved like grains of sugar in a cup of tea. But how could that happen? many wondered, as news of the

Jakaranda's destruction spread like a bushfire. How could the place that gave Nakuru life be deprived of its own life? And how could Nakuru survive if all it had was drawn from the Jakaranda?

The ruins of the establishment were still smoldering the next morning as residents from different parts of Nakuru and adjoining villages arrived to witness for themselves what had befallen their town's most famous landmark. The building's stone base still stood but the roof had been blown away, the rafters that once held it having caved in, the struts dark and sooty and fragile. People stood in groups whispering, wondering who could have been behind the arson. Yarns of all manner were spun about what could have happened. By now, it had been established that McDonald had been somewhat involved in the skirmishes that led to the torching of the house. It was whispered that *Kiama kia Rukungu* adherents had arrived at his doorstep and threatened to reduce him to dust, but McDonald's exact role in the incident remained unclear.

Religious folks dismissed those yarns and claimed the destruction was a natural disaster. They said God had unleashed an earthquake that shook the building to its core, then sent down a flash of lightning to torch the ruins. That no one perished in the accident, they said, was proof that this was God's warning to the world that the fire next time would be more devastating if people did not repent and turn to Him.

So, as different versions of what could have transpired started making their rounds, as was typical of Nakuru, McDonald's mythology grew larger than life. He always had a certain mystique, older men whispered, recalling McDonald's Years of Solitude in that very house that had been razed. Not to be left out, Gathenji the butcher reported that the marauding gang had arrived at the establishment earlier but were chased away by the customers. Yet very few who'd been at the Jakaranda added their voices to the debate; most were too embarrassed for not doing anything at all, and for even pointing the attackers to where Mc-Donald lived. Perhaps they, too, were deluded about McDonald's reputed prowess, and so had not taken the threat against him too seriously.

So let's end the speculation here and now and record the events as they happened. It is true McDonald was confronted by the dancing youths who invaded his farm, and whose paraphernalia suggested they were members of *Kiama kia Rukungu*. But looks can be misleading and McDonald had lived long enough to know that. He was somewhat hypnotized by a drummer who looked eerily reminiscent of a drummer he had encountered many, many years before in Mombasa, but whose name he couldn't quite remember. There was something familiar about the tilt of his head, even the way he thundered the drum with his hands.

McDonald tried to shake off the thought but he couldn't. At the ripe age of nearly ninety-two, he enjoyed great health, although his mind occasionally melded memories of the past with the present, so any exploration of the present was a laborious reflection of the past as well. His train of thought, as it were, started and ended with the literal train that he had come to build.

From his lofty perch, McDonald had the benefit of being able to watch the raiders under the glare of the security lights from his watchtower. The gang had to shield their eyes against the light when they looked in his direction, so had difficulty seeing him. As McDonald descended the stairs with slow, deliberate calculation, gun at the ready, his eyes never left the drummer, who moved toward the landing of the stairwell. McDonald trained his gun on the man, but the drummer kept jerking, moving to the throb of his drum as though the weapon held a particular pull. Soon, the rest of the gang surrounded McDonald, and he found himself in the middle of what felt like a cultural jamboree. There he was, an old, slouched white man, gun trained on the moving target of a gaunt man holding a drum between his legs. The space had been turned into an arena where two fighters were about to lock horns, urged on by the dancers who seemed to relish every moment.

The sight of the gun had not deterred any of the dancers, who shifted to a new song, flashing shiny swords that they retrieved from their sheaths.

> *Kataa kata!*
> *Kata mwanangu kata!*
> *Kataa kata!*
> *Kata mwanangu kata!*

McDonald had heard the song before, and it transported him back to Mombasa, back to the day the railway construction was inaugurated. He could see Nyundo—yes, that was the name of the drummer he had hired for the day—pounding the drum with all his might, drawing workers out of their huts. That had been McDonald's big day, and to grace the auspicious occasion, the telegram from London had confirmed that Charles Erickson, the colonial governor, would be coming to town.

Locals appeared to sprint toward the music, for the sound of the drum was a code that the Giriama had used for generations to mobilize the community. They met under the *mvinje* tree, which had outlived everyone in the village. Because the British could not pronounce *mvinje*, they called it the whistling pine due to the music made by its leaves. The locals' word was derived from *nifiche*, which meant shelter, because the tree had faithfully sheltered the community from the elements. If you met old Giriama men, and their throats were wet with palm wine, they would imitate the sounds of the *mvinje* then whisper what they had heard about the tree during their childhoods. If palm wine was still flowing, and the imbibing continued uninterrupted, they would indulge the magic associated with the *mvinje* and claim to have personally witnessed the *mvinje* descending a few meters to the ground—as a mother hen does to shield her chicks—and return to its normal height after the threat they were facing was over.

But the *mvinje* did not just offer protection to the people, the old men would confide, their voices steadier with the drink because they drank to remember, not to forget. They would laugh and explain how the *mvinje* nourished the sick back to health. Those who had leprosy only had to touch the bark to be cured. Children who had hookworm only needed to chew its leaves and the last worm would be rinsed out of their bellies. The *wazee* would drop their voices further and say women who had strayed from their husbands went to the *mvinje* under the cover of darkness and waited for its fruit to fall. If they ate the bitter fruit, their own wild fruit would descend from their wombs. *Dawa ya moto ni moto!* the old men would say and clap their hands together. Fire begets fire.

Beneath the tree were Nyundo and the other drummers, stripped to their waists, thundering the drums held between their legs. In the middle were a dozen female dancers gyrating their hips with such fluidity that one would think their bodies were boneless. They formed a ring around one dancer who balanced a gourd on her head while still thrashing her hips this way and that. The dancers were all topless—save for the ornaments dangling off their necks. The nipples of their round breasts stood erect. They wore tiny strips of cloth around the waist, which seemed to enhance the outline of their curves rather than covering them. The rhythm of the drum sped up and the dancers stomped the ground. Their generous bums tingled until the strips of clothing dropped off or disappeared in the crevices of their bodies. Then the throbbing beat came to an abrupt stop.

McDonald took the stage and made a short speech. There was a tremor to his voice that had refused to go away since the firing of the cannon, and his mustache still twitched at its edges. He was nervous about the locals' unpredictability and his inclusion of their dances was one of the ways he hoped to pacify them.

"Ladies and gentlemen," he started, "this is a special occasion when we witness the groundbreaking ceremony of the East African Railways. To commission this important project, the colonial governor, Sir Charles Erickson, has traveled all the way from Nairobi to lead us in the process. Without much further ado, join me in welcoming the governor." There was sporadic clapping from the few people who understood the language. The uncoordinated sounds came like falling donkey droppings. The locals cheered after taking the cue.

Charles Erickson was a small, thin man. He, too, spoke briefly, in an incredibly strong voice for such a small frame. He said the inauguration of railway construction was a landmark event that would transform the British East Africa Protectorate into a society where Christianity, commerce, and civilization could be cultivated.

"I should, if you allow me," Erickson said, "reorder the

hierarchy of those goals so that commerce comes first, followed by civilization, and then Christianity. Triple C, if you like. We shall deliver on those objectives using the rail that shall set sail from the spot where we are assembled today."

A hesitant round of applause started, before picking up pace as it spread from the Union Jack camp to the gathering under the *mvinje*.

"There are those in our midst who have christened this project the *Lunatic Express*. It is not the lucidity of its architects that's in doubt; rather, the term is inspired by the bravery of its dreamers. I daresay we shall turn these wild lands into orchards abundant with fruit. And I want to applaud the courage of five hundred farmers who have left the comfort of England to be the harbingers of change in the African wilds. They shall be rewarded with fertile land that locals have little use for, most of which is unoccupied. We are here to support their enterprise. The railway shall deliver their produce beyond these shores."

Erickson was then handed a pitchfork and shovel. He struck the ground once and scooped the soil. His assistant brought water to wash his hands and provided a fresh glove. Erickson flashed the gloved hand to the crowd, smiling his painful smile. People roared in laughter and waved back.

McDonald then stepped in. He was supposed to coordinate the cutting down of the *mvinje* tree to symbolize the clearing of virgin lands to pave way for the rail. He instructed African workmen hired for the day on what he needed done. But they all shook their heads and walked away. Fearing they had misunderstood his instructions, McDonald summoned an interpreter and relayed his message. This elicited a more hostile response. McDonald tensed. If his workmen disregarded his instructions in broad daylight, what would his boss think of him?

McDonald called over a British officer and told him what he wanted done. The officer took a machete from one of the African workmen and struck a blow to the trunk. It was avenged instantly: one of the local men who had declined to cut the tree repossessed the machete and struck the British officer in one fell swoop. A red film flashed on the blade. The Briton fell down instantly, bleeding profusely. Pandemonium broke out. Gunshots rent the air. Machetes clanged and produced sparks and bones snapped as humans fled for dear life.

McDonald woke from his reverie as the drummer walked toward him. He stopped only a few steps away and yanked off his mask. McDonald shrieked and dropped his pistol in fright.

"Nyundo!" he whispered, retreating as he did so. "I thought you were . . ."

"Dead?" Nyundo returned in Swahili with a smile. "I lived to tell the story."

McDonald's legs gave way and he dropped to his knees, holding his arms around his head before falling back into a crouched position. This could have been misconstrued as utter surrender—the crouching an act of supplication—but for McDonald it was a defensive position, as he readied himself to shield any blows delivered to his person.

Nyundo circled McDonald, then lifted his arm and let it fall only inches away from where the gun lay. He was testing to see if the white man was conscious, just as a boxing referee might. A dancer waved at Nyundo frantically, urging him to keep the gun away from McDonald, but Nyundo ignored him and went on with his assessment. McDonald sat up and said nothing.

The dance arena had now turned into a boxing ring, only

that one fighter was down and the other was pacing, waiting for him to rise. Nyundo smiled: "Now you know what our people mean when they say only mountains don't meet . . ."

McDonald nodded, looking stonily ahead.

"We come in peace," Nyundo said, grinning. "Isn't that what your people said when they first set foot here?"

McDonald still said nothing, reeling from the shock that the man he had long presumed dead was alive and well. "Get off my land," he finally growled, still downcast.

"This is not your land," Nyundo replied firmly. "Not an inch of our earth belongs to the white man."

"How do you know?"

"Because you couldn't put the land in your pocket and bring it back with you. You found it here."

McDonald was quiet again.

"I was there, from the very beginning. From the day you fired the cannon, to the day you felled all the trees in the *kaya*, uprooted from their roots by that bomb. A heart of darkness thrown wide open, like a book. I have seen it all with these very eyes." Nyundo paused for a moment, then went on: "The destruction of the *kaya* was a turning point for me. I kept asking myself: What would make a man leave his land of birth, go to another man's land, and impose his way of life on them? And as if that's not enough, destroy their culture? I lost my voice. People thought I was joking, but I had been too hurt to speak. So I let my drum speak for me . . ."

"Are you done?" McDonald asked wearily.

At this stage, the gang that surrounded him was mimicking how they would cut him down, and a slow, hesitant beat rang softly.

"Do you mean if I'm done talking or if I'm done fighting against the white man?"

"Whatever." McDonald shrugged, glancing at his adversary. Nyundo, who had been a young lad when they first met, was now in his seventies, but the person McDonald had first encountered hadn't changed much. The short, stocky frame did not seem to have added an inch in height or width.

"I'm not done talking, and when I am, I will decide if I'm done fighting or not."

"So, what comes first? The fight or the talk?"

"That's not for you to decide," Nyundo countered.

"It just occurred to me, if I am already dead, then I can't hear your story."

"It is not *my* story, you foolish man. It is *your* story. I want *you* to know I have walked in your footsteps since the *kaya* riots. I have witnessed the death and the destruction you have brought upon this land. A time will come when all shall answer for their crimes. There are things men shall answer to fellow men right here on earth." Nyundo nodded to his group. The beat rose once more and the gang retrieved their swords and swung them this way and that.

Nyundo appeared entranced as he went around the group, beating his drum while posing questions, to which the group responded in unison. When the beat softened once again, he returned and faced McDonald.

"I went to Kikuyuland and heard of Waiyaki, the one who was buried headfirst by your men because he resisted the railway cutting through his land. I went to Nandiland where Koitalel wouldn't let your men to build the railway through their land. Your men tricked Koitalel into what was meant to be a peaceful meeting, only to open fire when he appeared unarmed. To celebrate their cowardice, they cut off his head and took it to your queen. There are many other crimes, way too many to enumerate, committed by your men in your name.

"Despite my swearing never to work for the white man, I was dragged to fight in the big war in the white man's country. I took my drum with me, which I used to entertain the white soldiers. But I did not play the drums with my eyes closed. I saw the white men die. And I met black soldiers from beyond the seas. They said they had overcome slavery and encouraged us that we too would one day overcome white rule in our country. They said they used an underground railroad to defeat the white slave owners. I did the same when I returned. Our organized resistance went underground. Unlike yours, our railroad was not built using iron; it was laid in the hearts of people who were guided by a desire to do what's right. Those men and women formed our network that spread from village to village, town to town. Some provided the food, others brought the water. Yet others bore arms—all pilfered from under the noses of your men. But many of our supporters remained above board. Some even worked for you. Like Babu . . ."

McDonald sat open-mouthed. "Babu the surveyor?"

"Don't get too excited. That's our man. His code name in the forest was Guka. Patriot of the highest order. And when the history of this country is written, a chapter will be devoted to him. He was committed to the end. Or I should say, right from the start. The earliest I can remember was that incident at Fort Jesus when he made you wet your pants. And when our elders sat to think about foreigners who could be drawn to our cause, his name was mentioned repeatedly. Actually, nobody remembered his name. All they remembered was his pronounced forehead. *Sokwe mtu*, as we used to call him. And he used that fine head of his to formulate ways in which he could contribute to the movement without arousing any suspicions. So he beat you once more. We owe this freedom to him, for it is his generous contributions, and from a few others, that has kept us going. He printed all the materials we used throughout the war. He helped us in all ways, as our people put it, *kwa hali na mali*. And for investing in our freedom, our nation will honor and remember him. Now we are going to be free. To use the words of Nkurumah of Ghana, our beloved country is free forever. So it's your turn to leave. In peace."

Nyundo rushed forward and grabbed the pistol that still lay at McDonald's feet. McDonald froze, waiting to be shot. Even the singing from the gang stopped. It was dead silent. Nyundo swiftly dismantled the gun and removed the rounds of ammunition. He threw each bullet in a different direction.

"When bullets begin to flower," Nyundo said, "Africans shall reap the bitter fruit that the white man has sowed in our midst . . ."

McDonald attempted to rise but without success. He was trying to remember the note tucked in Turnbull's trousers after he was killed. It spoke of him holding the gun and the Bible, and reaping what he had sowed. McDonald decided he wasn't going to be killed on his knees; he would be on his feet. He tried to rise again and fell. Nyundo stretched a hand and helped him up.

There was loud grumbling from the young men in the gang. That's not how they had plotted the events. They had planned to harass McDonald and scare him out of the farm. Instead, Nyundo had decided to recall their past together and throw away the bullets that should have been used to silence him. The young men started ransacking the farm, kicking and slashing anything they found in their way. When they reached the Jakaranda, the torchbearer hurled his flame at the establishment. It landed on one of the tarpaulins near Gathenji's butchery and lit one side. In an instant, the blaze danced across the canvas, issuing a hissing sound before exploding in a ball of fire. Gathenji's butchery released two dozen black-brown mice who'd been hibernating under sacks of potatoes, and even more roaches, all fat and lazy. None of the roaches moved for some time, blinking in the flood of light, clearly disoriented. The few revelers present scrambled to safety, as did some bushbuck and antelope that had been at the watering hole. It took six hours to gut the building, and gone with it, the decades of history that harbored Nakuru's lore.

The Jakaranda ruins appeared to gain a new lease of life the following day as a six-vehicle convoy made its way into Nakuru, sirens squealing. Some thought the firemen had finally arrived. But they were wrong. It was Big Man and his entourage. He stopped by the ruins and shook his head as he observed the damage. He returned to his car and stood through the open roof, swishing his fly whisk around in greeting. The assembled villagers mobbed his car. Big Man said hooliganism and vandalism would not be tolerated by *serikali ya Mwafrika*, the black man's government. He would deal firmly and resolutely with it. He then turned to the police commissioner, who stood beside his car in dark blue attire with epaulets on his shoulders.

"*Bwana* Commissioner, I want those behind this arson brought to me in the next twenty-four hours, dead or alive," Big Man thundered. He scoffed at the roosters that had been left by the invaders at McDonald's house as a cheap gimmick to link *serikali ya Mwafrika* to the politics of death and destruction.

Big Man's convoy then drove to McDonald's lodge. Many white settlers had arrived to console the man. Addressing them collectively, Big Man explained, "I want you to stay and farm this country. There is room for each and every one of us, big or small, white or black, rich or poor. The people I want out, as I said the other day, know themselves. Those who cannot be categorized as either meat or skin. Those who hide in between, eating from two sides like *thambara*. Those who keep all their money under their mattresses because they have no faith in *serikali ya Mwafrika* . . . But tell them to make no mistake: I shall not stand and watch them ruin the future of this great country. In that regard, my government shall set funds aside to restore the Jakaranda, a building that gave Nakuru not just its life but its history as well. I thank you all. I thank Mr. McDonald particularly for being a founding father of the nation. A people without the knowledge of their past is like a tree without roots. Before the Jakaranda, Nakuru was nothing but empty plains."

20

Founding Father is a grand term one would hardly equate with a little man like Ahmad, the unlikely patriarch who extended Babu's lineage and also served as the founding director of Ahmad, Babu & Cordage (ABC), the firm that won him a state commendation on Independence Day in December 1963, alongside McDonald. Officially, Ahmad was recognized for his entrepreneurial spirit, for steering a large private company to profitability, for providing employment to hundreds of workers.

In truth, the recognition was yet another charade that denied Babu his rightful honor.

To understand how this came about, let's turn back the hands of time once again and return to September 1901 in Nakuru, when Ahmad returned from his brief sojourn to Mombasa, his penis still warm and moist after days of lovemaking with Fatima. On the one hand, he was remorseful and contrite; on the other, defiant and indifferent. He knew it was not right to steal another man's wife, especially one who had entrusted him with the cardinal responsibility of informing his family when misfortune struck. But at the same time, Ahmad felt quite justified in his acts: What kind of man keeps a virgin wife, not for a day or week, but for years? And what man in his right mind would let a woman of Fatima's beauty go to waste? *Babu should count himself lucky it's me who did it first*, Ahmad assured himself.

So that's how he rationalized things: it was Ahmad's duty of care that compelled him to violate Babu's trust in him. Furthermore, Babu's banishment meant Ahmad did not have to face him, at least not yet.

Three months later, a perfect opportunity availed itself. The news that Babu had been exonerated started making its rounds. Chief Lonana was convinced someone with blue eyes must have impregnated his daughter and he made it known he had no further claims against Babu. Indian and African workers pointed in the direction of the most famous blue-eyed men in their midst, Reverend Turnbull and McDonald, but some dismissed their suspicions just as fast. "Those two, aaaaiiii," some workers sighed. "It can't be. Tell us another one . . ."

Others were not as doubtful. "You never know, *ya Mungu ni mengi*. As Cow Man likes to say, God works in miraculous ways. His wonders to perform," they said. But that's where the conversation ended and everybody carried on with their lives, which, for the most part, meant rising at dawn and working till dusk.

As previously mentioned, Ahmad saw this as his opportunity to share some good news with Babu, thereby assuaging his own guilt over sleeping with Fatima. It would be a relief for Babu to learn that there was no case against him. Babu might even be able to petition McDonald to get his old job back. Ahmad made inquiries with other artisans and technicians who had dropped out of rail work to start their small businesses along the railway line. After consulting with a few people, he had a pretty good idea of where to find Babu. Since his presumed hideout was a little ways off, Ahmad planned on using the goods train that departed early in the morning after arriving from Mombasa the previous evening. But when the train arrived that evening, Ahmad received the letter from Fatima. He had initially panicked when a colleague alerted him to the missive. None of his relatives in Bombay could write because they were illiterate. He had no known relatives in the colony, not even a girlfriend. His heart beat faster at the memory of Fatima; yes, she could count as his girlfriend, even though she was married. But she couldn't write to him as that would be too risky. The memory of her erect nipple melting in his mouth shot a tremor through his body. He adjusted his trousers and sprinted to collect the letter from the train master.

He found it was actually a telegram, and even before opening it, he noticed there was a feminine feel to it: the brightly colored envelope, the leisurely loops on the letters that spelled his name. He instantly knew it was Fatima and he cursed under his breath as he opened the mail. *COUSIN ABDUL, WELCOME TO THE FAMILY. I'M WAITING EXPECTANTLY.*

Ahmad correctly interpreted the code to mean Fatima was announcing she was pregnant. There was no hint of panic in the note; if anything, there was a gleeful relish, an invitation to join her family, to populate it. Ahmad sucked the roof of his mouth; the act triggered a torrent of saliva. He felt like he was about to throw up. *This thing must be infectious*, Ahmad laughed quietly to himself as the nausea passed. *I am behaving like a pregnant woman.*

But it was no laughing matter that he had put Fatima in a family way. His narrative had to be revised. He'd have to tell his friend Babu a different story, for he couldn't simply walk over and blabber: *Man, you are in the clear. The girl you thought you impregnated has been confirmed to have been generous with others. It's definitely not your baby as you don't have blue eyes. Chief Lonana says he has no further case against you. Meanwhile,*

when you sent me to see your virgin wife in Mombasa—don't ask me
how I got to know she is a virgin—things happened and, you know, we
are family now. One big happy family, as I have put her in a family way.

Ahmad knew he couldn't say that to Babu. It was one
thing to steal a man's wife, it was quite another to impregnate her and produce a progeny to perpetuate his lineage,
even when that person was Ahmad who fantasized about
lining the railway line with big-eared tots. He considered
his options. He could persuade Fatima to elope with him.
Before Babu caught wind of their absence, they would
have crossed the ocean back to India. Folks there would
understand. They would shrug and say that strange things
always happen in Africa. In any case, why did that caveman need a wife if he couldn't consummate the marriage?
Alternatively, Ahmad could also hide in another part of the
colony and Fatima and he would live like a couple and no
one would ever suspect anything.

Ahmad concluded that he wasn't ready to face Babu.
He made no reply to Fatima's missive. He loved the sense
of power that conferred him. With a stroke of the pen, he
could commit a woman to eternal happiness or a lifetime
of grief. He read the note again and decided that Fatima
would be fine with or without him. She didn't need him;
she hadn't needed Babu. But he didn't know what to say to
her, so he didn't say anything.

Two months passed as he mulled over his options. The
rail construction had almost reached its zenith in Port Elizabeth. Technicians were about to lose their lifeline. Many
were talking of returning to India by the next monsoon,
inshallah. A new chapter was about to begin in the colony.
With the inauguration of the train service, goods would
soon start to be ferried to the dock in Mombasa for onward
shipping to England. Coffee and tea and rice and potatoes

and beans and maize and what-have-you. These would have to be packed in bags. Ahmad heard McDonald lament that all the sisal farms established to feed that need had failed—except for one place in the wild, the area around Babu's cave. Now Ahmad knew something else that Babu was unaware of—his land, just like his wife, was virgin territory, awaiting exploitation. While Ahmad was busy planting semen in Fatima's womb, Babu was busy planting sisal seeds in the wild. And from Ahmad's spectacular success with Fatima, who bore instant fruit without much effort, he knew he could get something for nothing from Babu.

Crucially, Ahmad possessed the information that Babu was a free man who didn't need to hide anymore. But he didn't tell him that when they met. Neither did Ahmad tell Babu about the impending birth of his baby with Fatima; instead, he told him of the potential business they could start with his sisal crop. And, since Babu was a fugitive, Ahmad said he would be the public face of the firm, now that the railway construction was coming to a close.

Babu had no objections. He was grateful for his friend taking the risk of meeting with an outlaw, even more grateful for providing an outlet for his sisal, the crop that he had been cultivating all this time without actually knowing what it was. He would till the land and provide the sisal; Ahmad would harvest and sell the crop to make bags that would bring them a bagful of money. It'd be a win-win situation. Ahmad had planted seed in Babu's domestic sphere, and Babu had planted seed in the wilds that would secure their futures financially.

Regarding his trip to Mombasa, Ahmad casually told Babu his wife was doing very well; he said she had a small but thriving business and she was part of a functional and lively community.

"What did she say about my—my problem?" Babu stuttered.

"She took it in stride," Ahmad lied. "Very strong woman. But I suppose she was distracted because she was on her feet all day serving customers at her shop."

Babu was quiet for a moment before he asked: "When you say she has a thriving business, do you mean her own enterprise or she works for someone else?"

"I honestly did not confirm, but it looked like her own. She closed it when she wished and—" Ahmad checked himself just in time. He was talking too much. Or did he unconsciously intend to tell Babu what he did with his wife when she closed shop? "And that kind of thing," he concluded abruptly.

"And," Babu pursued, "when you say she was *on her feet*, do you mean it literally?"

"Oooh, I forgot to tell you about that little miracle," Ahmad said with genuine enthusiasm. "Fatima is back on her feet!"

It was that little miracle that compelled Babu to travel incognito to Mombasa to see Fatima. Drawing on his escarpment experience, he masqueraded as a devout pilgrim, sadhu, and had his prayer beads, *misbaha*, draped around his neck over a flowing gown. He made his way on the rail that he had helped build, nearly squealing with pleasure as the train departed the station. It felt like a stolen moment, the gentle rocking of the train. He recalled each bend along the way, the conversations he'd had with Ahmad and many other workers. It was truly a journey down memory lane, some of it painful, some joyous. What stayed with Babu was the sudden realization that they had been out in the open for four solid years, making lairs just like wild animals. He thought about the friends he had made and lost along the way. Faces flashed through his mind but he couldn't produce their names as fast. Ahmad and Karim, it seemed to Babu, were among the only friends that had stayed the course—Babu and Karim having been reacquainted when the latter temporarily moved to Nakuru, before migrating to Ndundori. Great friends indeed. "God bless them," Babu muttered, using his *misbaha* for the first time.

Babu reached Mombasa without incident. He was excited about surprising Fatima. He was also somewhat nervous. He may have been hiding for five months, but he had been fleeing from Fatima for over two years, unable to cope with her illness, especially with the pressures of work on the railway. It wasn't called the *Lunatic Express* for nothing. But the main reason Babu had kept away was to avoid the curse that he suspected had befallen his wife, and all because of his foolishness. He had messed with a man of God, and soon after, Fatima had lost the use of her legs. If Ahmad were to be believed, though, Fatima was healthy once again. That could only mean that the effects of the curse had worn off.

It was on this optimistic note that Babu descended on Mombasa and quickly located Fatima's shop. There were not very many shops run by Indians in Mombasa, and those who lived there knew each other. Fatima, the wife of a railway technician, was known to all. Babu arrived at the shop with a broad smile on his face. The young woman he met did not recognize him, now that he had a full beard and was turbaned, and neither did he recognize her. He was looking for a scrawny little girl with tiny studs for breasts. The figure before him was a woman in full bloom. She was buxom, with wide hips, and the outline of her abaya confirmed she was supporting a ballooning belly. She smiled back at him and inquired what he wanted to buy from the shop. That's when Babu saw the gap in her teeth and confirmed he was indeed talking to his wife. Teeth, often used to identify corpses, are what he needed to identify his living wife. His wife who carried a new life that he'd had no part in making. A piece of Babu died instantly. He became the living dead.

Babu returned to Nakuru without any disguise. He felt, to use a popular Nakuru expression, like the man who went to a village dance lamenting his lack of shoes, only to find others who did not have feet. He had thought being an outlaw was the worst thing to happen to anyone, but he had returned from Mombasa feeling humiliated in the worst way. He had been cuckolded and the evidence was there for all to see. He did not have to hear the rumors from men in pubs or tea shops; he had seen for himself the fruits of Fatima's labor. He imagined her lying naked, sighing under the weight of another man, groaning with pleasure. He could not, try as he might, put a picture to the face of the man. Was he black, white, or brown? Had he been mechanical about his business, shedding his clothes carefully and piling them at the foot of the bed to avoid getting them creased, just in case he had to wear them to work, or had he torn them off in the throes of passion? Did that man know him?

Babu tried to focus his thoughts elsewhere. He had not impregnated Chief Lonana's daughter as alleged, yet he had been humiliated. So he had lost on all fronts: lost face at work, lost his job, and now he had to deal with the permanent disgrace of Fatima's infidelity and her illegitimate child. He needed to create as much space as he could between Fatima and himself.

On the way back to Nakuru, Babu considered his options. Perhaps he could try sneaking on board a ship and
returning to India—only he would be persistently questioned about Fatima once he was back home. And what
would he say to such inquiries? *Sorry, folks, but things didn't
work out between us, my wife got a man for herself and they did it so
well, they even produced a baby.* But was it not he who had left
her first, abandoning a crippled woman to fend for herself,
and had she not shamed him by seeking treatment and regaining use of her legs, thus creating a new life without
him? There was no way for Babu to extricate himself from
the mess and the relentless questions if he returned to
India.

There was also the possibility of abandoning Fatima
and starting a new life somewhere else in the colony. This
option seemed most plausible. He would lose nothing
by moving to a new locale where nobody knew him, and
where he would be saved from the embarrassing questions
about his wife. Back in India, their families would think
they were still together, so there would be no rumors of
their estrangement.

When Babu arrived in Nakuru, however, two things
happened that compelled him to alter his plans. First, he
found a portion of his sisal crop had been cleared by
Ahmad.

"Babu *bhai*, I vonder if you go back to India by foot,"
Ahmad chuckled when he arrived the following day. "I
take our sisal to ginnery. Now our money is spinning, it
vill fall like rain."

It struck Babu as odd how little Ahmad inquired about
Fatima, even after he mentioned he had been to Mombasa.
Maybe Ahmad was keeping a respectable distance so as
not to appear intrusive. All he asked about was Fatima's

business, of which Babu said little. Ahmad announced that he was leaving shortly with their sisal harvest and would return the following day to bring Babu his share of the proceeds.

But the rains did not come—the financial rains that Ahmad had promised—not even a trickle. Babu vented his frustrations through work, clearing more land and spreading new sisal seedlings. If Ahmad had found some use for the sisal, then he was sure his good friend would not swindle him out of his sweat. He would definitely bring him some money.

Yet Ahmad did not return, not the following day nor the following week nor even the following month. And Babu could not go looking for his friend, lest he expose himself to the authorities and risk arrest. It was in the third month after his trip to Mombasa that Babu decided to go back there. He was down to his last penny and life was getting unbearable. He regretted having fled from Fatima instead of confronting her, demanding some answers. He needed to know more about her business. There was no point in going around with bottled-up bitterness. He needed an outlet, and who better than Fatima herself? If the shop that he had seen was hers, he needed to know how she had come into its possession. Perhaps she had become a woman of low virtue and peddled her flesh for a living.

Once again, he traveled as a sadhu, just in case some old colleagues recognized him on the train. He went straight to Fatima's shop but she wasn't there. A young woman was holding down the fort, and she said that Fatima had fallen ill. "If you are a man of God, I think she could do with some prayers," the woman announced, glancing at Babu's regalia.

Babu was shamefaced as he headed where he had been directed, conflicted as to whether to proceed there or to flee back to Nakuru. Fatima had wronged him, but he had wronged her too. And if she was unwell, he was her only relative in the colony—if he discounted the father of her child, he thought bitterly.

Babu realized, rather belatedly, that he had not inquired into the nature of her illness. He recognized his mistake when he reached her doorstep. The piercing cry of an infant assaulted his ears. He turned to walk away but the door swung open in that instant. A middle-aged woman stood at the entrance not uttering a word, then shutting the door quickly. When the door opened again, a bunch of women stood by, waving him away.

"This business is for women only!" one shouted.

Babu glanced inside. An elderly woman sat in the center of the room. She was blowing a black horn in which herbs and spices had been stuffed, directing the smoke toward the infant that Fatima held in her hands. Babu retreated in panic.

Several women huddled to whisper among themselves. It appeared somebody had recognized him. He was invited in, but he remained rooted to the ground. Inside, the baby yelled at the full volume of its lungs. Soon, the women broke into song, holding the infant in turns, smiling into its face while humming. Babu scanned the room for any recognizable faces. Fatima, sitting in a corner, flashed a dainty smile.

"This must be the father of the baby," one woman addressed him directly, rising from her seat, glancing at Fatima for confirmation.

Fatima smiled and nodded.

Babu tensed. He might be her husband, but he wasn't the father of the baby.

The woman handed him the baby. "A baby is not held by the tips of the fingers. Come in and hold him properly," she said, and started singing; the other women joined in.

Babu stiffly accepted the baby. He was flummoxed. In one moment, he was being chased out of the room; in the next, he was being welcomed with merriment. The one thing he had promised himself was that he would have nothing to do with Fatima's baby; now it had been thrust into his arms, and half a dozen women were watching him intently. The baby stirred and yawned, a frown creasing its face. Then it stretched its tiny, spindly legs before releasing a trickle of warm urine that coursed down Babu's arms and hands.

"The baby has greeted its father!" one woman ululated, and the others joined in.

Babu cringed. The baby, created through the exchange of bodily fluids, was reminding him of its origin. *How vulgar*, he thought as he handed the baby back without uttering a word, then walked out.

Babu felt that the cold treatment he had received in his own house was the height of *madharau*. Actually, he corrected himself, it was Fatima's house. It did not feel like his home at all, although he had paid its rent without fail for the past four years.

Babu was also perturbed that the black horn, the totem of Nahodha's curse, had been used in Fatima's house—on her newborn baby. What was happening to his life? he wondered.

Babu was so lost in thought that he failed to hear his name being called; it wasn't until someone tapped his shoulder and told him someone was calling him that he realized it was Fatima. She was chasing after him, clumsily holding a *leso* around her belly.

"Where are you going?" she asked plaintively.

"I don't know," he said, which was very true.

"Are you coming back?" It felt like the plea of a child, seeking the reassurance from a parent that she was not being abandoned.

"I don't know," he responded, shrugging.

"We need to, to—talk . . ."

"No," he replied firmly. "We don't."

"Okay," Fatima said with equal firmness, though she didn't leave. "The women have come to help me. They know . . . know nothing . . . about us."

Babu started moving away.

"Wait!" Fatima commanded.

He stopped.

She walked over to him, gingerly unfolding a knot at the tip of her sarong. It was a clod of rupees. She gave it to him. "I have been honest," she said, looking him in the eye. "These are the savings from my *duka*. I set it up when my legs healed. I did not tell you because you never asked. But you kept the money coming. I kept it growing. I have my *duka* and now you have something to start a business of your own with." Fatima turned and started walking away.

"Wait!" Babu called out. "I want to ask you something."

"Let me ask you first."

"No, I asked first."

"You said you didn't want to talk."

"Now I do."

"No you don't!"

"Yes I do."

"No you don't!"

"Okay, you go first . . ."

Neither of them was smiling but the tension between them had dissipated.

"Why do you dress this way?" Fatima asked.

"Because I am now a sadhu," Babu smiled. "Or I aspire to be one."

"Seriously?"

"Well, maybe, maybe not."

"Is that why you didn't . . ."

"Didn't?"

"Do it . . . ?"

"Do what?"

"Abstain."

"What?"

"Since our wedding day."

Babu was silent.

"Do you still do it?"

"What?" Babu asked cautiously.

"Abstain."

"Maybe," Babu sighed.

"What about . . . about . . . the other problem?"

"What?"

"The other woman."

"Which one?"

"So, they are that many?"

Silence.

"The chief's daughter."

"I-I got many, many—"

"Women?"

"Problems."

"I should help you."

Silence.

"That woman," Fatima waved toward her house, "can help you."

Silence.

"She is the traditional healer who restored my legs."

"What's she doing to—to you?"

"It's the baby."

"Baby?"

"Protective charm. She did that to my *duka* as well. Exorcised the bad spirits before I opened the shop. She did the same to me when I told her about Nahodha's curse. She has very strong medicine."

"Yes, I can see that," Babu conceded.

"She has given me the black horn for keeps. She says I should use it when trouble blows my way."

"Blow me away then!"

"Don't tempt me . . ."

The 120 rupees Babu received from Fatima was nearly equivalent to the amount he had been sending her every year. And it was more than he would have received had he completed his contract with the railway. Moreover, she had managed to save money while still keeping her *duka* well stocked.

So, in spite of everything, their parting was amicable, their initially frosty relations having thawed somewhat. Fatima said she would stay on in Mombasa and regain her health after the childbirth; Babu would return to Nakuru and explore business opportunities to invest the money in. He felt as though he was being paid for his silence. From the two uneventful trips to Mombasa—uneventful in the sense that no one had bothered him—Babu was growing more confident that the authorities had either forgotten about him or were no longer interested in him. In any case, since he was not interested in pursuing any labor-related claim against the railway authorities, he thought he could comfortably settle back in and get immersed in fruitful work.

He did—by building the first white rondavel in the place, which would grow into Nakuru town before other workers arrived and put up their structures, thereby turning it into a proper settlement in only a few months. Farther afield, he established the first *duka* in the place, which would become Nakuru's commercial district. Fatima gave the business a great boost when she arrived six months later, throwing her energies and insights into the project. By the end of 1903, they had opened one more *duka* in Molo.

Over the years, Babu established an enviable business empire. The secret to his business, which he ran side by side with Fatima, was simple: he would travel across the Rift Valley buying food from white farmers and delivering it to the African markets. He was the bridge between the two races. Over time, the small *duka* that he had founded with Fatima's fund grew into a wholesale outlet that served Nakuru and adjoining towns.

In spite of his immense success, Babu remained down-to-earth, resisting overtures to join private clubs initiated by the Indian business community in Nakuru and beyond. Part of his reason for staying away was to avoid men from his past, such as Ahmad, who he once encountered at the funeral of a former railway worker. Ahmad had turned ash-gray when he saw Babu, before melting into the crowd. Babu had not seen him since Ahmad had swindled him with his sisal plants, and he did not want to see him again. He would keep away.

He lived a hermetic life, taking a packed lunch from home which he ate in between meeting with customers at the shop. That was actually part of his business success: the reliability of his shop remaining open, no matter what. He opened early and closed late. African businessmen who joined the trade had very different work ethics. Lunchtime meant closing to dash to the nearby eateries for *nyama choma*, washed down with a beer or two. And seldom did those who started imbibing ever return to work, postponing the reopening to the following day. When they did, battling a hangover from the previous night, they would start by restocking what had been depleted the previous day. It was due to these dynamics that Babu remained ahead of his competition.

Fatima stayed faithfully beside him, tactfully directing the business without getting in the way. Everybody thought them a perfect couple, and from the outside, they truly were. At home, it was a different story. Each observed the other's space, never crossing the no-man's-land that Fatima's son Rashid had defined in their bed, and which was maintained even after he grew up and moved to his own room and eventually out of the house. But in 1922, Fatima sensed something was distracting Babu. He would leave the shop early and disappear for hours on end.

That was the year that Babu joined the labor movement in the colony, and when trade unionist Harry Thuku was arrested, Babu was among those who organized the protests demanding his release.

But it was in the 1950s that Babu, by then a business magnate in the colony, contributed immensely to the liberation struggle. Using locals as conduits, he donated significant sums of money to *Kiama kia Rukungu*. And when he diversified his business and ventured into printing, he clandestinely published leaflets warning whites to vacate the Rift Valley. He became the freedom fighters' elder statesman, the father of the nation, or as they referred to him, Guka, meaning grandfather.

21

As it was in the beginning, when the train delivered to Nakuru the men who founded the township and shaped its future, so it was in the end, when the train also delivered their children to Mombasa to confront their secret past. And when the past meets the present, or to use the metaphor of the railroad, the trains intersect without the intervention of the stationmaster, it is likely to be a messy affair. And the triumvirate of Reverend Turnbull, McDonald, and Babu, whose life threads had run parallel to each other for decades, would finally come together. McDonald was the last man standing; Babu lay in bed for the third day, still weighed down by the history that he had sought to escape for sixty years; Reverend Turnbull, who preached about renouncing bodily temptations to save the soul, had been cut down by the lone fighter from *Kiama kia Rukungu* ten years earlier, in 1953.

Yet, it still confounds that the unraveling of those sixty years of history was heralded by a momentary clash in the dark between Rajan and Mariam on the staircase of the Jakaranda, producing sparks that would illuminate a history that had eluded their forebears, and herald their common heritage. In Nakuru lore, the term they use to explain such phenomena, like the coincidental meeting of strangers who later discover they are somewhat related, is *damu zinavutana*. Blood tugging toward the direction of its kin, much the same way gravity pulls objects toward the earth. Mariam's blood was pulling toward Rajan's.

Rajan inadvertently found himself sucked into a vortex of history he hardly understood. All he knew was that he was helplessly besotted with Mariam, so he had run after her as Babu whimpered on the floor like an old dog. Babu had spent years running away from Fatima; Rajan spent months chasing Mariam.

Unbeknownst to Rajan, Mariam was the daughter of the girl Reverend Turnbull had adopted and raised as his own; the girl whose mother was Chief Lonana's daughter Sene-iya. And the preacher had adequately prepared by envisioning a future without him and had left instructions on what should happen after his demise. He had bequeathed to his family, comprising his adopted daughter Rehema, as well as Rehema's daughter Mariam, a parcel he deposited in a vault of the Mombasa branch of the Bank of England, which was to be opened by Mariam or her mother Rehema. The only condition was that Mariam had to be at least eighteen years old to access it. Only months after writing his will, Reverend Turnbull was dead.

The timing of Reverend Turnbull's edict about the opening of the vault was rather apt. One might call it serendipity; others would call it divinatory insight—for 1963, the year that Mariam turned eighteen, was also the year the independent nation of Kenya was born. As though to test Mariam's competence in dealing with the affairs of her complex heritage, Mariam's mother Rehema had also recently died. That was when a grief-stricken Mariam, on the verge of losing her sanity, had set out for Nakuru from Ndundori with a rather foolish proposition: to venture to a place she had never been and to kiss a stranger. This might sound arrogant and foolish, but as it turned out, Mariam's instinct, like a magnet that pulls metal from a pile of trash, was pulling her toward her secret heritage.

So after that initial kiss in the dark with the stranger, Mariam had returned home with her two wishes fulfilled. As her mother's only child, and Rehema being a single parent, Mariam became the custodian of the family history when her mother died, and received all the family letters, including the one bequeathing her the parcel in a vault in Mombasa left by her grandfather, Reverend Turnbull. Mariam had planned on spending one night in Nakuru before taking the train to Mombasa, as the service was only available on Tuesdays and Thursdays. That's when she made her second trip to the Jakaranda and had her encounter with the man she would come to know as Rajan, reigniting the fire that her first kiss had lit in him. She had allowed the passions to consume her, reasoning, rather sensibly, that keeping the parcel in Mombasa for a few more days would make no difference since it had been waiting there for ten years.

Once again, her wisdom had prevailed, for Mariam's reunion with Rajan climaxed with Rajan taking her to meet his grandfather. Babu's meltdown upon hearing who Mariam's mother was only hastened her resolve to set forth for Mombasa and try to establish why the simple mention of her origins had elicited such a strong reaction. She fled Babu's home in tears, uncertain how to reassure his family that she had done nothing other than invoke the name of her mother, as Babu had requested; Rajan followed in hot pursuit, trying to catch up with her without knowing where she was going, or even why. He just wanted to be with her, seated beside her, parallel like the train tracks.

Mariam reached the train station ahead of Rajan and purchased a one-way ticket to Mombasa. Rajan caught up with her soon enough, as the train honked to announce its departure. Not knowing Mariam's destination, Rajan simply asked for a ticket to the end of the rail. The attendant, not humored by his philosophical quip, simply punched Mombasa as the last destination and issued the ticket. Mariam was already on board; Rajan scampered after her.

"Don't you know the rules, young man?" the ticket inspector scoffed, pointing Rajan toward the cabin for Indians.

Mariam, with her milky skin, was dispatched to the cabin for whites. So there they were, in the belly of the beast, gliding on the rail that their forebears had laid with their bare hands, going to confront a past that would reorganize their compartmentalized lives, or foster a collision from which none would ever be the same again.

They stood side by side for a reasonable portion of the journey, blowing kisses through the glass partitions that divided the cabins, giggling and laughing like little children. Before long, both exhausted, they gestured that they needed to get some rest and slumped back into their seats. Rajan felt somewhat conflicted about the trip, gnawed by memories of his grandfather on all fours, shouting for somebody to blow the horn, yet unwilling to blame the girl sitting across from him.

The train trip felt rather surreal, hurtling through landmarks featured in Rajan's songs, mostly from his grandfather's narratives. Rajan noticed the small mounds of earth that dotted the track. They were graves of men who had fallen by the wayside, and of whom Babu had said nothing in his recollections. At Mtito Andei, the train halted long enough for Rajan to step out and read the bronze plaque on a phallus-shaped monument at the station.

In Memory of 5,000 Men Who Laid Their Lives to Lay This Rail, it announced, the tiny letters below that listed the names of the deceased dancing in the sun, bequeathing them new life. Muted in the neat scrolls of the letters were the cries of grief that their families had unleashed upon receiving news of their demise, the message often delivered by a worker, sometimes years after the tragedy. For others, it was the sudden end of money dispatched every month that presaged their loss. Where a family was lucky, they would receive an urn bearing the ashes, or even a bone salvaged from the savage attack of a lion, wrapped in the clothes the deceased had last worn.

Not all deaths were violent: the prickly bites of mosquitoes or tsetse flies deflated life and sapped energy from their victims like a punctured tire., Before long, they were no more. Rajan was disturbed by the find, as well as Babu's silence on the casualties of the railway. Perhaps it was his grandfather's way of coping with the pain, Rajan thought, as this revelation led him to ponder what other traumas the old man had borne in silence.

Rajan flashed back to a long-forgotten memory when he had been about six and had seen Babu in pain. The year was 1947 and although Rajan did not know it, Babu had plucked hairs from his pate and thrown them into the fire, where they did their zigzag death-dance. And Rajan watched as Babu wept over the partition of his home region of Punjab, which had been split up between the newly established states of India and Pakistan.

Returning his thoughts to the present, Rajan wandered to the window and peered outside. When he was younger, he used to rush to the window of their house and watch the train hurtle down the valley. It always filled him with wonder to see a passenger by the window, absorbed by the landscape or simply lost in thought. He would wave excitedly and was elated when someone waved back. There was a strange fulfillment about being able to connect with another human being who he did not know. As the years passed, Rajan outgrew the habit but still enjoyed watching the train snake down the valley every week.

When he discovered Babu's old surveying equipment in the attic, all of which was in perfect working order, Rajan would climb up onto the roof of their house and pick out pretty faces by the train windows, focusing the lenses on his objects of desire until the train went out of view. He would zoom in on the images, pulling people who were a mile away to within an arm's length.

Long after the train was gone, Rajan would recall those images from his memory vault and wonder: *What was the story of those strangers? Where were they going and why?* Now, on the train himself, he wondered if a man or woman he had never met would notice his own face by the window, and if the memory of him would linger long enough to nudge their consciousness and wonder years later who he was, and where he was going. None of them would know that he himself did not even know where he was going, or why.

He looked across the cabin; Mariam was awake. He waved at her. She waved back, smiling, but a frown soon creased her face. She was thinking about the parcel she was about to receive, wondering how her knowledge of her past would reshape her future.

The requirements at the Bank of England were elaborate but Mariam had prepared adequately. She had every detail they sought to verify her identity. The parcel, wrapped in brown paper that had started yellowing, was not more than a foot long and a foot wide. Rajan signed to confirm he had witnessed the parcel was received intact. Mariam used the tip of the pen to rip the lining open. She took out the sealed envelope inside and opened it, reading briskly as Rajan sat and watched from across the table.

If I Die, The Last Word from Reverend Richard Turnbull,
Minister of the Gospel to His Beloved Family in Ndundori

I know by writing this I am rewriting my own history, per-
haps erasing a more venerated account that is likely to have
taken root by now. I am motivated to write this by several
things: Firstly, there is a war going on in the summer of 1952.
The armed Kiama kia Rukungu insurgents have warned me
and other ministers of the gospel against carrying on with our
work. I am not afraid of death, but this is not a quest for mar-
tyrdom. I have been dead for a long time.

My last word, however, should not be read as a statement
on larger things about life. Rather, it is a simple confession, a
gesture toward making amends for personal transgressions. By
sharing the truth, I am subverting the prospects of lies that I
have lived from being allowed to stand, least of all perpetuated
by others. I am, after all, human. I am writing to seek my own
redemption, to seek peace with myself. As I like to say, we have
all come short of the glory of God.

My daughter Rehema and my granddaughter Mariam
both need to know the story of their lives. Like John the Baptist
who foresaw the birth of our Savior, and delivered the truth
from an ancient time, I convey to my daughter Rehema the
truth of her birth. I am not just her social and spiritual father;
I am her biological father.

I confess to the despicable act of molesting her mother Se-
neiya, the daughter of Chief Lonana, barely a child herself, to
gratify my own flesh. I regret my own lack of self-control, and
even more, the lack of courage to own up to my failure. It is

true I coveted not just the beautiful land of Kenia, but also her beautiful children as well.

Moreover, I am ashamed for scheming, together with Ian Edward McDonald, to place blame on the young Indian man, Babu Rajan Salim. I am ashamed of having scared the young man away and pushed him into hiding. I was afraid his continued stay, awaiting the birth of the child, would expose my fraud. I am ashamed for hitting a man when he was down, instead of offering a helping hand and lifting him up, and for bearing false witness against him.

As though my transgressions weren't enough, I deployed schemes of deception to disguise my charitable act. I retained the suspected father's surname in Rehema's identity because I did not want to draw any attention to my own name. Like the biblical Cain, fated to bear a mark that distinguished him wherever he went, Rehema's surname, Salim, bears a permanent whiff of scandal although she is innocent. I should have been man enough to name her appropriately after myself. It was for this reason that I gave Rehema's daughter Mariam a different surname, unrelated to the Indian, though I admit still unrelated to myself or Mariam's biological father.

The identity of Mariam's father was kept a secret all these years as well. Let it be known her father is McDonald. His affair with Rehema came to my notice rather late in the day, and it broke my heart that a dear friend would violate my trust. We have shared many milestones with McDonald, but having him as a son-in-law is the one aspect I resent the most. This is just about the only instance when two wrongs make a right; I feel redeemed that I'm not the only one who has fallen short of the glory of God.

Rehema is not the only child I leave behind. The reason I deposited this note in a vault in Mombasa is to allow a bit of reflection on your journey back. Is this cardinal failure

*the only thing that should define my existence under the sun?
Mombasa is also where my journey began; see the land anew
and judge for yourself if I could have lived differently when
such beauty abounds.*

*But don't travel with your eyes shut, be on the lookout
for other big-nosed mulattos who dot the train stations. In all
probability, some will be your relatives, descended from the
loins of mubea, the minister of the gospel who failed his flock,
although it wasn't for lack of trying. If it's any consolation, I
have substituted the mounds of earth bearing the remains of
men who died building the rail with living beings, made beautiful in the eyes of the Lord.*

*As a final act of penance toward the Indian man, Babu
Rajan Salim, whom I falsely accused and scapegoated, I offer
the following: one quarter of any monies that may be paid by
my mother church upon my death. It is not to buy his silence
but to restore his losses against another injustice that I witnessed in broad daylight but never spoke out against. He was
shortchanged by McDonald and his henchmen over a grudge
they held against him, but which they could never prove: that
he had instigated labor unrest on the coast.*

*In this final act, I shall do what I have never done all my
life. I shall go against the biblical teaching which promotes the
idea of an eye for an eye. As recompense for bearing false witness against Babu Rajan Salim, I shall volunteer the following information in regard to the suspicious birth of his baby
boy, Rashid. His wife Fatima arrived at our mission hospital
on November 7, 1901, and soon went into labor. The nurses
reported everything went well until she was asked to give the
name of the baby's father. She instantly said it was Ahmad
Dodo. When she was asked to spell out the last name, she
came to her senses and said that the name shouldn't go in the
register. The boy's father should be registered as Babu Rajan*

Salim. I believe the boy's true father is the man she named on the pain of birth and that is Ahmad Dodo. If Babu does not know it already, then he should know he was cuckolded. And if he's aware of the deception but doesn't know the man, then he should look no further than Ahmad Dodo. We have all fallen short of the glory of God.

Written on this 20th day of October 1952 at Ndundori Mission
—Reverend Richard Turnbull, Minister of Gospel

When Mariam was done reading, she sighed and pushed the letter across to Rajan without a word.

22

ihii kionire uriro mbere ya gukawe—a boy discovers the marvels of life before his grandfather—Nakuru residents say of things that spare the old and afflict the young. Across the seas, another sage said: *The child is the father of the man.* This succinct truism encapsulated Rajan's travails. He now possessed knowledge of things that had eluded his grandfather all his life. Mariam now knew what her mother Rehema had never known. And Rajan and Mariam now knew they shared a common heritage: the Jakaranda was Mariam's father's house, and McDonald and Babu had a grudge that they had held for a lifetime.

Rajan and Mariam returned to the train station soon after leaving the Bank of England, somewhat exhausted by what each had discovered. They wanted to catch the night train to Nakuru to escape the sordid details of their pasts. And night travel would at least spare them the sight of the long-nosed children that Reverend Turnbull had said they risked encountering along the way. The dark of night would hide their secret blight—shield their tearful faces from prying eyes. They both found the night comforting.

They bought their tickets without incident. Rajan's face, now ashen with worry, persuaded the attendant that he was white. They sat together, snuggling, not in the impassioned heat of affection, but the solidarity of war veterans. Each wrestled with a mixture of emotions: anger, denial, bitterness. But it was mostly the exhaustion that lulled them into a fitful sleep through most of the fourteen-hour journey. Overnight, they had grown from carefree young people to burdened adults, pushed to the edge of a tidal swirl that threatened to drown their world as they knew it.

Suddenly, many things made sense to Rajan, like why his father Rashid, absent for half his life, was a taboo topic in Babu's household. It made a lot of sense, Rajan recognized, that Fatima and Babu found crafty ways of deflecting any conversation about his father. The official narrative was that he had gone to study in England, and had chosen to extend his stay after his studies. Now Rajan understood his father had been banished from the land possibly to save Babu the continued humiliation of being reminded of Fatima's infidelity. That was the compromise the couple had reached—to dispatch Rashid to London as soon as he reached eighteen. Rajan had few recollections of his mother, save the scant information that she had joined Rashid in England when Rajan was three. He couldn't put a face to the name, so he had come to regard her as an invention. Only that he was born of a woman—the proof of her existence was his own being.

Then there was McDonald's long-held grudge and his schemes of deceptions to deny Babu his just wages for honest toil. How much else had Babu been dispossessed? Rajan wondered, feeling his heart go out to his grandfather. Should he tell Babu what he had discovered? And if so, how much of it? Could he handle the truth that had eluded him for sixty years?

The horn blasted, interrupting Rajan's train of thought. They were approaching Nakuru. It was dawn and first light was struggling to shine through the dark clouds of dawn. Moments later, a wave of amber cracked open, suffusing portions of the water with a hint of soft orange so that it appeared as though Lake Nakuru was on fire. Mariam started to wake up. Rajan touched her face, planted a kiss on her forehead, and wandered to the window. He saw the sliver of light upon the lake, and the steam rising from the spring. But there was something wrong with the picture. Rajan had experienced the Nakuru dawn enough times to be able to sense that something was amiss. On clear mornings, one was able to see the silhouette of Mount Kenya, the mountain of God that had given the country its name. And depending on where one was standing, the snowcapped peaks melted into the sea as its shadow was superimposed on the Jakaranda. But the establishment was missing from the picture. So where was the Jakaranda? Where was the monument that defined the township? And how was his grandfather Babu faring? Would he be able to look him and his grandmother Fatima in the eye and reveal what he had discovered? Rajan shuddered at the thought, burdened by the family history that he knew he would have to bear alone.

Rajan turned to Mariam. He was about to inquire if she had noticed something was different about the town's landscape but quickly realized the Jakaranda now held a deeply personal meaning to Mariam. It was her father's house. And she probably hadn't spent enough time in Nakuru to notice the difference. Rajan disembarked with a mixture of panic and curiosity. He had an inkling that things would never be the same again for him and his family. He and Mariam were still holding hands, momentarily breaking their bond to upturn the collars of their coats to ward off the chilly dawn wind. A man stood in the way and they parted to avoid him. Another man roughly grabbed Rajan's hand and pulled him to the side.

"*Wapi* certificate of clearance?" the man demanded, producing a pair of handcuffs. They were plainclothes policemen.

Rajan flashed a grin, mistaking this as a stunt from adoring fans. "What certificate?" he asked, smiling.

"Don't show me your teeth, you think I'm your grandmother? *Wapi* certificate? If you have none, then you must be an alien."

"What do you mean by *an alien*?"

"*Weee*. I'm not your English teacher. I'm a policeman on duty. *Twende!* You will tell us more when we get to the station!"

"What's this nonsense? My grandfather built this town with his very hands. What kind of evidence do you need to know I belong here?" he protested as the shackles were put on his wrists.

"*Ala unanyeta?* Let's get going. You will tell those stories to your grandmother," the policeman responded.

Rajan grimaced as the grip on his wrists tightened. He was unsure if the man had used the line about his grandmother in jest, as it was a common slur among locals. Once outside, he was thrust into a waiting truck—the Black Maria, as locals called it—where other people had been consigned as well.

"I will go with him," Mariam said to the policeman, climbing into the truck after Rajan.

"We are not arresting *wazungu*, but if you want to come with us, who could resist such a beauty?" the policeman said. "We are now a free country, aren't we? Come one, come all!"

"So this is the ladies' man, eeeeh?" another policeman jumped in. "I will show you the real men around here." He grabbed Rajan by the back of his pants and dragged him to a corner of the truck. Rajan tiptoed to minimize the sudden pressure on his lower abdomen. *What's going on?* he asked himself for the umpteenth time. First, he could not locate Nakuru's towering landmark from the train, now he was being told he needed a special document to set foot in the place he had learned to play. Rajan concluded that either something had gone terribly wrong in Nakuru since he'd left or something was wrong with his head.

News of Rajan's sighting and subsequent arrest spread fast across Nakuru. And in keeping with the Nakuru tradition, those who witnessed Rajan's arrest added a new twist to the story. They said he had been arrested over suspicion of involvement in the arson attack on the Jakaranda. How could one bite the hand that feeds him? some wondered loudly. Yet others claimed Rajan had returned to perform his swan song before migrating to India, where he was betrothed to marry an Indian bride. The latter assertion was attributed to the mass relocation of Indians as the government deadline approached. Who would have thought the king of *mugithi* considered himself an Indian? some whispered. This is betrayal of the highest order. And why had the Indian Raj only discovered his Indianness after getting through with our girls? yet others whispered.

Regardless of which version, those who heard the news felt the need to visit the Jakaranda and witness what was unfolding. By midday, several hundred people had assembled at the ruins, adding to the number who had arrived earlier, the competing narratives giving way to even newer narratives, the latest version being that Rajan was being held after being caught in the act with a white girl.

Those assembled attracted other passersby, who stopped to watch what others were watching. What, exactly, none could tell. By nightfall, thousands of Nakuru residents and the neighboring villages of Karumaindo, Meciria, and Ituramiro had descended on the Jakaranda. At this stage, the gathering had gained sociopolitical meaning. They said they were keeping wake over the loss of their landmark, from where it was rumored Big Man was about to address the nation. By midnight, those who could manage had made their trips back home or sent for blankets and torches, food and firewood. A bonfire was lit on the ruins of the Jakaranda as a song rent the air:

Moto umewaka leo!
Moto umewaka leo!
Tuimbe haleluya, moto umewaka!

A preacher rose to offer a prayer. Before long, word spread that a holy visitation had been sighted at the ruins. The fire may have ravaged the place, but it had also renewed and strengthened it. The spiritual rumor drew even more people to the Jakaranda as some claimed that Reverend Turnbull, long presumed dead, had returned in perfect health to address the gathering at the establishment. *Haiya,* wonders will never cease, many villagers exclaimed.

On the second day, a contingent of armed police officers and army personnel were deployed to watch over the swelling crowds, issuing ultimatums for them to disperse before severe action was taken against them. But that only served to enrage the crowds who demanded to be addressed by Big Man. If their demand was not met, they said, they would march to the statehouse and seek an audience with him.

This idea soon blossomed into a chant: *Rajan for President! Rajan for President!* Yes, the aspirations of the young nation should be entrusted to the young. Those assembled said they would install Rajan as the people's president, and a group started its march toward the statehouse. A few politicians arrived to address the gathering. They said Rajan was too young to be elected to office, but he was certainly among the leaders of tomorrow. They pledged that once they were elected, they would lobby Parliament to amend the law and lower the age at which one could run for president from thirty-five to twenty-five. But that only spurred the roiling swirl of humanity to demand that the police produce the Indian Raj or else they would invade the station and retrieve him.

It was the latter assertion that threw the authorities into a panic and scuttled the plans to have McDonald address the crowd and issue an eviction order. He had been scheduled to speak to the crowd and order them off his land. Instead, the police considered the various options to defuse the gargantuan problem they had created for themselves. Releasing Rajan without charging him would leave them with egg on their faces, but when McDonald was consulted, he warned the authorities against underrating Rajan's capacity to cause trouble. "The fruit does not fall far from the tree," McDonald said, recalling the tribulations that Babu had occasioned him. He made no mention that the pretty young woman accompanying Rajan was his own daughter.

The police, convinced that his supporters would invade any station to retrieve him, shuffled Rajan from one place to another. As hours ticked away, the crowd swelled, surging toward the police barricade. By the afternoon of the second day of protest, police bayonets were touching the throats of the assembled young men and women of different races. The procession had now spilled onto the streets of Nakuru. Not many understood why they were in the streets in the first place, neither did they seem to care. All they had was a hunch that what they were doing was important; they were participating in the making of history, what they would one day proudly narrate to their children or their children's children. *Yes, I was there on that day people descended on the ruins of the Jakaranda. I saw it happen with these very eyes . . .*

23

From the Black Maria, Rajan and Mariam were led to a barely furnished room where a man in a blue uniform was hunched, scribbling furiously.

"This is Inspector Hongo, he will take your statement," said the plainclothes policeman who had not identified himself.

Inspector Hongo looked up, placed his official police hat on his square head, and hissed: "Yes?"

"*Yes?*" Rajan returned, unsure of what he was supposed to say.

"*Sema!*"

What was all this about? Rajan wondered. He had been asked to speak up, but what about? After an awkward silence, he started explaining how he had been picked up at the train station and hustled into the Black Maria.

"Do you know why you were arrested?" Inspector Hongo pursued.

"No," Rajan replied swiftly, hopeful that somebody sensible was starting to appreciate the ludicrous position he was in.

"All right, come inside and tell me more." The inspector motioned for him to enter through a half-door that swung open in both directions. "Mama, *unaenda wapi?*" he shouted at Mariam, inquiring where she was going as she followed Rajan through the swinging door.

"We are together."

"Not unless you want to be arrested."

"*Arrested?*" Mariam and Rajan chorused.

And that was it. A step through the swinging door made one an inmate and the other a free citizen.

"If I were you, I'd be busy seeking ways of securing his release instead of depositing your bum there." Inspector Hongo smiled, revealing sparkling white teeth and gums that resembled an overripe tomato.

Mariam refused to leave, insisting she would sit and wait during Rajan's interrogation.

"Suit yourself . . . Should you change your mind, there is room for more. We provide free room and board."

Mariam kept quiet.

Inside, Rajan's interrogation by Inspector Hongo did not last more than five minutes. He refused to answer any of the questions.

After several minutes of prodding, Inspector Hongo shut his big black book and announced: "*Sawa*, let's see how far your silence will take you. Would you have shown this kind of *madharau* if you were dealing with a white or Indian policeman? I know you Indians. Always trying to undermine *serikali ya Mwafrika*. Had you cooperated, I would have charged you with vagrancy or some other misdemeanor and let you go. That's what we have offered many Indians like you who have not applied for citizenship. The deadline for that came and went. Our very own father of the nation, Big Man, announced it, but since you are a strong-headed Indian who thinks the black man is nothing, including Big Man, you have chosen to disregard the instructions. Now let's see where that gets you . . . You are taking the next flight to India!"

Inspector Hongo's position wasn't far off the official position. Any Indian who did not cooperate with the authorities by offering hefty bribes, and who had been confirmed not to have complied with the legal requirement to regularize their status as decreed by Big Man, was being deported to their country of origin. But after only a few hours in custody, it was clear to the police that this was no ordinary man they were dealing with. Once they knew the street protests were somehow connected to Rajan's arrest, the police admitted this was what they called a hot potato. Too dangerous to handle. By nightfall of the second day of rioting, Big Man himself rang the station to inquire about the *ka-muhindi* who dared bring *nyoko nyoko* to the incoming *serikali ya Mwafrika*.

A crisis meeting was held that night comprising the highest echelons of police and army departments. The mobs were still in the streets chanting Rajan's name. Deportation was considered the best option. It was a time-tested strategy that had been deployed effectively through decades of colonial rule, and whose merit was still evident. Those who stood in the way of the railway construction had been removed from among their people and cast to the four directions of the wind. Me Katilili had been removed from the coast and domiciled in Kisii in the hinterland; the Talai leader of Kericho had been dispatched to Gwasi island in Nyanza; Waiyaki had been removed from Kikuyuland and was destined for Kamba land when he died. Later, when agitation for labor and political rights hit fever pitch, Harry Thuku would be consigned to Kismayo, on the border of Somalia; even Big Man himself had been dispatched to Kapenguria, in the northern frontier, away from his power base in central Kenya. Remove a man from his people and you have disabled him, for he draws his power from the people.

Rajan's deportation to India appeared ideal, but there was a question about his grandfather Babu's origins. The man had left the Indian subcontinent a Punjabi national, but Punjab had been erased like pencil marks off the map and its territory shared out between India and Pakistan. It was unclear which territory would accept him.

The second option open to the police was to deport Rajan to Britain, just as they had deported Indians who arrived in the colony to build the railway. Such Indians and their dependents were considered British subjects and so were eligible to migrate under a special privilege accorded all the British subjects across the Commonwealth. The latter choice was deemed favorably from a security viewpoint. No one would accuse the new government of kicking Rajan out; it would be reported that he had simply opted to settle in Britain to pursue interests other than singing. In any case, there was evidence he had lost his regular base at the Jakaranda. Moving on to new lands was both sensible and practical.

McDonald was roped into the discussions for three reasons: he was the owner of the Jakaranda, the epicenter of the protest; he was a retired army man; and thirdly, he had overseen the construction of the railway, the route through which Rajan's lineage was traced.

McDonald had had a very troubling time since the torching of the Jakaranda. The image that recurred in his mind with disturbing persistence was the day the flamingos arrived in Nakuru. The birds kept circling in his mind, making hissing sounds in his ears so that doctors who watched over him administered tranquilizers one night. But he couldn't seem to sleep.

"I see darkness everywhere," he kept mumbling, although the lights were on; or he'd wail that Nyundo had returned from the land of the dead to torment him.

In the morning he had dark shadows under his eyes, while his visions of the night resurged: the arrival of the flamingos and the return of Nyundo. A psychiatrist was called in to verify his state of mind, and confirmed that the old man was not hallucinating. He confirmed that McDonald had encountered Nyundo in the flesh, and the darkness in his mind was an echo from history. The doctor also verified that McDonald was aware that the Jakaranda had been razed to the ground.

"Doctor, I have been wondering if it was worth it at all," the old man lamented. "All that I worked for for over ninety years is gone forever."

"It's quite usual for us all to question our lives when we undergo traumatic experiences," the doctor explained gently, but McDonald interjected swiftly: "I'm not talking about the material loss, doctor, I'm thinking about my own humiliation by . . . by . . . a man I hired as a porter and drummer. I almost had to—to plead for my life. I, a soldier decorated by the Queen of England . . ."

"He did not threaten you, as I understood it."

"That's what I find frustrating, doctor. He did not threaten me. He should have shot me, and I would have died fighting . . ."

"He probably had a good reason for sparing your life," the doctor reasoned. "Maybe he was returning the favor."

McDonald shook his head and sobbed: "This is why it hurts. Saved by a nobody because I am nobody." So when he was wheeled into the room where government officials were mulling over their options to quell the uprising surrounding Rajan's arrest, McDonald was already in a foul mood.

When he was invited to address the meeting, McDonald made a short statement that confounded everyone: "I'd like to state up front that I shall recuse myself in this situation. I have known that young man all his life, so I cannot make an impartial decision about him."

There was a sudden hush in the room.

"Moreover," McDonald went on, "I have no more right than he does to live in this country." He glanced around the room. "D-did I talk about the girl in his company? I-I know her as well."

And so it was under the cover of darkness—on the third day of his incarceration—that Rajan was ferreted out of his last police base, blindfolded, and rushed to the airport. Mariam, not knowing that he had been sneaked out of the building, dozed outside the interrogation room, waiting patiently. Neither she nor Rajan had any idea about the street protests organized in his support, nor even where he had been taken.

In the one hour he was blindfolded, Rajan felt a certain comfort that he hadn't experienced in a few days. He did not have to make any decisions. It had only been three days since he'd learned about his secret heritage, the birth of his illegitimate father, as well as Mariam's suspect paternity. And his grandmother's infidelity. He had felt burdened ever since, unsure what was safe to share and with whom. A boy had grown into a man overnight, and even as the Land Rover trundled through the potholed road heading to the airport, Rajan resolved he wouldn't let his travails break him. He would endure it all. And if it required him to serve time, he was willing to. For, as Gathenji the butcher liked to say, prisons are not built for goats, but men.

Rajan was taken aback when his blindfold was removed and he found himself at the airport. Inspector Hongo had been right: he was taking the next available plane to India! *What's happening?* he thought in panic.

"Can someone tell me what's going on?" he shouted at the policemen leading him away, each holding a wrist.

One of them replied that he was being deported.

"Why?"

"Go ask your grandmother," the other responded.

Rajan snapped at the mention of Fatima. He tried to break free and tumbled down with one of the policemen. He kicked and clawed and bit and cried as exhaustion and the anguish of the past three days took their toll.

The policemen regained control and pinned him down before calling for reinforcement. A medic arrived and sedated him. One of the two officers who were to accompany Rajan to Britain to execute his deportation order reported to the ticketing office of Her Majesty's Air Service. He was directed to the immigration desk.

"If it's about Indians, sir, you need to start there," said the female attendant in a nasal tone. "You have to be cleared first."

The policeman obliged and went where he had been directed. Another female, a young Englishwoman, flipped through a file before dumping it and picking up another one. And another. Her face creased.

"Please give me a second, sir," she said to the policeman, wandering off to another desk where her superior was seated. The policeman noticed the English attendant had a generous behind which contrasted nicely with her small waist. Those were the fruits of independence, he thought pleasantly. Only months earlier, he wouldn't have even dreamed of coming to within an elbow of a white woman. And here he was. Who knows, perhaps he would ask her out next time he came to deport another Indian.

The Englishwoman returned with a file. It was the file that McDonald had compiled about the status of each and every railway worker after the construction was completed in 1902. The woman sighed and smiled apologetically. "We have a problem," she announced. "Your ward cannot be deported to England."

The past had finally caught up with the present to complicate the future. In that interlude, Rajan's present—lulled by his drug-fueled stupor—and Babu's past, drowned in hallucinatory reveries, had become one.

"Our records show his grandfather severed his ties with Britain when he deserted work. His privileges were taken away. He did not complete his contract as required, so he is not eligible to migrate to England as a British subject from the former colony of Kenia. In short, your ward cannot acquire a privilege that his grandfather was deprived in 1901." The woman paused and looked up.

The policeman was staring at her bosom. He turned away in embarrassment.

"There is another issue," she went on. There was renewed attention from the policeman. "The man's father is in England. Our records show he is a student, or has been a student for more than ten years. It is unlikely that he's been a student this long. It is likely that he graduated but never regularized his status. Whatever the case, a student lacks legal merit to host a family, unless they are his dependents and he is able to prove he is able to support them."

"What happens in such instances?" the policeman asked, puzzled and disappointed. He had gloated to his colleagues that he would be the first in his village to ride in a plane. He had to salvage things or he'd end up returning to his village with his tail between his legs. "As it is, the young man has lost his Kenyan citizenship . . ."

"This is unprecedented," the Englishwoman conceded. "I shall refer the matter to my bosses if you want. They can explore if there are other legal remedies available to us. As I said, it is quite unusual for a man to lose three countries all at once. If Britain is out of bounds, Punjab has been dissolved, and he failed to apply for Kenyan citizenship, the man is basically stateless."

"I'm afraid you have to make a decision now," the policeman said. "I received an order from above to deport him."

"I totally understand."

"I don't think you do."

"Yes, I do."

"Look," the policeman said, before dropping his voice, "Big Man himself has ordered it. And when I say Big Man, I mean the biggest man in the land."

"I totally understand," the woman replied.

"I don't think you do!"

"Yes, I do."

"If you do understand what I am saying, then you have to enforce this order now. Immediate deportation."

"I have given you the official position."

"What official position are you talking about? Who is more official than Big Man of Kenya?"

"I'm only following the law."

"Whose law are you talking about? British or Indian or Kenyan law? Big Man of Kenya is the law . . . You wait and see! You just wait and see. You will know this is the new Kenya! A free country led by a black man. You think we are still a British colony? Be careful, you might take the same plane to Britain! Just wait and see . . ."

The English attendant did not take the threat lightly. She had witnessed her former boss's deportation after he had fought with a local businessman over a woman. A small tiff at the pub had led to very serious consequences. As it turned out, the businessman was the branch chairman of the new Jogoo political party. That meant the businessman had very deep ties with the local administration. The Englishman had gone out for lunch, leaving his jacket slung over his seat in the office, dentures and glasses on the table. The next they heard from the man—he was phoning from Jan Smuts International Airport in South Africa, where he had been deported.

The Englishwoman did not want to risk such action against her. She rose from her seat to reveal her generous bum once more. Her finger pointed to a darkly lit passage close to the boarding area. "If you must deport him now, sir, I recommend you take him there. That's what we call no-man's-land."

The policeman wasn't listening. He was watching the woman's bosom. It appeared larger than he'd previously thought. He was thinking that if the bra was unhooked, the breasts would glide out like a roll of jelly. Those were the fruits of freedom, plentiful enough to feed the nation.

Still distracted by the Englishwoman's oozing sexuality, the cop absentmindedly deposited Rajan at the airport's no-man's-land. He was still in cuffs.

When Rajan regained partial consciousness, he tried to remember why he had been handcuffed and he couldn't quite place it. The dim light and the long passage called to mind the first time he'd met Mariam on the staircase of the Jakaranda. He shut his eyes and imagined her soft kiss with the strong lavender flavor. He turned on his side and the clink of the cuffs on the floor echoed the high heels that Mariam wore on that first night. He lay there and let the memory of that first encounter smother his tired limbs, soothe away his private pains, some old, some new. As he drifted off to a fitful sleep, he remembered Fatima's belated declaration that he had been betrothed at birth. He smiled and wondered who the girl could have been; her story would forever remain one of what could have been: a stillbirth that could not survive the birth pains of the new nation. Then, out of the blue, he heard Abdia's voice ring out, *Leeeeeeiiiilllllaaaaaa*, as the girl's pretty face filled the frame of his mind and he saw the trace of her taut breasts pushing through her thin blouse.

Babu slipped in and out of consciousness many times a day. After a brief hospitalization he was returned home, where a nurse watched over him around the clock. The doctor had recommended bed rest even though he had not suffered any fractures in his fall. He was considered mentally frail. Even when he was awake, he kept his eyes shut to avoid Fatima's questions. He did not want to look back on the past—the discovery that he had taken his beloved grandson to a school associated with Reverend Turnbull. Babu had also bequeathed the school a large endowment to support poor children in the future. Of course, he still had no idea that Turnbull had left him a peace offering in the form of a quarter of his savings. Neither did Babu want to wake up to the fact that Rajan had been dating Mariam, the granddaughter of Seneiya, Chief Lonana's daughter. That was all too traumatizing.

Still, there was a persistent image that lingered from the past, and which he had tried to unravel without success over the last few days: the strange dream that had

preceded the aborted pilgrimage to the Laikipia Escarpment, in which he had turned into a guinea fowl. The bird
had black and white spots, and it had elicited different
responses from workers from different races as it flew over
Fort Jesus. Some thought it black, others thought it white.
And while the guinea fowl in his dream was a flying bird,
the regular guinea fowl lived on the earth. Babu wondered
if the guinea fowl could be a metaphor for the Indians
of the British East Africa Protectorate. They had arrived
as British agents to toil on the rail; some, like him, had
worked for the British. Yet most never embraced the African life, nor were they absorbed into the colonial culture.
They had kept their space, retained their identity. But as
Babu had learned during his days in the wilderness, the
subtler prejudices of caste and religion had survived the
Indians' long sojourn across the Indian Ocean.

As he drifted off to sleep, Babu remarked to himself
that the guinea fowl was probably the Indian for a reason he had not considered before. It was a bird of flight,
in constant motion to forage where food was to be found;
Indians were similarly on the move, exploring opportunities in different parts of the world without putting roots
down. Babu smiled when he recalled the phrase he had
invoked whenever he was called upon to narrate the past
by his grandson Rajan: *We came in dhows to build the rail, and left
in planes* . . . Perhaps it was true that Indians did not come
to stay. They were mere *wapita njia*, passersby, their place
of belonging being that transience—the in-between world
connecting continents and cultures, heaven and earth,
land and sea—the space that the guinea fowl in his dream
could fly over and about, without being grounded like the
rest of its ilk.

EPILOGUE

When the whistle of the train heading westward blasts every Tuesday at 6:15 a.m., and rents the air again on Thursday evening at 5:35 p.m. to announce that the iron beast is slithering through the land toward the ocean where it all started, it is always a source of merriment for the locals. They will narrate how their week went and how the train intersected with their lives.

I was having my second cup of tea when the train to Mombasa passed, a girl will tell her lover to illustrate the length of time she was waiting at the coffee shop.

I knew I was late for work because the horn of the train sounded while I was still in bed, a worker will confess to a colleague.

Hotel check-in time is organized around the train arrival in the township, when tourists come by the thousands. They are met at the train station by tour guides ready to retell a well-worn yarn. They will point toward the imposing Jakaranda Hotel, whose replica was restored soon after independence, at an enormous cost to the independent government. Experts were flown in from London to ensure it was an authentic reproduction of the house that Ian Edward McDonald had built in 1901. Tour guides will point to the various aspects of the establishment and announce proudly: *That's the place that heralded the birth of this town.*

Then they will point in the direction of the school—now world famous for the top-class athletes it has produced—

and remind everyone that it was also built by the founder of the township, Ian Edward McDonald, although he established it under strict anonymity. McDonald, who had created the school in honor of his lifelong friend Reverend Turnbull, had made only one condition to the school founders: that his contribution would only be made public fifty years after his death. The school is also consistently in the news for its high-performing students, many of whom get appointed to the government cabinet.

The tour guides hail both McDonald and Reverend Turnbull as the founding fathers of the township and narrate their inadvertent trip there that permanently altered their destinies. There is a nature trail that simulates McDonald's first trip through the Nakuru wilderness, known to this day as the Great Trek.

But what has truly put Nakuru on the world map is the wildlife sanctuary around the Jakaranda, and the annual festival held every December to coincide with the migration of the flamingos, the alien birds that inhabit the lake that gave the township its name. The birds' first recorded exodus out of town coincided with the expulsion of Indians, which many believe was the birds' expression of solidarity with the community. It is not known where the birds hibernate for half the year, but they fly out every June and return every December. This migration is celebrated as one of the marvels of the natural world, reenacting the drama that Babu and other railway builders witnessed at the turn of the last century.

The Flamingo Festival, as the fête is known across the world, celebrates diversity and a multiculturalism whose embodiment is the mystique known as the Indian Raj, a local musician who became the conscience of his nation at the young age of twenty-two when he was arrested and nearly deported under a racist legal instrument that has since been scrapped. Portraits of the artist as a young man, with his hair pulled into a ponytail, are emblazoned on T-shirts, hats, photo albums, and other memorabilia that sell steadily throughout the year. The Indian Raj is many things to many people. When guides are dealing with younger tourists, they paint him as a Casanova who did everyone and everything in celebration of human love, but his story is refined to emphasize his sociopolitical consciousness when guides are dealing with mature or elderly tourists. The highlight of that version is how the young man, after being taken into custody by police on account of his race, turned the tide against his jailers when the entire nation rallied to his cause and insisted that Kenya could not declare independence as long as he was behind bars. Overnight, he became a prisoner of conscience.

The Flamingo Festival includes a procession that imitates the actual route taken by protesters in their demand for the release of the Indian Raj, a ritual that's undertaken in solemn dignity and often includes speeches by leading politicians. The procession ends at an intersection where, four years after his arrest, and with the young nation facing a general election, the Indian Raj was cut down by an assassin's bullet, triggering nationwide strife. The motivation for the killing was to prevent him from running for the highest office in the land, although he hadn't reached the requisite age to participate in the election, or even expressed an interest in politics. *Just imagine where this country would be had that young man lived*, tour guides remind their guests, before conceding that dimming the brightest stars is the natural order of things. Lightning strikes the tallest tree.

Music is a large part of these commemorations hosted at the Jakaranda Hotel, the all-time favorite being the *mugithi* dance that imitates the movement of the train that was inaugurated by the Indian Raj. An annual competition honors a breakout star who has interpreted the spirit of the Jakaranda Hotel of old in a compelling and refreshing manner. In the most recent edition of the fête, the star was a stand-up comedian parodying a butcher. He left everyone in stitches with his meat-stealing antics. His name: Karianjahe Gathenji—the grandson of the butcher who worked at the Jakaranda on the cusp of independence, and who displayed similar revelry.

Nyundo, too, has not been forgotten. There is an annual drumming contest in the schools. Beyond the school circuit, Nyundo is revered as a folk hero, and whenever there are tensions in the Rift Valley, as happens every election year, when rivals seek to drive others out under the pretext that they are the original owners of the land—the real intention being to prevent them from voting—old men whisper about Nyundo's warning. *Have the bullets begun to flower?* they ask silently.

In that sense, the dead have been resurrected powerfully, although it is the Indian Raj who encapsulates what brochures promote as the spirit of Nakuru. *The stone that the builder refused has become the cornerstone*, is the mantra used to market tourism in Nakuru. Yet this a historical misnomer: the man who Nakuru forgot is Babu, the first inhabitant of the township who died of a broken heart when he learned of his grandson's arrest in 1963, which further accelerated the push for Rajan's release. Babu's memorable assertion upon watching the construction of the original Jakaranda in 1901—that not being seen is not the same as not being there—retains a succinct truth. For it was Babu, guided by the alien birds, who felt the special pull toward Nakuru as a place that could provide nurture and nature to man and beasts.

Babu's vision was well ahead of his time. Although his assessment was based on what he could see on the land, over time archaeologists have confirmed that Nakuru is the cradle of mankind, the point of dispersal for all humanity, irrespective of race, color, or creed. Recently, geologists have made yet another find: vast deposits of minerals in the bowels of the Rift Valley, from precious metals to oil and natural gas. The most unusual discovery is a massive aquifer that could provide safe drinking water for the entire nation for a lifetime. And provide a permanent home for the flamingos.

That was probably what Reverend Turnbull meant when he said this was God's country, although his words were prompted by the land's natural beauty, or, as it later came to pass, the women who lived on it. Without a doubt, Nakuru is a stunningly beautiful place and many still covet it. The richest men in the world have made their holiday homes there, smack in the middle of the wildlife sanctuary that McDonald established, and where his remains lie. He died of natural causes at the age of 101. He received a state funeral and his grave is another popular tourist attraction.

Interestingly, no one remembers the women behind the pioneers, or their children. Just as no one remembers that the train, gliding along twice every week, rocking slowly, gently, smoothly, penetrating the beautiful countryside before squeaking its horn in joyful ejaculation, made a forcible entry into their land, raping and tearing it viciously, once upon a time.

END

Acknowledgments

They say it takes a village to raise a child, but I think it takes villages to create a story. This one has its footprints scattered around the world—starting in Iowa where the seed of this story germinated, nourished by conversations with fellow writers and ardent supporters, specifically Peter and Mary Nazareth and Chris Merrill of the University of Iowa.

In Nairobi, I thank my wife Anne for her faith and love, and for keeping the family going during my long seasons of absence; my other mother, Wangari Mwangi, helped steer the affairs of the family with love and devotion.

In Houston, I'm eternally grateful to j.Kastely, chair of the University of Houston's English Department, who navigated bureaucratic hoops to ensure my study was a pleasurable and fulfilling experience. My professors in the Creative Writing Program, Chitra Divakaruni, Alex Parsons, Mat Johnson, and Hosam Aboul-Ela, dedicated time and energy to offer valuable feedback and advice. The arts organization Inprint ensured I remained fully immersed in writing by providing steady checks, especially on rainy days, to keep my bills paid.

In California, I appreciate my friend, teacher, and mentor, Professor Ngũgĩ wa Thiong'o, for his solid support through the years, particularly for committing the time to serve on my doctoral committee. I'm equally indebted to Henry Chakava, my Kenyan publisher and friend, for his useful feedback on the early drafts of this book.

I also thank Mike Owuor, a patient and perceptive reader whose feedback helped enrich this book; and Professor D.H. Kiiru, for his steady support; my sisters Faith and Mary, for always being there for me.

Many thanks to my literary agent, Malaika Adero, for guiding me to a great publisher with ease.

During my sojourns at home and abroad, I made many great friends: Kim Euell, Dawlat Yassin, Charles Kasinga, Wanjikū wa Ngūgī, Sibusiso Mabuza, P.C. Wang, and Ivanka, to mention but a few. Thank you all for your friendship and support.